PRAISE FOR "BLANK"

BLANK whisks you through the life of a super-hero-she-god-dess-warrior-assassin with a healthy helping of mama bear madness. The main character, Carole Blank, draws the full range of emotions from the reader. I loved, hated, feared, adored, admired, and pitied her, sometimes on the same page. Deep characterization and tight pacing scream throughout this adventure. Fall in love with the strength and beauty of a fractured and deadly woman.

> ~ *LaDonna Cole, author of "The Torn"* ~

Kick ass!

> ~ *Katie Cross, author of "Miss Mabel's School for Girls"* ~

S.R. Karfelt's BLANK brings us all back to what we really want in life—a place to belong. Following Carole Blank through life wrenches the heart, fueling every emotion known to man—laugh, cry...get so angry you swear...you will want to find a character and kill them! BLANK has it all, and S.R. Karfelt has guaranteed that I will never see the world the same. Buckle up, America. You're in for a wild ride—and this Shieldmaiden is riding shotgun.

> ~ *Kelsey Keating, writer, blogger, actress,*
> *and shieldmaiden for hire* ~

Brace yourselves: Carole Blank's life is the epitome of mislaid hope and unapologetic misery. The prequel we've been waiting for since *Warrior of the Ages* chases an unprecedented assassin's journey through every layer of personal hell, accentuated by ardently candid voices in her head offering feedback on Carole's every thought and action. Get ready for a full-on attack of raw truth that will leave you achingly aware of the cost of loyalty, and the torture of unrequited love. Blunt, gripping, and extraordinary, BLANK follows the sacrifices of one woman on a quest to simply belong.

> ~ *Bailey Catherine, editor, blogger,*
> *and book critic at bellebubs.wordpress.com* ~

Some heroines are content to sit snugly inside the pages of their book, quietly and politely playing out their given roles. Carole Blank is not one of those heroines. Kicking, punching and screaming, she seized my imagination in a sleeper hold and refused to let go, making *BLANK* a white-knuckle read every bit as unforgettable as its main character.

~ Elle K. White, author of "Deep City" ~

Imagine a life of perpetual turmoil, with an insatiable need for heart-penetrating love. *BLANK* will transport you through one woman's private hell to a place of purpose and peace; that is if peace can be spelled C.I.A Covert Ops! If you enjoyed S.R. Karfelt's *Warrior of the Ages*, you are going to be over-the-top happy that you picked up *BLANK*, a novel that will intrigue men and women, alike. The internal dialogue of the characters throughout this story is so rich, so alive, so intense that you will never be bothered by the voices in your own head again. Tragedy and victory, love and hate, murder and the giving of life culminate in a tale that you will remember long after reluctantly setting the book down for the final time.

~ W. Franklin Lattimore, author of "Freedom Fight" and
"Freedom War," Books 1&2 of the Otherrealm ~

William ~
Welcome to the world
of Private Carole Blank !

BLANK

A SHIELDMAIDEN'S VOICE
WARRIOR OF THE AGES, BOOK TWO

S R Karfelt

S.R. KARFELT

VOTADINI PUBLISHING
HORACE TUPPER BOOKS

Cover design by Cory Clubb
gobolddesigns@gmail.com

Interior book design, all interior graphics, eBook design,
and Votadini Publishing logo design by
Blue Harvest Creative
www.blueharvestcreative.com

BLANK

This book is a work of fiction. The characters, incidents, and dialogue
are drawn from the author's imagination and are not to be construed
as real. Any resemblance to actual events or persons, living or dead, is
entirely coincidental.

Published by
Votadini Publishing/Horace Tupper Books

ISBN-13: 978-0-9895347-1-0
ISBN-10: 0-9895347-1-5

For Gram,
who showed me what a warrior really looks like.

ACKNOWLEDGEMENTS

Without my stoic and long-suffering spouse, I doubt I could ever have finished this book. Thank you, Dear Hubby, for your patience and low expectations in the housework and meal departments. Thank you for enduring my all night writes, my off the wall research quests, and my penchant for zoning in and out of conversations as my mind wandered to other worlds. I chose wisely.

Thank you to my Beta readers—Bailey Catherine, Abi Victoria, Elle K. White, Lindsay Hodges, Kelsey Rae Keating, LaDonna Cole, Katie Cross, Kimberly Robertson, and Frank Lattimore. Your feedback was invaluable.

For my editor and the staff of G.E.C., you trimmed and polished this labor of love into my ideal. Thank you for your patience and expertise. You took the path less traveled, and that has made all the difference.

For the Musers at Obey The Muse, thank you for the feedback, and thank you for keeping me company into the wee hours on all-night write nights, most especially Kimro, DMK, and LaD—I'm pretty sure we are every bit as funny as we think we are at 3AM.

Thank you Melissa Lougher, for sharing some of your experiences about your time as a Marine in the 80's.

Also a huge shout-out to Marines in the real world—for all you do, thank you.

To the Votadini resistance warriors, who make these stories possible.

And always and forever thanks to the Ragged Blue Monkeys (most especially the unforgettable Tom Mohan). Every word that finds its way into print is thanks to the time I spent living on the ragged edge with you, my fellow blues.

Thank you.
S.R. Karfelt

ALSO BY S.R. KARFELT

WOA—WARRIOR OF THE AGES
BOOK ONE OF WARRIOR OF THE AGES

CHAPTER
ONE

Roswell, New Mexico—September 1986

PINE HILL HIGH might be the first in the district to have a boy thrown through a second story window—by a girl. Since the school had double-pane windows, it seemed logical the boy-throw might result in death. Deciding murder might be an extreme, Carole considered the aerodynamics of throwing him feet first instead.

Her target stood 9.4 yards away from Carole with a ruler in his hand, furtively trying to measure the librarian's bust-size. The clueless librarian sat hunched over a stack of books, stamping them with the return date. Behind her the boy punched his fist into the air, his hand clenched firmly around the six-inch mark. He jogged silently in place with the enthusiasm of a marathon winner, and his friends at a nearby table performed a silent wave.

He's definitely going head first, Carole thought. *I'll take my chances.*

"He's only a child!" the voices inside Carole's head argued with her. *"You will not harm him!"* She ignored them. She scooted her chair backwards, grating it loudly over the linoleum. Mrs. Gonzalez glanced up. Behind her the moron now danced in place, tugging his T-shirt out to simulate large pointy breasts. Following Carole's eyes, the librarian turned her head in time to catch his genius. Date stamp still clenched firmly in her fist, the librarian stood, grabbed the idiot's

ear, and dragged him mercilessly across the floor by that bit of flesh. The boy's dancing skills came in handy as the big woman hauled him down the stairs.

Carole glanced desperately around, trying to find something—anything else—to distract her from her task. The moron's friends noticed her and bent studiously over their schoolwork. The part of Carole's brain that could still sense Mrs. Gonzalez dragging the boy through school hallways below her, could also sense that the boys at the nearby table were afraid of her. Their heart rates had increased, and they weren't even pretending to each other that they weren't afraid.

Am I really that bad? A glance at her bruised knuckles and Carole knew she could be. In her defense she only hurt them to protect herself, and even then the voices punished her for it.

"You hurt them when you judge them to be dishonorable. You have no right," the voices chimed in, inevitably reminding her of why she had skipped lunch for the dusty school library.

A draft of icy air blew across Carole and the sun-bleached hair on her arms stood up. The voices hated air-conditioning and they turned their attention to criticizing it. *"Artifice. Unnatural. Poison."* Ignoring them Carole returned her attention to the Encyclopedia Britannica and the section on mental illness.

The voices in her head went silent. They had nothing to say as Carole tried to diagnose them and that alone seemed ominous. The voices often argued about what books said. They argued what high-school teachers said. They argued every other thought that drifted through her head.

Carole turned her focus on the page and read. *Hallucinations (hearing voices)—check, that one is definitely covered. Delusions (often bizarre or persecutory in nature)—check. Disorganized thinking and speech.* Was her thinking disorganized? She'd always thought the same way, how could she know? She didn't talk enough to know if her speech was disorganized. She skipped to the next symptom. *Impairment in social cognition—check.* There was no denying even to herself, she was weird squared and to the tenth power. *Paranoia.* If she had to take the fire escape to exit the library it would take fourteen seconds. If she jumped the staircase and broke the window with the fire extinguisher, she could be outside in seven seconds. *Double check—paranoia is definitely covered. Social isolation?* Without glancing up, Carole knew she was the only teenage girl sitting by herself. She'd never had a single friend. Social workers surely did not count, not even Marsha.

Teenage boys were another matter. A good many of them certainly wanted to socialize with her, but she was working on fixing that problem. Sometimes a bloody nose said *no* much more clearly than words. Today's four detention slips crinkled in Carole's back pocket as she returned her attention to the page, mentally checking off social isolation. Her eyes slid to the next symptom. *Difficulties with attention.* She almost laughed, but a chill prickled over the top of her head. It wasn't easy to stay focused when the voices in her head interrupted all the time.

Schizophrenia. I have schizophrenia.

Not every symptom fit, but according to the manual she had until she was nineteen to achieve par. That gave her a couple years before—what? A complete psychotic break? *Should I tell someone?*

Carole shoved to her feet, the chair again scraping loudly. Who would she tell? Marsha? The social worker might believe her, but treatment was drugs and hospitalization. She could bear neither. The voices still hadn't said a word. Carole slammed the book shut and jammed it back on the shelf.

So she was mentally ill, but she couldn't think of one good reason to share that with another soul. It was hard enough being the foster kid, the girl who fought and dressed like a guy, there didn't seem to be any good or justifiable reason to officially add crazy to that list. Jamming her hands into the holey pockets of her jeans, she headed to class.

THE BELL RANG and Carole stood with the class, her eyes on her history essay. It had earned a D minus with *Stick to the facts!* scrawled in red pen. In the crowded hallway she crumpled up the paper and shoved it inside a planter where kids stuffed cigarette butts and hid love notes to each other. The plastic trees wouldn't mind.

Carole knew she probably shouldn't listen to the voices when they said everything different than teachers and books. If she was crazy, she shouldn't trust the voices. The problem was, when she could verify it, they were always right. She excelled in math and science because of what she learned from the voices. Wondering how that was possible, it occurred to her that even her mental illness wasn't normal.

Running a hand down the back of her head over the knots of her thick blonde braid, Carole admitted to herself that she believed the voices even though she hated them. They'd never lied to her, and that was more than she could ever say about people. As if to prove this point, three perfectly normal and popular girls slowed alongside her, shooting critical sidelong glances. Charlie's Angels' hairdos and new tops from the mall didn't make their snide remarks any prettier.

"Nice top—didn't you wear that yesterday?"

"I like your jeans, are they your mom's?" They giggled and hurried ahead of her, whispering loudly. "She's such a creep!"

"I can't believe you said that about her jeans! She punched Bob Miller in the face yesterday!"

"Nuh-uh! Not Bob Miller, are you kidding—"

Tucking her plain white T-shirt more neatly into her old-fashioned low-rise pants, Carole fell back a few steps and ignored them. Likely they'd be thrilled to be trapped in the locker room with Bob Miller. They were welcome to him, he was the creep. She had nothing in common with teenage girls. She didn't care about the hottest concert T-shirts, strawberry scented shampoo, or the coolest 80's pop stars. Carole hung back, waiting for the girls and the rest of the crowd to go up the stairs to the third floor. If she got trapped in the middle of the crowded stairwell and needed to escape, she'd probably hurt someone doing it. In her first high school she'd been in a crowded hall when the fire alarm went off. It had been a drill, but she had dislocated a football player's shoulder trying to escape. Apparently the quarterback's dislocated shoulder had affected the season, which was why she was now attending high school far outside of Albuquerque. Was there any place on earth more remote than Roswell, New Mexico?

For the fourth time that day a senior from the school basketball team moved into her line of vision, a tall blond with puppy dog eyes. He was quickly rising the ranks to stalker of the week. He brushed past Carole, dropping a tightly folded triangle of paper on top of her notebook. It looked like the shaped wad of paper kids played table-top football with.

The basketball player went only a couple steps before stopping in the middle of the hall, blocking traffic, to stare at her. Carole would have let the paper with her name scrawled on it drop straight to the floor, except the last thing she needed was someone from her grade to get hold of her latest love letter. Safely tucking it into her pocket for imminent disposal, she saw the familiar hopeful look, like she was waving bacon in front of a golden retriever. *What is it with some guys?* All she ever wanted with them was a worthy opponent in a game, or better yet, a fight. Obviously that wasn't what this boy had in mind. Boldly he reached for her hand. She yanked it away and glared. The boy put his hand against his chest and sighed, staring at her chest until she hid it with her notebook. *And what is that about?* She had absolutely nothing there of interest to them, her T-shirt rested against her as flat as this boy's. Possibly flatter. He licked his lips and swallowed a few times, like the bacon was coming closer, or maybe trying to work up the courage to speak.

Deep inside Carole had a sneaking suspicion that it wasn't her stick-like body he was interested in. She remembered the blissful touch of her mother's heart. That touch could explain the unnatural attraction she seemed to hold for guys, because it sure wasn't her looks. Sometimes when she'd snuggled close to Mom and Gran, the touch of their hearts had made it feel like she was floating. Squaring her shoulders, she shoved the memory away. Not feeling the least bit guilty, Carole made a rude gesture right in the boy's face. He turned away, stumbling blindly down a stairwell while an entire class of seniors shoved up it. His retreat reminded Carole horribly of a whipped dog.

The voices did not approve of her actions, and Carole tried to ignore them but they threw the word *"Dishonor"* at her and it cut.

The crowd on the upper cinderblock stairwell thinned, and Carole moved towards her class on the third floor. Her right foot just touched the second step when she sensed danger approaching behind. *How do I know?* The voices continued to rant about honor and integrity and she smiled faintly, it didn't matter how she knew, if someone wanted a fight they'd come to the right place.

Carole knew exactly how to defend herself, no thanks to the voices. They dropped the lecture in time to suggest a belated retreat. *Hah*, she thought. *Where is the fun in that?* Leaning to the right, Carole kicked her left leg back and knocked Bob Miller down the stairs. Apparently yesterday's punch had only encouraged him to bring friends this time. Three of his friends converged on her, eyes narrowed and mouths set grimly. One boy raced up the stairs ahead as they tried to box her in. Carole's smile widened, a thrill spread through her and her body responded: head butt, elbow to the left, right heel smashing back onto a foot, right leg up and a knee into a groin, spin around and a right elbow into a sternum, left fist into a nose. The nose smash felt so right that Carole indulged in some right-left punching for each boy's nose as a follow up.

EVEN LATER, WHEN Marsha showed up to talk to the principal, Carole was still pleased with her work. Plopped on a horrible orange plastic chair outside the principal's office, she listened to Marsha's polite arguing through the door. Sharp plastic weave bit through her jeans into her thighs, but Carole felt only satisfaction. *They deserved it! Four boys coming after one girl!* They'd have hurt her if she hadn't stopped them. They'd wanted to hurt her. She had sensed their dark intention as well as the fact that they were coming for her, felt it in her heart like poison. The voices didn't say very much, satisfied with a familiar lecture easily ignored. They didn't seem to know what to say about a girl who could fight like a warrior. Carole knew what to think, she was good at fighting, very good. Besides that those boys had deserved it.

Leaning back in her chair, she heard the principal delve into her fighting record. "…third time this school year, and it is only September!"

Marsha's reply was difficult to make out, she was using her Let's-Be-Reasonable honeyed voice, "…kind of a school where four boys attack one girl…throwing them out?"

"…play the girl card? That kid could bench press all four…"

Carole crossed one strong leg over the other. She probably could bench press at least two of those boys, her satisfaction increased.

"…dangerous…who knows what she was exposed to as a…background…foster children…."

Carole's satisfaction evaporated. Who knew what she *had* been exposed to as a child? She remembered Mom and Gran with joy, but she also remembered impossible things like grandmother's musical rainbows dancing inside her head. Maybe her schizophrenia came from drugs. They had been Hippies, Flower Children of the 60's. Maybe the voices were the result of a three-year-old exposed to psychedelic drugs. The thought was sobering. How many of her memories could she trust? Her mind drifted back, far into the past.

CAROLE USED TO fit in. Inside the car with the silver fins, plunked right in the middle of the front seat between her Mom and Gran, she had fit in perfectly. Her long legs were much shorter then, and stuck straight out in front of her on the green leather seat. That car was big and the inside baking hot. With the windows rolled down hot air blew over them spitting desert dust. It felt good. Carole could still feel it when she tried, could taste gritty desert sand between her teeth, and feel the blast of heat blow over her face. She could still hear the music and it made her heart starve to remember it. Mom drove, Gran wouldn't. Gran said driving killed her music. Carole could still see Mom's hair blowing half out the window and half in her mouth. She could see Gran's tie-dye T-shirt flapping while she tapped out a rhythm against the dashboard in perfect time to her music.

Music and bright colors had swirled through Carole's head, although the old radio had been torn out and sold long ago. Mom sometimes kept her sunglasses inside the hole where it belonged. Even without the radio the music played, following them almost everywhere. Gran made music echo inside Carole's mind and told her where it came from: The Beatles, Bob Dylan, or Gran's favorite, The Mamas and The Papas. One time Mom snapped, "Mother? Please stop with the California Dreamin'! She hardly talks because she's always listening to your head!" Carole enjoyed California Dreamin' weaving through her head with the dancing kaleidoscope of colors. The music and colors were part of Gran, and just like the touch of her heart warming Carole's, it belonged.

There was never any hurry in that car; it was a peaceful place, a happy place. Sometimes they stopped for days and took the suitcase out. Carole had very vague memories of eating sprouts or hummus spread on bits of stale pita bread. Those memories involved crowds of people she didn't know. She couldn't recall faces, just names like Sky, Summer, and Rainbow. Mom sometimes painted pictures on walls or canvas. People gave her money to do it. They never stayed long before Mom would put her paints in the trunk with their suitcase and say, "Want to go, Carole?" Gran would add, "It's waiting for us, Carole." One time Carole had asked Gran, "What's waiting for us?" Gran had looked out the windshield and gestured. "The skyline, Christmas Carole." Gran often called her that, Christmas Carole, though Carole could not remember ever celebrating Christmas with them.

She only remembered Easter, that one Easter. Carole remembered most of that whole day and in the right order. It had been very different than every other day. That morning Gran woke them up early. They were in a worn-out motel with orange carpet and lots of motorcycles parked outside. Mom made her take a bath in a tub that had dark cracks in it and black stuff in the corners. Carole had been afraid of that tub. Mom had been frowning so Carole didn't argue.

She tried not to think about what the dark stuff was, but the voices in her head had shouted at her. When she didn't listen to the voices they put pictures in her head. Pictures of black dreams rolled through her head while she sat in the water. Black dreams about falling into dirty water where a lady couldn't breathe and slimy dirt went into her mouth and nose.

Gran had come into the bathroom holding a frilly dress and asked Carole if she thought it was pretty. Carole had asked what it was. Mom and Gran argued then and neither one smiled or answered her question. Gran kept saying, "He deserves to know" and Mom cried while she tugged the silly dress over Carole's damp body. Then they were in the car again and Carole thought they were going to what was waiting for them, only this time in the scratchy dress that pouffed out and made her panties show unless she pushed it down. Sharp threads were digging into the back of her neck and her underarms, and she didn't like the way it felt against her skin. It didn't belong. It gave her a black dream about dirty food that a lady ate because there was no other food. Carole kept her mouth firmly shut to keep the dirty dress out.

Patting her leg, Gran told her that today was Easter Sunday and that they were going to pray and sing. Carole smiled, careful to keep her mouth closed, so that the dirty dress couldn't get in. She liked to pray, and she hoped they could have a campfire too. But this time it was different. They went inside a building to pray and it was very quiet and filled with statues and paintings that brought more black dreams to Carole's mind, so many that she started to shiver and the faint echoes of California Dreamin' faded instantly from inside her head. Gran took her hand and squeezed it. Her eyes looked like she didn't want to be in that building either. Carole wondered if Gran had the black dreams too. She wanted to ask her, but couldn't risk opening her mouth in the dress.

They sat in a row on a hard wooden bench. Carole kept her mouth firmly shut and looked around wide-eyed and frightened. Then she saw rainbow lights dancing across the carpet, across the people in the benches, it was nearly as beautiful as what came with the music that Gran made. This light shone from colored glass that decorated the windows. The singing wasn't singing like Carole was used to, it droned without a melody, but it touched her heart in the same place and the light coming in the colorful windows helped make it right. She might have liked Easter Sunday then, if not for her dress. Men in long dresses of their own walked onto the stage in front, chanting, and Carole craned her neck to watch them. They were very solemn and did not smile. They read and kind of not-good sang stories that made Carole remember more black dreams.

One man, whose almost singing might have been nice if he'd smiled, was talking on stage when Carole felt her Mom's heart moving. The touch of it strayed from her and Gran and went to that man's heart and shone on it. He stopped his sort of song and looked around. It took him a few tries to finish his song and it was different then, not as good as before Mom touched his heart. Carole wondered why Mom ruined the man's song. He had been happy and now he was upset.

On the steps outside the building the men in dresses were talking to people and everyone was saying, "Happy Easter." The man whose song had been ruined by her Mom turned to stare. When he looked at Carole she suddenly remembered him though she'd never met him before. Her young heart danced to his and she forgot about her dirty dress. She laughed because her heart and his went together and she tried to hug his leg. He knelt down to hold her away, grabbing her hands and squeezing them tightly. He stared hard.

He looked so scared that Carole's Mom told him it was okay and Gran told him they were staying in the skyline for Easter. That made Carole even happier. They'd never been to the skyline before, they usually just drove towards it. Gran lifted her up and held her and the scared man put his hand on her head and told her, "Happy Easter" in a shaky voice. Carole's heart danced around his happily. He loved her, she could feel it, and it made her want him to be happy too and not scared.

When they were back in the car Carole remembered she hadn't said Happy Easter to him. She pushed her hands against the horrid dress, holding the ruffles safely from her mouth, and lifted her chin to announce, "Happy Easter! Happy Easter! Happy Easter!" She shouted her words and let her heart go with them, hoping he would feel it. Her Mom drove the car fast and the tires made noise. Gran told her to just drive back to the skyline. She kept saying, "Give him a chance. Give him a chance." That was what Carole remembered of that day. It was the last time she sat in the car between her Mom and Gran. The last time she ever saw them. If they got to the skyline they didn't take her. She didn't remember how she got out of that car, but sometimes she dreamed that her blankets turned to metal and she couldn't get them off.

When Carole had woken up she was in a room that smelled like poison, with rows of beds that had bars on them as if she were a baby. There were boys and girls in most of them. She knew it wasn't Easter Sunday anymore. There were ladies who took care of them and they told her she was sick and hurt. They didn't answer her questions but she knew anyway. She felt it. Her heart already knew. Mom and Gran had gone just like in the black dreams. Something had come and hurt them and they were gone now. The ladies who worked there brought her food and tried to make her eat it, but she knew not to. She knew it was all dirty and she kept her mouth closed tight. Black dreams clawed at her because Mom and Gran were gone forever, and her heart burned like fire. The nurses got very angry with her and stuck needles in her and tried to make her eat. Carole knew music and colors were gone forever, they died with Mom and Gran. None of the nurses or the doctors in that hospital even touched Carole's heart, and they didn't seem to notice when her heart tried desperately to find theirs.

Then he came, the man in the black dress. He sat down in an old green chair next to her bed and asked her to please eat. She told him it was all dirty food. He looked at her like he believed her. He went away and came back with different food. Carole ate an entire loaf of hard bread, and soaked the crusts in good clean milk so she could chew them. The ladies who worked there said she was a willful child. He sent them away. He told her that *they* would not let him have her. He told her that *they* were sending him far away. He told her that *they* promised to take care of her. He told her that he loved her. That is what she always remembered about him. He loved her. She knew that before he told her, but she was glad he said it. He talked a lot, and his

21

voice went inside her head without his mouth moving like Mom's sometimes had. No matter how hard she tried later, Carole never remembered much of what he said. It was mostly about his duty and his oath, and that he loved her and that *they* would give her clean food, she remembered that part. He said he could do that much for her. He sat with her all of that day, until the ladies that worked there told him to go now.

THEY'D GIVEN CAROLE clean food back when she'd lived in the orphanage, but that had been years ago, and it seemed like she'd been hungry since she'd been dumped into foster care. She glared out her social worker's car window at barren desert whipping past. The thought of good clean food made her stomach snarl. Real food—the kind the voices approved of—was harder to come by in foster care. It was expensive. *So my father didn't even do that much for me.* The voices in Carole's head criticized that thought, calling it ungrateful. She pressed her lips together. Maybe it was her fault the orphanage had tossed her out, maybe not, but it made no sense to argue with the voices in her head. If they had to be there, she certainly wasn't going to talk to them. Marsha exited the freeway fast, and a shiver rippled down Carole's back. She hated cars. *But I can't walk all the way to Roswell and back in an evening,* she thought, turning to look at her social worker. Learning more about schizophrenia would require a car.

Marsha drove craning her neck over the steering wheel like a turtle, focusing her gaze out the windshield while simultaneously twirling the radio dial. Always in search of a song called Mississippi Cotton Pickin' Delta Town by what had to be the only African American country-singer, it astonished Carole how often Marsha found that song.

"I need a ride into Roswell," she said over the flickering static and choppy music as Marsha swirled the dial back and forth.

"Is that right?" Marsha had a drawl. "I need a week where you're not getting suspended from another school." Marsha had a look that could see right through you.

"I need to go to a library there—for research," Carole explained, trying to make it sound like homework.

"Mmmhmmm?" Marsha's root-beer brown eyes widened, calling Carole a liar without a word.

"It's a medical library." Carole decided honestly was her only chance.

"You want to go to a medical library in Roswell? What for?" Marsha squinted at her, grabbing giant sunglasses off the dashboard and jamming them on top her head where they perched looking like an extra pair of unblinking eyes peeping out of her afro.

Carole stared at her lap. Her jeans were threadbare, one boney knee poked through.

"You don't have a medical condition, you have a communication condition," said Marsha.

"There could be a reason I communicate by fighting." Smoothing the soft threads around the hole in her jeans, Carole came as close to the truth as she dared. Marsha was her only hope for a ride into town.

"You seem so much older than sixteen. Sometimes I think we still have your age wrong. That nun at the orphanage really had no idea when your birthday was." Marsha turned the car radio off just as it passed over California Dreamin' and a surge of relief went through Carole. In the twelve years since Mom and Gran had died she still couldn't bear to hear it. It was wrong anyway. Drug induced memory or not, there were no colors with the flat static sound, and without the loving touch of a heart like Gran's or her Mom's she couldn't bear to hear it.

"I'm almost seventeen," she supplied, "at Christmas. Sister Mary Josephine said my birthday was at Christmas."

"Did she now? By older I meant you're a smooth operator. If you think I'm driving you into Roswell so you can run away, you can forget it. You've been in foster care for over five years now, in seven different homes not to mention the four group homes, and I guarantee you every last place has been better than the streets. Don't you run on me now."

"I'm not going to run," Carole promised.

"Hmpf. Well, then I can tell you that I'm not taking you out of Pine Hill High, despite the fight. You're not going to blow through every high school in my jurisdiction. Pine Hill is suspending you for two weeks. That means you'll be Martin's slave at Happy Acres in the meantime. And do not get yourself kicked out of Happy Acres, because this is the longest you've been anywhere and the next stop is Detention Home. D.H. is better than the streets, but only because they have ice."

Carole looked out the window as they turned off the paved road towards Happy Acres. It was bumpy dirt road the rest of the way, and Marsha now drove her new 1986 Ford Taurus slower than the school bus usually went. The dust billowing around and trailing the car created a personal dust storm. They had to roll the windows up.

"How's it going at Happy Acres?"

Carole shrugged. The character building camp was visible in the distance, barely discernible from the junk yard next to it. Happy Acres was run by a group of Jesus freaks who were determined to show heathen foster children the error of their ways. It consisted of half a dozen dilapidated trailers, a garden and a pasture for Martin Happy's latest obsession.

Marsha's look could also stare words out of you, and she apparently didn't need to look out the windshield while driving to employ the talent on Carole.

"It's going good," Carole admitted, wishing the woman would look away or at least put her sunglasses on. Her probing gaze always whipped the voices into a frenzy.

"Act normal! Average! Typical! She sees too much!" Carole really had no idea how to do that, and her uncomfortable writhing only made Marsha stare harder.

Marsha stopped her car right in the middle of the desert road shoving the gear into park. Twisting her thin body to face Carole, she demanded, "The boys aren't bothering you?" Her tone dared Carole to lie.

Staring straight ahead, Carole asserted, "I can handle the boys. I like Happy Acres." She refused to look Marsha full in the face.

"Well, Hallelujah and thank you, Jesus! Am I to understand, Miss Carole, that you are actually *trying* not to get kicked out of someplace?"

"Yes."

"Huh." Marsha turned, put the car back in gear and continued her painstaking journey. When she finally parked in front of the ramshackle hodge-podge of trailers that was Happy Acres she gaped through the windshield.

"What are those things?"

"Emu, they're Australian birds," Carole said. "Mr. Happy is starting a farm."

"Is that what you like here? Those things?"

Smiling faintly, Carole pointed to a second fenced-in area. "No. I like the garden."

"The garden? I thought maybe you wrestled those birds. Good luck, Carole, I hope I don't see you again until after graduation. I'd appreciate it."

MARTIN AND ELSPETH Happy did not believe in boys and girls mixing together unsupervised. There was a boy's trailer and a girl's, with the commissary, the study trailer, and the Happy's trailer separating them. Despite their vigilance, every single night a boy or two ended up in the girl's quarters. Carole made it a point to run in the desert until everyone was really asleep. Even if she could have resisted the urge to ruin the romance of the week, she couldn't sleep through the ranting of the voices in her head condemning late night kisses and worse. "*It is wrong. You must never...*" So she ran under the desert moon.

Since she'd been suspended from school anyway, Carole didn't bother returning to the girl's trailer until nearly four in the morning.

She climbed through the window and quietly dropped her shoes on the floor, nestling into her cot conveniently located right beneath that open window. She slid the sheet up to her chin and closed her eyes. Sensing a boy's approach she peeked beneath her lashes and waited. He was hardly stealthy; the trailer floor creaked with each step. The six-year-old girl in the next bed opened her eyes. Donald Hitte became visible in the light of the alarm clock. He had long black hair and a pretty smile. Heather Carr, who he had abandoned in the next room, certainly liked when he visited her at night. Confidently he lifted Carole's sheet and slid beneath. Placing one long finger over her lips, and spoiling his chance for a fair warning, he whispered, "Shhh, Sugar. Heather will hear, and I don't want her coming after my favorite girl. You know how she is."

Carole rolled onto her side to face him, muscles tensing. Putting his free hand on her stomach, Donald ruined any chance for mercy by then moving it up towards her flat chest. Carole really didn't care how easy it would be to send him away with sharp words. She folded into a ball and threw her arms and legs out as hard as she could. Donald sailed across the little room, right over the wide-eyed six-year-old, and into the bedroom wall. The trailer shook with the impact.

Carole hurtled out of the bed and followed, landing on him with all she had. Part of her wanted to hurt him, and though the voices were shouting to stop, Carole followed her instinct. Grabbing a handful of his hair she shoved his head against the thin wall, leaving a slight dent. She hissed into his ear, "Next time you touch me I will kill you." Then she stood, and tucked the sheet around the six-year-old, tossing over her shoulder, "For now I think I'll let Heather deal with you."

The six-year-old whimpered and Carole hollered, "Hey, Heather? Lose anything? Your boyfriend just scared Claire, sneaking in here." Running a hand over the little girl's curly hair, Carole whispered to her, "Don't be afraid. Watch Heather, and if anyone ever bothers you like that, you'll know what to do."

Donald lay on the floor moaning. Heather rushed into the room and started cussing and kicking him. Barefoot, she lifted her foot and brought her heel down on him for maximum impact, furiously following when he tried to roll away. Carole crawled back into her bed, and turned onto her side. Holding her pillow over an ear, she closed her eyes.

AT NIGHT THE desert became bitter cold. Carole ran faster, but she should have taken a jacket. By morning she wouldn't be able to feel her feet in this cold. Of course her jacket was in back in the girls' trailer, where Heather lay entwined with Donald Hitte. Carole couldn't believe that Heather was stupid enough to take the boy back. She insisted that she loved him. In the darkness Carole snorted and hoped that six-year-old Claire told on them. They'd made the poor girl go sleep on the couch in the commissary trailer. None of the other girls would expose them, probably not even if Donald decided to spread the joy around. Carole left voluntarily, ignoring the temptation to tattle. She really wanted to stay at Happy Acres; inciting Heather's wrath would probably make that impossible. Besides, she'd promised to kill Donald if he touched her again, and every time the boy looked in her direction she found herself imagining ways to do that.

Running through the dark desert, Carole focused on the ground in front of her. Treacherous cacti and rocks littered the landscape. Sound echoed from the highway ten miles to the south, humming faintly through the night. Carole's keen senses took over as she ran. Like a vigilant sentinel, a place in her brain somewhere behind her left eyeball saw much better than her eyes could. It scanned for danger and obstacles, and she took care to avoid a family of javelina less than a mile away. Although she sensed the wild hogs in the distance, her eyes watchfully roved the landscape too. Not even the smallest insect escaped her notice.

From behind an outcropping of rock a figure suddenly appeared, casting a faint shadow in the starlight and catching her unawares. Surprised, Carole stumbled and skidded to a stop. She could sense the boy now, but why hadn't she sensed him sooner? Where had he come from? He stood not ten feet away, watching her. Behind him a crescent

27

shaped moon provided enough light to see his straight black hair and dark eyes. He wore jeans and a concert T-shirt, but no shoes despite the cruel cactus spines and sharp rocks. This stretch of land marked the edge of a reservation, but Carole never expected that to matter in the middle of the night. With an apologetic nod she turned towards the southeast.

He spoke. "Don't go."

Turning to ask why, she found him now close enough to touch and stepped back, disconcerted.

"You're very like him," he touched his chest, "here. I've never met another one. I think he'd want to see you."

Mimicking the boy, Carole put her hand over her chest. There was another one like her? She narrowed her eyes in the darkness. Was this boy a hallucination? Her schizophrenia in another form?

"Who are you?"

"My tribe calls me Fastest, everyone else calls me Jonathan Redfeather." He ran his hand over his Guns and Roses T-shirt. "You can call me Fastest."

"Why?"

"Because I am the fastest."

"I'm not your tribe, shouldn't I call you Jonathan?"

"You're like him, so you feel like one of my tribe. Although I've been watching you run, so maybe I should be calling you Fastest."

"My name is Carole Blank." She nervously slipped her hands into the back pockets of her jeans and studied the boy. He looked her age, and there was something gentle about him, though he stood too close. His head tipped slightly to the side and his lips rubbed together as he considered her.

"Blank? Your last name is really Blank?"

"I didn't have one, just a blank line after my name on my paper-work. My first social worker didn't like me very much."

"My people were once assigned last names too. Run with me, Carole Blank? I'll take you to Grandfather. I think he should see you, and he's too old now, to come so far in the middle of the night."

The cold and javelinas forgotten, Carole considered going with him although she could sense no one else in the nearby desert. *What if it was true? What if there was someone like her?* Standing next to this barefoot boy in the starry night, Carole reached out a hand and touched Fastest. He was solid. He grinned, his teeth very white in his dusky face.

"Did you think I wasn't real? I thought maybe you weren't either. May I?" He held up an inquisitive finger and she nodded. He poked her right over the heart and said, "Ah! It is stronger with contact. Grandfather doesn't allow me to touch his heart. He said it has been broken too many times. Do the rocks talk to you?"

Glancing around at the formations in the dark, Carole listened. No, the voices only came from inside her head, and they weren't happy about Fastest. She ignored them. "Does your Grandfather hear voices?"

Fastest nodded, "Yes, you do too then?"

"Yes," Carole admitted, her decision made. The voices shouted in protest, rumbling through her head. *"You must never tell. It is forbidden. They would destroy us."*

"Will you run with me to meet him?"

"Yes."

CROSSING THIS FAR onto reservation land was outright illegal and it could cost her Happy Acres. Martin Happy wouldn't hold with anyone bothering Native Americans. If he found out, Marsha would be there as fast as she could get her new Ford Taurus down the rutted desert road. Carole raced alongside Fastest, a thrill rising in her heart despite the danger. The voices criticized and threatened. With every step they got louder, until black dreams began to flicker at the edges of Carole's consciousness. They had ways of making her listen, but she stubbornly ignored them, her attention on the boy. He was fast, the fastest normal person she had ever met. If she could consider a boy appearing in the desert night and poking her to make sure she was real, normal.

"Take my hand, Carole," his voice labored slightly with exertion. "Only my tribe can enter on their own." Hesitantly, Carole put her hand in his. His touch seemed friendly, welcoming, and she trusted him instinctively. They took a few more running steps and the night changed around them, inky blackness closed over them and a gust of wind almost lifted Carole off her feet. Fastest grabbed her with his other hand, holding tightly and tugging her through the resistant blast. She thought he was shouting something, but couldn't hear him over the roar of wind. Then the wind was at their backs and they both slid onto the desert floor, skinning their knees.

"Sorry!" Fastest apologized. "I've never brought anyone inside before."

"What was that?" Carole's heart beat faster, but not from fear. The voices had stopped shouting, only faint warning whispers encouraging caution emanated from them now. They knew exactly what that had been!

"Grandfather calls it a veil, he made it. Look at the sky." Carole looked up, in the darkness the stars appeared brighter, the slice of moon closer. She breathed deeply, even the resinous earthy scent of desert night tasted stronger, cleaner.

The huts of Fastest's tribe were visible in the distance. They ran towards them but Fastest soon skidded to a stop.

"Do you sense him?"

Carole sensed nothing, and Fastest looked disappointed.

"He is very old. He says I am the only thing left for his heart, but he must have felt you coming," Fastest motioned with his head towards a rectangular stone, a monolith on the edge of the tribe's village. It seemed to be watching the night for intruders. Startled for the second time that night, Carole both noticed and sensed an old man beside it. She could have sworn seconds before that no one was there. He wore Indian garb like she'd seen some of the men do for tourists, leather trousers with fringe and a beaded shirt. Long colored feathers were attached with bits of leather ties to his frizzled grey hair. The face looked so ancient and wrinkled that it had surpassed old age and become something to be revered, a masterpiece of time. The eyes were black, intelligent and knowing, and riveted on her.

"Grandfather, this is Carole Blank."

Shaking his head, the old man stepped forward and pressed his hand right against her heart. "Can you feel me young one?"

Carole understood his question and she tried desperately to feel his heart. The surprisingly strong touch of his hand pressed against her chest as though he could bypass flesh and bone.

"I can feel yours, young one. It beckons though you hide it well." He stopped pressing and clasped his hands over her forearms, and she instinctively clasped his in return. He nodded approvingly. "I am Rutak Tural, and I remember you, Cahrul Strongheart. It would seem we never forget the heart of another, though you were a babe when I saw you last."

"I could feel her heart too, Grandfather. I knew she was one of your people," Fastest said. His grandfather nodded in his direction.

"She is one of my people, Fastest. They used to visit when you were a babe. I knew your grandmother, Cahrul. I declared to her, but she would not have me."

"You knew Gran?" The question came out as a disbelieving squeak, and tears welled up in Carole's eyes, willing it to be true.

"Oh yes, but I was too old for her even seventy years ago, she would not have me. She loved a man who fought in the Great War. He died before your mother was born in 1918."

Carole's heart sank. For one shining moment she had believed the old man. Gran hadn't been that old and her mother certainly hadn't been alive at the end of World War One. Rutak Tural released her arms and frowned at her.

"You do not know do you young one, who we are? And you don't believe me. You cannot sense my old, broken heart, but I can feel yours and the sadness there. I am sorry to feel the loss of your grandmother and your mother in it. I did love your Gran all those years ago. She was just a girl then, only forty-seven years."

The impossible story made Carole's heart sink farther. It would mean that Gran had been over a hundred when she died, and Mom—

Mom had been just a girl! Too young really, to have a baby. Carole saw her mother's young face in the mirror every time she looked in it. The old man interrupted her thoughts.

"This is a great sadness, Cahrul. You still do not believe me."

Rutak sighed, and sat down on a rock, crossing his arms over his chest.

"Your mother's gifting was painting. Her paintings grace half the churches in New Mexico. Your grandmother, her gifting was music and color. How I loved that woman, still do, love is not something that goes away." Carole reeled. Could what he was saying be true? "Do you remember her, Cahrul? Do you remember your grandmother's songs? Last time I saw her she put California Dreamin' in my head so that I still hear it sometimes."

The tears spilled over. It was true, all of it, all the memories flooded back, they had been real! *Rutak had known Gran!* He nodded at her.

"You believe me now."

"You called me—"

"Cahrul Strongheart."

"Am I Native American?" She ran a hand doubtfully over her blonde head. Rutak laughed a hoarse old man's whispery chuckle.

"No, no, it is because you have such a strong heart."

"And you knew Gran seventy years ago?"

"Yes, I was born in 1826. I am one hundred and sixty years old."

She looked at Fastest and he nodded to confirm the impossibility.

"He is. It is in our Tribal Histories. My people found him before we were forced onto this reservation."

"Yes, and they kept me because I could hear the rocks."

"Grandfather, will you listen to the rocks for Carole?"

"Cahrul," he corrected, pronouncing the name in a strangely familiar guttural way. "Come, Cahrul. Stand before me and I will listen."

"Take your shoes off," Fastest whispered. Reluctantly Carole stepped onto the backs of her shoes to remove them, then her socks. Sharp rocks and thin burrs that seemed to be part of the eternal dust of the desert jabbed and dug into her soft feet, biting hard. She stepped in front of Rutak, uncertain what to expect of talking rocks.

"Mmmm." He bent forward emitting a painful grunt. His gnarly hands patted the ground around her feet. He pushed a hand against her foot and she lifted it. Rutak again patted the ground and the sole of each stinging foot in turn, rubbing painfully against embedded cactus spines.

"Ahh, yes, yes. You do not eat dirty, the rocks are pleased. These feet will touch rocks in many places. Mmmh." Rutak groaned slightly then sighed. "Yes, not all are destined for lives of joy, you are a creature of service—you will only know joy when you serve." He continued to make sounds, most disproving or groans that sounded sympathetic, then a few chuckles. He straightened up slowly, with Fastest helping, into a more comfortable sitting position.

Fastest squatted beside the old man, looking up into his face as though making certain he was all right.

"We call him Grandfather," he told Carole, "though he had no children. He told our tribe to stay here, that the rocks approve. Then he made this veil to cover us, though we do not understand how a man can do such a thing. Grandfather told me the rocks want me to stay with the tribe and stop leaving the veil and going to rock concerts."

Rutak wheezed an amused ha-ha. "Your mother asked me to tell you that. The rocks want you to run and listen to their music."

"So sometimes he lies," Fastest groused. "Grandfather, did you never marry because of Carole—Cahrul's grandmother?"

Rutak tapped his chest, right over his heart. "She was the only one for me. Our kind must go with one who touches..." he wheezed again and again tapped his heart.

"What are we?" Carole squatted in front of Rutak, Fastest at her elbow. "Do you hear voices? Telling you what to do?"

"Mmmpf. You spend too much time alone, young one, if you hear voices telling you what to do. I have my tribe. You must make your own tribe. We are—few."

Looking from Rutak to Fastest for clarity she asked, "But there are more of us?"

Motioning with his arms to include the desert and heavens, he wheezed, "Droplets in the ocean." Then he closed his eyes.

Leaning towards him, Carole reached to put her hand over his heart, but Fastest slapped it away. "Don't. That just might finish him off. He's only sleeping. You're the most excitement he's had in a long time. You should go now, Cahrul. So I can get him into his warm bed."

Carole reluctantly slid her shoes on, holding onto her socks. "Can I come see him again? Tomorrow night?"

Fastest's dark eyes glinted and he lifted Rutak to his feet. "You can try. Go back the way we came. Put your hands out in front of you and feel your way out, it is very windy at the edges. It will feel hard beneath your hands, but the exit feels like wax paper and it smells like garbage. Push your way through. Goodbye, Cahrul Strongheart."

CAROLE RACED BACK the way she had come. The wind blew at the edges of the veil. She glanced back at the clear night sky exhaling a sigh of regret. It felt different inside here, fresher. Lifting her hands, she forced her way through the wind until they met something hard. It was bumpy and solid, as though she were inside a giant fishbowl comprised of dense bubbles. She smelled garbage first, and forced her way along the hard surface until the texture felt exactly like wax paper. She pressed against it and ended up in a face plant on the ground outside. Shoving the stinging heel of a hand in her mouth, she rose and looked behind her. There was no sign of Fastest's tribe. No sign of the terraced village made of earthen houses. She studied the desert landscape, committing it to memory.

Carole moved reluctantly towards Happy Acres. She jogged slowly through the desert night, the things that she had seen, that Rutak had told her, circling in her mind. Rutak was one of her people! Hugging herself she smiled into the dark and whispered into the night, "Cahrul Strongheart. My name is Cahrul Strongheart." Vaguely guttural it sounded pleasant to her ears, rolling off her tongue like Rutak's, "Kuhrul". Then questions started to nip at her. Why hadn't she asked about the black dreams? Why hadn't she asked about her parents! She suddenly remembered what Rutak said about the voices. Rutak didn't have voices telling him what to do. The diagnosis of schizophrenia loomed darker, and she shivered, wrapping her arms around herself.

"But he talks to rocks!" She laughed out loud. When the shapes of Martin Happy's emus were visible in the distance, Carole remembered a detail. Despite having moved barefoot across the desert, her feet were fine. The barbed pain of embedded cactus burrs had vanished miraculously with Rutak's touch. The only evidence of her visit with Fastest and Rutak was scraped knees.

THERE WERE SO many questions to be answered. Carole slipped away every night she could to search the desert for Fastest and Rutak, but she could find no sign of the veil. Sometimes she knew she stood near the place she had entered, but she couldn't get in. No strange wind kicked up to pull her through. Night after night she couldn't find the village, or the huge rectangular monolith, or any sign a tribe inhabited the reservation. Hopeful, she searched every night for a week. Determined, she searched every week for a month. By the time October turned into November her search became frantic, and as the months crept past doubt rolled in. Carole began to wonder if it had been real at all, or just another facet of schizophrenia. It had seemed real, not like a black dream, but real. *Could it have been a hallucination?* Maybe they were starting, her mental illness getting worse. Maybe by the time nineteen rolled around she really would have all the symptoms—maybe she would achieve par and become a perfectly normal schizophrenic after all. By graduation Carole stopped whispering *Cahrul Strongheart* into the desert night, and forced herself to accept reality, not childhood memories or hallucinations.

CHAPTER
TWO

Santa Fe, New Mexico—May 1987

"WELL, YOU MADE it, graduate. Know what? I'm proud of you."
Standing in the doorway of her brand-new corner office, Marsha greeted
Carole. "Did you learn enough about gardening at Happy Acres?"

"Yes."

Marsha didn't motion towards the comfortable chairs by her
polished desk. Picking up her leather handbag and car keys, she
shooed her assistant away.

"I made an appointment with the recruiter. Are you certain this
is what you want to do?"

Carole nodded. There really wasn't any choice. She'd graduated
high school before turning eighteen and had to leave Happy Acres.
Mr. Happy had offered her a job taking care of the emu, but even
if she had transportation and a place to live it wasn't for her. More
importantly she had to stop combing the desert at night looking for
another hallucination. If it was—*it was!* She corrected her thoughts,
refusing to be tempted to spend even one more night combing the
desert. Besides, she liked to fight and that is what marines did. It was
what she did well despite the disapproval of the voices. A small part
of her cared that they didn't approve, an even smaller part wished she
could please them, but the biggest part of her just wanted to fight.

For the first time ever Marsha touched her. She ran her hand down the thick blonde braid knotted tightly against Carole's head, tugging it over her shoulder and leaving it to rest across her chest where breasts had finally made an unremarkable appearance. Pressing her fingers against Carole's cheek, Marsha sighed.

"You are too beautiful to be taken seriously in a man's world. You never pick the easy path, do you? Marines don't have gardens you know, and they eat what is put in front of them."

The voices started to grumble and Carole shook her head. "I will manage."

"Yes, I'm sure you will. Well, come on then, they'll be expecting us."

THE CHURCH LOOKED exactly the same as it had that Easter Sunday fourteen years ago. The surrounding neighborhood didn't. Santa Fe 1987 bustled with upscale tourist shops and art galleries. Carole crossed the street against traffic and entered the adobe courtyard. Her heart ached with expectant memories. It had been right over there, at the front of the courtyard, that she'd felt the touch of her father's heart for the first time. The road had engulfed part of the old parking lot, but it had been close to that stop sign when her heart had last filled with the loving touches of her entire family. *That part had been real! Hadn't it? At least that much had, surely.* She forced her mind away from the memory, afraid to take comfort in possible delusion, crossing her arms over her chest as though to protect her heart.

The statue of Our Lady of Guadalupe stood in front of the church named in her honor. In the heat, a pile of flowers sat wilting around her stone feet, baking in the hot air, their sickly sweet scent mixing with the fumes of nearby traffic. Carole reached a hand towards the statue, but a watchful Priest shuffled closer and she pulled back. He wore the familiar black dress she remembered from that Easter so long ago. He began rearranging drooping bouquets, keeping a suspicious eye on her. A trickle of sweat ran down Carole's back. Did he know her father? Know where he was now?

"Mass is starting." The comment was a command and he headed towards the building. Carole took one step and stopped, unable to imagine what it would be like to step foot in that church again. She had an idea of what would happen if she asked for help to locate her father, a Priest. Resting a hand on the rough adobe wall, Carole watched people file into the church. Taking a deep breath, the pain in her heart abated slightly. Mom and Gran had loved her, whether or not her memories were accurate their love had been real, so had her father's. She still felt echoes of their love in her heart. Carole turned, pushing through the gate. She left, certain only that even now he still loved her, wherever he was.

LOOKING OUT THE window of the Greyhound bus, Carole took in the endless ocean and chunky palm trees of coastal South Carolina with stoic acceptance. She'd never before been outside the desert southwest, yet in the three day bus ride from southwest to southeast almost none of the countryside was unfamiliar or new. She'd seen all of these places in her black dreams. Just like returning to Our Lady of Guadalupe and finding only the surrounding neighborhood changed, these highways and buildings were new, but the geography—the slope of hillside, the rivers and waterways—looked almost exactly the same. Leaning her head against the glass, Carole pondered that. Not for the first time she marveled at the delusional depth of her bizarre brain. How did her aberrant mass of grey know not only what the country looked like, but how it smelled and sounded? No wonder so many schizophrenics believed the reality inside their heads, it was just as real!

Turning to the grey-haired lady beside her, she brushed her mental illness aside and focused on what she could control. "Excuse me? Mind if I borrow your scissors?" The plump lady put her crocheting down. Soft blue and pink balls of yarn rolled around her seat as the bus bumped down the road. A veined hand reached into a bag covered in glitter and rhinestones and she handed Carole shears.

"Don't mind at all, Sweetheart."

Carole jabbed the tip of the tool into her hair at the top of her head and started to chop.

"What are you doing?" For a grandmotherly type, the woman had a big voice that carried. It didn't compare to the shouted protests of the voices in Carole's head. Apparently crazy house liked her hair long. She ignored them all and continued to saw through her thick hair with the scissors. It made a crunching sound as she worked the blades through the fat French braid.

"Oh, honey, I'd never have let you use them if I'd known you were going to do that." The lady had one hand pressed against her cheek, and looked distraught.

Carole passed the scissors back to the woman and ran a hand through her hair. She felt lighter, taller, like she could run faster.

"I'm going to be a Marine," she explained, because the grandmother kept staring through over-sized glasses.

The woman shook her head. "What's a pretty girl like you want to be a Marine for?"

"I'll be good at it." Carole said with confidence. The voices made no comment about that, still lamenting her hair. She held the braid up and looked at it. It was nearly two feet long. She rolled it up and jammed it into her bag.

"Well, now the front is too long for the back. Hold still, I'll fix it for you." It took several minutes, as the bus stopped and started, but the woman chewed her thin lips and her scissors snapped sharply. Onlookers appeared appalled, but when Carole glanced in the bus driver's mirror she smiled at the results. Her messy hair stuck up around her head in all directions. Running her fingers through it, loose hair showered down.

"Thank you, it's perfect."

"You'd look good bald," the old woman laughed. "Good thing, 'cause you practically are."

THIRTEEN WEEKS LATER Carole still had that braid. Kneeling on the floor of her barracks she rolled each regulation item of clothing and tucked it tightly inside her canvas bag. These insignificant scraps of cotton were the only tangible remnants after her weeks at boot camp. The only two personal items she owned she jammed safely between the clothes. The long braid she kept only because of the voices strange obsession about women and long hair. It seemed to pacify them, though they still ranted every time she trimmed her hair. The second item a spattered, crumpled piece of paper with a recipe on it and *Carole's Bread* written on top, listed basic ingredients that were becoming harder to acquire. It was all she had of him, her father, the Priest.

"You don't get much mail." For the first time the Sergeant spoke to her in a normal tone of voice. He moved down the empty barrack, stopping at the foot of Carole's metal bunk, and looked down at her.

Carole rose immediately and responded, "No, Sir!"

"At ease, Marine."

In the thirteen weeks since she'd set foot on Parris Island, Carole hadn't received even a piece of junk mail. It seemed an odd subject for small talk on her last day. The Sergeant motioned for her to return to her task, and Carole watched him in her peripheral vision while she resumed packing. He looked uncomfortable and Carole automatically glanced towards the nearest exit. *Six seconds, including knocking him unconscious.*

"People noticed," he kept his voice low. "They also noticed you're an exceptional recruit. That's not necessarily a good thing for you." Bending as though to inspect her bag, he dropped a piece of paper into it, his voice a faint whisper, "Don't read it here. Look at it on the bus. Good luck, Blank. You're going to need it."

THE AIRPLANE BORE the orange and red bird of a popular overnight delivery company. It sat on the runway, engine sputtering and propellers whirring. The door stood open. Ignoring the voices, Carole obeyed her orders and climbed inside. Six marines glanced her way as though expecting her and a thickset one moved to shut the door behind her. Except for the pilot, they wore all black, like Carole. A tall black man with fine-boned exotic features fished a lighter out of his pocket. Clicking it to life he held it towards her. Carole tugged her handwritten orders from the waistband of her pants and held the yellow paper over the flame until the charred remains drifted down to mingle with a small pile of ashes.

The plane taxied down the runway, and every man but the pilot found a place to curl up among stacks of packages and mail. Within minutes their eyes were closed and their breathing even, except Carole. It was her first plane ride, and in the stripped down, rumbling craft, with the fumes of jet fuel in her nostrils, sleep was the furthest thing from her mind. But after a couple of uneventful hours, outside of the voices continuous bellowing about airplanes being forbidden and unnatural, she leaned against a pile of brown paper packages and tried to relax. She closed her eyes, trying to ignore the protesting voices in her head and growling hunger in her stomach. Despite the vibrating noise, rumbling staccato into her bones, she eventually slept.

"UP, PRIVATE." A rough hand shook her awake. Her five teammates were up and eating. One of them tossed her a canister of water and a foil packet of rations. Carole looked through the packet and settled on food the voices approved. She peeled wax off a piece of cheese, piled peanut butter on it and thankfully shoved the entire thing into her mouth. After a moment of studying the wax peeling, she ate that too. A couple of the men looked at each other but said nothing. One of them spread a blueprint on a pile of mail.

"This is the resort where you'll find your assignment, Blank. He'll be arriving about the same time we are. You're going to have one hour from the time you step foot in that hotel, to get in, swap discs, and get out. We're meeting here." The Marine pointed at the map indicating the corner of a parking garage. "If you are late, we will leave you."

All five of men gazed at Carole, varying degrees of incredulity in their expressions. They wore experience in their posture and quiet confidence on their faces. She knew her seventeen meager years probably seemed ridiculous to them. Carole sat straighter. They didn't know her. No one did. The tallest man stood and put his backpack on, threading straps under his legs.

"Do you have many jumps?" The other men began to follow suit and Carole grabbed her parachute, emulating them. She shook her head in answer. The tallest Marine frowned at her. "How many jumps do you have, Private?"

"This will be my first, Sir."

The rattle of the plane door rolling open and the force of incoming air blew past them, but Carole had no doubt the plane would have gone silent if not for the wind. The men all looked at each other. A thickset Marine yanked at the straps she'd buckled, loosening them. He tugged her parachute off and tossed it onto the floor of the plane near the pilot, hooking only lightweight straps over her body. He snapped goggles over Carole's head and adjusted them as he shouted instructions at her.

"I'm going down with you, tandem. I'll be your parachute by holding onto your back. My chute can carry both of us." One beefy hand grabbed hold of her straps and he briefly lifted her with one hand, checking her weight, and nodded an affirmation to the leader.

"Out of time, Wright," shouted the tallest, the handsome black man. The men deferred to him, but even if they hadn't, Carole would have known he was the leader. He wore his authority quietly, in every movement of his strong body. Holding onto an overhead strap, he motioned with his chin towards the open door of the aircraft.

Wright pushed Carole to the door of the plane, snapping his harness to hers and shouting instructions directly into her ear. "Belly first, Private. Arch your back and trust me." The voices in her head were frantic, and Carole realized that for the first time ever, they didn't know what to expect and neither did she. She was doing something new to them. The realization hit her as both terrifying and thrilling.

Wright shoved her. They fell and for several long seconds her mind stopped, fear almost took her. It was cold and the rush of wind strong, speech impossible. Strapped to her back, Wright wrapped around her like a human backpack. His strong legs covered hers and forced them into position. She arched her back. Beefy arms wrapped uncomfortably around her waist, but her mind was flying. It felt fantastic, the air so clean. Somewhere deep in her psyche she knew that this is how air should taste. Over the merciless wind she fought to suck in deep breaths, trying to eat as much of the clean air as her body could hold.

Lights appeared beneath her in the dark. Carole tried to calculate where they might be, she became uncomfortably aware of Wright's arms and strong legs wrapped around her. His hands pressed together, right over her heart, and she didn't think it was a coincidence. He tapped out the seconds right against her chest for what seemed twenty very long seconds. Finally Wright grabbed her hands and tugged them to hold onto his harness, squeezing, so she held tightly. With one hand folded across her chest, he used the other to pull his chute. The abrupt slowdown yanked her roughly, her hands involuntarily loosened on the straps, but Wright's left arm held her in a crushing grip. Then they were drifting down, and she tightened her hold. The lights below them grew larger and brighter. The voices in Carole's head seemed frozen. Drifting towards the earth suddenly felt unnatural. To be so high felt wrong, but the voices were silent and at least she'd finally found one way to stop them.

CHAPTER
THREE

Miami, Florida—July 1987

THE CLOCK WAS ticking. Carole had fifty-five minutes to complete her mission. The sticky heat of Miami waited politely outside as she pushed through a revolving door into the opulence of the city's crown jewel, The Vanderbilt Towers. The icy blast of air-conditioning raised goose-bumps. Glass and mirrors sparkled across the foyer, and a fountain shot geysers of aquamarine water into the air. Brightly colored exotic birds squawked from branches of tropical trees inside little jungles contained by marble and glass, right in the middle of the hotel lobby. Live music from a string orchestra drifted across the foyer.

Carole smoothed her short hair self-consciously. Captain Lincoln had soaked it with water from his rations bottle, and slicked it back with perfumed oil. He had also applied what felt like far too much makeup, all in the confines of a moving automobile with the entire team crammed shoulder to shoulder. All the while he'd instructed, incredulous that she barely knew the difference between eye shadow and blush. Unable to comply with the 80's marine motto of *woman first, marine second*, makeup had been the only lesson she'd paid little attention to in boot camp.

Taking a step forward and trying not to wobble in her heels, uncomfortably aware of the tight dress revealing far too much of her, Carole tried to ignore the voices. They'd recovered from skydiving, and were lecturing about propriety in clothing. *"Simplicity. Virtue. Clean."* Sometimes they sounded oddly similar to Sister Mary Josephine from the orphanage she'd once lived in.

"Good Evening, Ma'am. Welcome to The Vanderbilt. Are you joining us for the Ambassador's reception?"

Miraculously, a nod was all it took for admittance. The hotel manager led Carole right through the ballroom doors and past the guest list that she wasn't on. He escorted her to the bar and ordered her a white wine spritzer. She never had to say a word. It was a lucky break, because the dress wasn't conducive to gaining entrance through an elevator shaft. The escort and the drink made her appear to belong. The manager passed her his business card and strode off. Carole dropped it on top the gilt and glass bar and examined the liquid in her glass. Her stomach snarled with hunger. Not entirely certain what she held in her hand, she hesitated, tempted. No wavering fumes emanated from the drink, but the voices began. *"Filth. If you sully yourself you will cease to be!"* The voices had definitely recovered from the jump.

People looked in her direction, but with smiles. Captain Lincoln had been certain she'd be admitted without a problem. Corporal Horne had commented that her good looks were the only reason she'd been temporarily assigned to the Pact, as they called themselves. The remark still made Carole bristle. She spotted Ambassador Balto Nelson across the room. She sized him up, six feet of dark and handsome. He looked fit and fast, and standing in a crowd of beautiful admirers, she doubted he would ever go willingly with her anywhere. How could she possibly lure the man to the privacy of his hotel room? She'd never so much as held a man's hand with intention, she did not do seduction. Judging by his female stalkers, she was in the minority.

Clutching her glass of wine, Carole turned her back on several men standing at the bar. Hungry, she grabbed a bowl of nuts off the counter and headed in the Ambassador's direction, shoveling nuts into her mouth as she watched the man. By the time the nut bowl was empty, she knew how many men were guarding him, where they carried their weapons, where the ambassador hid the floppy disc, and that one of his bodyguards watched the Ambassador a bit more than the job required.

"Would you care to join me in a dance?"

Not even sparing a glance towards the voice, Carole shoved the empty bowl in that direction.

"Of course not," she snapped, moving closer to the Ambassador. She had to assume the dress, or the shocking lack of it caught his eye, because he looked right at her. Moving quickly behind a stone pillar, Carole hid, knowing she'd never be able to approach him unnoticed now. There was something very knowing in his look, interested and inviting. Conversation would definitely be required. Mentally she changed tactics. Her orders were to exchange the disc. Going to the man's hotel room was impossible; she couldn't go against the voices. Not like that.

Carole started towards the Ambassador only to be accosted by another man.

"Would you do me the honor?" He offered a handsomely tuxedoed arm and a friendly smile.

"I don't dance," Carole opted for polite refusal.

"That is a tragedy." The finely tuxedoed gentleman reached into an ornate display of tropical flowers and pulled a simple bloom with bright green petals tinged in peacock blue. It matched Carole's dress perfectly. He offered it to her. "It's your eyes in a flower."

Carole rolled those eyes and marched away, wondering if any woman had ever bought that line. Keeping to the outskirts of the room, she rebuffed both aggressive fools and polite gentlemen as she circled. Keeping an eye constantly on Ambassador Balto Nelson, several times she saw his eyes glance her way expectantly. He danced with beautiful women in exquisite dresses. He drank champagne and ate from plates of hors d'oeuvres. Throughout her wait, Carole realized the man had become aware of her every move too. She sensed it as well as she sensed time ticking away, and she beckoned to him with her eyes and her body, hoping to lure him away from witnesses. She only needed a moment, and if he fell for it, she'd use brute force. She simply didn't have the skills to do anything else. The voices were furious.

CAROLE TOOK A post in an alcove near the men's room, her mind ticking through the remaining time and narrowing options. Finally she saw the Ambassador approaching. He kept eye contact as he walked, stopping a bit too close.

"You are old-fashioned, yes? You wait for the man to make the move. I like that." He took her hand and kissed the back of it. The voices didn't like it. "What are you drinking?" he questioned, raising handsome brows over very blue eyes.

Swallowing to combat her dry mouth, where bits of nuts still resided, she paused only long enough for her mind to move over the crowd just out of view. Placing one hand on the back of Balto Nelson's head, Carole slid her fingers through dark hair, getting a good grip. He smiled with perfectly straight teeth, and she quickly cracked her skull against his as hard as she could. She felt it, but Balto's eyes rolled up until only whites were visible and his entire body crumpled.

Carole caught him under the arms and dragged him into the empty men's room. Her skull throbbed and she staggered in her heels while sliding the Ambassador across ceramic tile. She shoved open the handicapped stall with her backside and slowly tugged the Ambassador up and onto the toilet. Her floppy disc rested securely, wedged beneath a breast, and held safely in place by the far too tight dress. She fished it out. Balto's had been taped against his hairy stomach, and yanking the tape loose left a bald spot. Carole swapped the discs and considered her dilemma. When he woke, his mind would surely go straight to the mystery woman. She needed enough time to get off the grounds.

One of his bodyguards wandered into the bathroom.

"Ambassador? Are you in here?"

Carole sensed him bend to look beneath the stalls, so he already knew the answer. She took a deep breath, shimmying the tight dress up and over her thighs, ignoring what the voices had to say. She straddled Balto's lap and dropped right onto his gut, hard. He grunted, and a long groan followed. The bodyguard didn't say another word. He scurried out of the room and stood guard outside the entrance. Carole sensed him standing there with her inexplicable radar. Balto groaned again, of his own accord, and attempted to open his blue eyes, eyelids fluttering. Grabbing a handful of his dark hair, Carole knocked his head against the tile wall but the voices' protests reached such a fever pitch she didn't dare do it again. Balto's head lolled limply, so it seemed sufficient.

There were fifteen minutes left to make the drop point, and part of her mind could sense all the way to the far side of hotel and her team already leaving the parking garage. *They don't think I'll make it!* The thought made her narrow her eyes stubbornly. *They don't know me!* Unbuckling the Ambassador's belt, she ignored the shouted protests of the voices in her head. Tugging his pants down to his ankles, she left him sitting in a semi-coma state on the toilet. Then she moved like she'd never allowed herself to move in a public place, estimating forty-five seconds to cover her tracks.

The guard waiting outside the restroom was big, thick like Lieutenant Wright. Planning to take him down at any cost, Carole approached on the toes of her high heels. The voices shouted with renewed protest. He turned just a second before she reached him, his eyes sad, almost hurt. Carole read his expression a split second before her attack, suddenly reluctant to harm him. One brutal strike against his carotid and he faltered. Carole squinted through emerging black dreams, the voices punishment for disobedience and hurting people. She focused, roughly massaging his artery as he weakly tried to escape her stranglehold. The bodyguard lost consciousness and she helped him to the floor.

In seconds she dragged him into the men's room, ignoring images of divine punishment flitting through her head. Tugging the big man into the stall with the Ambassador, she paused only long enough to adjust the men's positions, suspecting that the bodyguard wouldn't mind this at all when he woke. Carole yanked her heels off and ran. Even racing away, far out of earshot when the two men were discovered, she sensed it. The part of her brain that saw far watched a group of men turn right around and exit the restroom without raising alarm. Apparently they didn't want to be the first to discover what she'd left behind. The voices were furious with her, spouting words like *"lies, dishonor, untruth."* Carole flew down the stairs, jumping entire flights in her rush. The Ambassador's reputation was collateral damage she was comfortable with. She just hoped he didn't have a wife to answer to.

LINCOLN CROUCHED AT the edge of the golf course with the other four members of the Pact, swearing very unlike a Captain. Carole approached between thin palm trees, toes digging silently in sand. Slowing and approaching with caution, Carole heard the Marines talking.

"How could they expect success—they sent us a girl! That is a Marine? She looks like she should be in high school!" A deep voice said.

"She does," another voice agreed, it sounded like the one called Horne.

"Never saw nothing like that in my high school, Imars." Carole recognized Wright's voice, goose-bumps rose over her flesh despite the humid night. *He shouldn't say that.*

Lincoln joined in the rant. "And you're not likely to see nothing like that again! Do you think that kid has a snowball's chance in—"

"Sir," Carole interrupted. "Mission accomplished."

Stepping from behind perfectly manicured tropical trees into the open of the golf course, she watched their faces change to various expressions of disbelief.

"How the—" Lincoln was interrupted again, this time by Wright.

"Sir? I see the lights of our ride. We're going to have to make a run for it." Wright glanced at Carole's dress and swallowed. "I have your clothes in my pack, if you need help changing."

"Never mind! She can run in that," Lincoln snapped. Carole noticed Lieutenant Brown grimace, and he smacked Wright reproachfully in the back of his head. Thankfully they weren't all going to act like the boys in foster care.

"What I'd like to know," Lincoln whispered almost under his breath, "is how she knew where we were?"

Carole pretended not to have heard.

CHAPTER
FOUR

Republic of Singapore—September 1987

THE HEAVY HUMIDITY affected her breathing, that and the bullet. Carole vaulted over a metal fence and bent low, running in a crouch. The gunshot had caught her just below the shoulder and laid her flat. It had probably saved her life, but it was difficult to be thankful at the moment. Likely the Pact had been expecting this all along, failure from *the girl*, as they had taken to calling her. She hated proving them right. Two months of successful missions would mean nothing now. The girl had failed as expected. A misty drizzle began to obscure visibility. *Thank God.* Even at night there were too many eyes in Singapore, and it was difficult to go unnoticed, especially a tall blonde leaving a blood trail. Asia had changed compared to what the black dreams showed her. Singapore at night teamed with life, non-stop activity, and bright light.

Dark Mitsubishi Lancers appeared to be the most popular car in Singapore, but in the sea of nearly identical vehicles, her sharp eyes found the license plate she wanted. On hands and knees, Carole scrambled over damp blacktop, past a row of cars. She slid into the one designated as her drop point. The driver twisted to look at her. It took some effort. The heavyset American appeared stuffed into the small car like a slug in a metal shell. Something in his body language registered as surprise but he blinked wide-eyed, as though feigning innocence. It triggered suspicion. *How could he have known my pick-up was a set-up? He acts like he didn't think I'd show up!* She almost hadn't survived to show up here or anywhere ever again. The voices whispered and warned. They sensed something off, danger.

"*Hide. Do not engage. Retreat.*"

With only dashboard lights illuminating the car, the driver's eyes were dark and she couldn't read them. His head moved as he looked for injury. Even in the half-light, the exit wound in her armpit revealed she'd been shot. Her left arm looked useless in her blood soaked shirt. It wasn't. "*Run,*" the voices urged. Carole didn't feel very cooperative.

"How did it go?" his eyes furtively darted to a leather packet shoved into her waistband. "You actually got the code!" He sounded incredulous, angry, and the reason why hit her. He was a traitor. The tilt of his head, the expectation of injury, and the condemnation of the voices convicted him, but it was the subtle reach for his weapon that sentenced him. Carole reacted without hesitation. Four innocent people had died that night, and she would not suffer a guilty one to live. Not bothering to pretend, and refusing to be shot twice in one day, she attacked. With her left hand she slammed his head against the driver window. It bought needed seconds. By the time he brought his gun around his belly, her right hand caught it in an iron grip and pressed the muzzle against his stomach. She forced him to pull the trigger. Inside the car it sounded deafening. She shook from the violence of the act, hating guns and intrigue and traitors. While her ears rang painfully, her gaze fell on the car keys dangling in the ignition. In scroll letters on a pewter key fob she saw the word *Grandpa.* She'd killed a man, a traitor, a Grandpa. Carole opened the door and vomited into the street.

"YOU'RE LUCKY TO be alive. Good instincts," the Pact's Captain told Carole while they huddled in the hold of a cargo ship. She barely heard the comments of the other men as she rolled that compliment around in her head. Lincoln turned his dark fine-boned profile towards the others and repeated it.

Good instincts. That is what she had. Grandpa had been a traitor to his country and she had killed him. Somewhere grandchildren would mourn, and she would have to learn to live with that. The words *good instincts* helped. Despite the voices, she was good at working off the grid because she had good instincts. Affirmation from another human being helped, and Lincoln gave her talent a name, a normal name. Not psychic schizophrenic like she'd been leaning toward, just good instincts.

"You are one lucky bitch. I'd bet there isn't even going to be a reprimand or a suspension." Corporal Horne, busy scrubbing her wound clean, smiled at her as though he'd congratulated her rather than used his derogatory nickname for her in front of the whole team. Apparently he considered it an endearment. "You were damned lucky Lincoln witnessed everything. When you kill one of your own, the outcome isn't usually very positive. You might want to consider that, next opportunity."

Horne picked up another bit of cotton batting, put salve on it and continued to rub vigorously. Carole sat on the table in her sports bra, the remains of her T-shirt beside her. Across the room Lieutenant Wright examined her with a bit too much interest. After his glance finally wandered to her hostile face, he busied himself checking the group's weapons. Ever since their tandem skydive the man watched her too closely. She'd have to do something about it soon. Imars, the weapons expert, stepped into Carole's line of vision, glaring at her.

"If you had a gun, you might not have gotten shot."

"Almost killed," Brown clarified across the hold, dropping a box of M16s onto the cargo floor with an echoing thump. He settled next to Wright, who quit shooting sidelong looks her way to pick through the weapons.

"Another inch to the left and you would be dead." Imars tried to stare her down. Carole didn't care, she stared back. She wasn't using guns. It was her risk to take. If she had to kill someone, she'd look into their eyes and know whether or not it needed to be done. The voices didn't approve either way, but Carole wasn't listening to them about it either.

Lincoln stopped beside her, defending. "Let it go, Imars. She could aim into the sea for a fish and hit a seagull in the sky. You don't want to be near Private Blank when she's armed. At least I sure don't."

It was true. She wasn't any good at it either. Not that she tried.

Imars huffed, but squatted beside the other men to help clean and load their weapons. Carole touched the knife at her belt. It was sufficient. When she looked up, Lincoln winked at her.

"It's not that knife anyone should worry about, Private." He patted her left hand, resting on the table. "It's these hands; they should be licensed to kill. In fact—" he paused to pour alcohol over her wound, ignoring her grimace, "I think they are. Unofficially of course, if you even existed, which you don't."

Imars chimed in from his spot on the floor, "It's easier to kill when you don't have to get so close."

The men all agreed with that statement, but Carole fought off a shiver. It shouldn't be easy to kill. Ever. Even the voices agreed with that.

THE WORLD FROM her black dreams was a familiar place to Carole. Over the next four months the real world became familiar too. Just like on her bus journey in the states, everyplace from Singapore to the Sudan, even Afghanistan and Colombia were all eerily similar to the places black dreams had paraded through her mind all her life.

Carole celebrated her eighteenth birthday in the cargo hold of an airplane somewhere over South America. Perched on top sacks of cocaine, with a pile of bananas in her lap, she ate her way through the fruit. Lincoln took a seat next to her and slapped the commandeered haul beneath him. It raised a puff of white powder.

"We'll be tossing our latest acquisition into the ocean shortly. Quite a way to spend Christmas, eh, boys?"

It did Carole's heart good to be included with the boys. She offered Lincoln one of her bananas and he grimaced, but told her proudly, "You're the only woman on any Black Ops team. I mean if you really existed you would be, which you don't, so never mind, but Happy Birthday. Your non-existent paperwork says you're eighteen today, which would be insane if you were real."

The rest of the team had stopped paying attention around the word "woman". Despite the growing list of successful missions they hadn't warmed to her. That included Lincoln, though he said all the right things, and sometimes, like today, seemed to mean them. Instead of truly being part of the team, Carole fit in more like a useful gadget they'd been issued but didn't quite trust. After a brief but annoying infatuation with her, Wright had finally given up when she'd knocked him unconscious one night at base camp. Horne hated all women, a fact which he proved anytime they were on break. The man wooed and dumped a new girlfriend in the space of a weekend. He had only one rule when it came to women, they couldn't be taller than his five foot ten inch height. Carole had almost a half inch of safety. Horne called Carole bitch anytime he had to address her for any reason, including at debriefings in front of superior officers, although he always said it in a polite tone on those occasions. It might have bothered her if she didn't have her own derogatory name for him, but she never said it out loud. Brown didn't pay much attention to anyone except to correct them for deviating even one iota from his plans. Imars had apparently dismissed Carole back in Singapore. He seemed to have no use for anyone who didn't employ his top of the line weapons, and the only time he talked to her was using hand signals during missions.

Carole rarely spoke to any of the five men unless protocol demanded it. She followed orders. She followed her instincts. She almost belonged with the Pact, and despite the condemnation of the voices and her outsider status, she was determined to be content.

CHAPTER
FIVE

North Korea—February 1988

"DAMMIT, THAT'S DISGUSTING. You're leaving bloody footprints. Why the hell can't you use a gun?" Imars glared at her from inside the ambulance. Carole grabbed onto the van's door to pull herself up and he shoved her back down with a wet boot to the chest. It took restraint she barely had to keep from pulling the jerk out of the van and throwing him into the snow. Exhausted and wounded she didn't need grief. The mission had not gone well.

Lincoln hurried to the rear of the ambulance, staring down at her. "It was supposed to look like an accident! What did you use, your teeth?"

Brown nearly panicked when he looked over the Captain's shoulder at her. "We do not want to get stopped in North Korea with blood literally on our hands. Take your clothes off and clean up in the snow." He rooted around in the van and tossed down a sweater and the white smock of an ambulance attendant. "That's all we have."

Lincoln jumped down to help her. Carole's hands were shaking as she pulled her jacket and jersey off. He stuffed them into a plastic bag, along with her pants. It didn't bother her to strip almost naked in front of the big man, and he appeared focused on cleaning her up and getting his team out alive.

"Brown is right. It will be a miracle if we get out of here without getting stopped. And if we do there is no way we're going to pass as Korean."

Within minutes Carole climbed into the ambulance and tugged on her dark wig. Lincoln took his place on the stretcher, working on covering his legs with padding used on burn victims. Watching her Commanding Officer disguise himself, Carole explained in Korean, in regional perfect dialect, "I didn't kill the physicist. It was a set up. General Samish lied."

Every head swiveled towards her. Lincoln growled, "Don't tell me this, Private. Do not tell me this."

"Shit, bitch, then who'd you kill?" Horne glared.

"General Samish and Ambassador Causer."

The confession caused momentarily stunned silence. Carole went through the motions of an EMT as her orders required. She jabbed a needle into the IV tube connected to Wright's arm. A saline bag hung above his shaking head. The entire pact watched her with expressions she couldn't bear to see. Her heart sinking, she dispensed the needle full of valium into Wright's line.

"We are so ff—" his words drifted off as he slipped away. Brown leaned over Lincoln and wrapped burn pads over his face. No one else said anything. Wright had about said it for them all.

IT TOOK TWO days to get out of North Korea. They weren't two days that any of the Pact could take pride in, or care to remember, and Carole knew it was her fault. But not once did a single member of the team say a word against her. It wasn't the elephant in the room, it was the elephant the men pretended wasn't there while trying to drag it out of the country, and it seemed to get heavier with each step. Wright and Imars would possibly lose some toes to frostbite. Carole had to knock Horne unconscious and stuff him into a trunk, something a misogynist would probably never forgive. Brown stopped speaking to anyone during the final sixteen hours, even with hand signals. By the time they crossed the border in the belly of a septic pumping truck, the men were ready to snap.

Standing in a snowy field, covered in filth, their contact refused to let them into his van.

"Give me break, you two days late! I give back other car, but I wait for you. Two days I wait! I no sign up for this," he gestured at them in disgust. "This my car. My family car. You know how much car cost in Korea?"

Carole turned on the men before they could kill the driver. She relieved Imars of his ever present gun and shot at the ground, coming far too close to Brown to ever be forgiven.

"Stop it! We're out now. We're safe. I'm sure we can find some-place to clean up and get a ride. Probably food too."

Lincoln marched right up to her and took the gun out of her hand, tucking it into his waistband.

"She's right, and we're all in far more trouble than this—shit." He tugged at his sweater. Like the rest of them he was covered in a mixture of the dregs of the septic tank and his own vomit. Lincoln turned to the driver of the van. "You need to call your contact. Have him send a message to Lieutenant Colonel White. Tell him we have a Judas Judge on our hands."

The driver stared at him a moment, then motioned with his head. "Get in, there no hot water for miles. When you get to base, you tell White. He there."

Five voices said the same word. Carole kept silent. This was her fault, and she had absolutely no proof to offer for failing in her mission. They didn't have to explain the term Judas Judge, because she knew she was Judas.

CHAPTER
SIX

Marshall Islands, South Pacific—March 1988

"HE'S LETTING US sweat," Horne said. They were the first words any member of the Pact had said in front of Carole in the two weeks since they'd returned to base camp. Camp was an island, technically part of The Marshall Islands, right in the middle of the South Pacific. Officially this particular island didn't exist anymore than Carole did. Without looking at her, Horne continued, "I've been expecting to be pulled out of bed at night for water-boarding. This guy has a reputation."

Lincoln dropped his rations tray on a table and started peeling a mango. "Ted White doesn't have people water-boarded. The man is an intelligence genius. Don't start trying to outthink him; your head will explode."

"Point is when a team no longer follows instructions they're no longer a team." Brown appeared to be talking directly to the large piece of fried fish in his hand. He hadn't even looked at Carole since North Korea.

Horne twisted in his seat to glare at Carole. Though they hadn't been speaking to her, they ran, practiced maneuvers, and ate together. In the close confines of the air-conditioned commissary, the stony silence had finally given way. She sat in front of a platter of grilled pineapple topped with avocado and black beans, slowly making her way through it, and ignoring him.

"Bitch, why couldn't you just have taken out the physicist? That was your mission. Not to decide who was guilty and hatch a new plan. That is not how it works." Carole kept eating and Horne addressed the rest of the team. "If the Colonel gets rid of her, problem solved. She's the one who didn't follow orders. She's the one who almost got us killed in North Korea."

"I'm guessing you put your opinions in your report, Horne? Shut it for now and do me a favor? Stop calling her bitch."

Horne inquired as to the appropriateness of a different name and Lincoln flew across the table, his usual resilient nature morphing into something dark and angry. Carole jumped out of the way as the rest of the Pact joined in the fray, half their bodies on the sturdy rectangular table, half off. Her plate, along with most of her dinner, ended up beneath Horne. The loss of the food bothered her the most. She understood the fight, understood fists better than the quiet subterfuge the men engaged in around her. If she was really part of the Pact she'd be in there with them, trying to knock a couple of Horne's white teeth down his throat. But she knew as long as she stayed out of it no one would get really hurt. These men respected each other.

The voices began to criticize the men, but she knew that Horne was right. She was the one who almost got everyone killed in North Korea. The Pact worked by different rules than she did. They followed orders to the letter. She followed orders until they interfered with the moral code that the voices had instilled in her long ago. Despite her occasional defiance, the voices were impossible to ignore. Besides, it wasn't just the voices—nothing in her would allow her to kill an innocent man, and the consequences of her actions were being paid by the entire team. She did not belong.

A squad of Military Police broke up the fight, placing them under arrest. MP's escorted them across campus, but they never made it to the brig. A young Private raced after them, halting the procession to announce orders in a voice that still crackled from the changes of puberty.

"Lieutenant Colonel Ted White sends word, Sir. Instead of the brig they're being sent to summer camp."

After executing an about face, the Pact marched obediently down to the beach, to wait on the docks. Apparently they were being moved to another island. Judging by the sympathetic looks shot in their direction, Carole had a bad feeling that the brig would have been a far more pleasant option than summer camp.

THE PACT STOOD at the dock waiting. Base camp activity buzzed around them. Most of the teams were there to regroup and train for missions, but the sound of rock music drifted from the main camp, the smell of a charcoal grill in the air. A helicopter landed on the far side of the complex, past the gymnasium, and several speed boats took men to waiting ships. Nobody paid any attention to the Pact. The men waited under guard by the kid still in the throes of puberty. He looked younger than Carole but smoked a cigarette while keeping one finger on the trigger of his M16. Carole knew this too, Imars would never forgive. She stood apart from the group, staring over the water and ignoring the prattling voices inside her head. They were urging escape before the Pact got her alone and retaliated.

Despite the overshadowing military presence, the islands were a tropical paradise. Clear turquoise water rippled and creamy sandy beaches ringed volcanic islands. Lush green vegetation darkened the interior of every island, hiding ugly barracks. Sunset eventually turned the azure sky flame-orange, ruby-red and gold. Palm trees became dark silhouettes. Carole focused exclusively on the scenery, ignoring the voices and successfully tuning out the arguing of the Pact. A coral reef grew beneath the water and she could sense teeming life. She focused on identifying marine creatures, using that part of her brain that couldn't be held prisoner by a boy with a machine gun.

A white speedboat pulled up to the dock, and two formidable marines with automatic weapons loaded them into it. The Pact leaned sullenly against the sides of the boat as it motored over the water. The sun set by the time they approached their destination, leaving only orange and red streaks and blinking blue boat lights striping the water. The boat motor cut off well before reaching shore. One of the guards poked Carole with the tip of his gun and growled, "Get out." She immediately did so, toppling over the side and treading water in the darkening ocean. A few members of the Pact argued about sharks and their still bleeding injuries before joining her in the water. Heavy splashes sounded as their supplies were tossed in behind them. The boat motor turned over, and the craft maneuvered back towards the main island.

Someone shoved a rubbery pack towards Carole's head, splashing water over her face. A volley of cussing followed. "Figure out a way to get that to shore, bitch." *Shoot*, she realized, it wasn't Horne, but Wright. The man had apparently gotten over any feelings he might have once harbored for her. Lincoln's long dark form passed by, swimming for the island in the distance.

Between alternately shoving and towing the bulky pack, the long swim tired Carole. She sensed fresh water, food, rope, and clothing inside the pack and in the endless water she sensed no sharks. That knowledge reassured her, but the men struggling around her didn't have that reassurance. The moon rose by the time they made land. Carole allowed the men to reach the beach first. Despite what the voices thought, she didn't think the Pact would hurt her, but it didn't seem like a good idea to give them any further reason to want to.

Tugging the case ashore, she dragged it over the beach, well out of reach of the tide. The members of the Pact simply dropped on the shore and went to sleep wherever they landed. Carole leaned against a palm tree and made certain they were all asleep. Judging by the few supplies they'd been given, the food and water wouldn't last long. They would have to work together to survive here. That task would have once been an unspoken given, but because of her everything had changed. Because of her the Pact was fragmented, and she knew it couldn't be fixed until she was out of the equation. *I don't belong.* Exhaustion finally allowed Carole to succumb to sleep.

FROM THE STORE of meager rations, Carole ate only cheese, peanut butter, and her share of water. That left more dried meat, noodles and energy bars for the men. Yet Horne said she was pissing him off, and that she ate like a spoiled child. Picking a large black beetle off a tree, she popped it into her mouth and chewed. Lincoln, always the leader setting an example, laughed and he followed suit. The insects had a strange minty taste to them, and they were protein. Carole could no more eat processed food than she could kill an innocent man, but she got hungry too. The voices didn't allow her to eat a processed granola bar, but they were perfectly good with beetles and woodlice. She could sense the tiny crustaceans crawling through the rotting trees in the jungle brush. They were small, but there were plenty of them. Grabbing an empty bottle, she headed towards the trees to gather her lunch.

The Pact spent day one mostly searching the small island. It took less than two hours to walk the beach and come upon their own footprints again. The interior of the island consisted of thick jungle, and they found evidence of many prior visitors. The remnants of huts, hammocks, snares, and tents had been reduced to sparse piles of rubbish. Useful supplies had obviously been removed to make life sufficiently painful for new arrivals. The only structures standing were manmade obstacle courses. According to the orders tucked in with their meager supplies, they were to participate in the various rope courses three times a day, employing specific handicaps. Lincoln took charge, announcing their schedule, which included the most basic course first.

During daylight the course took no real effort, although Wright swore at Carole throughout. Afterwards the Pact separated to dig through everything left behind on the island, looking for anything of use. With no freshwater on the island, their biggest need was anything that could be used to desalinate seawater. By dark they'd accumulated enough material to make a rough attempt at solar desalination. Tired, the men tucked down to sleep a couple hours before they'd need to wake and run the basic obstacle course in the dark.

Deciding it would be wise to sleep away from the Pact, Carole moved towards the trees. Sand stuck to her wet boots, trickling between the laces as she walked. Lincoln shouted after her.

"Not you, Blank! You don't eat much, but you drink your share. There's only enough water for another day. Let's see what you can do to fix our water problem in the next two hours."

"Sir? There's no light." Their supplies hadn't contained a single flashlight, and clouds blotted out the moon. Besides that, it would take the entire team to build anything big enough to supply as much water as they needed.

"Are you arguing with me?"

"No, Sir. Would you have me build a fire, Sir?"

"Absolutely not. I'd have you pull more than your own weight since you're the one who got us into this—situation. Build it in the dark, Judas, and wake us in two hours."

THE INCESSANT ROAR of the voices mounting their soapbox dimmed in comparison to the black dreams. Horrific visions of witch burnings, hangings, and a general assortment of torture paraded through Carole's consciousness. She was being punished far beyond what Lincoln could inflict on her. Maybe the voices had cried wolf too many times, or maybe the anger coursing through her veins helped, but Carole managed to stay focused on her task despite the divine retribution in her head. Forcing the scent of burning flesh and hair to the back of her mind, and using her extra senses she moved through the darkness unhindered by lack of sight, dragging branches, tenting poles and tying canvas to PVC piping. If she could trust her senses, and despite the background clamor, she thought she could, she sensed a pocket of water beneath the island—and it was very likely fresh. If she could trust visions she'd seen in her dark dreams, then a windmill could provide the energy to vacuum it from the ground—if she could fit the pipe properly through the opening in the rock. Carole shuddered as part of her brain watched a man in a town square being tortured, his skin being slowly peeled off his body.

Two hours later Carole stood over Lincoln, drinking from her rations bottle. The water tasted faintly brackish, but she had no doubt it was potable. The moon broke through the cloudy sky for a moment. Carole poked Lincoln with the toe of her boot. Hair had started to sprout on his normally bald head, and part of her wanted to dump water on it. To tell him if he gave an impossible task to the crazy marine with the legion of mad veterans in her head, it got done. She didn't dare, her head already screamed with pain, she certainly couldn't afford to antagonize her mad mental menagerie further. Lincoln ignored the boot.

"Sir? It's time to run the night course."

"Sod off, Blank," he intoned, turning over.

"That bitch is drinking our water!" Wright's voice cut through the night. With a head full of screeching pain, Carole didn't realize he was coming until he slammed into her, knocking her over Lincoln. The metal water bottle fell, landing right on Lincoln's forehead. He woke fully, swearing. Wright's weight crushed Carole into the sand, and pain exploded in her head as white light. Blackness came, blissful, welcome, then nothing.

She tried to stay there. There were no voices in the dark, no dark dreams, nothing. But from far off voices called to her, and Carole struggled to ignore them, she'd had enough of the voices. She needed peace. An unfamiliar physical awareness intruded, grinding against her. Hands pressed hard against her chest, rubbing over her breasts.

"Oh, God. Oh, God. You are so beautiful. Let me in, let me in," a voice whispered the words over and over, so low that she could hear them over the returning demented dissertation she was so familiar with.

"Stop him. Hide. Hide, hide, hide. He feels you."

Familiar body odor wafted up her nose, and a wet mouth lapped at her face. Carole twisted away. Clouds covered the moon again, but she knew who pressed against her. Wright's body odor always reminded her of the time one of Martin Happy's emus had been killed by coyotes and then left to fester in the desert sun.

"Get off me!" she shouted into his ear.

He ignored her, grinding against her, whispering softly, "God, oh, God, please!" He was a heavy, solid man. She'd hit the sand hard, and felt half buried in it. At that moment Lincoln and Horne located Wright in the dark, and hauled him off of her. Despite the dark, Carole sensed Lincoln throw Wright. He landed flat on his back in the sand, and to her horror he started to cry.

"Blank! Are you okay?" Lincoln shouted.

"Yes, Sir," she answered, but her voice sounded small. The sound of Wright's sobs horrified her.

"To the obstacle course, everyone, now! That includes you, Wright. Get there. That is an order!" Carole sensed Wright clamber to his feet and stumble into the jungle. Horne followed, grabbing his arm and leading Wright in the proper direction. Trembling, she rose to her feet.

"You will have no water until daylight, for taking it without authorization—and for spilling it!" Lincoln sounded furious. Suddenly Carole didn't dare tell him about the well, about the fresh water on the island. The voices were right, it was impossible for her to have found it in the dark night. She could provide no rational explanation for it.

"Yes, Sir. I'm sorry, Sir."

"Save it." Lincoln started to stalk away, then paused and turned in her direction. "What the hell do you do to Wright, you bitch? That man was a rock until you got to him! Leave him alone!" He stormed away then, and his words cut into Carole sharper than any had had the power to do in a very long time.

CHAPTER
SEVEN

Base Camp, South Pacific—March 1988

CLOUDS SLID PAST the moon, and occasional patches of moonlight lit the clearing like a ghostly spotlight moving soundlessly over the trees, before vanishing again. The obstacle course had been easy in the light of day, but night and tension took it to a whole new level. Standing at the head of the course, Carole could sense most of it. It consisted of walls to be climbed up and repelled down, wooden hillocks similar to a child's playground equipment dotted the area, the only difference being these were covered in rusty nails or metal and sharp bits of glass, a large parapet stood in the middle. The team would take turns defending, and then breaching it. Tunnels cut through the course, some manmade corrugated plastic and some reinforced earth, both clogged with refuse and mud.

The men spent the first half hour trying to calm Wright. Their method began with verbally tearing Carole to pieces. Keeping her distance from Wright, she could still hear the men's deep voices. *Bitch* seemed a term of endearment after other words floated to her ears: manipulative, calculating, traitor, scheming-lesbian, and tease being the most often repeated. Carole cringed to hear Wright defending her.

"You don't know, you don't know!" he said, crouched on the ground, rocking, rubbing his hands over his chest as though frantically petting a dog, and moaning.

Lincoln finally lost it. "Blank! You did this to him, you fix it!"

Carole stormed over to the Pact and slapped Wright across the face. He rolled backwards and landed flat on his back. Carole sensed a spot where his teeth cut his lip and blood trickled out of his mouth. Towering over him in the dark, she said what she meant. "Knock it off! I am sick and tired of you, Wright. What do I have to do to get the message through to you? I don't even like you. Leave. Me. Alone. If you ever touch me again, I will break your arms. If you don't think I can do it, get up and try me right now."

Wright growled two words at her, signaling a return to his senses quite succinctly. Horne hauled him to his feet, slapping him on the back with approval. "If you want to break her arms, we'll hold her down for you." Wright repeated the same two words to him, interlaced with several gasping sob sounds. The group moved towards the obstacle course, Brown and Horne dragging Wright by his armpits until he shook them off and lumbered forward on his own.

Lincoln set the scenario for the nighttime run. "Blank, Brown, and Horne team against me and Imars—Wright, you're rogue. If you get a chance to break any arms, go for it."

In all her time with the Pact Lincoln had been fair, until tonight. *Great*, thought Carole. She ran her hands through her short mess of hair, wondering why Lincoln would encourage hostility in the group. *He isn't, I'm not part of the group and he's not going to pretend anymore.* She had become the sacrifice if that's what it took to keep the Pact together. Carole pulled her mask over her head. If Wright came for her, she would have to hurt him. Horne shoved her towards the first wall, and she slid across the mucky ground. Grabbing onto a fat nylon rope she propelled herself forward away from her own teammates, focusing on the obstacle course and watching her back.

THE ABILITY TO know if her teammates would turn on her wasn't one of Carole's hidden talents. The voices expected the men to turn at any moment, but they'd been predicting attack and public execution since she'd been a child. Blessedly her team, Horne and Brown, seemed to automatically slip into their role of professional marine.

Carole climbed the parapet ahead of her team, behind her Brown and Horne struggled to catch up. Lincoln and Imars were up to something on the farthest wall. She suspected they were going to team with Wright at the last minute because he appeared to be attempting to rig some type of a trebuchet on the ground, something out of his skill set. No doubt their intention would be to take her down the next time moonlight broke through. Horne and Brown were still twenty feet below her, groping for hand and footholds, and safely out of the range of anything thrown in her direction. Carole slowly made her way around to the front of the parapet, out of the range of whatever Wright was planning, wondering if he'd decided to settle his feelings by eliminating her. She had no doubt that he'd get whatever he was working on functional if Imars helped.

Something felt out of place. Carole paused to take in the members of the Pact again. They were still at the same tasks, but the feeling niggled at the back of her mind. She was missing something, something besides water. The climb in the heat left her throat parched. Below, Horne's swallowing sounded like an open drain. She suspected he did it on purpose.

A shadowy figure shot out of the top of the parapet and dropped. With startling speed a man shot past Carole where she clung to the wall. Sensing him as he passed, she almost lost her footing, suddenly disoriented and dizzy. The only sound as he descended was the gentle whir of a repel line. Even the voices in her head silenced as a loud buzzing shock seemed to reverberate through her. A part of her mind reprimanded for not watching above. *Amateur mistake!* Another part noted that the entire team had gone still at the approach of what was surely the infamous Ted White. The Pact had been both dreading and anticipating the man's arrival. What Carole hadn't expected and what left her clinging to the wall was the fact that she too had been waiting for Ted White, but for an entirely different reason.

Carole could sense his heart.

Not since her father had been escorted from the hospital when she was three-years-old had she sensed the heart of another human being. The touch of a heart hadn't been a delusion, it was real. Tears filled her eyes and she clung to the wall, gasping, as joy surged through her. Ted hit the ground with a faint thud and skidded over brush. The moon broke through, lighting the clearing. Thirty feet below the first heart she'd sensed in fifteen years waited. Tears slid down her cheeks as she watched the men move slowly to where the Lieutenant Colonel waited. Dressed completely in black, with his head and face covered, she couldn't see what he looked like. It didn't matter, she could feel him. Leaning into the rough wood of the parapet she pressed her hands against her heart, feeling more awake than she ever remembered.

"Blank!" Lincoln's voice reminded her that there was protocol to follow. She wiped her eyes, not bothering to hook onto her zip line. Grabbing hold of Ted White's line, she dropped straight down, not caring who noticed the near-impossibility of the feat. She felt so alive. The Colonel didn't wait for her to descend. He moved towards the next wall and started to climb. It didn't matter to Carole. She knew he had to feel her too, how could he not? Strength surged through her, and she followed. She would've followed this man anywhere.

WITH NEW INSPIRATION the Pact worked together, tackling the obstacle course with a sudden burst of cooperation. Carole's body responded, climbing, running, and crawling, but her mind searched for every shred of information it had ever heard about Ted White. He was a legend in the small world of Black Ops, a Lieutenant Colonel at the young age of thirty-one. His reputation preceded him. Ted had a hand in the formation of every team, Lincoln had mentioned that months ago. Ted also had a hand in the dissemination and disbursement of every team member when the time came. Lincoln had mentioned that fact after they'd escaped North Korea. Carole wondered if Ted White also had a hand in the invisible members of the team, the ones who didn't officially exist—like her. Something about the way he glanced her way when he motioned for the team to follow him told her he hadn't. Balaclavas still covered their heads, but the faint tilt of Ted's told her she was being examined for the first time.

Once in a foster home a boy had brought a roadrunner into the house wrapped in a blanket. He'd carried it from room to room showing off to the other kids. Nobody was impressed because the creature didn't even struggle to break free. The small lump in the fuzzy spread might as well have been dead, because even when the boy uncovered the head it lay limp and unmoving, its eyes open and staring. At the urging of the other kids he'd unfolded the blanket completely. Carole never forgot that moment. The bird sprang to life, shot straight over the kneeling bodies of foster kids, over two dogs, across her bare feet, and up and over the piano before running straight out an open window. It had moved so fast she'd been the only one who could focus quick enough to really see it. That is how she felt now, as though her heart had merely been waiting for space to move in. She kept normal pace with The Pact, walking behind Lincoln, but her heart raced ahead to the space provided by Ted White.

Nobody spoke as they crossed the island. Ted White led them to a floating dock and clambered first into a waiting speedboat. He stood while the members of the team followed him aboard. Then he simply took a seat in the front, facing them. The hour long boat ride back to base camp was devoid of any conversation. The men were too nervous with the Colonel sitting shoulder to shoulder with them to speak, and he said nothing. Arms crossed over his broad chest, his head rested against a window, bumping faintly with the movement of the boat over waves. Carole was certain he had fallen asleep. She could feel it in the touch of his heart. It purred outside of hers, like a sleeping jungle cat. It was exquisite. *I want him.* The three words popped into her mind, and she blushed under the safety of her mask.

I want him forever. I want to jump into that heart and know him. I want him to know me.

The first rays of daylight lit the sky when the boat slowed. Pink and gray light stretched across the water and the Colonel rose, gracefully stepping over their legs in the close confines of the boat. The craft neared the dock and he leaned out, grabbing hold of the pier and tying the boat onto a large metal ring fastened there. Leaping effortlessly to the dock, his muscles rippled beneath black Gore-Tex clothing. It was the same clothing they all wore, and Carole realized she'd never once noticed, let alone admired, the fitness level of any of the other men. Ted White tied the other end of the boat to the dock, and paused beside a guard. Outside Carole's hearing he murmured something to an MP. Not once did Ted White turn and look at any of them. He moved down the dock with comfortable confidence, and jumped onto the beach. Crossing the beach, he tugged the cap off his head. From behind, his head of dark red curls stood out amongst a camp of buzz cuts, thicker than Carole's hair, shining in the early morning sun.

Mesmerized, Carole stared until the MP barked at them. "The Pact is to report to study hall for final debriefing and assignment."

She realized then that they'd all been staring after the Lieutenant Colonel. The group hurried to obey, exhausted but invigorated by the words of forgiveness. They disembarked and walked in a line behind Lincoln. The MP stepped in front of the last member of the team, Carole, with his rifle held across his torso like a sash.

"Not you. You are relieved of duty."

Not a single member of the Pact turned to look at her, not even Lincoln. They walked towards the study hall building without a word.

FOR TWO DAYS Carole was kept locked in a sparse cinderblock room under guard. The room had no window, and an MP stood armed outside the locked door. It opened and a tray of food slid across the threshold three times a day—if it could be called food—it was dehydrated and rehydrated, processed and preserved. Ravenously hungry, Carole refused to eat even a bite of it. Not one tray was removed. Six of them took up half the floor space in the room. The food dried a bit, hardening around the edges, but other than that it looked pretty much the same as when it had arrived. Carole suspected it was a test, so she drank water from the sink faucet and waited.

With her record Ted White surely knew she could escape. Settling against the wall, knees bent in front of her, she ran her fingers through her hair. What if he'd gone by the time they let her out? The thought made her heart burn. She needed to feel the touch of that heart again, and consoled herself thinking he must have felt her too. Surely he felt the same way. But anxiety continued to prickle, no matter how many times she reassured herself that he couldn't have left! In her mind she relived the feeling of his heart again and again. Head resting on her knees, she waited, eyes closed, trying to find strength to resist escape and stay put.

The metal door creaked when opened, pushing the trays uncomfortably closer. It wasn't mealtime and Carole blinked, lifting her head, hopeful. It was a General, and she took to her feet in one swift motion, saluting.

"Sir." Her unused voice croaked.

"At ease, Private." Heavy, corpulent, and red faced from the heat of the island, he moved trays aside with one booted foot, scattering utensils and making a path. Crossing to her bed he sat on the end of it, and it protested the act. The cot and mattress had surely been there since World War II, and flakes of rust dusted to the concrete floor. Bloodshot eyes blinked at her.

"You haven't been debriefed on the incident in North Korea?"

"No, Sir."

"And you're not going to be. Your report has been destroyed. If you had a record, we'd call this mission a failure. You went rogue on us, Marine. Do you know what happens to rogue marines?"

"They pay, Sir."

Nodding, his piercing blue eyes studied her. "Some think it would be a waste to make you pay for common sense. You were right, by the way, about Samish and Ambassador Causer. That doesn't really matter to me. You disobeyed a direct order. If it were up to me you'd disappear for real at the wrong end of a firing squad."

Carole didn't say anything and they just looked at each other for long moments.

"If you were a real marine this conversation would end with your court martial."

The General stood up. "Rogues do not officially exist in the United States Military. Some think you'd make a good fit with them if they did."

"Sir?"

"We're passing the buck. In this case that would be you, giving you to some nasty closet at the CIA. Mess up on them, and you'll wish you'd met my firing squad."

The General crossed the floor and went out the door without another word or glance in her direction. He left the door open, and the guard went with him.

THE PACT HAD left the island on a mission. Escorted to a room not unlike the one she'd been kept prisoner in, Carole showered and went to the mess hall for food. It was between meals, but the cook offered her a carton of milk, pointed towards some fruit, and handed her an entire pot of cold oatmeal. Standing in the kitchen, she wolfed it down, barely chewing, scraping every last gooey grain from the pot while he watched her.

"Hain't no one liked my oatmeal that much before."

"Thank you," Carole said. She took the entire bunch of grapes he'd pointed towards and headed for the door.

"You?"

She turned and watched his approach, wary. In her need for food, she hadn't paid him much attention. Beneath his white apron and baggy pants was a very fit man of about fifty.

"Are you familiar with Non-official Cover?"

Carole shook her head.

"We call it NOC for short." He pronounced it *knock*. "Someone will come for you in a week or two or three. NOCs learn to be patient. There's a joke we tell each other. NOC, NOC?"

"Who's there?" Carole supplied.

"Wait for it…you'll get it eventually, might even be funny when you do. Your password will be oatmeal." He winked, grabbed her empty pot off the counter, and headed for the sink.

Welcome to the CIA…or some nasty little closet of it.

AFTER AN AFTERNOON spent sidling through clusters of teams, desperately hoping to sense Ted White's heart, Carole heard enough gossip to know he hadn't left, and he didn't sleep in the barracks. The officers slept in apartments in a restricted section of the compound. She managed to last until dark before hunting for him. It didn't matter to her if he were in a bunk in a barrack full of men, she couldn't wait any longer. The urge to be with a heart that could touch hers felt primal, mandatory. Luck was with her. Darting around the restricted section, keeping to the shadows, she spotted him through a glass wall of windows. In the half-light his red hair looked wet, dark and slick, but his posture and movements were familiar, burned into her memory. He moved with the confident assurance of a man comfortable in his own skin. Carole gasped when he ran in her direction, and watched him jump, arms straight in front, falling towards the floor headfirst. He landed with a splash and she grinned, belatedly sensing water, her heart pounding so loudly it vibrated in her head. Ted was swimming in a pool in the officer's gymnasium, after hours. Alone.

Stalking him like a target from a mission, she made her way around the outside of the gym. Certain she could sense his heart—it moved in the distance like wind stirring treetops, more of a promise than a touch—but close enough for Carole to know exactly what that roadrunner had felt wrapped in the blanket: desperate to be free, to be where it belonged.

The doors weren't locked, and she slipped through, locking them behind her. Ted hadn't wasted power turning on the lights. A faint glow pointed the way via emergency exit signs, and Carole followed the splash of water. In the darkness Ted White's hair looked black, and she stood in the shadows watching him swim. With every lap, he neared close enough that she could clearly feel the gentle whisper of his heart against her own. Her own heart beat nervously, and she wondered that he didn't sense her.

What could she say? What if he sent her away? Despite the draw she *knew* he had to feel, he hadn't sought her out. How had he resisted? What if he hadn't felt her heart at all? That thought hurt. More than wanting him, Carole needed him. It had been years since she'd felt another heart. She couldn't walk away from it. In the shadows she made up her mind and lifted her chin stubbornly. He wouldn't say no. She wouldn't let him. The voices didn't say a word.

AT THE EDGE of the pool Ted pushed himself out of the water. Dripping he walked to a lounge chair and picked up a towel, drying sopping hair, vigorously rubbing the absorbent towel over his head. The remembered curls emerged as water ran down strong arms and dripped off his elbows onto the lounge. Silently Carole walked up behind him. He must have sensed something, because he immediately spun around to face her. Surprise furrowed thick brows and his mouth opened slightly. Ted had a classically handsome face, long-nosed and full-lipped, but what Carole wanted to see there was acceptance. For long moments she worried he would reject her, his expression of disbelief seemed frozen. Whatever thoughts were going through his mind didn't look welcoming. Pressing her fists against her thighs, she took a deep breath and instinctively allowed her heart to expand and move towards his. His expression changed to confusion, and one hand quickly reached to cover his heart. *He felt it!* But he took a step back.

"Private, why—what are you doing here?"

"I came for you," she said.

The Lieutenant Colonel slowly shook his head back and forth. "How did you get in here?" The hand stayed protectively on his chest.

Carole took a step closer. "I jumped the fence."

A quick smile flashed across Ted White's face. "You jumped a fifteen-foot security fence?" He laughed. "You're a very good liar."

The voices took issue with that. "I'm not lying," Carole said. Ted's smile vanished.

"You need to jump back out of here, because if you get caught—well—General Stanholt is itching for a reason—what I mean is you of all people cannot afford to step out of line."

"I had to see you."

Carole sensed Ted White's pulse accelerate, hers kept pace. She stood so close she had to tip her head back slightly to look up at his face. He swallowed and took another small step backwards, bumping into the lounge chair and causing it to scrape against the concrete floor.

"If you get caught in here, Private, I—no one will be able to protect you this time."

"Did you protect me last time?" she whispered, wondering. Ted's hand still rested protectively over his heart. Carole put her hand on top his. His sudden intake of breath made her smile.

"Please, Private." Ted leaned into her touch, so close. "This is a restricted area."

"Is it?" Carole put her second hand in place over his chest. Their hearts together made it feel as though she floated. "I'll take my chances."

Ted tilted his head, his lips neared. His eyes widened. They were an impossible shade of blue.

"Oh, screw it," he said. Grabbing Carole's arms, he shoved her down onto the lounge chair.

CHAPTER
EIGHT

Base Camp, South Pacific—March 1988

STANDING IN LINE for breakfast, Carole's gaze roved over powdered eggs, toast greasy with margarine, and bacon vanishing quickly beneath the hands of men she barely noticed.

"*Go to him. Connect. Show him.*" The voices were talking sense and everything had changed. The touch of a heart was not childhood's remembered delusion. It had nothing to do with mental illness or drugs. Last night proved that, Ted proved that. Running a finger back and forth across her metal cafeteria tray she considered his heart, her heart, they were one now. "*Almost,*" the voices corrected.

In time, she defended mentally. She couldn't force that. *You tried to force it last night,* she chastised herself before the voices could. Remembering last night, goose bumps rose on her arms. She had taken what must be given last night, Ted's body—or rather he'd taken hers. *After my golden invitation…but he certainly didn't mind.* Carole had bruises to prove Ted had been an enthusiastic participant.

"*That proves nothing,*" the voices argued.

Carole glanced at the men surrounding her, piling far too much bacon on their plates and arguing about sports. The Special Ops teams were fairly honorable men, but if she caught any one of them alone and—*hmmm.* Had it meant no more than that to Ted?

She moved down the cafeteria line, scooting her tray in front of her. Her boots pressed against her sore ankles and she thought about Ted's impossible efforts to get her canvas pants over her tightly laced boots. *Of course he wanted me physically, but I wanted him just as much!* A face remembered from childhood drifted into her mind's eye, Sister Mary Josephine lecturing about modesty, and the set of the Nun's pointed chin when she pronounced the word hussy. A secret smile quirked Carole's lips.

Hairy hands dropped a big bowl on her tray, interrupting her thoughts. She looked at the metal mixing bowl full of oatmeal and covered in bits of mango. It took up the entire tray. A quart of milk appeared under her nose. Carole looked up into the face of the cook, a cigarette with an impossibly long ash dangled from the corner of his mouth. She accepted the milk, and he spoke without removing the cigarette, his voice gravelly.

"There's more if that's not enough. That's the biggest bowl we got."

Carole grinned at him, and glided to a table with her food, the set of Sister Mary Josephine's chin still in mind.

The special ops teams ate with precision, within twenty minutes Carole sat on her bench alone. She downed every bite of the clean food, and glanced at the standard government-issue clock on the wall. She had the ability to sense time to the nano-second, but staring at the over-sized timepiece filled a few seconds. All she had to do now was figure out a way to fill the next sixteen hours. That's how long it would be before she could see Ted again. Subtracting the time it would take to consume lunch and dinner, she only needed to occupy fifteen and a half of those hours.

Leaning over her empty bowl, she idly scraped the sides of it, remembering last night and wondering how dangerous it would be to breach the officer's quarters in broad daylight. Ted had left rather abruptly. After realizing it'd been her first time, he'd sat on the edge of the broken lounge chair gaping awkwardly at her. He had walked away only to return, open his mouth wordlessly, close it again and finally nab his damp towel off the floor. He'd handed it to her, stared at the faint streaks of blood on her thighs, whispered, "I'm sorry," and bolted.

The sound of his bare feet padding across the damp floor had made her heart ache, but she'd managed not to cry until the door shut behind him. Yet they hadn't been tears of sorrow. Blushing she kept her head over her bowl, certain that the cook watched her from across the room. Last night with Ted had been the best seven minutes of her life—so far. Ted was so—but despite what the voices said, their connection was much more than physical. Licking the last bit of oatmeal off the spoon she thought about the touch of his heart. It felt like she'd been hungry for years and found ripe fruit. No it felt like—a kiss—the kind of kiss you thought would be gross, but it wasn't gross at all—it was exactly what you never knew you liked. Ted's kisses were so—

Hairy hands splayed on either side of the oatmeal bowl. Carole looked up into the knowing eyes of the grinning cook, her face flamed in embarrassment. She pulled the spoon out of her mouth with a pop.

"I have never," his cigarette still dangled and his eyes glinted with humor, "known anyone who likes oatmeal so much. Ain't natural, but I'll still respect you in the morning."

SLIPPING THROUGH THE glass door, Carole turned to twist the lock. A splash sounded from the direction of the pool and she raced across the length of the entryway, banging open the interior door. Ted's dark head appeared at the edge of the pool, watching her cross the room.

"You do realize this compound is considered impenetrable?" The sardonic tone made her laugh, and he added, "Don't get cocky. I sneak into it myself at least once a visit." Ted swam closer, stopping where an underwater light lit his expression. He gazed up at her, his tone now serious, "Is one of the guards letting you through?"

"Of course not! I go over the fence."

Jumping partially out of the water, Ted wrapped an arm around her legs and swept her into the pool, completely soaking her clothes and boots. Effortlessly treading water his hands slid under her thighs, and she wrapped her legs around his waist, her arms automatically following around his neck. Full lips pressed against her forehead and nose, before finding her lips. Holding her securely he leisurely finished the kiss. It was exactly what she never knew she liked, and her heart seemed to liquefy.

"I'm glad you came, but be warned, I have ways of making you talk," he teased with an undercurrent of question in his tone. She knew he wanted to know how she got in. Security was his job.

"I told you—" Carole considered then opted for outright honesty. She would never lie to him anyway. "I just jump the fence. The high jump is my—thing." Without warning Ted plunged beneath the pool's surface, taking her with him ten feet to the bottom, where he sat holding her in his lap. Carole leaned forward and kissed him, twin streams of tiny bubbles racing upwards. After several enthusiastic moments, Ted shot to the surface taking her with him. Sucking in a deep breath of air with a gasp, he tugged her along and swam to the side of the pool.

Exertion punctuated his words. "I didn't expect you'd come back tonight. I hoped you would—but I never expected you'd manage to sneak in twice." Ted offered a hand up as Carole climbed out of the water, onto the edge of the swimming pool. He pushed himself up on strong arms and sat beside her on the rough concrete surface. Warm water cascaded off Carole's soaking clothes, the smell of chlorine strong. Ted leaned close, water dripping off dark hair becoming rivulets over broad shoulders. His blue eyes searched hers. "Now I know how you got in. You swam through the water filtration system, because breathing is apparently optional for you." He yanked off her dripping T-shirt and tossed it. It landed with a wet plop in the middle of the pool. "With lungs like yours you could have been an Olympic swimmer, but your country needed you."

Carole shook her head. "I just jumped the fence."

Ted touched her cheek, and kissed her mouth softly, his lips moving gently, tenderly over hers, slowly pushing her backwards using his mouth as leverage. He only abandoned her lips to crawl over her, briefly perusing her body before finally looking into her eyes.

"You bribed the A-Shack guards—" he kissed the tip of her nose, "by promising to teach them your optional breathing trick."

"I really jumped the fence," Carole insisted. Unbuttoning her pants, Ted yanked them down, taking everything. It took effort, and soaked cotton clung determinedly to legs still sore from yesterday's attempts.

He tugged the uncooperative trousers, continuing to hypothesize in a teasing tone. "You used some type of metal eating acid and burned a hole in the fence—after disabling the motion sensors." Ted sat up and tugged harder, until Carole's legs journeyed to rest on his lap. Shamelessly, she laughed at the futile attempt that produced only a tangled mess of wet canvas and cotton refusing to budge further than her knees.

"Please take my boots off first!"

Ted went to work on the waterlogged laces and resumed his interrogation. "Chemicals are dangerous, where'd you get them here?"

"I jumped! Honestly!" she said.

Ted pulled a boot off and held it over her, slowly emptying pool water onto her face. "Tell me."

"I told you!" She didn't dodge the incoming water, and the answer came out half gargle. Chuckling, he tossed her boot into the middle of the pool, tugged her onto his lap and kissed her again, slow, drawn out kisses that made her stomach flip-flop. The kisses were delectable, but nothing could distract her from the touch of that heart turned playful. It romped in the periphery of her own heart, drawing her with a siren call. Carole pushed Ted onto his back, and crouched over him mock-complaining, "That boot will never dry in this humidity!"

"Tell me how you got in or the other one heads for Davy Jones's locker too."

"I told you—!" But Ted put a hand gently on the back of her head and pulled her close for another long kiss, and for several moments Carole lost contact with her limbs.

"I warned you," he said. Big arms reached around her middle and rolled her flat onto her back again. Playfully he turned his back on her, pretending to sit on her stomach while working on freeing the pants still dangling from a boot clad leg. "Last chance," he intoned over his shoulder. "These are nice boots."

"I told you, I jumped! It's the truth!" Carole laughed when he twisted around and emptied the water out of the last boot. She caught it in her mouth and spit it in a fine stream right back at him.

"A worthy opponent!" he chuckled, blinking and shaking his head so that more water splayed over her. "But you have nothing left to negotiate with." The splash of her boot was followed by the sound of her pants flung against the pool's surface.

"Neither do you now," she pointed out.

Ted tugged her to sit beside him at the pool's edge. They rested with their legs dangling in the water. "I can't remember what I wanted anymore anyway," he said. In one smooth movement he slid his trunks off and flung them into the pool too, where they briefly floated on the surface of the water. Ted rested a heavy arm on her shoulders. A hand explored the back of her head, smoothing her unruly mess of hair. Rhythmic and soothing, it made her want to purr. "Actually, it's coming back to me now," he said.

Carole leaned her head comfortably against a wide shoulder as the fingers played in her hair. The touch of his heart near hers felt expectant. It sat next to hers, side by side, like two lovers basking in the sun.

"Hmm?"

"What I wanted, it's come back to me," he said.

"What do you want, Ted?" Her heart leapt hopefully.

The hand moved to press gently against her torso, carefully avoiding her heart. Ted shoved her flat, although her legs still dangled in the water. "More," he groaned, splaying his body over the length of her.

THE SOUND OF an outside door clanged in the distance. "You forgot to lock the door?" Ted hissed, but the light of the emergency lights showed amusement dancing in his eyes. After nearly two weeks of nights spent together—totaling exactly 84.7 hours—Carole found herself as drawn to Ted's good humor as to his heart.

Completely naked with her bottom perched right inside a ceramic drinking fountain, Carole focused her mind further than her eyes could see. A guard pushed open the door to the pool area, not fifteen yards away. She froze, but Ted didn't. Languorously he continued rocking against her. She closed her eyes and bit back a gasp. *What is wrong with him? But oh! Nothing is wrong with him!* She tightened her legs around him.

On the far side of the room the guard crossed the floor, shoving chairs and lounges out of his way noisily. Good thing too because though Ted kept right on making love to her, a quiet chuckle sounded in her ear. Carole quickly clamped a hand over her lover's mouth. It made Ted laugh harder. The guard started to whistle Yankee Doodle, and Ted shook not-quite-silently against her.

The sound of a refrigerator hissed open, and the whistle morphed into the latest soft drink ditty about Dr. Pepper. Carole sensed him nab a soda, and then the refrigerator door slammed with a rattle of bottles and he shuffled back, shoving more pool furniture until he slammed through the door, and left.

A few minutes later Ted finished and Carole climbed down from her perch, rubbing a spot that would surely bruise.

"Why was that so funny? Aren't you worried about General Stanholt anymore?"

Ted kissed her forehead and grinned at her. "Sorry. I couldn't help but wonder what would happen if he was coming in for a drink from the water fountain."

Carole spun towards the east facing windows, her internal clock alert. "Ted! It's four-thirty!"

His smile vanished. "You've got to be kidding! Where are your clothes? Wait, here's my shirt, just wear this." He tugged the big cotton shirt over her arms. "Cut through the brush along the beach. We have to stop staying this late. If you get caught I don't know—just go!" He squeezed her bare shoulders gently before pulling the shirt over them, and kissed her, quickly buttoning the shirt for her while his lips danced over hers, scrambling her thoughts. "Tonight?"

"Tonight." Carole sensed half a dozen men outside the back door. She ran.

MUSING OVER THEIR late night escapades Carole promised herself that she would keep better track of time. She'd barely made it back before the entire camp woke up. Every night they said they weren't going to stay so late, that they had to stop risking discovery by the waking base. Yet every morning they each made a mad dash to get to their rooms unnoticed—every morning for two weeks. Carole grinned. They were both sleep-deprived. Bending, she examined a row of shells and sea glass filling the long windowsill in Ted's tiny apartment. Sunlight glinted off smooth bits of glass, most of it shades of blues and greens. A few bits of frosty glass at the end of the row were yellow and khaki. The khaki reminded Carole she'd forgotten to return the shirt from Ted's service uniform. At least she'd remembered her soaking wet boots after they'd spent twenty-four hours at the bottom of the pool. They still hadn't dried. She wondered what had become of her trousers left in the pool. Running a finger over the piece of khaki glass, the exact same shade as Ted's shirt, she shook her head in consternation. It wasn't like her to forget anything. Forgetting to return the shirt was bad enough, but how did one forget their own pants? Or underwear?

Worse than forgetting her pants, last night that guard could have caught them at the pool. It certainly wasn't like her not to sense someone approaching, especially someone with a gun. Despite that sobering fact, she smiled, remembering. The spigot had left an enormous bruise on her—Carole rubbed the spot, smiling faintly. Ted found humor in the oddest situations.

Carole looked out the large window at the view. The fifteen foot perimeter fence and patrolling guards didn't detract. Slender palm trees ringed the white beach in the distance, and the ocean stretched brilliant turquoise as clear as the sea glass decorating the room. Ted's trim apartment had white walls and concrete flooring like many of the living quarters in the compound, but special care had been given to this officer's quarters. A large orange rug filled most of the space, and photographs of the surrounding beaches covered the walls. It boasted a private bathroom, a tiny kitchen sink, a miniature refrigerator, a toaster oven, and about eight inches of counter space. Quite posh by military standards, though the table was a simple metal card table and the bed a standard issue twin complete with three inch thick mattress. Carole plopped down on it, rubbing her hands over the upgraded sheet and looking expectantly towards the door.

It swung open and Ted took one look at her before slamming it shut behind him. This was the first time she'd seen his face in the light of day. Even angry he was a beautiful man, tall and broad, a red-head whose skin tanned beneath freckles. Ted's full lips tilted upwards at the edges with a hint of perpetual good humor, even when angry. His face was broad and square jawed, his eyebrows dark despite waves of auburn hair curling around his head. Carole couldn't stop herself staring at that mouth as he hissed, "What if someone had been with me?"

"I knew you'd be alone."

"Come on, Carole! I didn't know I'd be alone until Captain Jeffries realized he'd forgotten his hat in the golf cart. That was two minutes ago!"

I knew, she thought, but shrugged rather than vocalize that. It wasn't something she could explain at this point in their relationship. *If ever.*

"Seriously, how the hell did you get—am I supposed to believe you hopped the fence in daylight and came in through the window?" She nodded, and Ted took off his hat and threw it on the little square table. Pacing, he unknotted his tie. "Right." He frowned at her from across the room. "What if you'd been seen?"

"I'm really good at what I do," she supplied.

Ted shrugged out of his jacket and placed it neatly over the back of a chair. Pins and metals decorated most of the left side. "So I've heard. Do you want a soda?" Voice cold, he moved to the tiny refrigerator and removed a Coke, popping the pop-top and disposing of the bit of metal neatly in the standard issue wastebasket. Holding the can up questioningly, he politely offered to share it with her.

"A glass of water would be nice," she said. Ted took a glass out of the lone cabinet and filled it at the tap. Opening the fridge he removed a tray of ice-cubes.

"No ice," Carole added. He popped the tray back in, and slammed the door a bit harder than necessary. Instead of bringing her the water, Ted set it on the counter, standing on the far side and crossing his arms.

"Why'd you come?" his tone sounded hostile.

The question seemed combative and she half-shrugged. "To see you in the daylight. We keep saying we're going to stop staying up all night."

Taking a sip of his Coke, Ted appeared to relax. He sighed. "You're a very resourceful stalker."

"I didn't think you'd mind so much, if I came here."

"Carole," he set the drink down, "if a man is going to have a stalker, it can't possibly get any better than you. If this," he motioned between the two of them, "gets out, it will only enhance my reputation. That would not be the case with you. You are on very thin ice after North Korea, so I really hope you trust whoever is letting you in here."

"Ted, I told you—"

"I know, I know, you jumped the fence." He smiled at her then. "You're very—"

"Resourceful?" she supplied.

"Actually, I was thinking stubborn and talented." Ted rounded the counter, moving towards her and unbuttoning his shirt.

TED SNORED. BRIGHT sunshine blazed through the window, and he slept with eyes squeezed shut against the light, wide open mouth snoring impressively loudly. He'd eaten onions with lunch. Stretched out on his long narrow bed, Carole perched on top of him, flesh on flesh. It was the only way they fit. Laying her head on his chest, she basked in the touch of his heart. It purred just outside of hers. She lifted her head and kissed his hairy chest, right over that heart. There was a tattoo there, a blue heart. It was hard to see in the tufts of auburn curls that covered it. Scroll letters filled it, so artfully arranged that it took a moment for Carole to make out the word. *Beth*. Lifting a hand, she gently traced the letters. *So it is your fault, Beth*, she thought. *The ragged edges of his heart were left by you*. Carole's lips pressed against the tattoo, and in his sleep Ted's arm tightened around her, keeping her comfortably against his body. Caressing his leg with hers, she nestled against him. It felt like they were floating in the sunshine. The voices had spent the entire afternoon emitting only a gentle *Mmmm* in her head. The voices in my head love you too, she thought and grinned. Oh, Ted, *I love you*, the words escaped without opening her mouth. They slid from somewhere inside her own heart to Ted's.

Ted jerked, snorting awake. "What? What are you doing?"

"Listening to you snore." *He'd felt it.*

He rubbed a big hand over her messy hair, then reached down and hauled her to sit across his torso. "I don't snore. God you're beautiful."

"So are you," she told him. He laughed at her, resting a hand on either hip bone. Running his thumbs up and down those bones, he appeared to be admiring her and she flushed under his gaze.

"You are an enigma, Carole Blank, and the most fit woman I've ever seen." One hand wandered off her hip and upwards, circling the perimeter before brushing gentle fingertips across her heart. Ted's heart beckoned like a brief whisper, and Carole gasped, certain he'd responded, but it stopped before she could fully discern the feeling. Ted jerked his hand away, sitting up. Grabbing onto his legs, Carole balanced in his lap while he craned to look at the clock.

"I have dinner plans with General Sands, what time is it?"

"1500 hours, Sir." Carole balanced precariously on Ted's mobile thighs.

"I like the way you say that." Ted heaved himself up, and Carole ended up momentarily airborne until he tossed her beneath him, lying on top.

"I prefer being on top—call me traditional. You know, for the most uncomfortable bed ever made, this is actually the happiest place on earth." Ted put a hand on either side of her face and brushed his lips across hers. For the moment, untraditional Carole Blank was in complete agreement.

"NO! CAROLE! WE fell asleep! Get up, hon! Did I crush you? I'm sorry. Are you okay?"

"Fine," she mumbled, sweaty and disoriented as Ted lifted his hairy body off hers. She didn't ever remember sleeping during the day. She let her mind reach outside and knew it was almost 1700 hours. Ted had dinner with General Sands.

"Get dressed. I'll go. Ted?"

"Hmmm?" He got out of bed all elbows and knees, leaving a series of little bruises behind.

"Can I tell you something?"

"You want to talk now? Oh God, Carole, you are a real woman after all, aren't you? I have five minutes. Can we talk later?"

"Tonight?" she grinned at him. *It's time.*

"Perfect," he promised, and then spent an entire minute kissing her.

Carole broke away to breathe. "I thought you didn't have time."

"I don't! Go before I throw you back down on this bed. I barely care what the General would say, but I don't think the bed would last another round." Carole climbed out of the rickety old bed and pulled on her clothes quickly, tugging her sneakers onto her feet. Ted scrambled around the apartment. She went to the window, pressing fingers against the glass pane.

"Carole! Are you nuts? You really do follow through on the illusion, don't you? Take the door. Everyone will be down in the dining hall now." Sensing that the hall was clear, she headed in that direction. It probably would lead to difficult questions if Ted saw her climb out the window and up the building with her bare hands, anyway. She reached for the door.

"Carole?"

Turning back to look at him, she smiled at the sight. One arm was through a khaki shirt, and the other through his jacket. Halves of both dangled behind him. Briefcase in hand, half full of random items, Ted shoved his tie inside, watching her.

"Yes?" she asked, enjoying his disorientation for some reason.

"Be careful."

"Not in the job description," she said.

Ted stopped moving for a couple seconds, eyebrows pulling together in a frown.

"Try? For me?" The blue eyes were the exact same shade of blue as the sky outside the window.

I love you, she thought, and smiled. The words would come easy now. Claiming his heart would come easy now. They were both ready. "Tonight at the pool?"

Ted nodded. "Tonight at the pool. Carole? Don't get caught."

COCONUT PALMS DOTTED the beach, and turquoise water met the color coordinated sky in a thin band of dark blue. Crystal clear water lapped white beach and only the sound of a helicopter ruined Carole's solitude. *Too bad we can't meet here*, she thought, wondering if Ted would be willing to risk it. Using her knife she cut into a young coconut, and drank sweet water from it. *Clean.* Slicing easily through the green drupe, a seashell became her spoon to scoop mounds of the gelatinous flesh from inside. She groaned, "Mmmm," with each mouthful. *Much better than woodlice!* Glancing towards the path, she sighed, sensing the approach of a team. Their enthusiastic marine shouts of "Oorah!" echoed distantly through scrubby jungle.

By the time the men appeared, running full speed towards the water, Carole was slurping her way through a third coconut. Likely three would be about as much as her stomach could take anyway. One of the men spotted her in the shade, separated from his buddies and jogged over to her.

"Sorry. Is this your spot?"

Shaking her head, she sucked the last bit of her meal down. "Go ahead. I'm going to swim along the shore anyway."

The man rubbed his stubbly chin, examining her, reminding Carole why she never wore her swimsuit around other marines. Pulling her legs up to her chest, she wrapped her arms around them.

"I think your friends want you," she said pointedly. Nearly a dozen men were attempting to unravel an enormous plastic banner, shouting at him to help.

Waving a hand dismissively, he said, "You can't swim here, you know about the sharks don't you?"

Carole just stared at him until he added, "This is just a thing we do for Colonel White when he leaves."

"Leaves?" Carole's heart seemed to leave her body, sinking somewhere through the strata of the planet and vanishing.

The young man ran a hand down his tanned torso. "Yeah, the Colonel always makes sure the Force Recon Marines get steak his last day, not chopped steak, real steak. It's our way of saying thanks."

Carole looked at the banner being unfurled. It said "Moorah" in big black and white cow-print letters.

"When does he come back?" her voice sounded far away.

"Shoot—not until next February. He only comes here for some old-fashioned amphibious recon training, for us I mean. He trains us."

Carole stood, though her legs barely felt capable of sustaining the position for long. She barely heard the man's sharp intake of breath.

"Hey, you might want to lock down early tonight. There's always beer after the steak, it gets rowdy, and—well—I don't think there's ever been a girl on the island before."

A helicopter skimmed over the tree line, and a deafening chorus rose up. "MOO-RAH." Carole didn't look up to see Ted, she didn't have to. She knew, and he'd known too. Just two hours ago, Ted had known he was leaving, and he hadn't even told her. Not only had he not told her, he'd lied to her, promising to meet her tonight—to talk.

The water was up to her thighs before she knew she was in it. Shouts of "Ooo-yah!" followed her. Diving beneath the clear water, Carole understood firsthand how a heart developed ragged edges. *Betrayal.*

CHAPTER
NINE

Deep Water, South Pacific—March 1988

INHALE. CAROLE BROKE the surface of the water and obeyed. *Dive.* One strong stroke and her forehead brushed the ocean floor. Sharp coral scratched against her chin, snagging the length of her swimsuit and digging into her legs. *Move.* Arms and legs cut obediently and she slid over bits of reef and sand. Deep beneath the surface, the weight of the water held her together. There was no light there, just pressure and movement. Far away the voices made only a faint keening sound. *Inhale.* Carole moved to the surface. Arms caught her, wrapping tightly, holding her against a too warm body. Deep inside her head she recoiled from the pain of the touch. It burned.

"What the hell are you doing?" A man's voice shouted at her. *Inhale.* Blindly she took a deep, long breath, filling her lungs as commanded. They expanded until they could take no more. "Stop it!" he ordered, shaking her. The command to dive didn't come, vanishing in a wave of fresh pain. The man struggled, hauling her from the water. Although his touch seared against her skin, Carole didn't fight him, but neither did she help. Limp and suddenly exhausted, she let this stranger drag her to shore. Lying in the sand, gravity attacked, pressing against her and she couldn't move.

"Are you okay?" A hand shook her, then moved, exploring across her body and down an arm. She was too tired to protest. The voice seemed far away. "God, I thought the sharks had gotten you by now for sure." A light shone in her face and pain shot through her head. She jerked away, squeezing her eyes shut. "You're bleeding! Look at me—gah, your eyes are blood red, keep them closed." The hands moved away and gravity stepped on her, pinning her arms and legs against the beach. "I'm going for help. Listen to me, Blank? Your name is Blank, isn't it? I don't dare touch you, let alone try to carry you. Stay here. Do not open your eyes, do you hear me?" Carole kept her eyes shut tight, but could still see the light from the flashlight right through her eyelids. "You're getting sand in those cuts, wait." The light disappeared and the hands moved away. Vaguely Carole sensed him move off. *Dive.* Rolling onto her stomach she planted her face in the sand, trying to obey, but her arms and legs couldn't combat gravity.

"Have you lost your mind?" He was back, rolling her over and jamming fingers into her mouth, digging sand out. "Be still!" he gently moved and tugged her, wrapping something around her. Against her flesh his touch burned but Carole remained cooperatively limp. It hurt far too much out of the water. She needed the pressure to hold together. One of his hands pressed softly against her forehead and the man leaned close. "The doctors will be in the officer's quarters by now. I'll go as fast as I can. I will come back for you. Blank? If you go back in that water again tonight, you will die." Then he moved. Carole sensed him running towards camp, towards the officer's quarters.

Lying in the sand she listened to the far off keening of the voices, and longed to return to the water. *If you go back into that water again tonight, you will die.* She thought maybe she already had, but gravity slowly lightened its hold against her body. After long minutes Carole opened her eyes and managed to sit up. The sound of plastic crinkled against her body. Recoiling, she brushed frantically against it. The voices were far off, still making their keening sound, but plastic against bare skin was forbidden and right now it hurt. Despite the darkness and her sore eyes, she recognized the MOO-RAH banner. Desperately tearing it from her body, Carole backed away, trying to escape the memory, and the touch of plastic against raw skin. *Move.* Eager to obey, she moved, her feet skimming over the sand, determination increasing with each step.

———⟗———

INHALE. THE COMMAND still echoed from somewhere deep in her psyche. Carole obeyed, closing her eyes briefly. They burned but the pain was fading. *Dive.* She shivered, needing to feel the pressure of water surrounding her. Soon, she promised herself. Standing outside a fifteen foot fence in the moonless night, it felt as though part of her still swam around the island. *Inhale.* Guards outside A-Shack opened the gate by hand. Two men in uniform swung the metal fence open in a slow-moving arc. *Move.* Distracted by the arrival of a supply truck the guards tended to their evening duty, their vigilant eyes abandoning the water pumping station. The small brick structure stood a dozen yards from the fence, typically guarded to keep the water supply safe. Carole used it as a springboard to clear the perimeter fence, as she had every night the past two weeks. This time the extra three feet of barbed wire circling the top of the fence almost brushed her back. She landed on her feet in a crouch, and ran.

Why did I come? The thought drifted through her mind beside the ghostly command, *Inhale.* No lights had been turned on inside the gymnasium tonight. It didn't matter. Light had never mattered to her. Sliding through the unlocked door and crossing the room, Carole could sense everything. Memories brushed past with every step: that broken lounge chair was the one they'd first made love on; and that one was where his heart had moved in tandem with hers for several seconds; the one propped by the wall had also broken beneath them, and Ted had laughed and rested his head against her chest; the floor near the shallow end of the pool was where he'd briefly pulled her head against his chest—before the intensity had made him move away; and the table by the planter where he'd—Carole pushed the memories away and sank to the floor. The hum of the pump and the smell of chlorine made her aching heart burn. She knew why she'd come. *I came because I said I would and I would never lie to him.* Their hearts were the same, but they weren't. Ted couldn't see in the dark. Ted couldn't see at all.

Dive. Carole obeyed the muted command, slipping beneath the surface of the still pool. Chlorine torched her skin, the pain fantastic. She welcomed it, now her skin felt like her heart. Momentum took her forward, then she drifted, a phantom suspended, before sinking slowly. The pressure helped, like her body might come into sync with her head again. Carole came to rest on the bottom of the pool, wishing it were deeper, that she could sink down further and further until the pressure on her body equaled that inside her heart too. Far off the voices spoke, but they were too far away and she couldn't understand them. Hadn't understood them since he'd left, it was almost pleasant— *Every cloud has a silver lining*—Sister Mary Josephine had used to say that in the orphanage—Ted had shattered her heart but dimmed the voices. His betrayal hit her physically there beneath the water. It felt like the time she had been shot in the back in Singapore, shoving her body against the rough bottom of the pool scratching her raw, salted, torn skin. *Move.* Carole obeyed again, shooting to the surface for a gasping breath. The voices' keening took form faintly, just one word, a long drawn out sound, barely decipherable—*Why?* Ah, the same question she'd ask if he were there.

THE SOUND AND shouts of masculine voices woke her, they were hard to decipher, as though traveling underwater. Carole lay on her cot, one arm flung over her eyes, protecting her from bright light streaming through the tiny window. Someone grabbed her arm, roughly tugging her onto her back. Blinking, she tried to identify the face, but nothing came to her. A garbled voice sounded from far away, but the mouth moved in a familiar pattern and she knew he'd asked, "Are you hurt, Private?"

"Fine." She struggled to sit up, but hands held her down. "I'm fine," her voice sounded far off and garbled too.

Hands moved over her, rubbing something painful against her skin. Identifying a doctor's touch, Carole sat up, pushing his hands away. "I'm fine! Stop!" she shouted. It sounded dim, but he heard it and his hands withdrew. Blurry faces came into focus with the sound of indecipherable arguing. She studied their mouths for a clue, deciphering words.

"...obviously not at death's door, Captain...those dirty wounds need cleaned or she'll be in trouble...coral reefs...look at her swimsuit...." Carole didn't like the way the doctor was looking at her shredded swimsuit. Neither did the Captain, because he stepped between them, blocking the doctor's view. Leaning, he peered at her legs and then her face. His dark eyes were familiar, and she recognized him from the team on the beach. He was the man who'd told her that Colonel White had left. He was also the man from last night. The man who'd dragged her from the water and wrapped her in plastic. Carole shuddered.

"I'm sure it looked worse in the dark. A little blood goes a long way." The doctor's voice sounded slow and garbled, but she made it out.

The Captain shook his head, still peering into Carole's face, perplexed. "I know what I saw!" The dark eyes looked hurt. She watched his mouth move. "I searched for you all night, for your body."

"Can't blame you for that." Catching the undercurrent in the distorted words, Carole glanced towards the doctor. The Captain turned and said something she couldn't hear. The doctor left. The Captain sat on the bed next to her with a wiry brush in his hand.

"This won't be pleasant." Leaning forward he attempted to rub it against her leg, and Carole jerked away.

"Private? You have dirt and sand embedded in those cuts. If they're not cleaned, you're going to be in trouble." Again he reached towards her. Carole backed against the wall.

"Go away."

"Don't be stupid, you'll get an infection. Look, I'm not going to hurt you. I'm a nurse." He looked like any of a thousand other young men on the island, young, thin, and sunburned. Only his eyes set him apart, dark and clear, with thick lashes and thicker brows. They were unusually kind eyes. Dipping his brush into a bowl of water, he squeezed a tube of soapy ointment over it. Then he looked at her, waiting for permission. What did it matter? What did anything matter? Plopping against her pillow, she put her arms over her eyes, blocking the sunlight, blocking everything. Focusing on the keening question of the voices, she barely felt the Captain scrubbing her wounds clean.

"You need to eat." His voice was loud, as though he knew he'd have to combat great distance between them. As though he knew the voices were keening and he was far away. "It's past lunch but I can find something. Are you hungry?"

Carole rolled onto her side, ignoring his protests as sheets wiped away freshly applied ointment. *Go away*, she thought, too tired to bother to vocalize it. *Leave me alone.* As though he heard her, the Captain finally left.

THE CAPTAIN CAME and went. Sometimes he washed Carole's arms, legs, and a spot on her chin, and rubbed salve into her wounds. The discomfort reminded her he was there. Other times he dumped trays of food in her room, where they stacked up, untouched. At first he didn't say much, but after a couple of days he griped at her about not eating. He liked to lecture about nutrition and health and wasting good food. After a trip to the bathroom, Carole locked her door to prevent his next visit. Later that same day she sensed him in the hall outside her room. From far off she heard pounding and yelling. She ignored it. The next morning someone seemed to have provided the man with a key, because he showed up again. Grabbing her arm, he hauled her to her feet. Briefly she considered throwing him into the hall and blocking the door with her only chair. It seemed like too much effort.

"You're coming to the mess and eating something if I have to drag you there. I'll give you two minutes to change or I'll take you in that swimsuit—though it's hardly a swimsuit anymore, so I wouldn't recommend it. You might want to wash and brush your teeth too, you smell." Releasing his grip, he moved away. Finding herself suddenly standing, Carole had to focus to keep her footing. Blinking she watched him head out the door to wait. He glanced back and caught her look. "Go ahead, but if you lock the door on me again, I will have the doctor take you in for psychiatric observation, Private. So you might want to rethink your plan." He shut the door in her face, but she could sense him standing outside it.

Thoughts seemed to move sluggishly through her brain, but she considered her options. Psychiatric observation probably wasn't very peaceful. A crumpled pair of canvas pants and a dirty T-shirt sat on top the laundry bag. Carole nabbed them, pulling them over her decimated swimsuit. She didn't care what she smelled like. Opening the door, the Captain scowled at her, dark brows joining over his nose.

"Shoes?"

Carole turned back into her room, and stuffed her feet into her boots, the ones that Ted had thrown into the pool. They were still wet. She crumpled to the floor, head on her knees, unable to move. The Captain came into the room and shut the door behind him, crouching beside her and putting an arm around her shoulders.

"Hey," his voice was soft. "He's not worth it."

"I don't know what you mean!" Carole lied. The arm tugged her closer in a half hug. The Captain pressed his forehead against the top of her head.

"Don't be stupid. I know what a broken heart looks like. Come on, you're going to eat, Private. I meant what I said. I will have you sent for observation." Carole moved then because there was little choice. Besides it was possible to live without a heart. Ted did.

MOST OF WHAT the Captain said got lost in the underwater flood she now lived in. Everything seemed far away. The next day consisted of more pretending to sleep and after once again being forced to attend meals, eating whatever food she could manage in the mess hall. Carole reluctantly showered, but only because after refusing, the captain had ambushed her in the hallway and dragged her into a shower stall, both of them fully clothed. Standing beneath a stream of hot water, he'd blocked her exit. Again Carole didn't care enough to fight the man. Maybe she wouldn't have cared about the shower either, but something in her became mortified when he started to wash her face with a soapy cloth. He held onto the back of her head as though she were a child, rubbing the rough cloth across her face, soap burning her eyes. She became aware then that he was whistling despite water running over his face and soaking his camouflage.

"Please!" she begged, getting a mouthful of soap and a mental picture of her pathetic condition. "Go! I'll do it."

"I was hoping you'd say that. I'll bring you clean clothes, and tonight you'll do your laundry."

The pleasure of hot water—and clean skin—seemed like a distant memory, but Carole went through the motions. Life was inevitable. It didn't care if she wanted to participate. She went to the mess by herself afterwards, and ate only what she knew the voices approved of, though they still weren't talking. Afterwards she walked to the beach and looked at the water. The faint commands of *Inhale, Dive,* and *Move* still swirled through her mind, but she'd stopped obeying them. *I've gone deeper into crazy,* she thought. Why? *Because it's safe there,* the answer popped into her head. A real voice sounded at her elbow, she'd barely noticed the Captain's approach.

"Don't go into the water, Private. I don't think it's a good idea." Why was his voice so far away? *He's not far away, I am,* Carole realized, shivering despite the heat of the day.

"Look, I know it isn't my business, but he's famous for this."

"I don't know what you're talking about." *Don't tell me this,* Carole thought. *Please, don't.* But she waited, watching the Captain's lips so she could understand every word.

"I don't know what I'm talking about either. I'm repeating gossip because I have a feeling you should know. I don't even know if it will help, but maybe if you're mad—Colonel White has a reputation with the ladies." Carole made a sound of protest, and the Captain held a hand up, stopping her. "Look, I saw your face the day he left, I'm not stupid. Don't worry, no one else knows. Colonel White's a great guy. He really is, at least if you're a guy he is. Most of us want to be him, but I have a sister, Private, and maybe I see things differently. He's famous for being a love 'em and leave 'em kind of guy. I'm just sorry you didn't know that. I'm surprised he didn't tell you that himself, because he's also known for being honest. He didn't tell you, did he?"

"No," she whispered.

"Maybe he thought you knew."

"No. He lied."

"Oh. I'm really sorry. You won't go in the water just yet though, will you?" Carole looked at it, clear and beckoning. *Escape.*

"No," she promised. He was right. She wouldn't come out again if she did. He nodded and turned to go, then looked back at her again.

"You can do better."

Something twisted in Carole's heart. No, she couldn't do better. Even if she wanted to, she couldn't. She'd made her choice, no matter how foolish.

"Not all men are liars," he said.

"I know," she said. *But they all leave*, she thought. The Captain left her then, and Carole forced one foot in front of the other until she was running along the shore.

PASSING NEAR THE helipad, a group of men watched her run. Pretending to turn a blind eye, Carole saw one of them motion to her. Reluctantly she stopped moving, making the man come to her to speak. He was a pilot, and looked about fifteen years old.

"You're my pick up, Private." Her eyes flitted to his and he whispered, "Oatmeal," and winked. For a moment she didn't understand. Then she remembered the nasty closet of the CIA she now belonged to. It was the code word. Motioning with his eyes to a helicopter, he added, "Ten minutes. You're going out with the mail."

Carole ducked into the trees and raced to her room. Banging the door open, she crossed the tiny space and grabbed her duffel, shoving dirty clothes into it. Dropping to her knees, she reached beneath her cot and pulled Ted's dress shirt out. She held her breath, afraid to smell him on it, afraid it would be too much if she did. Jamming the khaki cloth into her duffel, she zipped it. Lumpy shapes rested in a low spot on her mattress. Green coconuts. Carole unzipped her bag and forced two of them into it. Jabbing her knife into each remaining drupe in turn, she drank the water as fast as she could. On the way out the door Carole reconsidered and returned to her empty cot. She dropped her military issue knife on the bed and several seashells she'd gathered to scoop gelatinous flesh from green coconuts. It was all she had to give. It occurred to Carole that she didn't even know the Captain's name and she'd never once thanked him for saving her life. All she knew about him was he had one fortunate sister.

Twenty minutes later she sat on top sacks of mail in the back of the helicopter, on her way to her first official, or non-official, assignment as a NOC.

CHAPTER
TEN

Egypt—October 1988

IF IT WERE a closet it had been designed with Carole in mind. Moving across the globe, from assignment to assignment, without the need of paperwork or meetings provided purpose and enough isolation to disguise her peculiarities. Non-official cover suited Carole, and she wondered at times if she had been born to be a NOC. In South America Carole hiked through a rainforest for two days, with only a backpack, to deliver a map. A week spent crawling through a cave in Chile was a success when she emerged with some type of crystal that she couldn't identify. She turned it over without a single question about its origin or why it was in that cave. The work provided her body activity and distraction. It soothed like swimming in deep water. Egypt proved harsh, the desert rough by night or day, but she hiked it for a month to deliver a long series of numbers that she'd memorized. It took her weeks with a scientist holed up in a tent, before he could finally memorize the code, and she could leave and claim a successful mission. Her contact left her at a camp in the southern end of the country, on the bank of the Nile. Carole slept a lot in the desert heat, and as always she dreamed of Ted, even though she tried not to. Every night for the past seven months he'd haunted her.

"We're going to take you off active duty for a bit. It's time you had a break anyway. Where do you want to go?"

Carole roused on her flimsy cot, sand gritting between her teeth. Rubbing her eyes, grains of it scratched against her eyelids. In this desert, every crevice of the human body became infiltrated by sand. A man dressed in the traditional cotton gown and turban of an Egyptian sat on the bunk across from her.

"Why are you taking me off the active list?" She didn't need or want a break. Activity helped her function. It helped her forget, at least during the daytime.

Grinning through a full beard he motioned towards her prominent belly.

"When are you due?"

"December." Carole rubbed a hand over the mound. It moved, visible beneath her tight olive T-shirt. "And that's two months away," she protested. This Egyptian was the first agent who'd acknowledged her belly as though it weren't a disease. Once her stomach had become obvious, the only comments she'd garnered from those she worked with was encouragement to abort the inconvenience. It had started in late summer.

⋙⋘

DELIVERING A NOTE with detailed comings and goings of a local politician, she met an agent at a café in Ecuador. Usually her contacts barely made eye contact, passing her next assignment verbally and vanishing. In a crisp linen suit, Harry, as he'd introduced himself, pulled out a chair for her, insisting she join him for lunch. Unquestioningly Carole sat beneath a cheerful umbrella and took the proffered menu. Freshly roasted coffee wafted under her nose penetrating the distance to where she resided deep inside her own head. She squinted against blocks of bright sunshine striping the patio. A primal need for food roused her. The papaya juice looked promising, and some type of vegetable ceviche with corn and rice. A waiter passed with a tray of patacones, the refried plantains looked delicious. Could she possibly eat enough to satisfy her changing body? The agent offered to treat, and Carole ordered more food than the tiny table could comfortably hold.

"We can get you stateside to take care of that, but we need you in Peru by the following Tuesday."

Rolling up a crumbling corn tortilla, and rubbing it through a dish of soft butter, Carole asked, "To take care of what?"

Harry stared pointedly at the faint bulge of her belly. Carole folded the tortilla and jammed it into her mouth. It tasted clean, of local ground corn, delicious. She replied through the mouthful, "There's no need, it's healthy. We're both healthy." She swallowed. How she knew that, she couldn't really say, but she wasn't going to a doctor. She wasn't sick and it seemed perfectly capable of taking care of itself.

"For an abortion, woman. Not for your health!" Harry looked disgusted. Carole put a hand protectively over her stomach. *Kill it?*

"Oh come on, do you want a baby? You're not even married." That appeared to disgust Harry that much more.

Ignoring her pregnancy had been easy until this confrontation. If she was honest with herself, Carole did not want a baby. But what did that even matter? She was having one, and that was that, wasn't it? For the first time in nearly five months, the voices had something audible to say. The keening stopped, and for a moment Carole looked around, attempting to place what had just happened. The long drawn out mantra of the word *why* had become white noise months ago. She barely noticed it any longer, but when it stopped she was momentarily disoriented. Then the voices started to talk again, loud and clear. "*Life is sacred. You will not do this. Your will matters not.*" She slapped a hand to her forehead. They were back with a vengeance. A lecture began to ticker tape through her head so fast it was hard to determine where one word ended and another began, as though every word from the past five months needed said right now. Carole squinted at the agent, trying to focus.

"Tell me you don't believe in abortion," he smirked.

"I don't." *Apparently.*

A loud bark of disbelief escaped Harry. People looked at him, and he lowered his voice, "The Agency does."

"Is that an order, then?" The voices were shouting so loudly Carole had to read his lips to understand his reply.

"Someone will get back to you on that." Harry stood up and shoved a neat straw hat onto his head, glaring. "So much for women's liberation, right? You want a man's job, you want to sleep around, but when it comes to priorities you're Mother Earth following the Pope's agenda?" He leaned down, hissing into her face, "You're little more than an assassin! You don't get to have a conscience!" Straightening up, Harry smoothed his pale suit jacket. "Pay for your own lunch. Someone will contact you about this, so don't go far."

AGENTS HAD CONTACTED her after that, more often to discuss her condition than her assignments. The line-up had included several women who'd undergone the procedure and claimed to be comfortable with their choice. Of the four women claiming that philosophy, Carole believed only one. It didn't matter anyway. None of those women had voices in their heads. They had the freedom to choose their own destiny, and suffer their own choices. The voices didn't like her attitude, and they called in the black dreams to reinforce their philosophy on the sanctity of life. They showed her a variety of horrible ways to die if one didn't believe that life was sacred.

The last months had been increasingly difficult. Carole's body had been hijacked, and it demanded plenty of good food and sleep, both hard to come by in her line of work. The outside world still seemed too far away. Focusing on her assignments, while the voices lectured and paraded horrors for disobedience before her, took almost more effort than she had to give now. Sitting on the cot, in the middle of the Egyptian desert with gritty sand clogging her nose, Carole decided she wouldn't argue with this pleasant agent. With hands resting on robed knees, the man waited patiently for her to reply. Maybe she could find enough clean food and take naps now and then if she took a sabbatical. The thought appealed to her.

"It is getting difficult to fit through tunnels. How long before I can come back?"

The agent's white teeth grinned through a black beard. "Oh, you'll hear from us soon enough. You've got the makings of a lifer. Where do you want to go?"

Carole shrugged. "I could stay here." She slept well in the desert.

The agent laughed. "That's a good one. You could call your baby Sandy. It would certainly be his first meal. Nah, go stateside, good medical care if you need it. How about San Diego? Plenty of sunshine, but not so much sand."

"Okay," Carole agreed.

The agent rose. "Good luck with the baby; and your code word is sand. Appropriate, huh? You'll probably still be flossing it out of your teeth six months from now."

A MILITARY AIRCRAFT took Carole directly from Cairo into Guantanamo. Late arriving, an airman tossed her canvas bag at her. She caught it, wrapping the strap over her shoulder, ignoring his mortified look as his gaze fell on her belly. She swung the bag to rest against her back, and adjusted her jacket to disguise the large pregnant bulge. It hardly made her frail.

The airman recovered. "Can you run, Private? That's your boat to Miami on the dock. The next one doesn't leave until next Thursday." Over on the docks, marines were loosening the moorings on a boat. Carole rushed down the plane's metal steps and ran the short runway, heading for the wharf. She could feel the baby rocking around inside her, like a fat fish in a little aquarium. Boots pounding the pavement, she timed her steps. It was effortless to make the boat before it pulled away, but sensing the airman watching behind her, she didn't dare run too fast. Passing a column of marines, the familiar posture of a tall dark one caught her attention. Carole looked at Lincoln the same time he looked in her direction. Without breaking stride she kept running. There was nothing to be said. She didn't belong with the Pact, but something made her raise her hand in a smart salute. He didn't respond, so he either held a grudge or hadn't recognized her. Carole jumped onto the deck of her boat just as it pushed away from the dock. In the distance, Lincoln led the Pact in the direction of the barracks without a backward glance for her.

THE COMPLICATIONS OF civilian life struck Carole before she boarded the commercial jet out of Miami. Standing in Terminal D of the Miami airport, for the first time ever Carole was completely free. It was surprising to find that she didn't particularly care for this type of freedom. According to her ticket it would be necessary to change planes in Dallas, Chicago, and Boston before arriving in San Diego. The sense of that eluded her, and Carole triple checked her ticket before standing in line to question the airline staff directly. A tanned Miami blonde gave her a slow once over as she curtly informed, "It's correct. That's economy fare for you."

Directed to a second line, Carole waited another half hour. A grey haired woman with polished red fingernails shared, "There is a direct flight into San Diego, if you would care to upgrade to First Class. It's the only available seat." With several small paychecks in her back pocket, and a grand total of $10 in cash, Carole didn't think that option possible. Clad in her ever present camouflage pants and olive green T-shirt, she suspected the elderly woman knew that too. She patted Carole's hand. "I'll make sure you get seats in the bulkhead, it's more leg room in your condition. None of your flights offer meals, but you can get juice and peanuts. The flight attendants will give you as much as you want. Just ask."

EIGHT HOURS LATER, Carole stood inside Hopkins International Airport in Cleveland, Ohio, watching an October snowstorm blow across the runway. Both Dallas and Chicago and many bags of peanuts were under her belt. Boston had mysteriously given way to a flight into Cleveland due to unseasonable weather. Carole studied her ticket stub curiously, certain the bad weather centered over the Great Lakes, and unable to comprehend the logic behind the unscheduled stop. Military life now seemed more efficient than the voices had ever given it credit for. Wind rocketed against the glass wall, occasionally a colorful autumn leaf stuck before being swiped away by fat wet flakes of snow. Outside airplanes waited at gates, but all flights had been cancelled for the night. Destitute travelers lined up at payphones attempting to book hotel rooms. Tossing her duffel over a shoulder, Carole went in search of food. The hijacker straining against her T-shirt wanted food right now, and that fat fish refused to be ignored.

THE STORM LASTED into the night, though the snow turned to rain. Yellow vested linemen trudged through the dark to tend to airplanes. Stretched out on the floor with her pregnant stomach in the air, Carole sensed workers struggling through the cold rain outside. Wishing she could be outside with them, instead of listening to the laments of fellow travelers making sleep impossible, she gave up and opened her eyes. People slumped on seats surrounding her weren't the only ones complaining, the hijacker wanted to eat again. The cafeteria had closed hours ago, and rice and orange juice had consumed eight of her ten dollars already, even another orange juice would cost more than two dollars. Rising to her feet, Carole went in search of food, hoping to find a kindly flight attendant with access to those lovely little foil packets of peanuts.

BY DAWN THE storm gave way to a beautiful autumn morning. Streaks of pink appeared across the sky and planes were taxiing down the runway. Carole had a seat at her gate, a free carton of orange juice in hand and a paper bag in her lap filled to the top with packets of nuts. A brochure about flight attendant school had been helpfully jammed into the bag too. Zipped inside her duffel were half a dozen of the best apples she'd ever seen, donated for free by a pretzel vendor who looked freakily like her old nemesis from the orphanage, Sister Mary Josephine. Some people were very nice, Carole decided. Biting into an apple, she sighed with pleasure. It tasted as good as it looked.

A flight attendant called her zone. Carole held the apple between her teeth as she rose to her feet, clutching her bag of food and the duffel. Fellow passengers stared, and Carole tugged her T-shirt to hide her bare belly peeking out beneath it. The airplane took off a half hour later. Sitting in her window seat with plenty of leg room, thanks to the woman in Miami, Carole watched the outline of the Great Lake below her. Something about the light reflecting off the water appealed to her, but it soon disappeared into a view of endless flatlands. Sliding the shade on the sunny window down, she rested her head against it and closed her eyes. Ignoring the awful smell of airplane air and the somersaulting movements of the frolicking alien inside her, she tried to get some sleep.

CAROLE MOVED INTO an apartment above a row of aged shops. Located near the naval base in San Diego, the easy walking distance to a farmer's market and the waterfront sold her on it. The rent was cheap, and the tattoo parlor below an unexpectedly quiet neighbor. Most of the other apartments on the street were abandoned and boarded up. Homeless people gathered in the alley behind the row of half empty shops. They, too, were surprisingly quiet neighbors. Carole napped, ran, and ate. The bulk of her meager funds went to food. Using the bread recipe her father had given her, she made a fresh loaf each day and converted slices into French toast for dinner almost every evening. Long ago she'd memorized the expensive ingredients, but pressing her hand over the neatly written piece of paper provided a pleasure deeper than mere food could offer. How much of the memory of him had been real? Since meeting Ted, Carole suspected it had all been real. She kept the fraying yellowed page safe between two pieces of glass, right in the middle of the kitchen counter next to a stack of newspapers that she tried to ignore.

The newspaper collection began when a homeless lady traded one for a piece of maple sugar candy. Hardly a fair deal, especially since the newspaper had been six months old. But Carole had seen the woman picking through a dumpster behind the drugstore, so she'd agreed. She knew what it felt like to crave clean food. Later, fingering her way through a library book on organic gardening, Carole reached into her bag for a pear. Spotting the newspaper, she spread it open on her lap. Six-month-old current events unfolded before her, and she read quickly. Perusing the personal ads, she spotted an advertisement from a couple seeking a baby to adopt. Lisa and Tom listed a toll-free number and asked for a chance to love your baby. Rubbing her stomach, Carole considered it. The thought of foster care drifted through her mind, and she shivered. *Not foster care. A family, a real family, with a mother and father who would be there.* Strangely, the voices didn't protest. The idea took root.

AFTER THAT, ON market days Carole picked up the local newspaper too. A pile of them now sat on the kitchen counter, next to the cutting board with today's fresh bread. She kept the papers folded neatly, open to personal ads on adoption. Bob and Linda. Alice and Frank. John and Cindy. Mostly she tried to ignore them. *How can you choose a family by a name?* Carole stirred a pot of barley soup, opened the tiny oven door, and lifted out the day's bread. Depositing the pan on the cutting board, she made up her mind and reached into the pile of newspapers. Pulling out a random one, she chose Mark and Melissa. The voices said nothing about it, busy droning on about paint chips on a windowsill they wanted cleaned out. Taking a pencil, Carole circled the names and memorized the phone number. She'd find a payphone and call them after the holiday weekend. Monday. The voices still said nothing, and Carole picked up two worn green potholders, dumping her bread from the pan to cool. The choice made.

WALKING HOME ON Thanksgiving Day, a homeless man approached her, wearing what appeared to be his entire wardrobe and a red ski cap. He offered Carole a turkey sandwich. She gave him a bag of red grapes she'd just purchased, and sat with him while he ate both the grapes and the sandwich.

"I'm an outsidie," he told her cryptically. "I'm just an outsidie."

"Me too," she said. The man appeared to have taken up residence on a concrete porch with years of colorful old gum stuck to it. Carole settled into the abandoned entryway with him and leaned against a deteriorating old door. Peeling paint broke off where she touched, and she brushed red and green chips off her clothes. The man spoke in a side conversation to someone, though just the two of them rested in the doorway. Carole opened her paper sack and extracted a small container. She began to eat the vegetable and rice mixture with her fingers. Her companion felt his jacket pockets for a few moments and produced a mangled fork.

"More civilized," he told her.

Carole hid a faint smile by sticking her nose in the food and sniffing in the savory scent. A whiff of red pepper shot up her nose, producing a violent sneeze. Sitting cramped on cold concrete, it rocked roughly through her body. She felt a faint popping sensation deep inside her, it didn't hurt, but she knew her water had broken. She watched as it leaked through her trousers, a bit trickled a path down her leg, dampening her sock. The reality of having a baby seemed as far away as the rest of the world, despite the inevitable evidence. Turning towards the homeless man who also seemed far away, she asked, "Do you hear voices?"

"Just yours," he replied. "I'm not crazy. Hey, you're having a baby."

"Not until December," she insisted. She'd done the math.

"It's Thanksgiving."

"I know," Carole said.

"I think that means its November."

"I know its November." Her damp sock felt warm in her shoe. The man next to her watched the wet stain spreading down her leg, as he popped grapes into his mouth.

"I think you're having a baby in November," he pointed out. "It's a long walk to the hospital. You'd better get going."

Heaving herself to her feet Carole arched her back, rubbing a painful spot at the base of her spine. Fine, if it wanted to come a bit early, just fine. She wondered if Mark and Melissa would mind if the baby had already been born, and wished she'd called today. The homeless man patted his knee nervously, watching her. She told him, "I'm not sick. I'm just having a baby."

"Don't have it here!" he protested.

"I'm not. I'm having it in my apartment. Maybe I'll see you tomorrow." Picking up her bag, a bit more fluid gushed down her pant leg. How embarrassing, like wetting herself. She'd seen this in black dreams. Shoving the thought of black dreams out of her mind, she focused on the fact that having a baby was a completely natural act, even a couple weeks early. The voices agreed with that assessment.

"*Commonplace. Normal. Not unusual.*" What did the voices know about normal? That thought made her uneasy. On the second flight of stairs, Carole paused, placing a hand on her belly, a whisper of fear ghosting through her. What if this baby heard the voices? What if it saw black dreams too? She shuddered, and more water spilled out of her, splashing on the concrete steps.

She whispered a prayer, "Dear God, please don't let my baby have this, please." Ignoring the approval of the voices encouraging prayer, she worried. What would Mark and Melissa do if the baby they adopted heard voices? Would they give it to foster care?

Carole pushed open the door of her apartment and unpacked her bag of groceries: milk, cheese, sunflower seeds, and perfect green grapes. She passed an hour cleaning the tiny rooms, ignoring the voices along with the drops of water dripping in her wake. The apartment was small, just three tiny rooms including the bathroom. Old and worn, the furnished apartment could never really reach much level of cleanliness, but it had come with such old furniture and kitchen supplies that almost all of it was useable. It didn't have the modern synthetics and plastics that made the voices frantic and caused shivers to run up her spine. After a few days devoted to scraping old paint away, she'd only tossed out one plastic tablecloth and a pair of polyester sheets, replacing them with natural fabrics. Carole methodically emptied a dresser drawer, tossed clean towels in it, and put a stack of cloth diapers beside it. After considering for a time, she pulled the drawer free and sat it on her bed.

Then she sat on the bed and waited. The pain wasn't as bad as she'd seen in her black dreams. After reassuring her it was normal, the voices had nothing more to say about her baby or childbirth and never a word about Mark and Melissa. Closing her eyes, Carole allowed herself to do the forbidden, to revisit her time with Ted. The touch of his heart haunted her. Running her fingertips over her own chest she missed him so much it hurt. The pain from her heart eventually moved down to encompass her stomach, and then wrapped arms around her back and increased so that it took her breath away. She panted, trying to recoup between contractions, and tried not to think.

SOMEONE WAS SCREAMING, and in the back of her mind Carole knew it was her. The pain was so big, she didn't know if it was supposed to be like this. What if something was wrong? *Oh God, what if something is wrong with the baby? With Ted's baby? Not Ted's baby! Mark and Melissa's baby!* The screaming got louder.

It was dark outside, and her mouth felt desert dry, skydiving-with-her-mouth-open dry, swallowing sand dry. Water, there was no water. There was only pain. The screams came through her desiccated throat and made it raw.

"Hush, girl. It's supposed to hurt like that. It's what a baby costs."

Carole opened her eyes and a grizzled dirty face hovered far too close. She turned her head away and closed her eyes. She sensed an old man nearby too, sitting in the corner of the tiny bedroom. There was nothing she could do, and a wave of new pain took her.

Opening her eyes again, Carole saw that the old woman remained, grinning a mostly toothless grin at her.

"I think something is wrong," she whispered.

The old woman shook her head. "What's your name, dearie?"

"Carole."

"I'm Anne, but on the street my friends call me Happy. I've had six babies and thought I was going to die with every one of them—you're perfectly normal. A wee bit young though, there's no father then?" Anne, in her checkered housecoat with a purple rabbit's foot on a chain around her neck, looked disapproving.

"Of course there is a father."

Anne pursed her thin lips. "I meant a husband," she reproved.

"Of course I have a husband." Carole closed her eyes again. *It is true!* She argued with the voices before they spoke. The problem was simply that Ted didn't know he was. The problem was he was afraid. *"The problem is he doesn't want to be."* The voices were ruthless.

The man spoke from the chair in the corner of her room. "Should I boil water or something, Happy?"

"You watch too many movies, Junny. What am I going to do with boiling water?"

"I don't know."

"I need old newspapers. Can you get me some of those?"

Junny stood up and shuffled off as another pain engulfed Carole. She recognized Junny as the homeless man she'd shared her grapes with, and judging by Anne's appearance, she was homeless too. Then the pain took her away again.

A RING OF pain burned cruelly between Carole's legs. Anne caught the baby as it finally shot out of Carole's body, and wrapped it in newspaper. Carole leaned back and closed her eyes. It hadn't been bad, labor. The memory already receded from the fog she lived in. Anne poked her, grinning when Carole looked up. She forced the baby into Carole's arms. Carole reluctantly held it, lifting a flap of the paper to check the sex. It was Mark and Melissa's newspaper; the pencil mark circling their names rested against the baby's rosy stomach. It was a baby girl. Carole closed her eyes again, ridiculously feeling disappointed. She'd expected a boy—a likeness of Ted, although she'd never admitted it to herself until that moment. Her heart sank further as she thought of him, her missing husband who hadn't allowed her to touch his heart. What difference did it make? This baby would be Mark and Melissa's baby. Surely they would love her, even if she came too early, even if she heard the voices and had black dreams.

Something brushed Carole's heart then, something big and shining and full of light. It bounced against her heart. Carole's eyes shot open as the touch pulled her from the haze she'd been living in. It yanked her roughly out of the fog and she landed in crystal-clear reality, sitting on an old mattress with her newborn baby resting on her chest. She stared at her daughter, arms tightening around the impossibly small human being blinking up at her. The touch came again. Accepting. Open. Loving.

"Oh my God! Oh my God! Is that you?" she shouted.

The baby wailed and Carole's arms tightened, rocking back and forth in an attempt to comfort her.

"Is that you? Is that you? Oh my God! Thank you! Thank you!" The touch burrowed into her heart, making a home, taking up residence. *I'm yours, you're mine, we're us.*

Tears flooded her eyes, Carole rocked back and forth sobbing, clutching her daughter. Images darted through her mind. Dancing. Sunshine. Puppies. *Puppies?* Carole started to laugh through her tears. This is what the touch of a heart felt like! The touch of Ted's had been a dim shadow of this. This was what it had been like before they'd all gone. Her mom, her gran, and her father's hearts. This heart was even more than theirs, she was sure of it. This little girl's heart shone brighter, bigger, and bolder.

"This is real!" Carole shouted. "This is real! Do you feel it?" She tore her eyes from her daughter to look at Anne. The old woman stood beside her, rubbing her chest.

"What is that? Is that her?"

"Can I have some more of those grapes? Or maybe a banana?" Junny asked from the corner of the room.

Anne turned towards him. "Yes, take some fruit, Junny. You can go now." He shuffled off, whistling.

Carole's eyes turned back to her baby. She weighed about six pounds, but she was long and narrow for a baby. She looked slimy, covered in a thick white substance beneath the damp newspaper. Her eyes were big and dark blue, alert, her mouth an angelic little bow, her hair was either blonde or red, Carole wasn't certain because of the blood. She peeled the newspaper off her daughter, wiping streaks of ink from her, nestling her naked baby against her damp T-shirt. Quickly she touched everywhere, examining fine skin, and the shape of long thin baby fingers. They were shaped like Gran's! The toes were impossibly perfect, the cutest things she'd ever seen in her life, and there were no nails on them. The feet were long and narrow. The touch of the heart spoke, without words, yet Carole understood it. I *am* cute. I *am* perfect. I *am* yours, Mom. Carole tore her eyes away and turned them towards Anne's again.

"Do you feel that too?"

"Her sweetness? Yes, that is one very sweet baby girl. Sweeter than my own I'd say. What are you going to call her?"

Carole considered that. She hadn't thought of names! For a fraction of a second she considered Melissa—the woman who she'd almost—no, never! Shoving that idea far away, Carole thought. *Sandy?* She laughed. *No! Names?* For a moment she wondered what Mom and Gran's real names had been, wishing she knew. Then her rejoicing heart landed on Ted for a moment, and considered naming her daughter for him, the heart that helped create her. The memory of Ted and the faint touch of his heart didn't even hurt now. She smiled, thinking of Ted's heart.

"Beth. I'm going to call her Beth. I think it is her Daddy's favorite name!"

CHAPTER
ELEVEN

San Diego, California—March 1989

BETH AT FOUR-MONTHS-OLD looked like a thin cherub. Silky hair rested smoothly over her creamy forehead, intelligence shone through big clear eyes, and bow shaped pink lips smiled or protested beneath a perfect snub nose. Carole wandered down a sunny row at the farmer's market, frequently peeking at her daughter. Wrapped in a sling Carole had sewn from Ted's good khaki service uniform and one of Carole's own olive T-shirts, Beth's weight rested solid and reassuring against her mother's body. *I love you*, Carole thought, running a finger down the most perfect profile she'd ever seen. It took effort to turn her focus to a bin of vegetables and examine tomatoes. The yellow ones interested her. She could make a salad with the red and yellows mixed together, with some fresh mozzarella, basil, and balsamic vinegar. Her mouth watered at the thought. Nursing Beth had her eating twice as much as she usually did. Eating and nursing was a full time job, her favorite job. Running a hand beneath the sling, she smoothed Beth's silky blonde hair, so like hers, except it was soft and smooth and beautiful. The touch of Beth's heart tinkled against hers, pure as the note of a silver bell. *Mom, Mom, Mom, you're my Mom*, it said. There was something very open and honest about the touch of Beth's heart. Carole rarely passed a person who didn't reach out a hand to brush over the bundle always dangling close to her heart. Madly in love with this little person, Carole was deliriously happy.

A Hispanic man stopped in front of her, displaying a melon in each hand. Carole shook her head, refusing them. He leaned towards her and whispered, "Sand, and we leave in twenty minutes, so you'll need to come with me now."

Gaping at him, she dropped her bag of vegetables to the ground and both hands went to Beth. Hidden beneath the folds of fabric she yanked her T-shirt up and pulled her daughter to a breast. Beth bit on with enthusiastic vengeance.

"I need five minutes," she pleaded.

The man smiled, and patted the bundle suckling at her breast. "Take ten, we can run."

As she raced through the market Beth jostled against her, making little noises of annoyed protest, very faint noises because her mouth never once left the breast. Carole spotted Anne haggling over a cotton baby blanket she'd had her eye on for weeks. Only the purple rabbit's foot gave clue that Anne was the woman who'd delivered Beth four months ago. She might have been anyone's neat grey grandmother dressed in an emerald green gypsy dress smiling with new dentures. Rushing to Anne's side, Carole grabbed her arm.

"Remember I told you I'd have to go sometime?"

"Now?" Anne protested. "What am I going to feed that child? My breasts don't work like that anymore."

"God, how I wish they did," Carole said. She reached to run her hand over the woman's sagging breasts, drawing horrified glances from passersby. "Oh, if only they would." Carole felt something warm zing from her hands, sensed it moving invisibly over Anne. She held her hand there, wishing, praying, and certain she was beginning to suffer moments of delusion.

Anne didn't flinch. She rubbed her breasts too and said, "They wish they did too, but they don't. What should I feed her? I don't think she's big enough for your bread."

Carole shook herself. Wishful thoughts wouldn't feed Beth while she was gone. "Try soy milk, from that corner store where I get the sprouts. Mix it with a bit of goat's milk if she won't take it. Warm it a bit, and hold her close when you feed her. Use only those glass bottles I bought..." Carole's voice trailed off and she shivered at the thought of the rubber nipples, dropping her hand from Anne to rub Beth's little back. There was nothing to be done for it. This was what she did, she had to go. Anne would guard Beth with her life, and Junny would camp out in the entryway downstairs and help Anne if she needed anything. Carole pried Beth off one breast with a popping sound. Before Beth could shout, she pushed her mouth onto the other.

"Now that's a mother of the 1980's," Anne complimented. "Back in my day the doctors told us to use canned milk, that breast feeding was bad for them. I didn't listen to doctors then either."

Carole's eyes watered. Four months was all they'd had. It could be a year—she would ask. Surely they would let her come here sometimes, instead of camps, between missions. Surely—Carole could sense her contact waiting for her, sense the minutes ticking by double time. With only twenty seconds left, she pulled Beth loose. She came off the breast with another popping sound and made sweet grumpy sounds of protest, too sated to really fuss. Carole lifted the babe from the folds of fabric and looked into her four-month-old face. Beth gave her a milky drunken smile and burped at her. Carole kissed her forehead, cheeks and messy mouth, memorizing her, breathing her in. She pressed her face against her daughter's torso, wallowing in the taste of that sweet heart as it bubbled against her own. *Mom, Mom, Mom, mine, mine Mom*, it seemed to say. Finally Carole yanked the cloth sack from around her neck and draped it over Anne's.

"Love her hard. Make her feel it."

"Oh, don't you worry. I will do that." Anne took Beth from her mother's arms and Beth's baby heart bounced after Carole's as she ran off. The sound of Beth's cries and the touch of sudden tears reached farther than the touch of her heart, and Carole cried with her, not caring who saw her tears.

FOR MONTHS CAROLE prowled back alleys in Buenos Aires. Dressed as a homeless woman, she pushed a cart full of junk she'd secured from trash bins. Her mission was simply to locate another agent when he crossed her path, give him the code word, and take him to a drop point. The voices didn't like cities. They didn't like the food. They didn't like the touch of the dirty clothes that hung over Carole's grimy skin. They complained during the entire assignment. Carole wondered if Beth would ever behave as childishly as the voices, and the thought made her smile. Carole fit in with the homeless better than she did with most people. Sometimes she hoped that Beth would fit into the world they lived in, but mostly she hoped that Beth wouldn't hear the voices.

After Carole located the agent and made the drop, she spent weeks aboard a submarine. It felt good to be clean again, but the voices were frantic beneath the sea. Carole couldn't ignore them. She was frantic beneath the sea too. At not yet twenty years old, posing as a specialist in nuclear psychics seemed ridiculous, but she managed to pull it off. Keeping to herself, she simply listened to the reports of naval officers and said "Hmmm" a lot. There was a quiet young man on board, Petty Officer Leo Milton whose duty was cooking in the tiny galley. Leo kindly noted what Carole ate and put only those rations on her plate whenever she came through the galley.

The sub surfaced off an uninhabited island in the Atlantic. Outside a control room Carole hugged the wall so Leo could pass her. Leo tapped her elbow and mouthed, "Antler," the pass code.

Dragging a garbage bag, Leo hurried behind Carole as they moved through corridors. Carole focused her talents on passing unseen, using that part of her brain that saw through walls. Arriving at a hatch, Leo opened it. Carole helped him drag the bag through the hatch and they stood on top the submarine. The sun headed for the western horizon, but it wouldn't be dark for hours, and the water stood so calm it barely lapped the sides of the craft. The petite cook squatted on the hull and opened the trash bag, handing over equipment: a wetsuit with fins, a hand-operated desalination water tool, and a small packet of first aid supplies.

Leo riffled through a stack of photographs and handed them over one at a time. "This is the most important one. I know it's in black and white, but see the markings on the boat? It will come alongside the island in a week or so. You need to get on it. Take a good look at these men and this woman." He handed over their photographs. "You can take these with you to memorize, but burn them as soon as you get on that island. Do not interface with any of them. They'll know why you're there if they see you. Don't attempt to take them prisoner. You have to kill them, and as quickly as you can."

The voices started to shout, and Carole's heart sank. *Kill them?*

"Boarding would be best done at night so they don't raise the alarm, or detonate the weapon. The details about that weapon are need to know, and all you need to know is it's nuclear." Leo shook his head, looking at the sea glistening around them, reflecting the setting sun. "It's a dangerous world."

Carole nodded. Yes, it was very dangerous.

Leo tugged a small knapsack out of the bag and sat it beside the wetsuit. "Give me your clothes, everything. Your stockings, under-things, all of it, then put this on." Carole obeyed as Leo politely turned his gaze back to the water. She left her clothes in a heap and struggled with the tight wetsuit, forcing it up her legs and over her backside which had never seemed large until now.

"Wait, don't put your arms in yet. I need your blood." Leo turned his attention back to her.

Blood? Despite the voices objections, Carole complied, standing with the wetsuit squished against her midsection, naked from the waist up with one arm bent modestly over her chest.

Leo eyed her soberly. "Where wouldn't you mind having a scar?"

Carole shrugged. She'd prefer nowhere.

"Let's just use your upper arm. It will hurt more, but you can keep it out of the water swimming to the island. Sharks. Don't worry—I have bandages, and there is a first aid kit in your supplies."

Very matter of fact, Leo held Carole's arm out and sliced into it, catching the blood on her discarded uniform, and squeezing the

123

wound when it uncooperatively tried to clot. Leo remained conversational while Carole's blood spilled.

"I have to make it look like you've died. I could use a body part, even a finger would help, but you're going to need them all. If I take some toes, I doubt I can bandage it to keep the sharks off you. I have a torso in the freezer, but there was no place safe to thaw it."

"How are you going to make it look like I died?"

"An explosion. A fire on board is dangerous, but how many ways can someone disappear from a submarine? Some of the men will know there's more to it, and I'll deal with that as it comes. That's enough blood. I don't want to take much more, you have a long swim." Leo put pressure against the cut, pulled a vial of superglue from the pocket of his pants and glued the wound closed. "Let's hope it's waterproof. Pretty cool stuff." He wrapped the wound with gauze and then frowned. "Uh, you know, I probably just glued that bandage to your arm. Good luck—whatever your name really is. These terrorists have been trying to bomb a port city, and now they managed to get hold of a nuke." He handed Carole a knife. "That's all the weapon they gave me for you. Sorry. I hope you can kill with it."

"It's enough." Carole ignored the protests of the voices. San Diego was a port city. She took another glance at the photographs and shoved them inside her wetsuit.

"After you take the ship—" Leo recited coordinates and pass codes half a dozen times, though Carole could recite them back after the first round. "A team will come in and secure the weapon. Keep your head down." He watched as Carole slid into the water.

She bobbed in the water beside the submarine, and called back, "Good luck with the frozen torso."

Waving, he grinned. "We just got one of those new gadgets—a microwave oven—I might be able to thaw it in there if it will fit. I just worried someone would eat it if I left it unguarded."

LEO WAS RIGHT about the gauze and the superglue, the bit of fabric hung from Carole's arm and nothing she did would get it off. She trimmed it with her knife and left it to dangle. The submarine left a few hours after Carole made the island, so she assumed no one suspected she'd gotten off the vessel. There was no fresh water on the island, and Carole set herself to endure desalinated ocean water pumped through a little gadget made mostly of plastic. The voices would not stop shouting about it, and Carole wondered if they'd rather she just died of thirst. Cleaning enough ocean water to drink became a full-time job. Carole wondered how many agents died while waiting. The ship showed up though, a week and a half later. Sick of eating only seaweed, insects, and roots, she hit the sea in broad daylight. It was dangerous, but not as dangerous as the ship pulling away before nightfall.

Clinging to the underside of the ship, she climbed the barnacle encrusted, dented hull half way to the top and then got oddly lucky. One of the terrorists she recognized from the photographs climbed down for a swim. He ended up tangled in the rope, his head dangling in the water. Without the body strength to pull himself up he struggled for less than fifteen minutes, occasionally managing to emerge and get a breath before plunging again below the waterline, but never once did he manage enough of a breath to even call for help. Carole knew he'd spotted her clinging impossibly to the side of the hull, watching dispassionately. When he finally stopped fighting she resumed her climb, the sight burned into her mind, and her heart heavy although the voices didn't even reprimand her.

Swinging from the hull to grasp the rope he still dangled from, Carole let her senses creep upwards until she knew no one would see her board. When the coast was clear she simply climbed up the easy way and went below deck. Ignoring the voices lecturing about stealing, she took a box of raisins and a handful of apples and hid in a closet full of cleaning supplies. From the looks of the big vessel, she could remain there indefinitely without discovery.

Before she took even a bite of the stolen food, she sensed *it*.

Inside her head she could feel the metal of the ship, the people in it, but deep in the belly was something—other. It felt like a blank spot inside her brain when she tried to see it inside her head. Suddenly knowing what it was, she wasn't hungry. This weapon was her real enemy. Carole crept out of the closet. There were seven people on the ship, and three would have to be terminated. Killed by her own hands.

UNFORTUNATELY SHE COULDN'T sense which people were which with her mind, though she could tell the difference between the men and the lone woman. The voices were furious and they attacked with black dreams, trying to make her stop. "*You need permission. Permission. It is forbidden.*" The woman was on a radio speaking in Russian, and Carole waited outside the room for her to finish. Then she realized that she could understand the language she'd never learned.

"I miss you too, baby girl. Mama will be home by Christmas. I'm kissing you, do you hear me? I'm kissing you!"

A man's voice sounded in English. "Get off Trina—it can be traced."

"Bye bye, baby. I have to go. Listen, here's my kisses for you. I love you. Mama loves you, baby girl."

The radio cut out, and the woman objected in English. "I haven't seen her in months! She's starting school and she's scared."

"You should be scared. We're sitting on a bomb that we know nothing about. We'll probably blow ourselves up with it, if we even manage to get into any American port with it."

"Did Miller look at it today? He said something needed tweaking, whatever that means. I don't trust him."

"He went for a swim. He'll get to it."

"That was his priority? The thing is radioactive and he wants to go swimming?"

"He smells like a sewer."

"We all do. Also Miller's fault. Go get him, Thomas. I don't want to die of cancer."

Thomas exited into the hall and Carole followed him long enough to identify him. He looked very strong and capable, so she used her knife when she stepped in front of him. Cutting his throat, she held his eyes. When the light started to go out, she lowered him to the floor.

Trina had to go next, and Carole felt regret about ending the woman whose daughter was starting school someplace far away. Entering the cabin at an impossible speed, she knocked Trina from her chair and jammed her knife into her throat.

"I'm sorry," she whispered, the Russian words unfamiliar on her own lips. "I have a daughter too, but I am not trying to kill yours." Tears ran out of Trina's furious eyes as the life left her body.

The last man was already dead. He'd shot himself in his cabin. Carole could only identify him by a scar on his neck. His room was filled with books on nuclear bombs and radiation. Carole knew something was terribly wrong on the ship. She could feel it. The weapon seemed larger than when she had first boarded; the blank spot in her head bigger.

There were four other men on board, but at noon they went to the dining cabin and Carole simply locked them inside. She returned to the radio room, walked over Trina's body and sent the message as she'd been told. By that evening she couldn't bear to be near the weapon and she swam back to the island to wait.

No one came. Carole drank barely potable water, ate roots and waited. She remembered the joke. *Noc Noc. Who's there? Wait for it.* After a few days she went back to the ship to let the men out of the galley. They were four young, strong boys from Tanzania. They spoke no English, but fortunately she discovered she could speak some Swahili. The black dreams were very good teachers of language. Leading them to the deck top she told them that they had to get off the ship because it was poisoned. Although they seemed strangely docile, only one came with her.

FOR SIX WEEKS Carole lived on the island with Fazil. She taught him how to clean salt from the water, and he taught her how to build a makeshift shelter. They lived in companionable peace together. It was the first of September before a ship arrived. It dropped anchor a good ways from the pirate ship, but boats went back and forth and the people in them wore hazmat suits. Carole built a fire on the shore and waited some more.

ANOTHER WEEK PASSED before a team arrived at the beach and used a Geiger counter to check Fazil and Carole's radiation levels. They were given pills and examined. Their supplies and clothes were confiscated and destroyed. Carole endured the humiliating process of being publicly naked and washed down with Fazil at her side. Then they were both taken from the little island to the big ship for further examination.

"You're an unusually healthy young woman. What nationality are you?" A military doctor stood curiously at the foot of her bed. Fazil watched from his bedside beside her.

Shrugging, Carole replied, "I have no idea, why?"

The doctor flushed, and waved the question away with his hand. "Idle curiosity I suppose. The radiation didn't affect you very much. Fazil has no thyroid left, but yours is fine. We've done what we can for both of you, but as a physician I would estimate Fazil will not live to be a very old man—and he will never have children of his own, or enjoy the good health he deserves. You, however, will likely live to a very ripe old age. Of course, Fazil was exposed much longer than you were."

"How is it possible that the radiation didn't affect me?" "*Don't ask!*" The voices warned, "*Hide! Don't draw attention to yourself!*"

The doctor sat down on the bed beside her and looked over her chart, frowning. "I didn't say it didn't affect you at all. It's thrown you into very early menopause—maybe it will reverse in time, but I doubt it."

"What does that mean?"

"Your reproductive years are over. I'm sorry, Agent. Considering what might have happened to you, I strongly urge you—both of you—to be thankful you're alive." He shut her folder, stood and addressed them both. "I'm afraid the men who remained on the ship weren't so fortunate."

CHAPTER
TWELVE

San Diego, California—September 1989

SHOVING HER WAY from the very back of the aircraft so that she could get out first seemed to be a social faux pas. Carole did not care. Even grey-haired old ladies hissed at her and fussed. Carole glared her way past flight attendants and silently dared anyone in first class to complain out loud. After weaving between passengers crowding the aisles and fishing for their carry-on luggage, she waited first in line to depart the aircraft. The flight attendant opening the door tossed more glares in her direction, and then Carole ran. She had no intention of collecting the expensive suitcase full of new clothing provided at base camp. All she'd really wanted for her efforts was a direct flight to San Diego, and they'd denied her that. Sprinting out ground level automatic doors, she hopped into the first taxi she saw and bellowed her address at the driver.

A mile from her apartment they got stuck in traffic. Carole pushed the door open, threw a ten dollar bill at the driver and ran. It was a Sunday night. Beth would be ten months old in exactly two weeks and twelve hours. She'd been alive longer without her mother than she'd been with her. Carole ran faster than allowed, and the voices protested. People on the street stopped and stared. Rounding the corner onto her own street, her heart pounded with excitement.

Several Hells Angels, a biker gang that liked to hang out at the tattoo parlor, watched her approach. One offered her a ride on his bike. She shook her head and dashed to the alley behind the shop. Junny wasn't there. Carole took the stairs two at a time, a cold sweat breaking out. The door was locked—maybe they'd gone somewhere. She dashed back down the steps, into the alley, and found Junny's old porch. The key was wedged behind an iron number seven, stuck there with a wad of old gum. It came off with several inches of green gum still sticking to it. Carole ran back up the stairs and jammed the key into the lock and burst through the door.

There was a television on the kitchen counter, turned on. A thin man came out of the bedroom in just jeans, his torso so hairy it appeared to be one with his beard. He gaped at her. "How the hell did you get in here?"

"Where's my daughter? Where's my baby?" Carole screamed. Panic squeezed her heart and she closed the distance between them. She'd kill him! But first he'd talk, he'd tell her everything. He backed towards the bedroom door and held his hands up in surrender.

"Hold on, hold on! You're the—I think the baby's okay. I'm Anne's son, but—well, just hold on a second. My mom wrote a message for you." While Carole stood, shaking with anger and terror, the man edged past her. He dug through a pile of newspapers and mail on the small kitchen table, shooting worried looks in her direction. "They arrested my Mom when they came and took the baby. She wouldn't give her to them."

"They arrested—where's my baby?" The scream tore her throat like a razor.

"Here! Here it is." Backing away, he held a piece of paper out. Carole snatched it and read.

Dear Carole, I tried, Sweetheart, but child protective services came with the police and took her. I couldn't stop them. I'm sorry. Junny followed them. He said they put her with a family at a new apartment building over by Saint Patrick's church. Anne

A sob tried to come out, but it got stuck in Carole's heart. It felt like it would rip through the wall of her chest.

Beth was in foster care.

Carole spun on her heel and ran out the door. She didn't care who saw, she jumped the flight of stairs, turned and headed towards the street.

"Hey, Babe, you want that ride?" A biker rocked his hips in a suggestive gesture and his friends laughed.

"Someone took my baby!" Carole gasped, unable to stop tears of terror running down her face. Her hands shook. "I think she might be at some new apartment building over by Saint Patrick's church. Do you know where it is?"

The guys stopped laughing. One of them offered to make a new baby with her, but the man she'd addressed scooted forward on his seat. "Hop on. I know where everything in this city is."

Four other bikers followed behind as he took off. Thundering bass barked, echoing in the motorcycles' wake. Carole hung onto the man's leathered torso, her entire body shaking with grief and fear. She would *kill* them for touching her baby. *Kill* them. The voices shouted at her and she didn't hear a word they said. For the first time in her life she felt truly angry. A red veil seemed to drop over her vision, as though the blood she wanted to shed had risen from her own heart. She wondered if the scalding tears sliding down her cheeks were blood too.

The bikers stopped right in front of a new apartment building. Compared to the huge rectory next door, the building looked small, only three stories high, but planters full of bright flowers and little trees arranged artfully on the roof gave it an upscale appearance. Carole jumped off the bike and the bikers followed her. Running up the steps to the front door, she found it locked. She looked for something to break the glass door, and reached for a flower pot. A biker grabbed her arm.

"Hold on. This is what we do at these places." He used two big fat hands and pressed dozens of rows of buttons on the intercom at the same time. Several voices replied within seconds, asking who it was. "Pizza," he answered, and the door buzzed open.

Carole raced into the building, ready to kick every door down. On the first floor she ran from door to door and put a hand on them, sensing nothing. Mounting the stairs to the second floor, she made it halfway up and sensed Beth's heart in the distance. The tears stopped then. She'd found her. In four steps she was in front of a heavy metal door with 202 in shiny brass letters over a peep hole. A hefty biker with a mane of black curls peered down at her.

"You sure this is the one?" She nodded and he produced a heavy flat wire and slid it into the keyhole on the door handle. "These places give the illusion of security at the front door, so no one uses their deadbolts." He shook his head in disgust, jiggling the wire until the lock clicked. Cautiously he opened the door, looked in, and gestured for Carole to go first. Five bikers followed her into the apartment, leaving big dirty footprints on brand-new cream-colored carpeting.

The television was on in the front room. It was brand-new too, as was the beige sofa and oak dining room set. A purple car-seat dotted with silver stars rested against the closet door beside a man's shoes. A woman's pink sweater with pearl buttons draped over a dining room chair. Carole took a deep breath. *She* was Beth's mother. Behind her, she sensed one of the bikers close the door behind them and twist the deadbolt. They made their way towards the hall. A man moved at the far end of the dark hallway, his voice a deep hissing whisper. "Be quiet, Kimberly, I just got her to sleep!"

The man saw them and froze. Disbelieving, Carole stepped backwards into the Hells Angel behind her, her knees gave out. He caught her under her arms and stood her neatly back on her feet.

How?

The man standing in front of her was Ted White.

They stared at each other, both momentarily stunned. Ted glanced at her friends and growled, low. "How did you get in here?"

Carole continued to gape at him. Her new friend behind her put a big tattooed hand on her shoulder and squeezed it. The gesture helped immensely. She held firmly to her feet and took a deep breath.

The biker answered for her, "You have something that belongs to this little lady, and we're here to get it back."

Ted held the man's gaze briefly; then looked at Carole. "She's my daughter too, isn't she?"

The hand dropped off her shoulder. Unable to answer, Carole thought indignantly, *Of course she's your daughter!* Her shock began to give way to anger. Did he really think there was any doubt about that? And why had he taken her if he thought Beth might not be his? Adrenaline still coursed through her veins. Part of Carole wanted to knock Ted to the floor, kick him a few times, and go to her daughter. Even in her sleep, Beth's heart beckoned like a whisper. Carole stepped towards it but Ted held up a hand.

"Wait, don't wake her, she just went to sleep!"

Carole's mouth opened in surprise. *The audacity!* Words finally came. "I haven't seen her in six months! You took her! I thought she was in foster care!" Fear and despair singed the last words.

"She'd have been better off, you left her living in squalor!"

"How dare you! I did not!"

"You left her with some half-crazed homeless woman! That old woman was breastfeeding her! Carole, she had the baby crawling around on the floor—naked—on top of newspapers like a puppy!"

Anne had managed to breast feed Beth? Carole's heart rose in wonder and amazement. *How?* She defended her friend, "Newspaper is clean, nearly sterile. Did you know that? This carpeting—" Carole stomped a foot on the brand-new carpet, "is not."

"If I'd have known you were a virgin, I wouldn't have touched you that first night." Ted threw the inappropriate statement at her, but it didn't even sound like he believed it. The Hells Angels had gone completely silent. Carole could sense their rapt attention behind her as they listened to the private details of her life.

"Really?" Carole fought the urge to break his nose.

"Really. You lied to me."

She gasped—rage rekindling, but the Hells Angel behind her grabbed her arms. "I lied to you?"

"Yes! You showed up at the pool one night, and threw yourself at me. I never had a choice!"

"Oh, please—" Carole paused as the rage subsided. It was true, probably truer than Ted knew. The man behind slowly released her arms.

"Not once, but every night for weeks. You never even told me your name."

She glared. "You knew my name."

"That is not the point. What kind of a woman does that? All that sex—it's all you did. I've never had a woman—you practically rubbed me raw night after night. And after the way you'd treated Wright! What else could I think? I heard him. I *saw* how he behaved at summer camp, he cried! Wright didn't cry when his mother died. Everyone thought you had an affair with him and ripped his heart out afterwards!"

"You know that's not true!"

"I didn't know that night! I heard what they said about you. I read the reports. Wright was in love with you, and you slapped him across the face and laughed at him!"

"It was the only way to get him to pull himself together!"

"That night, I'd assumed you were a—"

Carole tensed. If he said it she'd knock his teeth right down his throat.

"And why didn't you tell me you were pregnant? What right did you have to—" Ted motioned down the hall, where the reassuring touch of Beth's heart beckoned for Carole's even in sleep. She glared at Ted.

"You left without a word, and worse than that you are the one who *lied* to me, Ted White! Even if I wanted to contact you—which I didn't—I couldn't have."

"Carole, you could have told anyone and they would have let me know." He sounded hurt. His big shoulders slumped, and even in the dim hall light she could see dark circles under his eyes. He looked exhausted.

What did any of this matter now?

"How did you find out?" she wondered.

Ted rubbed a hand over his eyes and shook his head. "Blind luck. I ran into—" he glanced at the bikers behind her and continued cryptically, "your old friends. Lincoln told me he'd seen you—and you were pregnant out to here." Ted made a gesture. "At first I didn't think much of it, not really. Maybe to be surprised that you'd keep a baby."

Carole's gut twisted, is this is what he'd really thought of her? But why would he lie about it now?

Ted avoided looking at her while he talked, bracing one big hand against the wall. "Then it just popped into my head one day a few weeks later. I saw a woman pushing a baby in a stroller down a street in DC—anyway I did the math. I thought, it was, you know, possible that it could be mine. I thought about the pool, and the first time, you were so strange. You are so strange. But I called in a few favors. Found out where you lived. Ran a check for newly issued birth certificates for the months of November and December in San Diego, and got a copy of the one with your name on it."

"You snoop!"

Ted smacked an open hand against his chest. "That birth certificate has my name on it too! Under *father!* Imagine how I felt when I saw that!"

"You left!'"

"Men do that after one night stands!"

"*One. Night. Stand.* I am nobody's one night stand! Of all the—if you thought I was a one-night stand, why did you lie about leaving?"

Ted clasped both hands behind his head and stared at her a moment. "I had to go—and I knew you were getting attached. I didn't want a scene."

The frank answer hurt, and she knew it wasn't true.

"Are you going to lie to me again, and tell me you weren't attached?"

Ted looked away for a moment, staring at the blank white wall, then back at her almost angrily. "Why did you name her Beth?" Pronouncing the name, his voice dropped low, emotional. Even in the dim light of the hallway, the pain in his blue eyes was evident.

"For you," Carole whispered.

Ted made a sound and looked at the floor for several seconds. "You don't even know who she was."

Carole lifted a shoulder in a faint shrug and told him, "I know she was your heart."

"God." Both Ted's hands covered his face for a moment; then they slid down so he could look at her, his blue eyes searching.

"I have to see my daughter, Ted. Now." There was nothing more to be said in front of an audience, but maybe she hadn't chosen as foolishly as she thought. Maybe.

"Yes, you have," the voices said.

Moving to the side of the narrow hall, Ted gestured as the Hell's Angel had done minutes earlier, inviting her to pass. "Just, please don't wake her. She's very colicky, cries all the time."

Behind her one of the Hell's Angels asked, "Got any beer?"

Ted made the same gesture towards the kitchen, and sighed. "Help yourselves."

THIRTEEN

San Diego, California—September 1989

BETH LOOKED LIKE a different baby. The only way Carole could be certain she was hers was the touch of that open heart, but even that felt a bit different. Beth was so long she took up more than half the length of the crib; she'd never fit in the dresser drawer she used to sleep in. Carole examined the skinny bump in the crib with its narrow bottom in the air. Beth whimpered and turned her head towards Carole, cupid mouth working in her sleep, a deep furrow between soft brows. Ted followed as far as the doorway, hovering anxiously. Carole ignored him, she'd been dreaming of this moment for six months! It was impossible not to touch Beth; the heart was beckoning but agitated. There was an edge of discomfort to it that had never been there before. Was it because her mother had left her? Guilt wretched in Carole's gut, had her daughter been miserable the entire time? The blonde hair grew thick now and longer, the tips curled along the collar of her pink sleeping gown. Carole's hand slipped over the white bars and rested on the silky head. Her heart sang with relief just touching Beth's again. The touch had changed, but this was her baby.

Carole's fingers brushed over the silken hair; amazed how much her daughter's head had grown. She ran her hand all the way down to rest on the tiny rump. It crinkled beneath her hand. Appalled, she knew what was wrong, why Beth was agitated. Disposable diapers. Something about them seemed to penetrate right into Carole's hand with an unpleasant tingle. Anxious to ease her daughter, Carole lifted Beth up to her chest, tugging the diaper off and tossing it on the floor.

"Oh, God, you have done it now." Ted warned from the doorway. "Why did you take her diaper off?"

Beth's eyes opened sleepily. They were light, like the summer sky. Her mouth a perfectly shaped tiny bow, yawned sweetly, and the eyes blinked dreamily. The anxiety in her heart faded away and swam around Carole's in greeting. "*Mom, Mom, Mom, my Mom,*" it said with a little shiver of relief. Beth didn't make a peep of protest at the sudden pantsing interrupting her nap. Carole hugged her to her chest and rocked back and forth. "Oh, I'd forgotten how sweet, how very sweet—"

"She is sweet," Ted agreed, coming to stand beside them. "Even when she's wailing—and I can't believe she's not now—there's something so engaging about her. I've never seen her awake when she wasn't crying before."

Carole pressed her lips on top the blonde head, spreading kisses and breathing her in. Beth snuggled against her chest, burrowing in with hands, feet and face.

"It's the diapers. Plastic bothers her." Carole swayed back and forth with Beth buried against her chest, brushing her cheek over the top of Beth's head. "What are you feeding her? Some food bothers her too."

"Ugh," Ted groaned. "She throws up everything. Formula. Cereal. Everything. And I have to wrestle it into her. I've had her to almost every pediatrician in San Diego. I just can't believe she's not crying!"

Carole fought back her own groan. The man was poisoning their baby. "How long have you had her?"

"Six weeks. I have to go back to Washington next week. I just hired a nanny for her and I made an appointment with a pediatric specialist in DC because she's lost weight. Please tell me you're going to be here for a while—because if you are—"

"I am. I'm on leave for six months."

"That could work. I have to be in DC for six months. I'll be frank with you, Carole, when I found her in that dump with that woman, I got a lawyer. She hasn't even had a single shot or immunization has she? I'd been thinking of suing you for custody of her, if you came back."

Carole tensed, backing towards the door. She could be out of here in twelve seconds; she'd have to move carefully with Beth in her arms. Intuitive, Ted moved to block the doorway and put both his hands up in defeat. "I hadn't seen you with her. I hadn't realized how much she needs her mother. If you promise to live here—I'll pay for everything—maybe we could work this out. Six months with you, six with me. I can be back here by the time you have to leave again. What do you think?"

Carole studied him a moment, remembering the night she had chosen him. Of course she would share Beth with him; she wanted to share everything with him. Not split custody, they belonged together. The faint touch of Ted's heart lingered just outside her own. Loyal. Patient. Loving. Distant. She looked him over. Ted was a big man, very tall and broad shouldered, ruggedly handsome with deep blue eyes and full lips that were made for kissing. Impulsively she kissed him, and despite her own good height she had to stand on tiptoe to press her lips against his. Between them, nestled in her arms, Beth sighed. *This is the way it should be.* Abruptly Ted pulled away, his hand moved towards his mouth before dropping awkwardly, as though he'd thought twice about wiping the kiss away. It would have hurt less if he'd slapped her. Carole hid her expression in Beth's hair; it smelled sweet, a faint chemical scent.

"Whatever you need, Ted, but I can't live here, and neither can Beth. The chemicals in the carpet and walls bother both of us. That's why I chose an old apartment. And she can't have shots, they could kill her. You'll have to trust me on that."

Ted ran a large finger over Beth's hair, and then brushed fingers briefly over Carole's, as though apologizing for his rejection. "I think, concerning Beth, I do trust you, but I don't understand you. You're going to need to explain some things, and, Carole, who are those guys with you?"

"I don't know. They gave me a ride over here." She could sense them in the kitchen, snooping through things. "I think they may have stolen your wallet off the kitchen counter," she blurted the comment without thinking of a way to explain how she knew that, so she quickly asked, "Why is Anne in jail?"

"Obstruction of justice, she wouldn't give me Beth."

Carole rotated Beth to gaze into the sweet face.

"Anne was just trying to protect this baby. She knows Beth can't wear disposable diapers or eat formula. Anne knows how to take care of Beth, she wouldn't cry all the time with Anne. You have to get her out of jail. Today. She didn't do anything wrong, and what happened to Junny?" At Ted's look she explained, "He lived in the stairwell of my apartment. He followed Beth here. It's how I knew where she was."

Ted considered that, then walked to the bedroom window and pulled up the mini-blind. "That wouldn't happen to be him, would it?" he pointed.

Gazing across the street, Carole spotted Junny perched on the church steps across the way. She smiled. "Sure is. I knew he wouldn't leave her."

"You keep some odd company, Carole. I thought Washington put a tail on me."

"I choose wisely when it comes to my daughter."

"Did you—do what you did at base camp just to have a baby with me?"

"You honestly think that?"

Ted shook his head, admitting, "No. I just don't understand why you came to me like you did. You didn't even know me."

After his betrayal, it took effort to say it out loud, but it needed to be said. Ted apparently did not believe what his heart told him. "I love you."

Backing away as though she'd spit on him, he bumped into the doorframe before hurrying through the door, and down the hallway. She heard him talking to the Hells Angels, offering to buy drinks at a nearby bar. They all left together. Carole found the big cotton blanket that Anne had been haggling for the day she left. She spread it on the floor, and lay down with Beth tucked against her chest. The baby heart moved against hers like music, vibrating with a contented purr. At last she was heart to heart with her daughter as she'd dreamed of being for the past six months. "But I never dreamed Daddy would be here," she whispered, her heart swimming with Beth's again at last. Smiling, she closed her eyes, and drifted into a contented sleep.

⚜

VOICES FROM THE front room woke Carole. The television was on, and for a brief moment she thought that's what she'd heard. Then Ted's deep voice said, "I'm sorry, Kimberly. I don't know what else you expect me to say."

"I don't know what you expect me to say! I'm supposed to be attending Georgetown by the end of next week! I turned my life upside down for you and that baby—got into graduate school—"

"You're still going to DC—"

"But I don't have a job now, do I?"

"Kimberly, Beth is staying here with her mother."

"Beth's mother is an irresponsible teenage girl! She needs a nanny herself! You expect me to believe you're going to leave that baby with—"

Ted's voice rose in anger, interrupting. "Now you're crossing a line. I'm doing what is best for Beth, and her mother is none of your business. Look, the only thing that's changed is that Beth is staying with her mother."

"You know what, Ted? The only person who ever believes your lies is you."

"Excuse me?"

"You haven't left that baby in six weeks. You're not going across the country without her. What's changed is you don't need me. I think I can figure out who my replacement is."

"Kimberly, we can talk about this in Washington. Use your ticket, and I'll see you there."

"I will use my ticket, but I won't be seeing you." The front door slammed and Carole heard Ted wretch it open.

"Kim! Come back, Kim!" Ted called after the woman then shut the door. Seconds later Carole sensed him in the kitchen making coffee.

Just inches from her face, Beth grinned at her. Wetting through her pink gown, it ran partially down a skinny baby leg and pooled momentarily on Anne's nice blanket before soaking right through to the carpet. Carole grinned back. She leaned forward, nose to nose with her baby and whispered, "I think we're going to Washington with Daddy, are you okay with that?" Beth's grin got wider as though she understood and approved. She had two little teeth in the bottom of her gums, and two matching on top. It was the most gorgeous thing Carole had ever seen, and then Beth did something worse than wet in her gown. Her face turned pink for a moment, but the grin got wider.

A TRIP TO the store to get some real diapers moved to the top of Carole's priorities. Even a baby as sweet as Beth got nasty without a diaper. Carrying her still grinning, stinky baby into the bathroom, Carole filled the tub with plain water, and wiped her off with wads of toilet paper while looking for soap to wash her with. It didn't need to be anything fancy, just something plain that wouldn't irritate Beth's sensitive skin or nose. There was baby shampoo, lotions and oils, but Carole ignored them. The medicine cabinet held only huge boxes of extra-large condoms. For a brief moment that discovery produced no reaction. Then she spotted several used ones in the trash can. They looked like stray fingers from rubber gloves, knotted neatly at the end, and Carole's heart sank. Disgust welled up. Her mind flashed back to the island after Ted had left, to the Captain standing on the beach talking to her. *He's famous for being a love 'em and leave 'em kind of guy.* She could think of many words, but love wasn't one of them.

Carole tried to push Ted's extracurricular activities out of her mind, and sat Beth in the tub, kneeling beside her. Beth slapped the water and gurgled with laughter when it splashed her face. *Besides, it happened before I told him I love him*, she reassured herself.

"*Unfaithful. Adulterer. Forbidden.*"

She argued in defense of what the voices had to say. *He was just running. He's afraid of me, but at least he can't pretend away my feelings now, and I know he feels the same way I do.*

But Ted's heart and actions told her two very different things.

Carole had settled on warm water and a cotton washcloth to clean her daughter, and she rubbed. Beth turned uncooperative, squealing and struggling to escape and Carole focused on the task at hand. Within moments Carole was smiling as Beth held onto her fingers and took tiny steps through the tub, on the tips of her toes. Those toes were still just as sweet, and they had perfect little toenails now. After examining Beth and delighting in the changes that had her sitting up sturdily on her own, hanging onto the side of the tub by herself, and gabbing happy sounds, Carole let the water drain. Wrapping Beth in a cotton towel, she dried her off and headed for the living room.

Ted sat on the sofa with a plate of eggs and toast. Last night's beer bottles sat on the coffee table, next to another box of condoms and his wallet. She glanced at his knuckles, noting they weren't bruised and wondered how he'd gotten it back from the bikers.

Ted stood up. "I didn't know you were up. I can't believe she's not howling! She's never slept so long. I kept checking on you two, but she looked so happy!" His index finger touched Beth's button nose. "She looks so much like you. That heart shaped face, and her mouth, look at those lips. Isn't it strange to see yourself in another person? She's like a little clone of you, nothing like me at all." He sounded disappointed.

Carole grabbed Ted's hand and put it against Beth's chest, right over the happily galloping heart. "She's exactly like you inside. It's what makes her so sweet."

Snatching his hand away, he stumbled on his words. "Yes, well, is that like being pretty on the inside?" Forcing out a chuckle, he gathered Beth into his arms. "I made you breakfast. You might need to pop it in the microwave to reheat it."

Glancing down at Ted's eggs, Carole knew they were the supermarket kind the voices forbade. Brushing her messy hair off her face, she decided to be as frank about food as she could be without telling Ted she sometimes listened to the voices in her head. "I'm a vegetarian and I have the same kind of food sensitivities Beth has. I suppose she got that from me too. I'll run down to the store and get some groceries. I'll take her with me—"

"No!" Ted moved slightly to one side as though blocking her. Looking at Carole's expression he apologized. "Kimberly, the nanny, said it's better to keep babies away from crowds the first year."

"That's ridiculous."

"She's an expert in childcare. She helped write a book about it."

It didn't matter if she'd written an encyclopedia, Carole knew it was ridiculous. She was about to say so when she noticed a big blanket on the floor next to the play pen. A glance took in two foil condom wrappers laying on the edge of the blanket, torn open and empty. Carole's stomach dropped out. They had not been there yesterday. Ted had been with someone. Pain shot through her heart like an icy knife. This morning while she slept in the other room with Beth, he'd been with someone! *The nanny?*

Beth squirmed in her father's arms, her face going red as she stopped breathing along with her mother, and then she screamed an agonizing shriek of pain. Ted frantically examined her as though expecting to find a visible injury. Carole knew her daughter felt the pain in her own heart, and wasn't afraid to voice it. Ted lifted Beth to kiss her scrunched up face and cooed useless words of comfort to the wrong person. *Control it, control it,* Carole thought, trying to force the pain away. Beth should not have to feel this. The conversation with the mysterious Kimberly suddenly took on more depth.

The voices condemned. *"Fornication. Dishonor. Dirty."* Carole shivered faintly at the thought of those filthy words, and Ted with Kimberly, last night? This morning? Beth cried harder. Woodenly

Carole went into the nursery and got her shoes and wallet. Beth was still screaming when Carole returned.

"I'll be back in a couple of hours," she told Ted without looking at him.

"Take my car," Ted took keys out of his pocket. "It's parked right by the—"

"I don't drive," Carole interrupted, and left.

ARMS LOADED WITH groceries, Carole returned. Beth's screams met her in the hallway. She knocked for several minutes before Ted opened the door. Carole tried not to look, but her eyes wouldn't obey, they darted back to the blanket by the playpen. The wrappers were gone. Strangely that didn't help much and Beth's howling increased accordingly. Frowning and bouncing Beth in his arms, Ted cooed through the wailing, trying futilely to coerce her into taking a bottle of formula.

"The peace sure didn't last very long," he lamented.

In the kitchen Carole warmed a mixture of goat's milk and soy, poured it into a bottle, shuddering as she attached the rubber nipple. She took her daughter into her arms, interrupting Ted's patient resignation, and began the process of trying to force the nasty nipple into the sweet mouth.

"I know, I know, sweet. I know, I know. It's good inside." Beth struggled, moving her head from side to side, grunting.

"I wish you'd nursed her," Ted lamented. "Kimberly—the nanny— said it is healthiest for the baby."

"I did," Carole told him. "The first four months. Then I had to leave."

"Maybe," Ted interjected, "you could try nursing again? Would it work after all this time?"

I wish. The thought made Carole's breasts ache with longing. Maybe it would after a time, but she didn't dare. Her own body had been poisoned.

146

"I don't think it would be safe, after my last assignment. I was exposed to—something."

Ted's eyes widened. He bit his lower lip, and leaned in close. For one wild moment she thought he was going to kiss her, but his lips stopped at her ear.

"Never," he breathed, "allude to your work, even with me. You're a ghost now—whatever your cover story is, you need to believe it yourself."

"I work for the UN," Carole responded with conviction, brushing the rubber nipple across Beth's mouth, leaving a milky trail. "My mother was Swiss, and I picked up the language firsthand. I'm hoping to become a reviser in time." Ted's eyes widened. For a moment Carole thought he really believed the part about her mother, but he shook his head slightly, his face sagging with the weight of a frown. He ran his hand over his mouth and glanced towards the windows. When he finally spoke, he barely whispered the words.

"If there had been any choice—but a Judas Judge violation is treated as war time treason. It took every contact I had to keep you alive after North Korea."

"Why did you?" Carole mouthed wordlessly. She knew why, but she wanted him to know it.

"I had to," he whispered with a frown, as though still trying to puzzle it out.

Carole turned from him with the same type of patient resignation he had for Beth. Carole held her daughter close to her thin T-shirt, near the breast that longed to do its duty, and thrust the rubber nipple into her mouth. Some milk finally hit Beth's tongue in her determined frenzy to dislodge it. She latched on with a vengeance, sucking hard.

Ted grinned, delighted. "She's sucking so hard the soft spot on top her head sinks in." Looking up into that rugged face, Carole waited, expectantly. He smiled at her. "Is there any chance at all that you'd be willing to go to Washington with me?"

Figure it out, Ted, and soon. "Of course." *Please.*

Ted's smile was brilliant; he had very straight teeth, rectangular and masculine.

Leaning down, Ted kissed Beth's forehead. Her eyes were closed as she focused on sucking with all of her might. He ran a big hand over the silky hair. "Thank you, Carole."

CHAPTER
FOURTEEN

Washington, D.C.—October 1989

THE VOICES DIDN'T like air travel. *"Unnatural. Dirty air. Dangerous."* It was one of their issues Carole usually felt comfortable not cooperating with. Fumes of jet fuel drifted past, and she ignored it, trying to wave the air away from her daughter.

Planes are safe enough, she defended mentally. *I hope.* Beth perched contentedly on Ted's lap, smiling her rabbit-toothed grin. Carole shifted uncomfortably, her defiant opinion on the safety of aircraft wavering. For once Beth didn't seem tuned in to her mother's discomfort. She blew raspberries and belted, "Da, da, da," for the entertainment of the fellow passengers. Strangely, the passengers seemed to enjoy Beth as much as her father. Not just the grandmothers on board either, but businessmen and the flight attendants alike made over Beth, begged to hold her, and showered compliments. Several times Ted tore himself away from their bubble of contentment, handed Beth to Carole, and wandered into the first class compartment. At first Carole didn't think much about it, but on his third trip—when she sensed him pass the men's room—she allowed the stealthy part of her brain to follow him.

The plane was full, there was one almost empty seat and that was between her and Ted with Beth's car-seat strapped into it. Inside

Carole's head the familiar flesh and bone that made up Ted's body stood next to that of a vaguely familiar woman. When Ted returned after an absence of twenty minutes, Carole didn't return Beth to his outstretched arms.

"Is something wrong?" He buckled his seatbelt.

"Are you in love with Kimberly?" Carole only knew one way to ask questions, and that was to simply ask.

Ted stared at her, his mouth agape. She knew he wanted to ask how she knew about Kimberly, so despite the objection of the voices to too much candor, she explained. "I know who she is because I heard you talking to her that day she came to the apartment."

Closing his mouth, Ted firmly pried Beth out of her arms and held her against his big chest. After patting Beth's hair for a while, without looking at Carole, he simply said, "I don't love her." He continued patting the golden head for a bit more and added, "I'm not comfortable talking to you about her."

"Are you comfortable having me in Washington with her?"

Ted's dark blue gaze met hers firmly. "You're Beth's mother. I'm comfortable having you anywhere that benefits our daughter."

Carole liked the way he said *our daughter*. It was the first time he'd said it.

"Beth comes first, Carole." He looked worried. "Can we agree to that much, right now?"

"Absolutely, but Beth was better off with Anne than your Kimberly."

Ted made a sound of disagreement, but said, "Well, we'll need someone to watch her when you have to leave, I can't always be there, and Beth is used to Kimberly. Besides, you said Anne won't come to DC."

"She's not comfortable traveling further than she can walk," Carole admitted.

"I'm not comfortable having Anne near Beth anyway."

"Are you comfortable with Anne living in your apartment in San Diego by herself?"

"Not at all," Ted laughed faintly. "And neither are the neighbors. I agreed because I owed her something after having her arrested, but everyone who lives there all pretty much works for the government and votes the same. She doesn't fit in. I'd say they're not any more comfortable than I am, having Anne there."

"Is it because she's Jewish?"

"Is she Jewish? I didn't know that, but it's not because she's Jewish, Carole." He looked at her like he sometimes did, like he was trying to figure her out but was afraid to. "It's because she dresses like a bag lady, likes to spend the weekends living in the park, and starts conversations about the time she spent in prison."

"She was only in jail, and that was because of you, and that experience was no small thing for her. She was in a concentration camp you know. Lost all her family there, her husband and five of her children, except for Aaron, but he was born later. His father was one of the guards in the camp."

"Oh, God, Carole. I had no idea."

"There are reasons people are the way they are."

Ted was still staring at her when the flight attendant brought them little trays of striped steak. Carole refused to even allow it to be placed in front of her. Ted ignored her warnings and tried to coerce Beth into some of the mashed potatoes. She obligingly allowed them to be put into her mouth, and then blew them onto his nice shirt with an expression of such distaste that he laughed.

"I suppose you warned me."

"They're not real potatoes. She'd eat real potatoes. Those are some sort of rehydrated thing."

"How can you tell that? They look the same and they taste the same."

Carole arched a disbelieving brow. *Really?* They sure didn't look the same to her. She dug a banana out of a bag. "I can always tell, and I bet Beth can too."

"How?" Ted seemed genuinely curious.

Mashing a bit of banana between her fingers, Carole popped it into her daughter's mouth. "Well, when I look at food I can almost taste it before I taste it."

"You mean like smelling it?"

"Sort of, but it's more about looks—and stuff, you know?" Obviously he didn't, and how could she explain the poisonous waves emanating from bad food? Or the metallic taste that filled her mouth if it touched her lips? "Like when I look at this banana—and it's not true of all bananas they're not all created equal—I just know that it is good. When I look at that food," she grimaced, "it makes me think of muck."

"Uh, okay—it tastes all right. Not good, but not muck either."

Carole smiled at him. "You think I'm weird."

Diplomatically, Ted only said, "I think you make beautiful babies."

TED LEFT FOR his job right after checking into the hotel. Beth and Carole were in a room next to his, there was a door between the rooms, but Ted kept his side locked. Carole bathed with Beth, and tossed on her usual olive pants and T-shirt. She tucked Beth into tiny cotton jeans and a heavy sweater, marveling over the baby-sized clothes. They headed out into the city together. Ted and his Kimberly had provided a ridiculous amount of girly-pink clothing, but Beth needed clothes that weren't synthetic blends, and that was hard to find in baby clothes. Carole ended up at a second hand shop, miles from their hotel. With new old clothes in hand they had to walk several more miles to find the kind of soap the voices approved, and a Laundromat to wash the new purchases at. Carole relished the little adventure with her happy baby, reminded of when Beth was a newborn. Carole wasn't used to complete strangers approaching her, even men tended to shy away from her anymore, but Beth grinned and gabbed at everyone, and they in turn returned open admiration. In the Laundromat Carole enjoyed Beth's popularity, but kept a watchful eye as her daughter was passed from person to person.

Returning to the hotel after dark they were met by police officers in the hotel lobby. Ted sounded impressively furious when he asked her where she'd been. Holding up her sack of clothing, she told him, "Shopping." The police cheerfully passed Beth around, and left.

"CAROLE, THESE STREETS aren't safe," Ted groused in the elevator, long fingers caressing Beth.

Despite the bellowing protests of the voices to elevators, Carole couldn't stop herself, she grinned at Ted and he had the grace to smile.

"I know you can take care of yourself, but you had Beth with you."

"I can take care of Beth too, try not to worry. I'm very capable." Ted moved his hand from Beth to touch Carole's cheek tentatively. It made Carole's heart sing, and Beth tilted her head flirtatiously. Carole wondered if the little moppet was always going to betray her feelings to the world.

The elevator doors opened with a ping, a woman stood waiting with her arms crossed. She glared when she spotted Ted. After one disbelieving glance at his fingers pressed against Carole's cheek, mascara blackened eyes widened and she spun on polished heels, stalking away. Ted followed without a backward glance.

Beth started to cry.

THE NEXT MORNING Ted knocked on Carole's hotel door. "Why's Beth crying like that?"

"It seems she does that when I'm upset. I'm going to take care of it today."

His eyes went to Carole's single piece of luggage, a military issue canvas sack, packed and sitting on the hotel bed. "You're leaving!"

"No, Ted, I told you I'd come here with you and I will. I'm going apartment hunting. If I find something, I'll leave you a message at the front desk."

"Wait, wait." Ted pushed his way through the door and shut it behind him. "Look, I'm trying to find an older apartment in the Georgetown area. Something you're not allergic to where I can have one floor and you can have another. I figure it would be much easier for us to take turns keeping Beth that way."

"Is Kimberly going to live there too?"

"Carole, that's none of your business."

Going to the bed, she hoisted her sack onto a shoulder, settling Beth comfortably against the other.

"Unfortunately it is. I told you I love you and I meant it. When you go with her, it hurts me. I try to hide that from Beth, but I can't. She's too sensitive and she suffers too."

"Oh for pity's sake, Carole. What are you talking about? Beth isn't even a year old."

The look in his eye was so condescending, Carole sighed. Dropping her bag on the floor, she shifted Beth and tried to explain. "You followed Kimberly to her room from the elevator last night. After you spent about ten minutes outside her door knocking, she came out. She'd changed into a dress, something polyester," Carole shivered, "and you went down to the hotel restaurant for drinks at the bar. Then you caught a taxi and I assume you went to dinner somewhere west of here—I couldn't sense where, it was too far. But you both ate seafood—I'd rather not explain how I know that. You came back here at midnight. You had two bottles of wine. I think it was red, but I'm never sure because they both feel similar because of the sulfites. Beth was sound asleep at first, but then you spent the night in Kimberly's room just down the hall. That was plenty close enough for me to sense about everything you were doing, and Beth started howling. I left the hotel, Ted. I didn't want to know. Beth and I wandered the streets out of range of your tryst. It didn't help though, because when you hurt me I can't control hurting Beth."

Ted yanked Beth out of Carole's arms, his blue eyes suddenly dark and dangerous. "What do you mean you're hurting Beth?" He jerked Beth's little shirt up and examined her flawless body. Beth chuckled when he poked around her belly. Her red-rimmed eyes attested to her long night, but she was happy now that her father was there, because Carole was happy now. "What the hell are you talking about? Were you watching us? Did you follow me?"

"Don't be ridiculous! Of course I didn't follow you. I tried to get away from knowing what you were doing. And you know perfectly well I wouldn't hurt our baby! How can you say that? I'm talking about hurting here, Ted!" Carole smacked a hand against her still aching heart. On cue, Beth's face fell and her lower lip quivered. The demonstration couldn't have been more profound. "I can't let what I feel hurt Beth. I need to stay far enough away that I can't sense what you do."

"Are you telling me you're psychic?"

"If that's what you want to call it. I don't know what it is, but I do know I can't control the way I feel, or the fact that Beth can feel what I do."

"So you're both psychic." Ted gave her his famous Lieutenant-Colonel stare. "You expect me to buy that because you knew where I spent the night? Don't forget, I know what you do for a living. I'm the one who recommended you for the job, and as you mentioned yesterday, you're very good at what you do."

"You forgot your wallet in Kimberly's bathroom; she's going through it right now. For breakfast you ordered room service, you had eggs and some type of pork. She had fruit with whipped cream on it, though she's eating the pork you didn't finish while she goes through your wallet right now. You have your badge in your right pocket and change in your left—two quarters, a nickel and three pennies. You have scratch marks on your back, four of them on the left side. You're wearing boxers and your undershirt has a loose hem in the front. There's a man in the room across the hall and he's going to walk outside his door—right now." The sound of the door opened and closed. Ted turned and looked out the peephole. Carole continued, "I think he's going running. It feels like those thin pants runners wear. He's about five foot four, a hundred and thirty pounds, probably Asian." Ted turned back to her, looking pale. "And the elevator just stopped at this floor, the door is opening—now." The loud ping sounded down the hall. "I lost track because I went out of range last night, but would you like me to tell you how many prophylactics you used this morning? Including the one that broke?"

Disbelievingly, Ted shook his head. "That's insane. How do you do that?"

Taking a deep breath, Carole tugged her daughter out of his arms. Beth sucked busily on her fingers. "I have no idea how I do it. How do you not? As for insane, I've considered that too, but if I am that doesn't explain why I'm right, does it?"

"Can Beth do all that too?" Ted seemed horrified by the magnitude of that idea, and it was a feeling Carole shared.

"I can't be completely sure, but I don't think so. She's different than I am." Carole put her face against Beth's clean hair and breathed her in. A dark wave of nausea rippled through her.

The voices were furious. "*They will destroy us if they know! You forfeit your life!*" It had been a very long time since they punished her. In her mind she saw a lion leap almost playfully towards a woman, ripping her head off her body effortlessly. For a moment the body remained erect, and Carole was sure the head clenched in the animal's jaws knew what had happened. Carole's morning oatmeal raced up into her throat and she choked to keep it down. In her arms Beth made gagging sounds and vomited spectacularly across the hotel rug. Carole had to squint to see Ted through the horrific images of torture flitting through her mind.

"What the heck?" he said, "I didn't know a baby even ate that much."

Carole whimpered. "Ted? Is there any way you could take Beth for a few hours? I don't feel very good right now."

He must have seen something in her face, because his expression went from fearful to sympathetic. "I have a meeting—but Kimberly could, if you're okay with that."

"I don't think I have much choice. Please ask her to stay here with her though? So I can feel her."

"Okay. Is she sick?"

"No, no. I am. Take her?" Ted gathered Beth into his arms but all Carole saw was the lion licking the stump where the head had been. A wave of horror washed over her and Beth started to sob.

"She's going to cry the whole time, isn't she?"

"Probably." Carole sat down on the bed. She couldn't see now. The dark dreams were covering her eyes. "I'm sorry," she whispered.

"It's okay. Kimberly's used to it. Do you need anything?" He sounded concerned, and she wished she could see his expression again.

"No, just go, please."

The door clicked as he pulled it open, adjusting Beth. "Carole? I'm sorry I make you so sad."

"You make me happy too." The black dreams were taking her, she couldn't hear all of his response through the snarls of lions, but it sounded like he might have told her she frightened him.

CAROLE KNOCKED ON the door of Kimberly's hotel room, on the other side of the door Beth's cries ceased. The door whipped open almost immediately.

"So you're the teenage mother? You look older." Sharply beautiful, chic and made-up beneath waves of flowing hair, Kimberly didn't look any more like a nanny than Carole looked nineteen.

"Thank you for watching her." Carole held out her arms for Beth, who coyly leaned back in Kimberly's arms and looked at her mother upside down.

"They can do genetic testing now, to prove paternity." Kimberly made no move to release Beth.

Carole simply held her arms out.

Kimberly tightened her hold on Beth. "We'd adopt her. She'd be better off and you could have your freedom."

"I want my daughter."

"Of course you do, it's your only hold on him." Kimberly thrust Beth roughly into Carole's arms. "He doesn't love you, he wants the baby."

Beth whimpered, little emotion barometer that she was. "I know," Carole whispered, and even though she didn't completely believe that, it really hurt. She allowed her feelings to show on her face. Kimberly looked like the kind of person who liked to kick when you're down.

"You're a slutty gold-digger."

Bingo. All's fair in love and war, Carole thought.

From the hall behind Carole, Ted walked up to her side, surprising only the nanny. He glanced briefly into Carole's eyes before turning his gaze on his girlfriend. "She'd be wasting her time, Kimberly, since I don't have any gold—and if she's a slut, what are you?"

"Ted! I'm just telling it like it is," Kimberly defended herself.

Ted took Beth out of Carole's arms. A wide grin stretched across Beth's face, and she happily patted his chest.

"Is that it? Do you think I have money? Everything from White Enterprises went to creditors when my father died. I'm still paying off the loans for his state funeral. Didn't you hear the Washington rumors?"

"I don't care if you have any money." Kimberly wasn't much of a liar. Beth stuck a tiny finger out at her as though she recognized the lie too. Carole gently slid Beth out of her father's arms, lifted the tiny finger to her lips, kissed it, and walked away. Beth giggled louder with each step.

CHAPTER
FIFTEEN

Washington, D.C.—November 1989

AFTER KIMBERLY LEFT, Ted unlocked the door between his hotel room and Carole's. Beth avoided the portable crib housekeeping provided, and slept nuzzled against her mother at night. Carole sensed Ted sometimes creep into her hotel room to watch them. Beth would giggle then, in her sleep. Carole suspected Ted knew that meant she was awake, that she was the one thrilled to have him so close. If Ted's fingers accidentally brushed against Carole's over dinner, Beth would sigh and hold out her arms to her father, opening and closing her hands in a pick-me-up gesture of impatience.

Sometimes Ted would bring organic fruit or fresh vegetables from a farmer's market near his office. He'd leave the produce for Carole on the round faux wood table in her hotel room without saying a word. Beth would tear herself away from studying the patterns on the draperies or from an attempt to splash in the hotel toilet, and crawl across the room and up her father's leg until he lifted her to hang onto his neck. Ted obviously adored the choking hugs. Carole supposed it was the main reason he became thoughtful about bringing food she could eat. She also suspected Ted would do whatever it took to make Beth happy. Ted started to rest his hand against Carole's on the dinner table, and sit next to her on the tiny loveseat in her hotel room. With his leg pressed against hers, Carole once again felt the touch of Ted's heart in hers. Faint compared to Beth's, but it was the heart of the man she loved.

One evening Ted knocked on the door between their rooms.

"Can I come in?" At Beth's joyful screech, he shoved open the door. Carole sat at the little hotel table with Beth on her lap, feeding her applesauce and bits of pumpkin. Ted paused beside Beth and kissed the top of her head, gently brushing fingers through Carole's tousled hair. Food dropped out of Beth's mouth with her enthusiastic *ha ha ha*. Ted plunked down in a chair across from them and dropped a deck of cards on the table. He tapped the pile with a big finger and slid the top card off, bending it slightly so she couldn't see.

"What card is it?" he asked. The back of the card had a picture of The Washington Monument on it. Carole shrugged, and Ted lifted another card, peering at her questioningly. "Come on, guess what card it is."

"Why?" she wondered.

"It's a test—if you're really psychic you'll get at least half of them." Carole laughed, and Beth mimicked the response, chuckling while bits of pumpkin dribbled down her chin.

"I never said I was psychic, and whatever I am doesn't work like that."

"On demand?"

"I can't see through things, Ted, not like that. I can tell you exactly what those cards are composed of organically. I can tell what's in your pockets because I can sense the organic composition. For instance I know you have thirteen bills in your wallet, but I can't tell what denomination they are. Coins I can tell, the metals are distinctive." The voices protested, and Carole closed her eyes a moment, running a hand over them as black dreams began to flicker.

"It hurts you to do it, though? Gives you a headache?"

Doing it doesn't hurt, Carole thought, *just telling you about it*. She said only, "Sometimes."

"I hope Beth can't do it."

"Me too."

"Do you need me to take her for the night?"

Sweat broke out over Carole's forehead. Images of babies taken from their parents flitted through her head. What if Ted told what she could do? Would someone take Beth from her? *I trust him*, she reminded herself. *He has my heart, I have to.*

Nodding, she closed her eyes. "Would you? Please?"

"YOU COULD WALK about anywhere you'd want to go from here," Ted crowed. "It's old, but clean. What do you think?"

The little walk-up apartment measured about thirteen feet wide, and not all that much longer. Windows in the front looked out over the proud old neighborhood and park across the street. A tree grew right up against a window in the back. The place had absolutely no amenities, there was no air-conditioning, and the old fireplace had been bricked shut. Carole could have slept comfortably on the hardwood floor. She put Beth down, and the baby dropped to her knees to crawl the length of the rooms.

"It's brilliant, but I know I can't afford anything in this part of town."

"I'm paying for it."

"Surely you can't afford this, your apartment in San Diego, and your own place here."

"It'd be cutting it close, so I was thinking—we could share it."

"What do you mean?"

Ted tore his eyes from Beth and looked into Carole's face. "I think we should get married."

Beth started giggling as she raced away faster. Ted grinned, "So you're not completely opposed to the idea?"

Tears formed in Carole's eyes and she shook her head. "But you said you don't love me."

"I'm sorry. Don't cry, Carole, please. I want us to be a family. I think we owe it to Beth to try, and I think we could make it work."

The tears spilled down Carole's cheeks, but from the far side of the room, where Beth now stood on shaky legs to tug dirt out of a potted plant, their daughter started to laugh deep belly laughs.

"Is that a yes?" Ted asked.

TED MOVED INTO their Georgetown apartment on a weekend, insisting that Carole stay in the hotel until they were married. It struck Carole as ridiculous. To her they married the night she went to him in The Marshall Islands. Luckily Ted couldn't bear the separation from Beth for long. He arranged for the wedding on a Tuesday morning before work. Dressed in his full Lieutenant Colonel regalia Ted showed up at the hotel early, a custom-made dress for Beth artfully arranged in a white box. Carole packed their things into her canvas bag, and Ted dressed their daughter. Beth rolled back and forth across the hotel bed giggling while he wrestled her into yellow silk. In honor of the occasion Carole sported chocolate brown trousers and a creamy satin blouse. She also wore her first pair of heels, knee length leather boots, but heels just the same. Briefly she considered slicking her short messy hair back, but settled on looking like herself for the occasion. Ted nabbed her canvas bag, swinging it over one capable shoulder and Beth onto the other. Glancing at Carole, he did a double take and smiled, offering a hand. Carole took it, her heart floating.

TED HELD BETH, who laughed almost maniacally throughout the civil ceremony. He kissed his daughter instead of his bride when it came to that part, and The Justice of the Peace insisted on taking a wedding photograph of Ted holding Beth. After using his own camera, he never even offered to make them a print. Afterwards Ted went back to The Pentagon, and Carole went straight to the supermarket and bought a steak. She walked six miles home, carrying groceries and Beth, her heart still floating.

THE APARTMENT HAD once been one long room and the main walls were brick. The kitchen made up the middle, with only the counter serving as a divider from the front room. Behind the kitchen, oak and glass doors separated the bedroom area. Light from the wide bedroom window lit the house through the glass walls and open arch-way. Ted had made a small alcove to one side of that, draping frilly curtains from floor to ceiling. Beth's white iron crib sat tucked inside. The space in front of the kitchen counter had been designated as the living room. Leather furniture marked off the boundaries and across from it a steep column of stairs went down to the outside door. Ted had installed a sturdy gate to protect Beth from attempting to crawl down. Carole jogged lightly up the steps and latched the baby gate behind her. Beth already slept soundly against her shoulder, exhausted from her day of wild laughing.

Tossing Anne's colorful blanket on the floor, Carole lay Beth down to nap in the kitchen. The touch of the sweet, innocent little heart swam around hers while she made a marinade for Ted's steak and slid it into the refrigerator. Carole made her bread recipe, muffins of grated carrots and applesauce, and a pumpkin maple cake. Peas, carrots and spinach were cooked and frozen into cubes to supplement Beth's meals. A squash casserole went into the oven with twice-baked potatoes, and she mixed a green salad. Every recipe that Beth would eat, Carole wrote on index cards in pencil for whoever would be the new nanny. The thought of Kimberly sent a slight ripple of worry down her back, but she shoved it away. Carole's wedding ring felt uncomfortable on her left hand, heavy platinum encrusted with diamonds. It was surely an heirloom, something that Kimberly would have appreciated from Ted's wealthy past. Carole forced the thoughts away. Kimberly was before they married in his eyes. Ted had taken a vow and he was a man of honor. She ignored what the voices had to say about that.

THAT EVENING TED came home with whiskey on his breath, ate his steak, gave Beth her bath and went to sleep on the sofa in front of the television. Curled in her crib, Beth cried all night. Carole turned her thoughts towards the dark dreams hovering at the edge of her consciousness, looking for anything she could see about mothers and daughters. Knowing she had to break the connection. Beth was becoming a frightening mess. After a wakeful night of self-induced black dreams, Carole woke to a morning with a colossal headache, no answers, and a sobbing baby.

EARLY THANKSGIVING MORNING, Carole found Ted asleep on the couch again. *It's going to take time*, she told herself. She'd have to be patient. Carole tried to imagine what it was like for Ted, married to a woman for the sake of their child, a strange woman. Even though he knew more about her than anyone ever had, it only seemed to distance him. It made her glad that she'd never told anyone before, and not just because of the punishing black dreams. Focusing on stuffing the first turkey she'd ever cooked and deep in thought, Carole's attention wandered from Beth's toddling steps and quick crawls as she snooped around the apartment. Just as Carole slid the bird into the oven, some maternal sense warned her to look up. Beth teetered on the top step of the steep open staircase. It was a long way down. Ted sprawled on the sofa much closer, but Carole didn't think to cry out. She shot over the kitchen counter with every ounce of energy she possessed. Ted had noticed Beth too. He managed two steps before Carole flew past him, jumped the railing and landed on the stairs below Beth. Carole caught her daughter as she toppled, snatching her neatly out of the air. Beth laughed a real belly laugh, and Carole glanced through the railing at her husband still standing near the sofa, his mouth hanging open. After a long moment filled with only the sound of Beth's chuckling, Carole walked slowly up the steps and tugged the baby gate closed, latching it. She heard Ted's gulp. The dash across the apartment should have been impossible, and for Beth she'd done it in plain view of Ted. The voices didn't say a word.

The next few hours, Carole was painfully aware of the way Ted watched her. Seated at their tiny Thanksgiving table, Carole addressed it straight out. "I really don't know why or how I can do those things."

Ted pulled the loaf of Carole's homemade bread across the table. Beth did a face plant into her slice, sucking a hole through the middle and making a happy nom-nom sound.

"Mother bear syndrome," he said without meeting her eyes. "I saw on television once where a mother lifted a car off of her son. Human beings are capable of amazing things."

Carole knew he didn't believe his own explanation. "I think my mother and grandmother could do some unusual stuff too. I can remember things—but they died when I was three, so I'm not sure how much is my imagination. I think my grandmother could do this thing with music where I'd hear it in my head."

"She was a singer?"

"No, not exactly, she didn't actually sing, and they weren't her songs. I'd see it too, but it was all inside my—"

"It's probably better if you don't speculate like that, Carole. It's probably your imagination anyway."

Frustration won out. "Okay, I'll stick to facts, Ted. I can hold my breath for twenty minutes, and run a mile in under four minutes, I always could, at least since I've timed myself. And I can measure time in my head, and weight. Beth weighs eighteen pounds seven point two ounces right now. You weigh two ounces under two-oh-four. If you eat all that turkey you'll probably—"

"Carole! Please, don't! It's Thanksgiving! Can we just have a normal dinner?"

"That's just it Ted, I really don't know what normal even is."

"Could you try?"

She was very good at pretending. "Yes, if you like."

"I would like it, Carole. Very much." Ted pulled the glass butter dish across the table. Carole tried to think of something normal to say while he buttered his bread and the shouting voices punished her indiscretion. After an uncomfortable silence during which she couldn't think of a single thing, he said, "You make really good bread, the best I've ever had. Tomorrow's Bethy's first birthday so I ordered her a cake made with organic flour."

THE ENORMOUS ORGANIC birthday cake came iced in mounds of frosting bright with food coloring. Obligingly Carole snapped pictures while Beth rubbed it into her pretty hair and proceeded to stuff handfuls into Ted's mouth, flat out dodging all attempts her father made to slip a piece into her mouth. Sitting on a chair beside the birthday girl, he said, "Beth, no like cake?"

Beth regarded him solemnly for a moment, both pink frosted hands in the air, fingers spread wide. Then she stunned both her parents by replying, "No, I don't," in perfect English. Nothing Ted or Carole could do after that could drag another such response from her.

That night, Ted tucked Beth into her crib and left for a beer. Crawling into her bed alone, a little voice spoke inside Carole's head. It sounded very different from the voices that had plagued her all her life, and it said something she'd never heard before.

"Mom? I'm thirsty." Carole sat straight up, her mind racing. *Oh my God*, the voices were changing! This could be the psychotic break she'd been expecting since high school. "Please, Mom? Some milk? In your cup, not the yucky one Daddy uses." Trembling, Carole flipped on her bedside lamp and hurried to the archway. In the alcove Beth's crib sat in a sea of pink and white stripes. Her daughter sat up, watching expectantly. She looked at her mother's empty hands. "Don't we have milk?" Beth asked out loud.

The memory of the earlier sentence, the one that Ted had witnessed, kept Carole sane. "Just a moment," she managed, and rushed to bring it as demanded. Beth took it in her one-year-old hands and tipped her head back and drank greedily from the cup.

"It's so good," the voice said in her head.

"Beth?" Carole leaned over the crib to look at her daughter. "Please don't do that."

"What, Mom?" The voice in her head asked as she continued to slurp the milk down.

"Talk inside my head like that," Carole whispered.

Beth spilled milk down her gown when she stopped drinking and said out loud, "What's the difference?"

"I like it when you talk with your mouth, and I don't think Daddy can hear in his head."

"Okay, Mom," Beth said in her head, sucking from the cup again.

Carole was still up when Ted came stumbling through the door.

TED WASHED IN their narrow bathroom and fumbled through the bedroom closet for pajamas. On his way to the living room, he paused beside the foot of Carole's bed. "You're up?"

"Yes. Beth wanted a cup of milk."

He must have heard something in her voice. "Did she talk again?"

"Yes."

Ted sat down beside her, a grin on his face, "Really? What did she say?"

"She said, 'Don't we have milk?'"

"Are you kidding me? That's amazing. Don't you think that's amazing?"

"I think it's a little disorienting."

Ted threw his head back and laughed loudly. He looked down at her with an amused smile. "Welcome to my world."

Carole smiled back at him, a genuine smile that lit her heart. He had a point. "I guess now I know what it's like, but I don't think she gets this from me. I can remember my Mom worrying that I didn't talk when I was three. Maybe this is from you, were you a progeny?"

"Probably," Ted admitted slyly.

"I love you." It slipped out. She bit her lip. It usually sent Ted scampering. Tonight he rubbed his hand over her messy hair and swallowed.

"Soft, like Beth's. Only you can look breathtaking in an old T-shirt. Carole, you are truly beautiful."

"So are you."

Ted leaned forward. Cupping his hand behind her head he held her firmly and kissed her like he meant it. Carole's heart puddled in her chest and melted into an ache somewhere low. She wrapped her arms around him and pulled him down to her. It had been so long.

Ted was rough, and he tasted like whiskey. She didn't care. She loved every touch, every taste of his mouth, every sigh and groan that came from his lips. She loved the weight of his body on hers, the way he pinned her against the bed and tried to get closer, and closer. Preoccupied, he left his heart open and unguarded, and Carole wrapped her limbs around him, trying to get closer, trying to touch that elusive heart.

"No!" he pleaded as he finished. Rolling away, he breathed heavily for a couple of minutes and started to get up.

"Please, don't go. I won't do it, if you don't want me to."

Leaning to kiss her he said, "I'm coming right back. I'm just going to get some—protection for round two."

Protection? "Ted, do you mean those rubber things?"

Sighing, he shook his head. "Don't tell me, you don't like latex. They don't have natural ones, I checked. I'm assuming you won't take the pill?"

It hurt. He didn't want more children. "It doesn't matter, I can't have children anymore," she whispered it.

"What do you mean?"

"The same reason I couldn't breastfeed anymore."

Settling in beside her, Ted ran a hand down her naked flesh and she shivered.

"Are you all right otherwise?" he whispered back.

"I think so."

"I'm sorry, Carole."

She was quiet and he leaned close, whiskey fumes in her face. "I mean it. I am sorry. A few minutes ago, I was thinking that it was too soon. That we needed time—and now, now I just feel—sad."

"I'm sorry. I should have told you before you married me."

"Don't be stupid. Come here." Ted started kissing her. By morning she was sore, tired, and extremely happy.

"MOM? DO WE have any bananas? The good kind, not Daddy's?"

"Beth? If you don't say it with your mouth, I'm not going to give you anything."

"Moooom!" Beth fussed loudly. Carole tugged her out of the high-chair.

"Really? You can speak in perfect sentences and you are still pooping in your diaper?"

"Change it," Beth said sweetly.

On the changing table in the pink and white striped alcove, with the pink and white striped bedding, wall hangings, and curtains over a painting of a fake window, Beth assisted with the changing process by issuing orders. "No wipees, they itch me."

"Aren't you picky?" Carole grinned at her.

"Soft diapies."

"But of course."

"No yucky powder."

"No, never."

"It makes sneezes and itchies."

Carole picked up the baby powder and tossed it, and Beth grinned approvingly. The door opened and slammed and Ted crossed the hardwood floor with heavy footsteps.

"Da!" Beth cooed, grabbing her feet like any one-year-old and wriggling with joy. "Da! Da! Da!"

Ted leaned over Beth to smile into her face. "How's my girl?"

Beth squealed happily. Carole froze, dropping the sodden diaper to the floor.

Ted picked Beth up and she snuggled against him. He glanced at the nasty diaper on the floor and said, "Yuck, Mommy, glad you had to change that one." He went to the kitchen. "Do you want some nana, Sweetie? Nana and some of Mommy's cookies?"

Carole left the diaper on the floor and headed for the front door, grabbed her running shoes and bolted out. She got a block away before she bent over double and opened her mouth in a silent scream of agony. Did Ted not realize how keen a woman's sense of smell was? She could recognize the scent of another woman in seconds, especially when it was on her husband's mouth. Carole retched. It felt like her heart was being torn from her chest. Again.

WHEN CAROLE RETURNED, Beth slept blissfully unaware, tucked in her little alcove. Ted sat watching TV.

"You forgot to clean that diaper, Babe. I put it in that bathroom pail to soak, and washed the other ones. They're in the dryer downstairs—no, don't go, I'll get it in a couple. Go take your shower. I bought some of those nuts you like from that shop on the corner. The almonds with cinnamon only, no sugar, they're in the kitchen. Want some?"

"I'll shower first." Did her voice always sound like that?

"How about a cup of your tea? I picked up a jar of that honey you like too."

"That would be nice."

She sobbed, sitting on the shower floor. It was impossible to hold the tears in. Did he think gifts could fix it? *What am I going to do?*

The voices answered for her. *"You've made your choice."*

No sound came from Beth, and Carole was certain her pain was so large that it wouldn't fit into Beth's sweet baby heart. Thank God.

THE TEA SAT waiting on her bedside stand when she came to bed. Ted had already tucked into the far side, pretending to read a magazine. His casual nonchalance shouted his crime at her, and the voices, the same ones that insisted she had no choice but to stay, condemned him. *"Fornication. Dishonor. Death."*

Carole tried to ignore them and sipped her tea. Ted had only slept beside her once, and some sick and desperate part of her heart found a drop of comfort in the fact that he was there again tonight. After what he had done. Surely he regretted it. Surely he would never do it again. *Please. I am a fool.*

"Your choice is made," the voices heartlessly reminded.

"Carole?" he reached over and ran a hand slowly down her back invoking a shiver of grotesque hope. "Are you very tired from your run?"

"I'm not tired at all." He'd brushed his teeth and showered. For the first time ever Carole forced herself into his arms, wondering if this is the way it always felt for Ted.

SPRINGTIME TRIED TO come early to Washington, DC. Buds and cherry blossoms argued with unseasonable snow flurries. Ted brought Carole an arrangement of pussy willow he'd cut himself. It grew along the edge of the park across the street, the park where he took Beth and spent Saturday mornings, the park where he chatted

171

with pretty joggers and dog walkers. At first Carole had watched him from the window in the front room. Even after she forced herself not to look she still sensed him. While pushing Beth gently in a swing he'd accept a phone number, laugh with friendly young women, kiss a hand or sometimes even willing lips.

He usually gave Carole flowers after a tryst; mostly roses and daffodils, but lilies were his favorite. Today the offering of pussy willow sat in the middle of the table in an expensive crystal vase that said only one thing to Carole. *I did it again, sorry.* She avoided looking at the immoral gift. She'd never liked picked flowers anyway. She didn't like gifts. If her heart would ever let her kill him, she'd find a way to do it with flowers.

Busy grinding seeds to make her bread she pulverized them a bit more than the recipe called for. The ringing telephone interrupted.

Ted hollered from the front room. "Can you get that, Babe? I think Beth is going to tie her own shoes."

"The potty would be more impressive," Carole groused, and went to the phone. "Hello?" She held the device safely away from her ear, she didn't completely trust it. Sometimes she wondered how much of her behavior was from the voices and how much was her own strange phobias.

"Montague. Pirate ship in the park—ten minutes." The phone went dead. Carole looked at her half-mixed bread. Ted would never have the patience to finish it. Beth would be stuck eating oatmeal, fruit, and vegetables for a while.

Emptying her pockets of money and identification, Carole tugged on socks and shoes. Hurrying to Beth's alcove, she changed the crib sheets and folded all her clean clothes from the laundry basket. Flitting past the bathroom, she dashed in, cleaned Ted's stubble out of the sink, scrubbed the toilet, washed her hands and brushed her teeth. She put Beth's little toothbrush right beside Ted's. Then she dashed to the front room. Beth sat on the floor with her shoes on the wrong feet, tugging at the laces with her tongue sticking out.

"Did she do it?"

"Maybe tomorrow." Ted grinned.

"Remember she can't eat nuts or popcorn."

"I know that, why—do we have some?"

"No, just wanted to remind you because I have to go to work."

Ted's expression went dark and he looked away from her.

Carole squatted beside Beth and told her, "Mommy has to go bye-bye."

"To work," her sixteen-month-old corrected.

Carole leaned forward and kissed her forehead. "I'll be back."

Ted didn't look at her as she walked towards the steps.

"Hey?" He called, as though an afterthought. "I think I might get transferred. If you're gone awhile, call my office before you head home, I'll leave a message with my secretary."

"Back to San Diego?"

"Likely." He shook his head as though in disbelief. "I suppose we'll be bunking with Anne."

"Oh. Well, you'll have a sitter. Ted? I love you." Because despite it all, she did.

"Bye, hon." He kept his head turned towards Beth. Carole wondered, if it weren't for Beth, what she would do.

Carole jogged down the steps and into the spring sunshine, her step lightening as she went.

⚞⚟

CHAPTER
SIXTEEN

Santa Fe, New Mexico—April 1990

WEST OF SANTA Fe, the Desert Veil Casino and Resort sprawled across acres of desert. Mammoth adobe buildings covered half those acres. The main building had the look of a museum, in an Art Deco meets Native American style. Gaze flitting over décor, Carole glided through the adobe entrance, stilettos gnawing on her feet. A pile of realistic auburn curls itched against bare shoulders, and rhinestone studded sunglasses covered half her face. Inside the lobby, a western-themed three-story stained-glass window illuminated an elaborate curving staircase. It filled the lobby with a column of bright desert light. Life-size bronze sculptures hid in cool shadows. Carole peeked curiously over the rim of her glasses. Something about the space drew her. It felt open, empty, both cool and warm, like the desert itself. Within her mind she could sense the enormous casino in the basement level just below her, but right here, this place reminded her of old memories of New Mexico.

"Welcome to the Desert Veil. Are you here for the Southwest Singles Go for Broke Weekend?" The native hotel manager, wearing a leather sport coat and bolo tie, didn't wait for her answer. He snapped his fingers at a bellhop. "Karl will take your luggage."

Reluctantly Carole handed over her suitcase, pretending not to notice that petite Karl almost dropped it from the weight. Though her contact had given it to her just moments ago, she knew there was a high powered rifle, tripod, and silencing equipment inside, all swathed in sparkly, sequined gowns and more uncomfortable shoes.

"Miss…?" The manager asked, ushering her to the front desk.

"Anderson," she supplied, sliding two fingers of her left hand into the tiny pocket of her incredibly tight slacks to hide her wedding band. How could she have forgotten her wedding band? The distracted manager hurried to greet more guests. With her ring now safely tucked in her pocket, Carole plopped her designer bag on the marble desk and fished out a phony credit card.

"I have reservations," she told the clerk. Something about the stance of the waiting bellman made her think he'd seen the ring maneuver. Oh well, a judgmental hotel employee was the least of her problems. Shooting a twenty-year-old drug dealer seemed a far bigger problem. This assignment worried her. The voices were incensed, their enraged tirade made it hard to focus on a back-up plan, and she had only fifteen hours to complete the mission.

Standing at the front desk while she checked in, the bellman stared rudely the entire time she gave false information to the desk clerk. Dark eyes roved from her ridiculously heeled shoes, over the shiny tube top, to the curls of her wig, and back again. Carole resisted the urge to kick him across the lobby. Shoving the sunglasses further up her nose, she settled the huge handbag over a shoulder, and took the room key from the clerk.

"If you need anything, Miss Anderson, anything at all, just dial the front desk."

Carole ignored the clerk's comment, which seemed to be directed at her tube top. Several men lingering at the lobby bar raised their glasses at her as she headed for the stairs. She ignored them too, and followed the bellman, still studying her through critical eyes, up the stairs. With obvious effort, he lugged the heavy bag. It thumped against each wooden step up three flights of stairs. Carole hoped it damaged the gun. It would be a justifiable reason to not use the weapon.

After dragging her bag down a sunlit hallway, the sweating bellman insisted on unlocking the door for her. Carole saw his eyes dart to the outline of the wedding ring in her tight pants pocket. Once the door finally swung open, she dismissed his condemning looks and left her little critic to haul her suitcase over the threshold. The room continued the southwest theme, and she crossed posh carpeting patterned with a turquoise abstract of the horizon and rising sun. Sliding a glass door open she stepped onto the balcony. Peering across beautifully landscaped desert towards a building of luxury suites, she put both hands on the railing. The drug lord's suite stood within easy shooting distance of her room, on the third floor, just opposite hers. At night even a poor shot like her couldn't miss. *I can't do it*, she decided. *I won't. Not like this. What if the hit is innocent?*

The bellman loitered annoyingly in her room, tugging and shoving the suitcase onto the luggage stand. Carole reached into her expensive handbag, fishing for a small bill in the obscene pile of cash. The disguise of wealthy divorcee with a gambling problem made her as uncomfortable as the assignment. Changing her mind, she chose a larger bill. Maybe Karl was a family man. Turning towards the sliding glass door, Carole sensed danger a split second too late. The small wiry man hadn't been judging her, he'd been reading her. Her gaze slid over his cold expression to the gun in his hands at the exact moment he fired it. Carole toppled off the third floor balcony, backwards, the last thought in her mind a reprimand that she hadn't sensed the weapon. *Fatal error.*

IS IT NIGHT? Or have I gone blind? It doesn't matter, Carole concluded. Each beat of her heart thumped further apart than the last, every shallow breath demanded greater effort. And the pain, how could one woman hold so much pain? It wouldn't take much longer to die, the voices reassured. Unable to feel the bullet wound, she remembered the angle, knew it missed her heart because she'd stepped almost imperceptibly towards it at the last moment. It had hit a lung, and she was bleeding out, barely able to breathe. Not sure if she was face up or down, unable to feel her body, Carole reasoned that she must be lying face down. Probably alongside someone's balcony. The wig had to have fallen off. *They'll find my suitcase,* she worried, *and the gun, and my cover will be blown. No!* She tried to move, or thought she did, but couldn't tell if it made any difference. *Maybe the bullet hit my spine? No, the angle was wrong. I fell, maybe I broke my neck.*

"Don't move. It will make it worse," the voices warned. "*Time is short. Make your peace.*"

Carole timed her heartbeats. *Ten minutes left? Maybe. Oh God,* she prayed, her mind drifting to Ted and Beth.

"Hush, Cahrul. Do not try to move." The name and voice sounded vaguely familiar, but thoughts of Beth crowded out any curiosity.

"She's dying, losing too much blood. There's nothing we can do." The volume of these voices rose and fell like a child playing with a radio dial, vibrating oddly as though they spoke into a fan.

"No, I won't let her. Get Rutak."

DOES PAIN REALLY have no limits? Unbearable is a mythical word. You will bear what you must, there is no choice. A droning chant wove through the pain, chasing dark philosophical thoughts. Carole's heartbeat steadied, and impossibly the pain increased. The world was pain, chanting, and her slow steady heartbeat. Peaceful, pain-free darkness hovered near, but when it approached, Carole willed herself closer to the pain. The voices criticized, even in death.

"*Do not fight! Accept the inevitable. Let go.*"

"Grandfather? Can you help her?" That voice sounded familiar. Refusing to obey the voices, Carole tried to place it.

"You have seen me heal worse."

"Will you be all right?"

The whispery chuckle that followed touched someplace deep inside Carole's slowly beating heart. Familiar longing ached there.

"I have been all right for a very long time, Fastest, too long. I am tired of all right." *Fastest?*

An unfamiliar voice objected. "No, Grandfather! Do not do this! What is she to us? A killer!"

"Cahrul is one of my people, and a warrior. It is my duty to help her."

"We are your tribe. You will choose her over us?"

"Cahrul is flesh of the woman I will always love. I have given my all to the tribe. I will give my last as I wish." A door slammed. It echoed through Carole as pain, shattering her into pieces, and she was gone.

CHILDREN'S LAUGHTER SOUNDED muffled through thick clay walls. Inside her head Carole could see through walls to youngsters running nearby, could sense a native village of small terraced huts sloping around her. Opening her eyes, a square adobe ceiling greeted, and just below it narrow rectangular openings ringed the walls. Columns of light filtered through those high windows, and dust motes hovered in the air. Several wooden beds were crammed into the small earthen house. Carole sat up too quickly. Ignoring a wave of dizziness, she cautiously touched her chest. There was no pain. Tugging off a neon green concert T-shirt that had certainly not been in her suitcase, she examined her naked body. A small red scar marred her right breast. Reaching over her shoulder, she found much larger creases on her back. The exit wound. *Healed.* Taking a deep breath, clean desert air painlessly filled her lungs. A twisted rope mattress swayed beneath her, jostling a bowl of clean water against her hip. Lifting it to her lips, she drank thirstily. Although warm, it tasted fresh, and she gulped half of it before it hit her. Her heart lurched and she nearly dropped the bowl. Carole knew exactly where she was.

It's the veil. Where Rutak Tural and Fastest live.

This wasn't a hallucination, this was real. The taste of the desert air had never been so clean, water so pure. *This means it has always been real!* Tucking the bowl beside her, Carole searched as far as her mind could go, wallowing in the touch of clean land. *Since this is real, that means—!*

A man entered the low adobe doorway, bent forward. Long hair hid his face while he shifted past the bright fabric serving as a door. Carole immediately tugged the Ramones T-shirt back over her head. The man moved lithe and graceful, seemingly unaware of her brief nakedness. Shining dark hair brushed bare dusky shoulders, and he pushed his hair aside and tilted his face up to meet her eyes. She recognized him as the man from the picture of her hit. This was the man she'd been sent to kill. Carole's breath caught and her fingers threaded through the rope mattress beneath her, holding on. Though time had altered his features from boy to man, she knew him.

"Fastest," she gasped, sudden tears burning her eyes.

Fastest took a seat on a bed next to her, so close his knees touched her rope mattress. His dark eyes red rimmed, his face sad, he said, "We have a bit of a problem, don't we, Cahrul?"

He knew. She opened her mouth and then shut it, unable to find words. Fastest smiled faintly.

"We both know I can't outrun you, so perhaps we can talk before you get down to business?"

"I didn't know it was you." So many thoughts crowded Carole's mind, she couldn't focus. *This is real! The veil is real!*

Fastest crossed strong arms over his naked chest. "Such a relief, Cahrul. Would it have mattered?"

Would it? She didn't know. If he was guilty, did it even matter now? *Yes! The fact that he really exists changes everything. Doesn't it?*

Clever dark eyes watched her. "How do you feel?" He nodded towards her chest.

Pressing hands against it, she remembered and glanced down. "I got shot."

"You sure did."

"How long have I been here? What day is it?"

"You were shot yesterday."

"That's impossible."

He smiled faintly. "Oh, we're both pretty familiar with impossible, aren't we?" Then the smile faded. "What happened to you? That you would come after any man with a gun?"

A sob almost choked her, catching her by surprise, but anger flared in her heart. "Does it matter what happened to me? I used to come back here—every night—I scoured the desert for you—for your Grandfather! In the end I thought I'd imagined this place. I thought you and Rutak were a hallucination! I thought I was crazy!"

Fastest leaned forward, placing dusty desert hands over hers. "I know you came, I saw you, and I'm sorry we hurt you. Remember what Grandfather told you that night? We couldn't be what you needed. You had to find your own tribe." Carole yanked her hands away.

"Then you have your answer, don't you? I found my *tribe*!" The words were bitter. *They didn't want me!* The truth was worse than a hallucination!

Fastest folded his arms across his brown chest again. Dark eyes studied her intently. "Did your tribe tell you why they wanted me dead? Or do you not require reasons to murder a man?"

Carole flinched. Despite everything, those words hurt. Fastest's hand immediately found her shoulder and squeezed gently, as though to soothe his would-be assassin.

"I'm sorry. Grandfather said you will have your reasons. Of course he also told me if they are justified, I'm not to resist!" Fastest pulled his hand away again, crossing his arms, but Carole felt certain his anger wasn't at her right now.

"Rutak told you to *let* me kill you?"

"If it is justified." The words were measured. "But I do not plan to cooperate no matter what your reasons are."

Carole bit back a sudden inappropriate smile. Surely Rutak couldn't expect that type of cooperation from his grandson! Fastest's dark gaze turned cold and Carole's amusement faded. *Had* Fastest become a foe? She needed to know she wasn't duty bound to kill him.

"You run the casino as a front to launder drug money."

Fastest's mouth dropped open. "I do not!" He glared. "That's what they think? Is that why they're so determined to off me?"

Carole shifted. The rope mattress swayed. "Have others come after you?"

"You're the third. Karl is quite astute at spotting assassins."

"He killed them?" Carole remembered the man's expression. *Yes, he'd killed before.*

Fastest frowned. "You'll judge Karl? For protecting me from killers and old friends?"

"Drug money buys guns over the border. It costs innocent lives there and here. When you don't see the consequences it's easy to kill. Does that make you less guilty?"

"If you cannot bring yourself to believe me, do you think Grandfather would have allowed my tribe to have any part in drugs? Or money laundering?"

"Where did the money come from for that casino, then?"

Scowling, Fastest stood and reached into the pocket of his jeans, digging. He dropped a handful of small rocks in her lap. Several scattered and dropped onto the dirt floor. She picked one off her lap, still warm from Fastest's pocket.

"Silver? Silver hasn't been mined in New Mexico since—oh, it's here inside the veil."

"Why do your people assume everything my people do is illegal?"

Carole looked up at him. "There are photographs of you at a drop. I saw them, but I didn't recognize you. Never even thought of you, why would I? I thought you were a figment of my imagination! You looked angry in them, different. Your hair was short."

Gathering his long hair in his hands, he pushed it over his shoulders. "My hair has never been short." Suddenly he sucked in his breath, and muttered in his native tongue. It sounded like swearing to Carole, and her brain struggled to make sense of the words. The word Kiyag stuck out, it sounded like a name.

"You know who it is?"

"I *might* know who it is."

"Who is Kiyag? Is he here?" Carole shifted weakly on the rope mattress, knowing she would be unable to do anything about Kiyag even if he walked into the hut right now.

Fastest chewed his lip, eyeing her. "He is my foolish young cousin, and I don't know that he's done anything illegal. Unless stupid is a crime."

"People die because of stupid choices, and someone who looks very much like you is costing lives every day."

"Well, we all look alike to your kind don't we? If you have to kill someone, it may as well be me or my stupid cousin?"

"I don't have a kind. And even if I do just walk away, someone else will come. You have to go public about the silver, Fastest. It would explain how you have money. They would know to look elsewhere."

"Do you think I will be safe if I go public about that? It's not like I can show them the mine."

Carole knew he was right. "I'll find your cousin Kiyag. Guilty or not he might know enough so I can find out who is. I'll kill them."

"Good God, Cahrul. You say that so easily."

"It'll buy you time. Find a way to justify the casino."

"Don't do me any favors, especially ones that involve killing anyone. Karl has my back."

"Why do you want a casino anyway? You have this veil to live in. Why leave it?"

"Why leave the reservation? Well, I'd like my people to have choices outside this veil. It's not big enough for all of us, and some of us want a life in the real world. The casino seemed a better money making option than what Kiyag *might* have done." Running a thumb over his bottom lip, he grimaced faintly. "But there are some who find drugs and gambling equal vices. Grandfather never approved of the casino. I should have suspected something when he suddenly wanted to come see it. The rocks must have told him that you were coming."

"I didn't imagine that either. The rocks really do talk to him?"

"They must have told him you would need him last night."

Carole pressed her fingers against her chest again and breathed deeply, painlessly. "He saved my life. I think I heard him chanting—"

"Praying."

"Then I woke up here. Can I see him?"

Fastest stood quickly and wove between the cots to a sideboard along the far wall.

"It's late. You need to stay in that bed for now, and you need to eat. Grandfather said you lost too much blood, to force you to rest if need be. If you promise not to kill me today, I'll feed you."

"I'd rather you didn't joke about it."

"What makes you think I'm joking?" He filled a plate with beans from a crock, and grabbed a handful of tortillas. Returning to her side, he handed her the plate and sat facing her. "Eat. We all obey Grandfather around here."

Scooping some beans onto a tortilla, Carole argued before taking a bite. "You don't. You said you weren't going to listen to your Grandfather about letting me kill you."

"Was that supposed to be funny? You don't have much knack for humor."

Shoving a huge bite into her mouth, she spoke around the food. "Did you ever stop going to rock concerts like he told you to?"

The ultra-white teeth she remembered flashed in his dusky face.

"You do remember the details, don't you?"

Forcing a swallow, she sat the plate in her lap. "I remember all of it. Every word. Rutak is the only one of my kind I've ever met. After that night I thought he'd explain everything to me. Instead I ended up thinking I was completely crazy."

Fastest moved smoothly to sit beside her. "We were afraid you would think that." He smelled like desert and his clean hair hung nearly to his waist, it brushed against her arm, and he tapped his chest. "There is great love in you. I don't understand how you can kill people. I don't judge desert predators for being what they are, but it is much more difficult to see a human being like that." Fastest stood and for some reason she wished he hadn't. *Am I a predator?*

"*Yes,*" the voices answered.

Carole picked up the sloshing bowl of water at her side and sipped it. A wave of dizziness washed over her, and she leaned forward, splashing water onto her plate. Unable to focus, she closed her eyes shutting out the bright light. To keep from passing out, she dropped flat, swaying slightly on the rope mattress. Fastest bent over her and took the plate from her. She sensed him deposit them carelessly on the next bed.

Not meaning to she whispered her thoughts out loud, "You are real. This place is real. It changes everything. I'm not crazy."

"We'll debate the sanity of assassins later, Cahrul. Rest." She heard the splash of water as he refilled the water bowl against her hip. He moved her hand to rest beside it. Fastest's touch was gentle, kind, surely the result of caring for Rutak all these years. Carole tried to force her eyes open. *What if I fall asleep and it all disappears again?* Questions flitted through her mind. She needed answers.

The ropes on the bed next to hers creaked and she sensed Fastest sink onto it, and heard him sigh, a long sad sound. Then his hand was back, stretched across the short gap, spreading a woolen blanket over her. She didn't protest when he tucked the ends beneath her. Maybe he wouldn't vanish if he was touching her.

"I'll stay with you for a while. Please rest."

"I used to think, when I searched the desert for this place, that you and I would be friends," she whispered, unable to believe she'd voice the thought. "That's sad isn't it? I saw you once, and anyway, I don't have friends."

"Perhaps if you did not try to kill them," he whispered back, "you would have friends."

"Don't. Don't tease."

"I'm not. You might want to think about it."

Carole didn't answer him. They hadn't wanted her. She wished she hadn't said so much. After long minutes of scrambled thoughts, exhaustion won out and she slept.

CAROLE WOKE, SWEATING despite the cold desert night, and for one terrifying moment thought she'd imagined Fastest. Alone on the rope mattress, she groped for her blanket and sat up, her mind searching through the night for him. Wrapping the thin woolen blanket over her shoulders, Carole made her way to the sideboard for food. Shoveling cold beans onto a tortilla with her fingers, she tried to locate Fastest among the sleeping tribe. The small terraced village sloped around her, and her mind skimmed over unfamiliar families as she ate the clean food.

She almost missed him. The hollow space of a kiva had been dug just yards east of the houses. Carole could sense a wooden ladder jutting from the underground structure, surrounded by a ring of stones. Finishing the last of the food, she revisited the spot with her mind. Moving downward, always an unpleasant task, instead of sensing earth she found open space. Fastest lay sprawled on the ground inside the kiva. She tensed until she felt his heartbeat, his breathing, the tears on his face. A horrible suspicion entered her mind. Wiping her mouth, she closed her eyes and focused. The ground beneath Fastest had been disturbed recently, and she forced her reluctant mind beneath it.

"No!" she whispered into the night, knocking a clay pot from the shelf. It rolled across the dirt floor. Though the life that had been Rutak Tural was gone, she sensed the shell that had housed him, his body buried in the ground. Carole ran into the night.

A WOMAN SAT huddled on the ground at the top of the kiva, swaddled in cloth, just a dim figure in the night. Carole ignored her, heading for the opening.

"Don't," the woman warned. "Jonathan needs to mourn. When he needs comfort, the tribe will see to him, not you."

Ignoring her, Carole headed for the ladder. A beam of light flashed directly into her eyes and then blinked off. The old woman

S.R. KARFELT

stood, slapping the flashlight against her hand. The light blinked
back on.

"I think the batteries are going. Don't you dare ignore me, young
lady. Turn right around and march back to your hut. Rutak Tural did
not give his last for you to waste it. You never did follow the rules very
well, did you? Not when it didn't suit you. Do you have a problem with
your hearing? I said *march!*"

For some reason Carole responded to the command, turning
towards the huts. The old woman shuffled behind her with a heavyset
gait, rocking from side to side as she moved. The flashlight blinked in
and out with an occasional thwack. Inside the hut, Carole slid weakly
onto the nearest bed, exhausted, wondering if she'd have managed the
climb down the ladder into the kiva. The woman's flashlight finally died,
and she lit a lantern, casting a glow of warm light inside the hut.

"Aw, Carole! Your hair! All that beautiful hair gone, that's a sin."

Blinking through the light, Carole caught the dark outline of
the woman and her mouth fell open. She sat straight up in the bed so
fast that it felt like her brain slid forward inside her skull. She could
feel her heartbeat inside her head. The woman was a nun, and not
just any nun.

"Sister Mary Josephine?" *How on earth?*

"Oh she remembers the name, but not the manners?"

"Good evening, Sister Mary Josephine," Carole intoned automatically, childhood memories flooding her mind.

"Good evening, Carole. Would you like a drink of water?"

"No thank you, Sister Mary Josephine," she whispered. *It's not
possible. I have lost my mind, completely and utterly lost my mind.*
Carole lay back on the bed and closed her eyes. Overwhelmed and
exhausted, she couldn't process it, and dove into unconsciousness
without even trying to fight it.

DAYLIGHT CAME, AND Carole had to pee, but refused to open her eyes. She could sense the bulk of what was surely Sister Mary Josephine sitting in a chair near the entryway of the hut. What on earth was the nun who ran Rio Rancho Sisters of Mercy Orphanage—the very orphanage she'd been housed in until she was ten years old—doing here? Inside a veil where the only other of Carole's kind that she'd known had just died? Could this possibly *be* a hallucination? It felt real, but didn't they? Didn't all schizophrenics think their hallucinations were real? *Oh God, I've lost the ability to recognize reality. Maybe I'm in a coma. I hope I'm in a coma.*

Fastest made little sound as he pushed through the flap over the doorway, but Carole sensed him. "She's still sleeping?" He sounded worried.

"No. She's just pretending. I don't think she can go much longer, she needs to use the latrine."

Carole rose immediately and faced the nun. "Good Morning, Sister Mary Josephine." It was real. No part of her mind could have recreated the acerbic nun so perfectly. Her face sagged a bit more and her hook nose seemed larger than last time she'd seen her, but the sharp green eyes were exactly the same, and she'd never noticed in childhood, but they were beautiful. Carole glanced towards Fastest, clad in the same jeans from yesterday, smudges of dirt dusting them. She moved to him and after a moment's hesitation, awkwardly took his hands.

"I'm sorry about Rutak. I don't know what to say. It's my fault he died, isn't it?"

He leaned forward and briefly touched his forehead to hers. "No. It was his choice. He said for you to use his gift wisely, Cahrul." The dark eyes, ringed with darker lashes, teared up. "And to thank you for giving his death meaning."

Carole's own eyes remained dry, but something twisted in her heart. Regret spread there, aching through her. Fastest put his hands on her shoulders and squeezed gently.

"Grandfather said you would understand that, and it would comfort you."

The ache intensified. "I do understand, but I'm selfish. There are so many things I wanted to ask him." She glanced towards the nun questioningly. *Why is she here?*

"Your questions can wait. You need to get dressed before the ceremony." But from the remembered tilt of Sister Mary Josephine's stubborn chin, Carole knew she'd get no answers from her even after the ceremony.

CHAPTER
SEVENTEEN

The Veil—April 1990

INSIDE THE BATH house Carole washed from a basin, scrubbing dried blood from under her arms and torso. Rubbing a cloth down her legs she found it dried between her toes. Surprised to realize how much blood she'd lost, she understood now why she was tired, despite the miraculous healing. Examining her body in the bright light streaming from openings high in the walls, she found not even the thin red scar remained on her breast. A heavyset woman stood in front of a large silver-framed obsidian mirror, braiding glass beads into her long frizzy hair and curiously watching Carole in their reflection.

"Grandfather's prayers still work in you. By night you will be strong again."

Moving to the mirror, Carole turned to search her back for the thick scar of the exit wound and found only a thin line. The woman unfolded a pale linen garment and slid it over Carole's head. The thin fabric felt soft against her skin, and slid down the length of her body. The gown hugged her hips and most of her legs in long neat pleats, leaving only her arms bare. Both waistband and collar were blue, and colorful clay beads dangled. Carole ran her fingers through her freshly washed hair, and the woman handed her a plastic toothbrush still in its package.

"Take it with you when you go. Grandfather didn't like the outside world brought in, but sometimes we cheat. There's tooth-paste on the shelf."

OUTSIDE IN THE bright desert sunshine, Fastest waited wearing only a bit of linen across his hips. Turquoise beads decorated his glossy hair, hanging in a curtain down his back. Carole crossed the ground barefoot, trying not to wince with each step. Fastest moved gracefully to meet her, and led the way, his bare feet used to the invisible burrs infecting the ground.

"The entire tribe will fast today, except for infants, even the oldest of the elders. We assumed you would too."

"Of course," she said.

"You'll need to rest after the ceremony. This won't take long, but it can be taxing. Grandfather said your kind do not mourn death like we do, but he was with us for a very long time. We can't let him go easily, and this will help us to heal. I think he would forgive us that."

They ascended the path towards the kiva, where hundreds of the tribe had already gathered. In the distance Carole could see Sister Mary Josephine directing youngsters away from the proceedings. She asked Fastest how the nun was tied to his people.

"When I was a kid I saw her here with Rutak a couple of times, and right after you'd been here she came. I asked who she was that time. I always felt free to ask Grandfather anything, unfortunately he felt free not to answer me, but I figured she had something to do with your kind."

"Maybe, but she's not my kind."

Fastest explained he'd met two others of her kind since he'd seen her last, both men, and he'd disliked them both. "All I really know about your people is they live in remote places far from large bodies of water— or perhaps it was close to water, I'm not sure. I know, Cahrul, that you want information about your people, but I don't know very much."

190

"I didn't mean to interrogate you, especially not today," said Carole, looking around. They were in the middle of the village. The large open space appeared to be the main camp. Bowl shaped, with earthen benches dug in a circular pattern, it had been built stadium fashion. Fastest and Carole stood on the topmost spot of the dirt arena, looking down. People were spreading out, most standing in rows, but below a few men were gathering in the center. The women wore linen dresses like Carole, but most of the men were almost bare, like Fastest, wearing only the smallest bit of fabric.

"Tell me what to do," Carole said, noting the women heading towards the easternmost edge of the bowl.

Fastest's white teeth flashed briefly. "Follow your heart. That is what your people are best at, isn't it?" He left her then, and made his way down the rows of dusty and weedy steps, to gather at the center of the camp with dozens of men. Despite his advice, Carole's heart told her nothing. The voices told her she didn't belong there and to leave, so she stayed right where she was instead of heading east with the other women. Watching as the tribe followed their hearts to their places, she noted with surprise that in the sea of dusky bodies there was a handful as light skinned as she was.

Almost as one the crowd quieted. Instead of facing towards the bottom of the earthen bowl, everyone turned to face east, where most of the women stood. To Carole's surprise she realized she wasn't the only woman who hadn't joined them. There were about a dozen women standing near her, most very old, and Sister Mary Josephine stood among them, dressed in her black habit, her old-fashioned long cap dangling down her back. The women on the eastern edge began doing something, and Carole focused her attention. At first they appeared to only rock and tear at their hair. When Carole realized the dark globs sticking on their gowns, and drifting to the ground was hair, she spotted a silver knife being passed from woman to woman. They were cutting their hair off. Yards and yards of dark glossy hair were being sawed away until woman after woman emerged with hair horribly similar to Carole's.

Her eyes cut to the men at the bottom of the circle. They had their own knives, and she watched as Fastest yanked his gorgeous beaded hair taut with one hand, and hacked at it with the blade. By the time he finished his scalp glistened raw and bald. The light-skinned man to his left took the knife. He scraped the blade through short dark hair, leaving one wide bald path down the middle of his scalp. To her dismay he then used the blade to cut his flesh. From his shoulder, across his chest, down to his hip he meticulously sliced before passing the knife to the next man.

A silver blade had made its way to her group, and Carole watched curiously when Sister Mary Josephine took it, mentally contemplating the fact that she'd never seen the nun remove her cap, even the times the orphans had been taken to the local swimming pool when she'd been a child. The nun didn't break tradition. Lifting the wicked knife to her face, she lightly slid it across her forehead, just once. A scarlet ribbon of blood appeared instantly, and she held the bloody weapon out for Carole to take.

It was heavy in her hand, solid. Carole lifted it to her hairline, surprised at how the sharp edge easily cut a swath through her already short hair. Hefting it a second time, she cut another path on the opposite side, leaving twin stripes in its wake. Being the last woman in her group, she held onto the weapon, unsure what to do with it. The men to her left had their own knives. Sister Mary Josephine held out a calloused hand and Carole gave it back to her, but the nun grabbed her arm, straightened it, and sliced just below the crook of Carole's elbow, repeating the maneuver until she'd left dozens of shallow scratches all the way to her wrist. Obediently Carole held out her left arm, knowing it was required.

The nun handed the knife back to her, glaring meaningfully. Carole understood. Rutak had given his last for her. More than his entire tribe, she owed him a sacrifice. Carole had never hurt anyone for the purpose of causing them pain, but she knew how. Lifting her arm into the air, she repeated the marks from under her arm to her elbow, and again with the other arm, cutting deeper than the nun had. Expertly she ran the razor sharp blade between her fingers and against the sensitive tips. Without bothering to lift her gown she attacked her thighs and calves, shredding material along with flesh. In turn she lifted each foot to extract payment from the soles, and inflict pain between her toes. She'd begun work from chin to chest, cutting only as deep as she dared when the nun snatched the knife off of her, a horrified expression on her face.

To the east the women began a hair-raising keening that sent shivers straight through Carole. A rhythmic chorus rose and fell, "Ah! Ahh! Ahhh!" The voices in her head had been criticizing the semantics of the ceremony, and fussing about possible infection from the cuts and shared blade, but they hadn't protested her sacrifice. They surprised her and took up the tribe's scream inside her head. The sound vibrated sharply through her and made goose bumps shiver painfully over her wounded flesh. Instinctively she joined in with a heartfelt shout of pain, feeling it. Pain for her loss, pain that she'd never know the things Rutak wouldn't tell her, pain that she loved Ted and he ran to other women to escape it, pain that she left her daughter to hunt people like animals—at the bidding of those she was sworn to obey. "Ahhhhhhhhhh!" The sound ripped through her body, and she stopped only to draw breath and repeat it.

After a time Carole rocked back and forth to the sound, and sensed that most of the crowd did the same. Her skin burned horribly, especially where salty tears dripped off her face and landed in shredded skin. Words started to come out. First it was simply *no*, a word soldiers were forbidden from saying. The faces of those she'd killed flittered through her mind, and she screamed *no* throughout, as though she could take back what she had done.

Carole could almost see them.

Grandpa. "No!"

General Samish. "No!"

Ambassador Causer. "No!"

Miller—the terrorist who went for a swim and drowned with a foot tangled in a rope and his head dangling in the water, right in front of her dispassionate eyes. "No!"

Trina—the Russian mother whose daughter started school while her mother's body decayed in the hull of a ship. "No!"

Thomas—the foolish nuclear engineer who hadn't even fought back when she slammed her knife into his throat. "No!"

In the end she shouted their names to the desert, knowing she'd done her duty. She was a soldier, and her pain was part of her sacrifice. Her shouts weakened, and she rocked slower, and in the end her words turned from sin and regret to those she missed. "Gran. Mom. Gran. Mom. Happy Easter." She knew she wasn't making any sense, but the words rasped from her sore throat, as loud as she could manage.

Deaf now to the keening pain around her, she swayed in place, unable to manage another coherent word. She looked in confusion at a face that appeared right in front of her, recognizing him as the man who'd stood beside Fastest, and shaved his head and cut his chest. Why was he looking at her like that? Why were his golden eyes so familiar? Why was he crying?

"Cahrul?" he rasped in his own hoarse voice. "My shieldmaiden daughter? Could ilu be this good to me?"

My father is here. The Priest.

The ground spun and reached up to grab her, and everything vanished.

PAIN ROUSED CAROLE, sharp stinging pain all over her body. And arguing.

"Don't you dare heal those cuts! She made them for Rutak." Sister Mary Josephine's scathing voice demanded obedience. "She'll be fine. The boy knows what he's doing. Didn't Rutak himself disinfect your wounds with clay when you were a boy on the reservation?"

"I'm sure you saw evidence of that when I lived at the orphanage. Clay gathers in deep wounds and leaves a tattoo, especially on light skin. I still have the marks." Carole recognized her father's voice, though she hadn't heard it since she was nearly four years old.

Fastest's strong hands were firmly rubbing what felt like dirt into the cuts on her arms. If she had any energy at all, she'd cry. He rubbed so hard that she swayed back and forth, like a boat on choppy water. It took a disoriented moment to realize she lay on a rope bed, inside a hut, with the remains of her dress bunched up around her thighs and her father and Fastest ministering to her self-inflected wounds.

"Son, don't put that clay on her neck. She'll have orange stripes for the rest of her life."

"My name is Jonathan Redfeather," Fastest's voice replied politely, though he sounded as frustrated as her father. "Sister, why didn't you stop her?"

"She doesn't listen to me!" The scathing voice replied. "I had to pull the knife out of her hands. Even as a child she never listened to me. She wouldn't have ended up in half the trouble she got into in foster care, nor have wound up here *shot* if she had!"

"She's the one who got shot?" her father hissed. "Foster care! I left my daughter with you and you put her into foster care?"

"I tried to keep her, Joseph. Things have changed since you were at the orphanage." The scathing voice sounded genuinely contrite. Carole struggled to open her eyes. She wanted to see contrite on the nun's face. She couldn't quite manage it.

Gentle hands slid softly over her bare feet. Despite the tender touch, the burning pain from the dirty cuts increased and she groaned.

"You're not doing your healing thing on her, are you?" The contrition had gone from the nun's voice.

"Not for the cuts, Sister." The hands slid up her fiery legs. Strangely Carole began to feel better, stronger. It came in waves of energy from the touch of those soft hands. *My father's hands.* They reached her hips and stomach, and moving upward, paused to linger right over her belly. She opened her eyes, struggling to focus. Whatever he was doing to her seemed magical. Despite that, she couldn't quite manage to sit up, but her father's face appeared over hers. He smiled. "You look so like your mother, so like Keight!"

Carole gazed into wide eyes. His lashes were ridiculously long and when he blinked at her, it reminded her of Beth so much her heart ached.

"I remember you," she said. Her voice sounded froggy. Interrupting Fastest's painful doctoring, she lifted an arm and grabbed her father's hand so he couldn't get away. He held it tightly and leaned closer to kiss her forehead, her nose, and then her lips, the way she sometimes did to Beth. Tears burned in her eyes. "What's your name?"

"Joseph Tural, Father Joseph Tural."

"Tural? Like Rutak Tural?" Carole searched his face for any remembered similarities to the old man's face, but found none. He smiled at her question and shook his head. Joseph looked pale, slight, and graceful, and she suspected if he didn't look so worried, and if his head hadn't been shaved in a sort of awful reverse Mohawk, his plain features would have been kind. The type of face you'd trust instinctively. The long-lashed golden eyes that reminded her of Beth's were the wrong color, but the open, honest clearness to them was the same as her daughter's.

There were so many questions she needed answers to. Head pounding and skin on fire, dizzy and aching, she asked questions while she had the chance. "Couldn't you have *visited*? Or written? So I'd have known your name? What did you just do to me? Can you heal like Rutak? How does it work? What are we? Why can we do—stuff? Do you hear voices?"

Joseph's dark brows pulled together. "Don't you remember anything I told you?"

It took a moment to understand exactly what he meant. For a brief second Carole thought she'd missed something while being transported from the main camp to the hut she now found herself in. She tried to remember how she'd gotten there, and what had been said.

Realizing that wasn't what he meant, a sudden flash of angry heat shot through Carole. He still loomed close, gazing at her face, and she used their clasped hands to form a fist and roughly pushed him away with a punch, yanking her hand free. The voices violently protested the act, bellowing in her head, and Carole shouted over them.

"Do I remember what you told me? You mean when I was three years old? Did you think I would?" Though physically shoved away, the touch of his heart didn't go. It rested right beside hers, and it eased her anger, because she sensed the place in his heart where she belonged. It had been empty and aching all this time too. Knowing he'd shared her pain, she relented and admitted, "You said you loved me. I remember only that."

"If you only remembered one thing, that was the most important." Joseph leaned close again, gently brushing the back of his fingers over her cheek. The touch of his heart, reassuring that she was indeed loved by her absentee father, kept her from pushing him away again.

Fastest, kneeling beside her cot with his bowl of clay, rose swiftly. Sister Mary Josephine loomed over Carole, hands on hips in a familiar gesture remembered from childhood. Carole could only assume shoving a Priest had caused it. Fastest hooked his arm through one of Sister Mary Josephine's elbows and none too gently turned the nun towards the doorway, tugging her width through the narrow opening. The leather hide swayed from their passing.

"Don't try to sit up. You look ready to pass out again. I'm afraid my healing isn't comparable to Rutak's. Sip this." Joseph pressed a cup to her lips, and Carole sipped several bitter mouthfuls before turning her head, sensing a sedative. She had too many questions to sleep.

It worked quickly, warming her veins and numbing her lips, but she fought it, needing answers. "How do you heal? Rutak healed my gunshot wound, overnight!"

Joseph exhaled a breath, and Carole felt the anxiety the mention of her gunshot wound caused. It grazed his heart like a real bullet.

"It's just prayer. Prayer works. Everyone can do it to an extent. Rutak was unusually proficient, even for one of our kind. I'm not nearly as talented."

"I felt the strength of your prayers," Carole argued, trying to sit up.

"Well, yes. As I said, most of us can do it. Don't strain yourself, be still. You've lost too much blood. I'm not that talented at healing, so you're going to have to rest. I'm afraid my gifting lies elsewhere."

Despite Joseph's command, and the voices advice that she heed it, Carole continued to struggle to sit up. "Gifting? What is a gifting?" Firmly grasping the rope mattress beneath her, she used it to push herself up. The room seemed to spin uncomfortably to the left, and her arms felt too weak to hold her up, spots of grey blotted out her vision. A split second before her head slammed back against the cot, the voices intoned, *"It is disrespectful not to obey your father."*

CAROLE DREAMED THAT her blankets turned to metal that night. Beth was caught beneath them too, and kept trying to tie her shoes. Bleeding from his heart, Ted watched from a helicopter, ignoring the blood soaking the front of his uniform. He appeared to be trying to reach them.

The dream changed and Carole became a little boy with long dark hair, running barefoot in the sunny desert beneath the veil. Rutak rubbed orange clay on his sore feet, and called him Nomno. All the kids from the tribe begged for Nomno to live in their huts. Ted's helicopter hovered overhead, but Carole didn't care now. She liked being that little boy. Nomno had four puppies, but a rattlesnake bit one, and him, and Rutak healed Nomno but the puppy died. Carole cried.

Sister Mary Josephine came to take the little boy to the orphanage and he cried then. The puppies couldn't come. Rutak said the rocks wanted Nomno to go now, and Rutak gave him a new name. He wasn't Nomno anymore, he was Joseph Tural. So in her dream Carole stopped being Nomno and became Joseph Tural too. Joseph had to live at the same orphanage she once had, and carry trash down to the same incinerator in the same church basement just like Carole used to.

Joseph didn't mind the incinerator, the orphanage, or any of the rules, and he liked people. He prayed for them a lot and shot right up into the sky when he did, floating through the heavens to talk to ilu about people he loved. Carole liked flying with Joseph though she knew it was just in his head, and that she was really still Carole trapped on the ground, under her metal blankets, while the voices told her she was going to burn up and die.

There were paintings in the north porch of the church where Joseph worked. They were orange, yellow, and red, like the desert under the veil. Those paintings reminded Joseph of his flying time with ilu. It was his job to put a drop cloth down when the artist came, and to carry buckets of water and clean the brushes afterwards. He came early one day, and the artist was still painting. It was a girl. Her hair was covered with a paint splattered bandana, and she wore a big ugly denim dress filthy with splotches of bright paint. It didn't matter because Joseph felt the girl's heart.

Only she wasn't a girl, she was a young woman, and Joseph wasn't a boy anymore either. He was a man now. She had a car and they left together. Somehow Joseph remembered how to get to the veil, and they went there, to the desert, to be together. Her name was Keight and without the bandana and dress she looked like a painting herself. Joseph remembered to tell her that he would become a Priest later that year. It was too late now for Keight to reject him because of that, but she said she wouldn't have anyway.

Rutak didn't mind Joseph and Keight being there, and gave them a shady hut to live in for the summer. Keight painted on the walls inside, and they played in the desert in the mornings. They had puppies and each other, and every day was perfect. Sister Mary Josephine came with Keight's mother when it was time to become a Priest and fly to ilu all of the time. Carole recognized her Gran and she cried with happiness. Joseph didn't, he said he was sorry to Keight's mother and called her Mother Klare. Gran told him not to be stupid and put Going to the Chapel by The Dixie Cups into his head with dancing rainbow lights. It made Carole cry harder, but Joseph laughed and so did Keight. Keight said goodbye to Joseph, kissed his cheek, and hopped into the big green car with the silver fins and drove off into the desert.

Joseph was flying with ilu then, telling Him about the people who needed Him, but a little girl shouted Happy Easter at him, and he fell back to earth, landing on his knees, hard. Keight and Klare had gone to live with ilu, and someone was shooting at his little girl. Ted and Beth were in the helicopter together. Ted was bleeding horribly. It ran out the open door of the aircraft and dripped all the way to the ground to land on Carole. Beth perched precariously at the edge of the doorway sitting in all that blood, wearing a spotless yellow dress, focused simply on tying her shoes.

A man screamed and Carole woke up.

A MAN'S SCREAM seemed worse than a woman's. Carole had experienced it far more in black dreams than real life, but it set her heart hammering in her chest no matter where it came from. This time it came from her father, on the cot next to hers. Early morning light pinked the hut. She saw Joseph wrestling to wake from a dream, head thrashing from side to side, hair from his inverted Mohawk brushing against the cords of the rope mattress. Instinctively she knew he was dreaming the same dream she'd had, knew her father had once been a little boy called Nomno who the children begged to dream with. Knew Joseph shared himself, his heart, in his dreams. The shared dream hadn't scared her, and she didn't understand why it scared him.

"It's alright," she said, reaching to shake him gently. "Beth is fine. Ted takes care of our daughter when I'm gone."

In one unnatural movement Joseph shot to his feet, reminding Carole just how startled Ted must feel when she did it.

"Get up!" he shouted at her. Instinctively she responded, mirroring his movement, the voices in her head instantly on alert. "Find shoes!" he commanded. Carole blinked in the dim morning light, searching the hut. Joseph leapt over her bed. "Scan! You can scan can't you? Find shoes!"

"Scan?" she said, but her mind already made the connection. Ignoring his bid for footwear, she searched for any sign of danger. She sensed nothing to be afraid of in the peaceful village, but her father's anxiety made her tense, ready to run.

"Can you see with your mind? You don't need eyes to find shoes do you?"

Carole had often considered the talent as radar. She moved her mind nearer and sensed several pair of sandals outside the hut under a bench. "They're outside the door. Can't you do it? Scan?" she said, unable to stop herself from questioning even as her mind again scanned through the village, searching for trouble.

"No. It's a warrior gifting, a shieldmaiden gifting in your case." He crisscrossed the hut, nabbing something from under a bed. "I think you might have noticed my gifting last night. How old is your daughter? Beth?"

"A year." He didn't respond, so Carole added, digging among some utensils on the sideboard for a weapon, "She has your eyes."

Joseph moved to her side, clutching a metal canteen. "I saw her in your dreams. She looks like you and Keight." There were tears in his eyes. Carole noted they weren't tears of joy.

"Why are you afraid?" Carole unscrewed the lid from his canteen as he held it out, and filled it with water from a pitcher. Spotting a dull butter knife in a tray full of spoons, she palmed it.

"Because there are others here like us, two Warriors of ilu!" he said. "I saw them yesterday. They'll surely seek you out." He pulled the canteen away before Carole finished filling it. Water spilled onto the desert floor beneath. Carole followed him as he hurried outside.

Together they bent beside a bench and rooted through piles of dusty sandals. Carole's mind raced as her hands searched for a pair of shoes that would fit her. Memories from somewhere drifted into her mind. Somehow she knew what Warriors of ilu were. Every hair on her body now stood at attention. They were fighters like her, only they'd trained for it. For years. Fear prickled up her spine, though she saw no reason for it. *They're dangerous but we've done nothing wrong.*

Her father nabbed a pair of sandals and tugged one onto a foot. "You're remembering? It happens when our kind get together. It's a type of ancestral memory. The more time we spend with our own kind, especially touching, the more you'll remember. You have good reason to fear Warriors of ilu. It's forbidden to take a mate outside of our kind. If they realize what you've done—what your Ted and Beth are—likely they'll kill you, and them."

Carole finally located a pair of mismatched sandals that would fit and sat her dull knife on the bench to strap them on. Joseph strapped his second shoe on. Carole tightened her shoes and reached for her knife. Her father's hand shot out and stopped her.

"No. You can't win a fight against them, and it would be wrong to kill them."

"You said they'd kill me, Ted, Beth! I won't let anyone hurt my family!" She brushed his hand away and her fingers clenched the knife tightly. Joseph shook his head.

"Did Rutak never tell you? Our people are so few, droplets in the ocean he used to tell me. Just go, and don't ever try to come back here. Keep your family away from our kind."

"I don't even know any of our kind!"

"I'd assumed as much. You're still alive." Joseph gently removed the useless knife from her hand and put his fingers through hers. "You still don't sense anyone coming?"

"The tribe is rousing. Nobody seems to be heading in this direction. I don't sense Fastest or Sister Mary Josephine at all."

"Keep scanning. Let's go."

THE VILLAGE AND desert were open and exposed, but the steeped huts, and the rise and fall of the land made moving through it unseen easy. Carole and Joseph stepped silently, tucking against adobe walls, and behind brush to keep from being noticed. Scanning helped, and Joseph knew every step and stone from his childhood home. After yesterday's fast, the hungry tribe woke with breakfast in mind, washing quickly, and hurrying towards the main camp for a communal breakfast. Within minutes Carole and Joseph passed the large monolith boulder, and moved in the opposite direction from everyone else, safe from detection.

Carole sensed relief fill Joseph's heart.

"What drew you to a man like Ted?" he gasped, jogging across open desert.

Hurrying through the empty desert at his side, Carole glanced towards him, her reply unstrained. Matching Joseph's slower pace took no real effort. "It was the first heart I'd felt since yours. I needed him. I had to—I couldn't bear the thought of being alone after that."

A faint smile touched the side of his wide mouth. "I sometimes feel their hearts too. Is your Ted a good man?"

The question gave Carole pause, but she answered honestly, shaking her head. Joseph didn't slow or look in her direction, intent on getting out of the veil. "No," she said.

"You were drawn to the heart of a bad man?" His words were strained with exertion.

"I think—I think I've made him bad. He's afraid of me."

Joseph nodded sagely, as though that were perfectly understandable. "I'll speak to ilu about him."

"What are we, Jo—Father? Why are we different?" She stumbled over calling him father, and he squeezed her hand tightly.

"Everyone was once very much like us. They changed, we didn't, but we're all just people, Cahrul. What sets us apart is our choices."

"If we're all just people, why does it matter who I married?" Carole argued.

"I doubt it does to ilu, but your choice is forbidden to our kind. The exit is just ahead." He panted, "We can talk later."

"But I didn't even know I had a kind!"

"Didn't you?" Joseph argued. "And would it have mattered?"

Carole wondered if it would have.

In front of them a strange wind blew, signaling the edges of the veil. Carole remembered how to get out, to feel the hard bubbled invisible surface, and sniff for the whiff of garbage—signaling the entrance to the dirty world outside. The smell of garbage blew past Carole's nose and she slowed, turning towards it. Joseph stopped moving altogether, skidding to a standstill. Before she could turn her head and ask why, Fastest came jogging through thin air, stopping not three yards away.

Beside her Joseph blew out a sigh of relief, before anyone could speak two impossibly fit men appeared right behind Fastest and slid to a stop. Carole knew who they were even before she sensed fear fill her father's heart. Warriors of ilu.

WITHOUT HIS HAIR Fastest looked different, older, and stubble had begun to pepper his scalp, turning patches of sore-looking skin black. The warriors were dressed like Fastest, in jeans and running shoes. The tallest wore a black concert T-shirt. The fabric stretched so tightly over the man's broad chest and eight-pack abs it made the name of the band indecipherable, telling Carole no matter how strong she was, she did not have the bulk and strength of that man. *Speed. I can best him with speed,* she reassured herself. The second warrior stood smaller but bare-chested, revealing an unimagined level of fitness. *He'll be fast too.* Dark blonde hair rested on his broad tanned shoulders, but Carole's eyes were drawn to the enormous sword strapped to his waist, resting against faded blue jeans. *Surprise. I can best him with surprise.*

Judging by the expressions on their faces, they hadn't expected to see Carole and Joseph at the edge of the veil, but none of them looked hostile.

"Hey!" Fastest grinned at Carole and Joseph. "Sneaking off? Did you hear Bert & Ernie here were looking for you?" Carole's father stiffened beside her, but Fastest's black eyes glittered mischievously revealing no reason to be afraid.

"*Yet,*" the voices whispered.

The bare tanned fellow smiled widely, moving closer, routinely shoving the sword behind his leg. "Jonathan calls us that, but I'm not Bert, my name is Bakrahn and my brother is Estrellas." The big guy—

204

Estrellas—nodded at her, his grin so wide he appeared to be in pain of some sort.

"Why are you looking for me?" Carole managed, trying to ignore the waves of her father's fear moving against her heart. *They can't know about Beth or Ted,* she reassured herself, eyeing the hilt of Bakhran's sword. He kept his right hand positioned as though to grab it at any second, but he seemed relaxed and wore the same idiotic smile as his brother.

"Why else?" Fastest intoned. The stupid smile seemed to be contagious among the three of them. "They wanted to meet you because they've never seen a girl before."

"He means like us," Bakrahn explained. "We've never seen a female Covenant Keeper before."

"They all wear their hair like that I hear," Fastest said, pointing at Carole's shorn hair with the two bald paths striped through it. Neither man seemed to mind it. They kept right on grinning at her. The voices were having a fit, and her father's hand clenched hers so tightly it hurt.

"Tell her, Bert," said Fastest to Bakhran, "Tell her what you want." Carole shot him a dirty look, but Fastest only seemed further amused by it.

"I want—we both want—to give you our declaration." The half-naked warrior, Bakrahn, launched into what sounded like a sales pitch. "Choose as your heart leads. We have a small clan in the Sierra Nevada. There are twenty-eight of us. You'll be our first woman! If you want you can meet everyone else and then choose a husband, but Estrellas and I are the best fighters, and the youngest."

Carole went still, every muscle in her body as tense as her father beside her. Fastest burst out laughing, a wheezing series of *hee-hee-hee* practically choking him. For a moment Carole hoped that the whole thing had been a joke, but the two warriors turned confused looks on Fastest. He bent forward bracing his hands on his knees, gasping for breath.

"Are we missing something?" broad-chested Estrellas asked. Despite Fastest's teasing, the sharp-eyed, big warrior didn't look like he'd miss much.

Fastest managed to stand, and dug in his pocket. Trying to talk around his laughter, he sounded like he was having an asthma attack. "F-finesse for starters, guys, but also instinct. C-Cahrul's already got a guy. I'm not one of your kind but even I can spot a girl who's already in love, and—" He stopped chuckling and fished something out of his pocket, turning his attention on Carole. "Obviously very married. I can't believe you were ducking out of here without this rock. I didn't think your kind did wedding rings. I had to pry this swag out of Karl's clenched fist!" Fastest flicked a ring into the air. The familiar platinum and diamond ring from Ted's wealthy past seemed to move in slow motion as it spun towards her, sparkling in the sunshine. Joseph released her hand and nabbed it out of the air.

"You can't be married," Bakrahn said.

Fastest's dark eyes went from Carole's face to Joseph's and back. He sucked in a very loud breath as realization dawned. Somehow he knew, and if Fastest caught on so quickly, Carole had no doubt that so would the warriors.

Confused, both Bakrahn and Estrellas looked from Fastest to Carole.

"No! She can't be married," said Estrellas, "her heart has the touch of a unjoined woman."

Suspicion was beginning to dawn in Bakrahn's shocked eyes.

"*Run!*" Joseph's voice sounded only in Carole's mind. "*Focus on what your eyes see, not your mind! Go, protect your family!*"

Before Carole could react or wonder, the desert ground beneath her vanished, replaced with swirling whitewater. It rapidly rose to cover her ankles. For a moment Carole remained frozen, the icy pressure from the water almost knocking her down as it climbed to her knees and higher.

Joseph pushed her towards the veil's exit, the touch of his heart against hers loving but firm. "*Focus on what your eyes see, not your mind.*" For a moment it made absolutely no sense, but Carole concentrated, focusing on what her eyes saw, not her mind. Suddenly she knew it wasn't real. There was no water. She felt it, she thought she saw it, but it didn't soak her soiled dress. There was no bank containing it, or source for the water, and she hadn't sensed its approach. It had just appeared. A boulder also appeared magically beneath Joseph, confirming her assessment. Water swirled around his robes without dampening them. Carole now stood hip deep in the flood, but completely dry, and knew with absolute certainty this flash flood was a daydream of her father's making, just like his dream from last night.

Trying to obey Joseph's command to run, she stumbled forward a few steps, but her gaze returned to those struggling in the swirling water. They didn't know it wasn't real. Fastest had fallen flat on his back beneath a whirlpool, and appeared to be calmly holding his breath. Both Warriors of ilu seemed to be trying to tread water as waves crashed over them. With the ground firm beneath her feet, Carole managed several more steps forward. Hands against the edge of the veil she felt the hard bubby texture she remembered. She glanced back at her father. *How will he get out? Will Fastest be harmed?* From here she could easily see right through her father's daydream. The warriors were struggling. In the guise of helping them her father shoved Estrellas further beneath the waves. Face buried against the ground Estrellas took in mouthfuls of desert dust. He appeared to be in danger of suffocating on dirt.

Bakrahn lunged after Estrellas, moving through the desert with jerky, swimming movements, but managing to keep to his feet. With his back to Joseph, Bakrahn took a deep gasping breath and ducked down, tugging uselessly at Estrellas, managing only to throw more dirt over his head. Bakrahn struggled, fighting against the weight of imagined waves, still managing to keep to his feet. Joseph reached as though to push him over. His hand bumped the sheathed sword jutting past Bakrahn's jeans, and his hand closed on the hilt.

In that split second Bakrahn abandoned his reach for his brother and spun in place. He pulled one mighty fist back and punched Joseph full in the face. Joseph's head snapped back so hard and far he bent over backwards, head down, his feet swinging a full circle up and through the air, spinning around in a complete circle, his dark robes flying around him before he landed flat on the ground.

Carole slid to her knees, all the breath knocked out of her body with her father's. She knew the water had vanished for everyone. Ice hot pain froze her heart. In that split second she knew that Nomno, Father Joseph Tural, her father, had once again become someone new, only this time she couldn't know his name or follow—not even in her dreams. He was dead.

Fastest, lying flat on the ground, shot into the air and double round-house kicked Bakrahn in the head, first one side and then the other. Caught off guard, the warrior dropped straight to the ground, unconscious. Estrellas hadn't risen from his imagined drowning, dirt clogging his mouth and nose. That part of Carole's brain that lived to fight watched, but the pain in her heart knew only Joseph.

Fastest roared at her, "Go, Cahrul! I can't keep them down long without hurting them! Ernie's going to suffocate!"

"FATHER!" Carole screamed. "Father!" It came out a hair-raising primal sound echoing across the desert as she raced to his side, throwing herself into the dust beside him, unwilling to believe what her heart knew. Clawing over his dark priest robes, she ran her hands up his spine, searching for his injury. "I can fix it, I can fix it. How do you do it? How? You said we can all do it! You didn't tell me how! Fastest! Help me! You have to help me!"

Behind her the part of her brain that always watched, knew Fastest gave Bakrahn another faint kick in the head.

"Go! Your father is gone. There's nothing you can do, and you will die too if Bert wakes up!"

"No!" she wailed. "No!" She knew it was true. He'd gone from inside her heart in a horribly familiar way, taken the same path as Mom and Gran, his presence, his love, vacuumed away and gone with him, leaving only icy hot emptiness behind. "No!" She covered her father with her body, screaming her agony into the very earth. "NO!" *I need him! I need him! Give him back! Please! ilu? Please!*

Fastest ran to her, wrapping his arms around her middle and hauling her to her feet.

"He's with his God now! Did you not feel his spirit soar? Don't be selfish. If he is watching you, don't cause him pain!" He pushed her roughly towards the exit. "Father Tural died so you wouldn't have to! Rutak died so you wouldn't have to! Do something with your life! I have a car parked on the far road, this side of Happy Acres. Go! Take it. You have to get ahead of these warriors!"

"Why'd they kill him? He's just a Priest! He didn't do anything!"

"He reached for his sword! You don't attack a Warrior of ilu and live to talk about it, not even in your dreams." Fastest ran back to Bakrahn and kicked him another good one. "Rutak taught me that long ago! You have to go! Ernie's suffocating, and I can't keep kicking this guy without really hurting him!"

"They'll kill you!" Carole realized. "We have to kill them! I'll do it!" She moved towards Bakrahn. Fastest planted one hand on her chest and shoved her towards the exit.

"Don't you start that! What is wrong with you? I'd let them kill me first. Grandfather would never forgive me if I hurt Bert and Ernie, and neither would your father!" He dashed to where Estrellas still hadn't moved, and bent beside him. "I'll give you a two minute head start before I help him! I hope you can still run fast. Then I'm dragging them out of the veil. They can't get back in again without help, so I guess that means I'll be living in the veil after all."

Standing near the exit to the veil, wind and the scent of garbage blowing over her, Carole looked back at her father's body prostrate on the ground. How could this have happened? What could she have done to prevent it? Why did everybody she loved die?

"For the love of God, would you go?" Fastest shouted at her.

"I—I can't drive!"

"The keys are under the driver's seat. Figure it out!"

The image of Ted and Beth in her dream floated into Carole's mind; Beth perched on the side of the helicopter, Ted bleeding. They were still alive, and she needed to keep them that way. She ran.

CHAPTER
EIGHTEEN

Republic of Singapore—July 1990

FOR FOUR MONTHS Carole lived with a street gang and went by the name of Ka. Half of her heart seemed to have died in the desert with her father. The other half starved for Beth and even Ted, for any shred of reassurance they might provide. At least she'd done what she could to ensure their safety. If Ted ever figured out why he was being transferred from city to city around the globe, he'd surely never forgive her. Apparently her skills meant something to someone. After flat out lying that she'd killed Fastest, the powers that be had agreed to her request. Carole had no doubt that wherever in the world her kind hid, it wasn't in cities.

The gang leader squawked a high pitched order for attention, and she tried to focus on what he said. This assignment was dangerous. She couldn't afford to allow her thoughts to stray. Fortunately her heart was better off dead in the desert, and starving for Ted and Beth than in this warehouse in Singapore. There was no love here. Not a man in the gang had seemed drawn to her. Most of them, she was fairly confident, were terrified of her.

"Cargo ship come tonight. Girders and rebar. Usual. Chi-nu usual too. We guard heroin, we skim heroin. You get caught. You die. You let someone else skim, I kill you myself."

Rin, a wisp of a young man, led the Chi-nu. Seventeen years old, he stood just over five feet tall and weighed about a hundred and twelve pounds. His entire upper body was black with tattoos of demons. He was the singularly most evil person Carole had ever known. When Rin spoke to her, the voices went completely silent, allowing her to focus on the innuendo in every comment. The focus may have saved her life over the months. The life Rutak Tural had given his last for. The life that had cost her father his. If she could eradicate this demon and his kind, their sacrifice would mean something. Carole tensed, focusing on the leader as he turned soulless eyes in her direction.

"Ka!" Rin had a grating high pitched voice, and he spat every word that crossed his lips. "You will tell me how you skim, so we can continue when you die!"

Remaining seated, legs crossed yoga style, Carole leaned forward in a reverent bow. Rin did not like that she was taller, and he verbally contemplated killing her for it at least weekly.

"I will tell you, Rin, before I die."

Rin laughed, a series of rat-a-tat-tat ha-ha's, cold like verbal gunfire. He liked the answer, though, because he motioned her permission to go. Rin had very little use for women, and leaving the warehouse Carole was careful not to turn her back on him.

CAROLE'S ABILITY TO skim kept her alive, her height the least of her troubles among the Chi-nu. Rin had allowed her in the gang for purely mercenary reasons. As the first female admitted into his inner circle, he seemed to search for a reason to get rid of her. He hated Americans, and though she spoke flawless Chinese and passed herself off as Australian, Rin said it was the same. Until she came along he'd recruited skimmers from the street children of prostitutes, and stole baby girls from a local Monastery where they were regularly abandoned. If the stolen babies were pretty, he sold them to nondescript ships that passed through port. If they weren't, he put them in his ugly doll collection in a warehouse. For the first time in her work as a NOC, Carole had gone rogue. Maybe it was simply because she was a mother, and maybe it was because of Rutak's charge to use his gift wisely, but one day she'd dropped into the Monastery and walked right into the Abbot's office and told him how the babies were being stolen. It put an end to Rin's baby trade and the loss of income pissed him off, but he never suspected her.

Carole moved lightly over worn concrete sidewalks, and lifted a wallet from a drunken sailor leaning into the face of a pretty prosti-tute. The voices raised a ruckus about dishonor and stealing, but Rin liked wallets and this was life on the street. Good or bad, she was an excellent thief. She wondered what her father would have said if he'd known about her work. Would he have judged her like Fastest did? Glancing up and down the street, she felt fairly confident that she wouldn't run into one of her kind in the squalor of these streets. Racing down an alley, she headed uptown.

After what had happened in the desert, the four months among the Chin-nu were bearable for one reason, Friday's skimming. Once Rin freed her, Carole had the entire day to prepare and meet the ship. Most skimmers spent the day devising new ways to hide the heroin. Carole spent it with Beth. Almost. Disguised as Ka, Carole dressed like an Asian punk rocker, her short hair dyed black and spiked. She wore black lipstick, shaved off her eyebrows, sported her gang's tattoo on her neck, and had seventeen piercings on her face alone. Uptown shopkeepers didn't allow her through their doors.

Sensing Beth in the distance, Carole jogged closer. Hiding behind a rack of brightly dyed dresses displayed on the sidewalk, she soaked in the touch of her daughter and felt grateful that the closet of the CIA she now belonged to had done this for her. Risking a peek around the dresses, she spotted them.

Beth's new nanny was a canny native of Singapore, and Friday was market day. The petite and pretty nanny wheeled Beth in a stroller while bartering for goods. Beth twisted in her stroller and bellowed, "Hi, Mom." Sometimes Carole regretted coercing her daughter into speaking only with her mouth, because everything Beth told her was loud and clear to anyone who understood English, which was the bulk of Singapore.

"I like chewy bugs!" Beth leaned forward in the stroller, using her hands to emphasize her words. Nanny parked the stroller next to a bin of vegetables, negotiating price with a shopkeeper. Beth shouted at Carole while pointing at a bowl just out of reach. "Daddy won't let me eat them, but nanny does!"

The nanny dropped a couple of the deep fried Asian delicacy into Beth's reaching hands and went back to arguing with a shopkeeper. Beth talked while she munched on the big brown bugs, her advanced vocabulary marred only by her chewing.

"Why are you hiding in black hairs? Where's the yellow ones? Does your face hurt like that, Mom?" Carole shrugged and shook her head in answer to the questions. She pretended to look over a bin of mangoes, shooting covert grins at Beth, who munched her treat and narrowed her eyes, studying her mother's piercings from the distance. Beth finished chewing and added, "Monkeys eat poop."

At the conclusion of the nanny's finagling, the petite woman passed Beth another bug, turning the stroller away. Carole dared follow, but kept well behind, coming only close enough to feel Beth's heart occasionally before dropping safely back to avoid the nanny's attention. Beth continued to bellow random tidbits in her direction, switching from English for the grand finale. "Nanny keeps the change!" The comment, spoken in clipped, neat Malay, made several heads swivel in the nanny's direction. The tiny woman with waist-length dark hair defended herself to passersby in rapid-fire Malaysian.

The random expositions of her daughter reunited Carole with her heart. The dishonor and evil of the Chi-nu, and the ache for her father, coupled with the chronic black dreams unleashed by the voices over her work, made the months move slowly. But for four heavenly hours every Friday, Carole followed Beth and her nanny, and Beth had yet to disappoint. At noon nanny took Beth to preschool and left her. Able to sense her, Beth shouted out a farewell to her mother. Today it was a profound, "Diqi eats crayons, Mom. I eat chalk." It was time to go then. The preschool didn't take well to a gang member lurking around, ogling the children.

Nanny took the market haul back to the apartment. It was a small space over a restaurant that specialized in duck soup. Ted met her there for lunch. Carole had only followed once and knew better than to do that again. Besides, it was time to change into her skimmer disguise.

UNLIKE RIN, LONGSHOREMEN had uses for females, and Carole ignored the voices and used what little advantages she had. Friday afternoons she showed up at the dock wearing indecent jean shorts, a tank top that would fit Beth, flip flops, and clutching a kid's Kuti-Kuti lunch box. The ship docked. Some people departed and new ones boarded. Carole's job was simply to stand watch over whatever crate she was pointed to that day. Her boarding process usually involved some grabbing and groping, but Carole moved fast, and when she elbowed some dock rat to his knees, the bulk of the men loved it. Skimming was the easy part of her assignment.

There were eyes on her the entire time, and she knew that there were bets placed on how long she'd last. She also knew that the men were planning on doing worse than slitting her throat and tossing her on the garbage scow once they caught her. She wondered if they thought she was deaf or didn't care if she heard them argue over who would get to do what.

Disguised as her alter ego, Ka, Carole sat on the crate and ate her lunch. Most of the crew bet on that lunch as the vehicle for skimming the heroin. It actually contained a box of brown rice, a cup of miso soup, and two pieces of fruit. After consuming her lunch, she painstakingly repacked the empty boxes, sat patiently on top of the crate, and at sundown she left. On her way off the ship they searched her empty boxes, and found nothing. Tonight the captain made her open her mouth and he shone a flashlight inside, then conducted his weekly pat down, taking his time and grinning throughout. Then he patted her on the head, told her she was a "Good Girl" and let her go, at which point Ka spit at his feet, made an obscene gesture and left.

RIN CAUGHT CAROLE as soon as she entered the warehouse through a top window. With the rest of the gang at his back he had her dragged down the catwalk. At a nod from him, they started to yank off her clothes. Carole beat two of them unconscious, then stood in front of Rin and yanked the tank top and shorts off, spinning briefly, completely naked, before pulling her clothes back on herself.

"Where you hide it, Funt?" Rin invented his own obscenities, and Carole felt they were certainly fouler than the run of the mill ones the gang used.

Carole glared at him. "Where I always keep it, in my lunchbox."

"No bugging way, Girlie! I watch you myself since you leave ship. It empty on ship, it empty now. Check her on inside!" he ordered the gang.

Carole yanked open the box to reveal the mountain of powder. "They touch me again and I throw it."

"Don't get bitchy. You do good work here, Ka, I let you live. We go to your home now."

Anxiety prickled up Carole's spine. Her home?

"We go Australia in morning. Except Milo. I kill Milo. He boring. Play with ugly dolls tonight. Last time." Rin walked off like a runway model.

CAROLE HID ON the roof of the duck soup shop until midnight, when the nanny climbed into the shower. Ted lay watching TV as she dropped through the open window and landed behind him. Ted's

215

reflexes were impressive. Ducking a lamp he threw at her, she hissed, "Ted! It's me!"

"Good God, Carole! What the hell are you doing? Why are you dressed like—are those piercings real?"

"Listen, I only have a few minutes. Do you have a pen and paper?" Ted kept an eye on her, and dug through a pile of stuff on the coffee table to produce them.

"You're on assignment here?"

Carole didn't bother to answer, he surely knew she couldn't. She wrote down two addresses, carefully disguising her handwriting. "I don't know if you can get this into the right hands or not. This one—" she pointed to the top address, "has several million dollars of heroin inside a chimney vent on the roof. This other one—God, Ted—I don't know what else to do, that pig is going to just leave those babies to die I know he is. There's dozens of little girls in there—"

"You know we have to stay out of human trafficking right now."

"They're Beth's age, Ted."

He took the paper, and a ripple of sorrow traveled through his heart so deeply Carole felt it.

"I'll figure out something—Carole? Why don't you stop? Tell them you want out. I know enough people in Washington. I think I could get you out safely now." He was serious, he looked worried.

"It's what I do, Ted."

"Don't you want to have a normal life? Keep your own daughter safe? I could take an assignment someplace quiet."

Carole ran her hand over her spiked black hair and grimaced, thinking of her father's merciless death in the desert. Rutak's message stirred in her memory, it always came to her in Fastest's voice: *Use his gift wisely.* She had the ability to stop people like Rin. Besides there was really only one way to keep her daughter safe, staying home with her wasn't it. Beth and Ted were far safer moving from city to city than they ever could be settled someplace quiet.

"What is a normal life? And there is no safe, it's an illusion, a game. I keep Beth safer doing this than I could at home. I need to go, Ted. A couple more months and I'll be back." She could sense the nanny wrapped in a towel and combing her long dark hair. "I'm going to duck in and see Beth. I'll go out her window. Make sure you lock it behind me?"

"I'm being transferred to New Zealand. Christchurch I think. Call the office to know for sure."

"I will." Carole paused beside him, wondering how the agency knew Rin's plans so quickly. A surge of anxiety welled up in her. Ted's transfer was because of her, what would he do when he realized that? Ted eyed her nervously. She had become the disguise. There would be no kiss, no hug. Nanny now played the part of wife.

"When I packed our stuff to move here your wedding ring was missing." His blue eyes glanced at her hands, at the ragged fingernails she'd colored in black magic marker, at the vulgar words scrawled on her hands. Unable to bear it and certain he could read Chinese; Carole hid her hands behind her back.

"I lost it," she whispered. Ted made a slight movement, his large body bent inwards just briefly. Disappointment and resignation were clear in his eyes when they met hers.

"Oh. It was my mother's."

"I'm sorry," she whispered, remembering her father snatching it out of the air in an effort to protect her. She wondered if he'd been buried with it still clenched his fist. She didn't think he'd like that. Fastest would have known that. Maybe he'd given the ring back to Karl. A ring meant nothing to Carole, but hurting Ted did. He wouldn't look at her, standing tall and staring blindly at the floor.

"I love you, Ted. I miss you." She darted into the nursery, and closed the door behind her, leaning against it. The part of her heart where Ted belonged felt so hollow it hurt. She had a feeling that nanny didn't sleep in Beth's room at night. It took great effort to shove that knowledge away. It was time to keep Beth safe.

SITTING UP IN her crib, Beth waited. "Hi, Mom."

In the shadowy nursery, a red neon light blinked into the room through the window, the word *Duck* intermittently visible across the wooden floor. Carole leaned over the round crib, her heart racing for Beth's. She saw her daughter grimace as their hearts touched.

"Mom, what's wrong?"

In the other room Nanny sat on the couch beside Ted now, and Carole knew he wasn't even trying to hide it. Why should he? He was married to a spy, a NOC, an assassin, a woman with unnatural talents who had forced herself into his life and showed no respect for things that were important to him. Surely he was aware that she could sense his movements from inside Beth's little room. Was he trying to hurt her? Or make her jealous? Or both?

"Mom?" Beth sounded scared, and Carole pulled the touch of her heart a safe distance away from Beth's. The voices screamed their protests, but she did it anyway, knowing it was the only way to truly keep Beth safe.

"*Life is love. It is what we are. It is all there is.*" The voices argued and it felt like a door slammed shut deep inside her heart. Forever.

Beth shuddered and her voice went high with fear, "Mom, what's wrong?"

Perfectly calm and in a phony voice as though she were speaking to Rin, Carole replied in a closed off, empty tone, "I don't think Daddy likes my earrings on my face."

"They're ugly, Mom."

"I know. I'll take them off next time I come home."

"Where'd you go?" Beth asked.

"Places."

Shaking her head Beth pointed at her mother's heart and then to her own. "You goed someplace away here, I miss you. Did Daddy make you sad?"

"Daddy makes me happy, he is the best. I love Daddy. I miss him so much." As pathetic as that was, Carole meant every word.

"Mom? Come back in here, now." Beth patted her chest.

Leaning over the crib, Carole smoothed Beth's pretty hair. "It's Daddy's turn, okay. He'll fill up the space. I take up too much room and he can hardly fit, so I'll stay outside a little to be fair to him. Is that okay? For Daddy?"

Beth frowned at her, soft brows pulling together and her pretty mouth turned down. "I love Daddy." She lay down in the crib, the big eyes blinking up at her mother, the scowl still on her face. Her lower lip quivered. "Make bread when you come home?"

"I will. Bye Baby."

"Bye, Mom."

Ignoring the protesting of the voices, Carole opened the window and slid out. It had to be like this. It wasn't even Ted's fault. The only way to make Beth believe she was a normal little girl, to be certain she didn't search for the touch of a heart, was to leave her heart alone. If being with their kind made them remember, she needed to stay as far from Beth as possible. Besides, Beth wouldn't remember what they'd had, she was too young. Carole's fingers slid onto the rough concrete of the duck soup shop, and she pulled herself upwards, climbing until she reached the roof. Once on top she curled into a ball, pressing her hands against her chest. There could be no one else in the world like Beth's Daddy. She would do this for her daughter. She would keep her family safe.

CHAPTER
NINETEEN

Alice Springs, Australia (Outback)—August 1991

"MR. WHITE, IT'S not going to work out, I'm sorry." Miss Kathy said it like she meant it, standing in front of the classroom door. Beth knew the teacher wasn't really sorry, but Miss Kathy liked Daddy. One time Miss Kathy saw Daddy parking his car and said he was a stud. Beth decided Miss Kathy was a bad girl and a liar. A liar because she said she didn't eat sweets, but she sneaked and ate snacks out of the school cupboard all the time. Beth glared at her while holding possessively to her Daddy's big hand.

"Are you throwing my daughter out of preschool?" Daddy didn't like Miss Kathy, even when she was pretend nice.

"Of course not!" But it was a lie, Beth could feel it. They were throwing her out. She held tighter to Daddy's hand. He wouldn't let anybody throw her. Miss Kathy said, "Take her to the base doctor. There're all types of reasons why children behave like this. She probably just needs something to calm her down a bit—and once she is feeling better, we'd love to have her back."

"Ha!" Beth interrupted, pointing a finger at her teacher. "That's not true! Daddy? That's not true!"

Miss Kathy gave her *the look*. She didn't say, "You're trying my patience today, Beth" like she did when Daddy wasn't there. She was thinking it though. Beth just knew it. Miss Kathy handed Daddy her folder with all her art projects inside and said, "She's a sweet girl, Mr. White, but we have thirty preschoolers and she disrupts the entire class."

Beth sniffed. "You're trying my patience today, Miss Kathy."

Daddy snorted beside her and squeezed her hand. He was trying not to laugh.

"See what I mean, Mr. White? Three-year-olds don't talk like that."

"Ha!" Beth bounced on her toes, thrilled. "Yes they do! I'm three and I do!"

Daddy picked her up, and told Miss Kathy "Ga 'day." He hid his face from the teacher while they went to the parking lot, so Miss Kathy wouldn't see him laughing. Beth loved when Daddy laughed. He laughed all the time. She loved Daddy.

MOM DIDN'T THINK it was funny. Mom didn't think anything was funny.

"Carole, she's just smarter than the average bear."

"I think I might be," Beth piped up and considered that. Bears weren't very smart, were they? She'd have to think about that. Maybe there were books about how smart bears were.

Mom put a bowl of bean soup in front of her and a big piece of hot bread and butter. It was Beth's favorite food ever. Mom was no fun, but she cooked best. Beth glanced at Daddy's plate and shivered. Daddy ate really yucky food.

"You have work, Ted, and so do I. We'll have to find a new place. I can look tomorrow. I think the Catholic school might consider taking her early."

"They won't, I asked. I could get her a nanny."

Mom went very still and Beth watched her. Mom was so pretty, even though she didn't like to smile. She didn't like nannies either.

Daddy did. When Daddy didn't like stuff he said it out loud. When Mom didn't like stuff, she stopped moving.

"It's the third preschool, Carole. It was funny, but maybe I should have the base doctor examine her."

"She's not taking pills, Ted. I don't care what the doctors say. Nothing. Ted? You wouldn't give her pills and not tell me, would you?"

Beth watched her father while chewing on her slice of warm, buttery bread. He would. He broke Mom's rules all the time. She wondered if she'd like pills as much as ice-cream.

"Do you want to come to the pediatrician's with us?" Daddy asked Mom. Beth took a deep breath, pleased. Daddy almost lied. She shivered slightly. It hurt her when people lied; it felt like she couldn't breathe. She didn't let them lie. That is why Miss Kathy didn't like her.

"IT'S CALLED TOURETTE'S Syndrome," the doctor said.

"No it's not!" Beth bellowed. Mom put a hand on her shoulder. That was Mom's way of telling her to shut up. Beth listened. Everyone listened to Mom if they knew what's good for them.

The doctor looked at her like he was waiting for her to lie, and wrote something in his folder. "It's a neurological problem where the patient can't control random physical impulses. There's therapy and medication—"

"You're nuts," Daddy interrupted. Mom almost laughed and Beth tossed back her head, looking up at her and hoping to see it. She'd felt it, bubbling near her heart before Mom caught herself and stopped it. Mom kept her heart hidden and quiet, not like Daddy's. Right now Daddy's heart was mad. He picked Beth up and held her against his shoulder. She could feel his heart close to hers, trumpeting and pounding, like the horns soldiers played to make you wake up and the sound Mom's shoes made when she raced out of the house because Daddy liked nannies. Beth sighed and put her cheek on his shoulder, patting him. She liked nannies too. Daddy opened the door and left.

Mom followed. Beth could see the doctor shaking his head back and forth behind them.

"OUR DAUGHTER DOES not have a neurological problem. She just speaks her mind," Daddy groused. When he was mad he drove too fast. Beth loved it. They bounded down the road through the bush and the Jeep bounced really hard. Mom's heart was tight and small because she didn't like fast. Mom didn't like cars, though she never said it. Beth could feel it. Mom turned around to check her seatbelt and car seat and told her to hold tight.

Mom said, "I agree with you, Ted. The problem is not everyone wants to hear what is on Beth's mind."

"Because she's honest? I admit it's disconcerting. She points out my fibs too, so I know how it feels to be on the wrong end of it. Mrs. Glick asked how she looked in her dress, I said really nice—Beth just shouted, "Daddy! You don't like it! Why'd you say that?" And I saw General Sands on the golf course Tuesday. He said I was probably getting transferred stateside by New Year's. Beth started hollering why did he always say that when he was making us stay right here. I got away fast as I could." Daddy chuckled and Beth swung her legs happily in the little backseat. She listened closely when her parents talked, to make sure that they said only true stuff. They needed her help. Everybody did.

CHAPTER
TWENTY

Territory of Hong Kong—September 1994

CAROLE'S ASSIGNMENT HAD taken seven months to complete, and she needed to see Beth and Ted. She raced up seventeen flights of stairs, wondering if Ted had taken an apartment in the high-rise as punishment for her long absence, and wishing he hadn't refused his assignment in Buenos Aires. She hadn't had a peek at kindergarten-aged Beth the entire time. The building seemed as modern as one could be, all glass and mirrors and whisper-quiet high speed elevators. Carole thought poor Beth could not sleep well in this tribute to technology. Carole had to knock on apartment 17847 for long minutes, stubbornly refusing to push the doorbell.

At least she could sense only Ted and Beth inside. Beth was tucked in bed already and Carole waited impatiently. Ted opened the door and the expression on his face told her she had come home at a bad time. He looked good, as always, his hair shorter than usual but very sophisticated and slick-looking, clad in a nice tuxedo. *He has a date,* flitted through Carole's mind, her husband had a date. God, it hurt just as much every single time. Surely she should be used to it after five years of Ted's indiscretions.

"Oh, you're going out? It's okay. I need a shower and time with Beth anyway."

Ted opened the door all the way, inviting her in. "She's sound asleep. It's good to see you. You look fabulous, Carole."

The comment surprised her. Surely she looked exactly the same, except for the latest patch of swollen red skin where another tattoo had been removed by laser. This time it had been on her shoulder, much less noticeable than the ones on her neck and face had been. Yet time seemed kind, and she healed remarkably well, certainly another attribute of her kind. Or maybe on the other side her father was talking to ilu for her.

Her latest mission had been a failure. She hadn't been able to stop the bombing. Eighty-five people had been killed but she had lived, sustaining fractured ribs, a broken hand, and a severe leg break. Last night on the ship she'd dreamed of her father. He said he'd pray for her, and her broken and injured bones had healed impossibly fast, a fact she had tried to hide from the doctors. She stepped painlessly into the apartment now and took a look around.

The apartment looked clean, not in that dusted and neat way so much, but clean and comfortable as the voices demanded. That fact surprised her. The floor was polished bamboo, and the walls were woven grasses. Carole spun in a circle, taking everything in.

"It's nice!" She wished she'd thought to talk to her father in her dream and ask if he'd ever spoken to ilu about Ted. She turned her scrutiny almost worriedly on her husband, reminding herself that it had only been a dream, and that she always healed too fast.

Handsome as ever, Ted's smile welcomed her. "It is nice, isn't it? I was hoping you'd come before we got reassigned. Beth takes the elevator without a word of complaint. They're glass, and you can see the city outside. I think bringing nature indoors is a brilliant concept."

"*Artifice. Illusion. Trickery.*" Of course the voices tried to spoil it. Ted surprised her when he stepped forward, wrapped his arms around her and hugged her.

"I thought something happened to you."

It had, but she'd survived it, so it didn't matter now. He smelled so good. She leaned against his broad chest, wallowing in the moment. Beth slept nearby—her heart just out of reach—the way

Carole always kept it now. It still felt like home, the warmth of it like a nearby hearth.

Ted rested his cheek against the top of her head. "Come with me? Tonight? It's just a hideous black-tie event for some Washington contacts, but, Carole, I hate the idea of going anywhere when I haven't seen you in so long. I'd cancel if I could, but I don't dare."

The greeting made her tingle right to her fingers and toes. "I don't have whatever women wear to black tie events." For once she wished she did. All she owned were cotton slacks and T-shirts.

"You have a dress!" Ted snapped his fingers, "and shoes too! Beth got them for you for Christmas. Of course she took the liberty of unwrapping them for you too, but they were beautifully wrapped until Christmas Eve."

Ted grabbed her hand and tugged her into an enormous master suite. Carole looked around at the wall of glass overlooking the lights of Hong Kong. Jungle plants were artfully arranged from floor to ceiling and she looked at Ted in surprise.

"I got a promotion, not to this level of posh, but one of the delegates went stateside and offered me this place, so I took it. Good decision too, otherwise we'd have been stuck in that mess in Buenos Aires. I'm getting things done here, and there's a nice school down the street. Beth is—hanging on there."

"Not any better?" Beth's tongue had caused more than embarrassment the past few years.

"Tomorrow. Tonight it's just us." Carole's spirits soared. Ted went to a closet hidden in the living bamboo wall, and walked inside. A moment later he trotted out holding a tiny embroidered dress, very traditional Japanese, but her eyes went to the heels that dangled from his long fingers.

"You bought those for me?"

"Beth chose them, so you have to love them."

Ted's humor was infectious and she laughed at him. "But can I walk in them?"

"You can hold onto my arm."

Carole took the clothes and headed into the enormous bathroom.

IT USUALLY TOOK Carole less than five minutes to bathe and dress for the day. She slipped inside the glass enclosed shower and took her time, shampoo and conditioner. She nabbed Ted's razor and shaved, something she rarely did. She brushed her teeth with Ted's toothbrush, and ran some of his hair oil through her cropped mess, slicking it back with his comb. After slipping the little dress over her head and strapping on the heels, it had taken her almost fifteen minutes. Made of good silk, the dress felt okay against her skin, but the style of the dress and that it was a dress made her uncomfortable. It was the first dress she'd owned since she'd been in the orphanage in New Mexico. She paused in front of the mirror. The dress was too tight, but she liked the shade of blue, it matched Ted's eyes. Tiny flowers and birds were embroidered over it in brilliant colors. The shoes were the exact same shade of red as the red flowers. As young as she was, Beth had an eye for little things.

Carole stepped into the bedroom where Ted waited, his mouth dropped open. "Carole, you are stunning. There ought to be a law that you have to dress up, at least now and then. Wait!" He darted over to the double dresser and fished around. "Beth filled your stocking with make-up." He glanced at her expression and put the lipstick down with a grin. "Okay, baby steps." Carole laughed and something made her take his hand. The doorbell rang. She could sense a young female standing in the hall and her heart sank a bit. Was this the date? She tried to let go of his hand, but he threaded his fingers through hers.

"That would be the babysitter, Kimmy Lee's only twelve, but her mother is in the apartment next door. Come on, our car will be waiting downstairs."

THE CAR TURNED out to be a limousine, and it took them into the heart of Hong Kong on a Saturday night, leaving them at a chic hotel. Ted greeted every person as though they were old friends, from the doorman to the United States Secretary of State, who stood with his wife. He spoke to the Japanese Prime Minister in the man's native language. The men all greeted Carole with polite interest, bowed graciously, kissed her hand or shook it, and turned their conversation to Ted. Most of the topics involved either politics or sports, but Carole felt fairly certain that most of the conversations had nothing to do with what was said. There was subterfuge in every idle comment, and Ted appeared quite good at this type of cloak and dagger politics. He remembered where everyone lived, their families, what they liked to drink and what sports teams they followed. Ted's comments and questions seemed to soothe tension or initiate conversation. He moved from group to group, welcomed with fresh enthusiasm by each new assembly, and disappointed regret following each departure. Carole had never been so bored in all of her life.

Standing at Ted's elbow, with an untouched flute of champagne in her hand, she occupied her mind with escape plans, recognizing concealed weapons and shooting covert looks of hostility towards men who stared openly and admiringly at her. At first she thought there was something wrong with her dress, like a gaping seam exposing her lack of under-things. Once she ruled that out, she thought her clothes were inappropriate, considering most of the women wore long sweeping gowns, artful make-up and had hair like a country western singer. Then she noted the winks, raised eyebrows, and lascivious interest in eyes raking repeatedly up her legs and over the too-tight dress. Because she stood next to Ted, not one of the men dared express open interest, and Carole soon turned her attention back to escape routes.

FOR DINNER TED and Carole were seated at a round table with five other couples. The women in the group were plainly curious about her.

"I'd heard a rumor that Ted was married!" At first Carole stared blankly at the woman, then Ted started to chuckle and she realized it was meant to be a joke.

"She travels so much. When she is home we don't like to share her." Ted squeezed her shoulder.

"What is it you do, dear?" An elderly woman with probing bug eyes seemed very interested in the answer. Ted stiffened at her side.

Carole lied. "I'm an interpreter for the U.N." The voices protested her lie. They were exceedingly hard to please. Apparently the only acceptable lies were the ones they suggested, and they suggested plenty of them. She ignored them. The CIA had provided her cover from the first. It was just rare that she had to use it. Carole simply didn't socialize.

Ted recouped, apparently remembering the cover story himself, but sticking with facts. "Carole's a whiz with languages."

A redhead on the far side of Ted leaned forward, her eyes unfriendly. "That's probably where Beth gets it from then? That child is amazing."

"You know Beth?" Carole asked.

"I was her nanny for a while when Ted first moved to Hong Kong." Carole tensed. She studied the attractive redhead. Tiny, like many of the nannies Ted chose, she also had an impressive expanse of shiny hair—another trait Ted seemed to have a penchant for. Her date was an older man. Ted hurried to introduce them.

"Carole, this is Alexa. She did nanny for Beth until she started school. Alexa's date is with the Chinese Embassy here in Hong Kong." The gentleman was so old he just stared blankly into the distance, his head nodding up and down.

"Yes," Alexa gave Ted a dirty look. "Kim was kind enough to let me tag along when my date fell through."

Carole reached for her glass of water and took a sip. So Alexa was the date, but at least Ted wasn't going with married women. It wasn't exactly a silver lining, but the small consolation was all she had. She felt Ted's hand on her thigh beneath the table and he squeezed, explaining, "And that sardonic remark was meant for me as the rest of the table knows. Alexa has been kind enough to accompany me to functions in your absence."

Carole met his eyes in surprise. What was he telling her? He'd never once explained any woman to her before. She smiled at him, and then turned the smile towards Alexa. The woman didn't return the gesture.

CAROLE WIGGLED THE dress up and sat on the toilet quickly. Several glasses of water and lemon slices were a poor substitute for food, and her growling stomach wasn't the only side-effect. The food was artful and sparse, and beyond a few wax beans and a tomato salad there was nothing she could dare to eat. This entire night she felt very out of her element. It was low-grade torture. Sitting in the peaceful seclusion of the ladies room, she tried to figure out the automatic toilet paper dispenser.

"So that is the elusive Mrs. Ted White?" A woman's snarky voice echoed through the ladies room, and Carole placed it as belonging to the bug-eyed woman. "That dress is really something. Martin drooled in his plate all evening."

"Guess so." Alexa sounded bored.

"I thought he was on the verge of divorce—or maybe it was that they're Catholic, and just staying together because they don't believe in divorce. I heard something like that before. That dress didn't look very Catholic. So much for Washington rumors."

"He married her because she got knocked up. He doesn't love her." Alexa's voice sounded hateful. But those last words never lost their power over Carole. She leaned forward and put her head in her hands.

"You keep telling yourself that, Alexa. He sure looked happy, and that woman is stunning."

"I've been *helping* Ted for seven months. I think I know how happy he is."

"I hope you have more respect for yourself than to let a married man use you."

"Like you wouldn't let Ted White use you."

The snarky woman laughed. "Touché, as much and often as he wanted to, but now you're out in the cold, Wifey is back and you're with old Kim Fong, or is it Fong Kim?"

"We'll see."

"Don't kid yourself, Alexa. Ted White's philandering is infamous, but he's devoted to that kid of his, and no man alive would walk out on a woman like that."

"Oh, Ted's just grown a conscience because the kid asked some nosy questions. She came home early one day just when things were getting interesting and asked if we were having a sleepover."

"Hah, were you?"

"I don't think there would have been any sleeping involved!" Alexa laughed at her own joke. "Anyway it doesn't matter what his wife looks like because sooner or later she'll head off to wherever the U.N. is, and that man has needs."

"Oh, really? Needs? I wouldn't know about those firsthand. Martin is happy with the bi-annual dash, as I like to call it. Did you know Ted was engaged to one of the Kennedy's once? It was a match made in heaven for Washington. Word was he was going to go into politics like his father, and she had the background. Huh, it couldn't have been a Kennedy it had to have been a Republican. Maybe it was an Eisenhower cousin, I forget. It was a while ago."

"What happened?" It sounded like this was news to Alexa too.

"It was all very tragic—maybe that's why I was thinking Kennedy. It might have been a Vanderbilt, I can't remember. Anyway the wedding was on the Cape in June, huge affair, everyone was invited and they went. Except Martin and me, we were in Europe that summer. So anyway, on the eve of their wedding, his fiancée drove into Hyannis Port to pick up her wedding dress with Ted's mother. Driving back they were in a horrible wreck and they both died at the scene—she might have been one of the Hemingway's, I can't remember, but her first name was Beth. I remember that, because it was Ted's mother's name too."

"God. Are you sure they both died, Joyce?"

"That's not the best part. Turns out the fiancé had had a drunken bachelorette party and a fling with an old flame, days before, and Ted found out about it at the funeral!"

Alexa snorted. "That sounds like typical Washington exaggeration, Joyce."

"His father told him. That man was such a lush, always drunk. Anyway, the thing is the rumor was that the old flame was Ted's *dad*, Mr. Filthy-Rich Theodore White Senior of White Enterprises," Joyce finished with a flourish.

Carole flushed the toilet, stood, yanked her dress down and slammed the stall door open so hard it echoed through the sparse modern bathroom. Holding Joyce's gaze in the mirror she stalked to the sink, and calmly washed her hands. Both women suddenly had nothing to say. Joyce looked delightfully horrified, her bug eyes darting from Carole to Alexa a bit hopefully. Alexa defiantly held her ground, but when Carole moved close to nab a paper towel off the marble sink the woman flinched away.

Conversationally Carole told Alexa, "The U.N. is in New York—City." She painstakingly dried her hands while Alexa's mouth opened, and then wisely closed again. Tossing the crumpled towel into the trash, Carole stopped in front of the mirror to smooth her dress and her already smooth hair. She gracefully crossed the shining granite floor, her heels clicking with each step. Placing one hand on the door, she paused to look back. "By the way, Alexa? Joyce? My father was very Catholic." She marched out.

IT HAD BEEN ages since Ted had touched Carole like he meant it, but tonight it felt like he did. They usually went through the motions of being married almost every night whenever she was at home, but Ted kept his enthusiasm with his heart, far from Carole. A sick needy part of her, one that she spent a lot of time hating, delighted in his eagerness now. Wrapped around him, fingers entwined in that glorious hair, Carole wondered how he could bear to be with anyone else. They could have everything, if only he'd reach out and take it. If only he'd let her in. Pressing her bare chest to his, heart to heart, she groaned and bit his shoulder.

Ted didn't pull away this time, but he did put his weight onto his hands, creating as much distance between their hearts as he could without stopping. Carole knew to leave his heart alone or he would stop. The touch of it drew her now, despite all his dishonor and cheating. At this moment all that seemed far away. Like a bee to a flower under the hot sun, she simply needed. Like a breath of air, water in the desert, the desire for his heart felt primal and mandatory—and rejected. Grimacing, she forced her heart to stop reaching, and moved it away from the lure of Ted's. It hurt, and the voices chimed in their protests, completely ruining the lovemaking for her.

"Love is your purpose. You must—"

Carole's mind drifted, scanning into the kitchen in search of good food. A bowl of cooked rice and a dish of raw vegetables caught her attention, and she simply waited for Ted to finish so she could find something to supplement her meager meal from the dinner party.

Fifteen minutes later, wrapped in Ted's dress shirt, Carole sat on a wooden kitchen chair with chopsticks in hand shoveling cold rice and vegetables into her mouth. Ted wandered in wearing pajama bottoms, looking pleased and tousled. He kissed the top of her head on his way to the coffee maker. Carole was glad he'd enjoyed it and wished she could have too.

"Thanks for tonight. There's so much going on," he said.

For a moment she stopped eating, thinking he meant between them.

"Hong Kong passing from Colonial rule is a diplomatic quagmire. I'm lucky to be here right now."

Carole resumed her meal.

"I figured out why they keep sticking me in the middle of nowhere." In the cool kitchen light Ted's blue eyes glinted darkly and a chill tickled its way up Carole's back. She set the chopsticks down and waited while Ted set the coffee pot to working. He leaned against the granite countertop and eyed her.

"It's Beth. She said some very politically incorrect things about the Chinese in school this past week. I lied and told them she had that Tourette Syndrome thing. They'd have thrown her out if I hadn't."

Carole hadn't realized she'd been holding her breath. She inhaled deeply. He didn't know the real reason. *Thank goodness!* Ted would be furious if he found out her work was meddling in his career. It was the only way to keep them safe. Safe meant close to her. Safe also meant cities where her kind wouldn't be.

"*You're allowing Beth to take the blame!*" the voices bellowed, shaming her. She shook it off.

"Do you punish her when she talks like that?" Carole stirred her rice. "Don't coddle her about it, Ted! You saw how dangerous her mouth could be in Somalia."

Avoiding her gaze Ted yanked out the coffee pot before it was ready. For a moment the only sound was scorching coffee as he quickly poured some into his cup and jammed the carafe back on the machine. He pulled out a chair, settling next to Carole.

"I think she's stopped having nightmares about that, but I know she remembers. She's been begging me to let her sponsor a kid with one of those ministries that feeds them."

"Food won't give that boy his hand back."

"Carole, don't be hard-hearted about it. Beth was four years old and that boy *was* stealing."

"He was starving! Are you justifying Beth's mouth?"

Ted sat his coffee cup on the table. "No! I'm saying she didn't mean to cause the boy harm. She didn't realize what would happen! You weren't there! Don't judge!"

Oh yes I was, Carole thought. But of course she couldn't say that because Ted had no idea his plane had touched down in Mogadishu just so she could interfere in his plan to spend six months in the Alps. She couldn't know for sure where her kind lived, but she had a bad feeling there'd be some of them in the Alps.

"Negative reinforcement can be very inspiring," she said.

"I just think it would be better to keep her out of Africa for now."

Carole couldn't argue with that, but she had a feeling that's where she—and therefore they— would be headed next.

"Is that where they're sending you?" she asked innocently, shoveling the last of her rice into her mouth while the voices called her a liar.

"I can probably get a few months delay until you go back to work, but I have a feeling that's what they're thinking."

"Do you have a choice?"

"They'll pretend to listen to me, but the fact is I'm not taking Beth into the middle of any civil wars. I'll go civilian first."

Uh-oh. "So her mouth has gotten worse?"

"Yeah." Ted put a big hand over hers, folded his fingers through it and drew it to his lips for a gentle kiss. He sighed. "I'm so glad you're home."

"MOMMY'S HOME!" TED'S enthusiastic shout echoed through the apartment wall. Carole sensed Beth burrow deeper under her blankets. Apparently their morning girl no longer had to be up before dawn. Staring up at real cherry blossoms dangling over the bed like a canopy, Carole stretched. She wouldn't mind sleeping longer either. Ted hadn't been much interested in sleep last night. She grinned, scanning through the compact apartment. Ted playfully tugged at Beth's blankets while their daughter stubbornly yanked them back up. Ted dug beneath them and teasingly yanked on Beth's skinny legs, slowly sliding her out from the bottom of the bed.

"Mommy's home, sleepy bones! Get up!"

"Oh, man!" Beth groused.

"Old man? Did you call me an old man?"

"You know what I said, Daddy," came Beth's pragmatic answer. "Why do you pretend like you don't understand me? You always do that!"

"It's more fun," came Ted's honest reply.

"Oh, man!" Beth said again, adding, "The fun's over if mommy is home!"

Carole's heart sank a bit. *It's true. I'm definitely not any fun.*

"Mommy cooks."

Beth scrambled to sit up and bellowed, "Mommy cooks good!"

"That's fun," Ted tried.

"It's good, not fun. Ice-cream's fun though, but Mommy won't let us eat it. Can we get it after she leaves?"

"We can get ice-cream with Mommy."

"No we can't!" Beth argued knowledgably, and Carole smiled again. *That's true too!*

"Well, we can take her to do something else that's fun. We'll take her skating!"

"She won't like the music. She won't smile!" Beth warned, and Carole sensed her daughter bounce to her feet and run to her dresser, tugging a top and leggings from a neat drawer.

Ted crossed behind her and helped pull her nightgown off over her head. "Yes, she will so smile. Mommy smiles all the time!"

Beth rounded on him as though he'd hurt her. "Don't LIE!" Hands protectively over her chest she screeched at her father, "Don't you lie, Daddy! Mommy does not smile all the time! Mommy never smiles!"

Carole sat up in her bed, sensing Beth's heart pounding rapidly in her small body. *It hurts her! Lies hurt her!*

Ted calmly dug through Beth's dresser drawers and handed her fresh underpants. "Exaggerating is not lying, Beth. Your mother smiles sometimes. I've seen her."

"It is so lying, Daddy!" Beth's voice came out high-pitched and teary. "Don't zaj-zaj—exajerade-exaggerate on me."

Ted's sigh had to be noticeable to even Beth, because she let that argument go and wiggled into her silky top. "When did you see Mommy smile?"

Ted chuckled lightly, and though she couldn't see his face with her scan she had a feeling he was blushing. Carole laughed out loud, knowing when Ted saw her smiles.

Beth's voice sounded in a loud whisper. "Uh-oh! She can hear us!"

"THEY'RE CALLED ROLLERBLADES," Ted told Carole.

"In-line skating," Beth corrected, zipping in neat little circles between her parents while Carole knelt, strapping a pair of the ugly wheeled boots on.

Beth had been right, the music was horrendous. Carole knew Beth understood every word of the Japanese lyrics too, and so did Ted. She shot a disapproving look up at him.

"Told ya," Beth caught it and sagely complained to her father.

"Hey, Miss Know-it-all, if you want someone to skate with you'd better stop being so fussy. I'm not even trying to squeeze my big feet into those little skates ever again."

"Last time you did!" Beth argued.

"I had blisters for weeks!"

"You did not!" Beth stopped moving to scream at her father, drawing many polite Japanese looks towards the loud American kid.

"Beth White," Carole warned. Guiltily Beth refused to meet her eyes, and went back to weaving around them, her skates making a skit-skit sound.

"I had blisters," Ted amended.

"You fell," Beth corrected.

"Almost broke my—"

"LIAR!" Beth bellowed the scream with such enthusiasm she went pink in the face. The bulk of the people skating nearby moved away, giving them wide berth even though they weren't even on the rink yet, apparently seeing a need to prepare for it.

Carole rose easily to stand on her skates. She scooped Beth up under her arms, lifting her until her daughter was nose to nose with her and looking fearfully into her eyes, her thin body dangling limply below Carole's strong hands.

"You will not speak another word until I'm done skating and we leave this rink. Do you understand me?"

Beth's clear eyes were wide. She nodded.

"And if I hear you sass your father again, I'll paddle you so hard you won't be able to sit for a week. Am I exaggerating, Beth?"

Tears flooded Beth's eyes, and her lips quivered. She bravely shook her head.

"Carole!" Ted whispered her name in protest. Ted didn't believe in spanking children. Carole didn't believe it should ever be necessary more than once.

DESPITE THE UNCOMFORTABLE height of the skyscraper apartment, Carole liked the open space. If she kept her scan to herself, she could forget they weren't in some sunny flat in a quieter city. The plants were a comforting touch, and the smell of her baking made it feel like home. Beth sat on a high stool next to the granite countertop and worked on writing out and adding up a long list of products and prices. It seemed a bit complex for a kindergartener, and she gnawed her thumbnail, focusing.

The months had flown. Ted had received a temporary transfer to South Africa and had begun making arrangements for the move. He seemed comfortable with taking Beth there. Carole expected to get her phone call to leave soon. Things were good between them. Last night he'd allowed her to rest against his bare chest and hadn't pushed her away. She'd lain there until she'd sensed his heart pounding a worrisome beat beneath hers, and realized he was terrified. *If I had more time—maybe—maybe we could figure it out!*

"Do they harvest silk in Africa, Mom?" Beth glanced up from her papers, gaze sliding blindly over the pile of bell peppers Carole expertly rinsed and sliced.

"Prob—actually, I don't know for sure." Carole admitted and Beth went back to her list. Both Ted and Carole had decided to answer

Beth's questions only if they were absolutely certain their answers were verifiably correct. She seemed calmer. Maybe being thrown out of kindergarten had been for the best as Ted purported at the time.

Head bent over her peppers Carole peeped briefly at her daughter. Beth had exposed entirely too much information about her teacher's political leanings on crowded parent night. A lot of people in Hong Kong probably felt like Ms. Tanaka had about China and America. Maybe a lot of people in the Kowloon district also thought that headmaster Sato was a limp dick. But nobody wanted to hear a child expose her kindergarten teacher's real thoughts on all three subjects.

After the suspension Carole had resisted the oft threatened paddling to ask Beth if she knew what a limp dick was, to which her daughter had replied, "An ineffectual man." Ted said spanking to punish the truth was wrong. Carole still felt in two minds about it, but had resisted because the voices encouraged it.

Beth scratched her head with the back end of her pencil for a moment, and then furiously erased some numbers.

"What are you working on?" Carole asked.

"Estimating the gross national product of China for the next twenty years. Can I have a calculator for Christmas?"

Carole bit back a laugh. Beth would be six soon. "No you can't, but if you can manage not to get thrown out of school in South Africa, maybe they'll let you use one there."

"It is going to be higher than people realize, I think. I have trouble doing really big numbers without a calculator."

"Did you use a calculator in kindergarten?"

"No. Kimmy Lee's Mom lets me use hers when I go to their apartment."

Carole turned to open the oven door and pulled out a loaf of bread. Shoving the door shut with her foot, she set it on the cutting board and patted the glass encased recipe her father had written so long ago. Ted had had it laminated and sealed in glass for her a couple Christmas's ago. Turning back to her peppers she tried to keep the conversation going with Beth.

"Does Kimmy babysit you over there sometimes?"

"Yep. When Dad goes out, she comes here. When he wants his back rubbed, we go there."

"Oh." Carole faltered chopping a red pepper, nearly catching her own finger. Beth noticed, her clear eyes watching from across the countertop.

"Are you okay, Mom?"

Keep it honest. "Yeah. I didn't know Mrs. Cho was a masseuse."

"Miss Cho. She only does it for Dad."

Carole froze.

Beth blinked at her. "Is that okay?"

Never let it hurt Beth. Carole forced her mouth to supply an honest answer. "It's a little too nice."

Beth's head tilted slightly, as though trying to decipher her words. "Dad likes it."

Carole nabbed a small plate from an overhead cupboard. "Would you like a slice of bread while it's hot?"

Beth's sucked in her breath with an enthusiastic sound. "May I have butter on it, Mom, please?"

Carole turned her back to get it, hiding her face. She should know better than to spy on Ted, she regretted it every single time, but unable to control her scan she allowed it to drift through apartment walls, searching for Ted. He was there. With Kimmy Lee's mom. Hot tears scorched her eyes. Carole purposely pressed her hand right on the hot glass bread pan for several seconds. The gasp of pain that escaped her had nothing to do with her burning hand.

"Mom! Are you okay?"

Carole turned back with the bread in her good hand and slid it quickly across the counter. "I burned my hand!" Ignoring Beth's sounds of sympathy, she hurried through the apartment to the bathroom where she could cry in private.

CHAPTER TWENTY-ONE

Shanghai—March 1999

"DADDY, CAN I drive?" Beth knew he'd say no, she was only ten and a half, but she liked to make her father laugh. Stuck in gridlock during rush hour, she could sense tension in his heart.

"Do you think we could get there faster," Dad patted her knee, "if you drove? Roll up your window, sweetheart, rough neighborhood."

"It's too hot!" she protested.

"Oh, we'll get double scoops of ice-cream to cool down. We'll be there soon."

"How soon?" Beth rolled the window up. Sweat trickled down the back of her dress.

"Mmm, by next weekend I'd bet."

That made her laugh and it might be true in this mess. It was part of the fun though. They hopped in the car and just drove until they found whatever Beth felt like searching for. Dad called them quests. Tonight they were questing for halo-halo ice-cream. It was her favorite, and his. Maybe the only food they both liked, and that made it even more special.

"I think I'm going to need a bowl, a big one." Beth was hungry. "You can have my Jell-O if I can have your cherries *and* nuts." She negotiated the exchange with her Dad while thinking about her Mom's cooking: fresh bread, rich soups, and stews. Her stomach growled. She should learn to cook for herself, the problem was she'd rather go hungry than take the time to do it. Most every day when Mom was away, she simply ate rice and vegetables.

"I should probably stick to just the two scoops," Dad teased. "I'm getting fat."

Beth smiled at her big, strong father, and then a street vendor caught her eye. "Ooo, Daddy, can we stop there? Look at that fabric. You should have a tie made from that, it matches your eyes. Please, can we?"

"Not in this neighborhood."

Traffic started to move, and Dad accelerated. The little car shot forward. Beth tugged her notebook out of her schoolbag and penciled in the location and description of the fabric. She had four notebooks listing random treasure she'd spotted everywhere they'd lived. They had yet to have purchased a single thing. She didn't care, she just liked knowing where the best honey was, or the best silk—and she'd bet that bit of cloth she'd just glimpsed was perfect. It wouldn't make her skin crawl to touch it.

"Whoa!" Dad's grip tightened on the steering wheel, and the little car lurched, escaping a big black sedan swerving too close. "Hold on!" To avoid an accident he headed towards the sidewalk and one little tire banged against the curb, pushing the vehicle back into their lane. The car jerked, and began to bump up and down. "Darn!"

"Did we hit that car?" Beth was certain they hadn't, but something was wrong.

"No, flat tire. Looks like our quest just turned into an adventure."

Beth clapped her hands, smiling. "Can we look at that fabric?"

"We'll see—first we'd better look for a new tire. I don't think this tin can called a car has a spare."

Dad pulled close to the curb and put his flashers on. People shouted behind them and made gestures out their windows. "Look at that, Bethy, they love Americans here."

She pushed the lightweight door open and scrambled out. Traffic never slowed, and it was impossible to open the driver's door. It took Daddy several minutes to pry himself from behind the wheel of the tiny car, and wiggle across the passenger seat. Beth slapped both hands over her mouth to keep from laughing as he crawled out the passenger door onto the sidewalk, hands first.

"Want to see me do that again?" Daddy teased. Beth dropped her hands and laughed out loud.

"Maybe you'd better have just one scoop," she said.

"Oh you!" He rumpled her hair. "I'm still fit and trim, for a General."

Beth put her arm around him and leaned against her big strong dad. He was perfect.

"Not the best neighborhood to get a flat in," a man commented in a friendly voice, speaking perfect English.

Ted's arm tightened around Beth slightly. "Oh, things happen for a reason. Maybe you have the best halo-halo ice-cream in Shanghai here?"

The man had very interesting eyes, lit up and happy. Beth liked him. He looked like the kind of man who didn't lie. "I'm afraid not, but we have other things here just as wonderful."

"A spare tire for my Big Wheel?" Daddy always joked that his car was a toy. Beth didn't know what a Big Wheel really was, but he said it all the time and she laughed because that's what you did when your Dad told a bad joke.

"As far as that goes, I have a telephone you can use. It's going to cost you though."

Daddy rolled his eyes. "But of course, it is Shanghai."

"Not money. I just want to talk to you about being the kind of man your family needs. I want to talk to you about love and truth."

Beth looked at the neon sign in the dirty store window. It blinked *Jesus* in green. Daddy frowned when he saw it, and glanced up and down the street. "Is that a good idea around here these days?"

"Depends on who you're trying to please."

"I'm just trying to make a phone call," said Daddy, squeezing Beth's arm to let her know it was okay. "Not make the evening news in any part of the world."

"Have a little faith." The man pulled open the door of his shop. Little bells attached to the handle with bits of twine jingled.

"I have a little faith." Daddy tightened his arm around Beth and pulled her closer. "It's patience that I'm running a bit low on, Mister." But he winked at Beth and they walked through the door together.

BETH WORRIED, AND Mom wasn't there. Daddy cried a lot at night. She could hear him talking to himself through the bedroom wall, but she couldn't hear what he was saying. Lying across her bed, on her stomach, she thought about her problems. The Marlow School had kicked her out. Dad had said it was okay, that she was too smart for Fourth Grade. He always said that when she got kicked out. It didn't bother her to get kicked out. People lied and she made them stop and they kicked her out. She didn't mind going to new schools. She liked new places. She rolled over on her bed, and picked up her new Bible. Loiling, from the Jesus church had given it to her the day they got the flat tire. She liked Loiling, but thought he might be why Daddy cried so much now. Beth just wasn't sure why the truth would make Daddy cry. Loiling didn't tell them anything bad. She wished Mom would come back. Mom would know what to do. Mom always knew what to do.

"CAROLE!" DAD'S SHOUT scared Beth. She jumped off the bed and raced down the hall. Mom stood by the front door, her face too white. Dad was scaring her too. Mom looked over at her and didn't say anything, but Beth knew that look. It meant give us a few minutes. Usually Mom gave it to her when they were going to talk about why she got kicked out of school and now what would they do with her.

This time Beth knew it wasn't about her, but she did the same thing she always did. She slid down the hallway out of sight, and listened.

Daddy hugged Mom, she could hear Mom's bones crack a little bit. Daddy always did that when he hugged you, it didn't hurt. Beth liked it, and she thought maybe Mom would too. Mom's voice sounded worried when she said, "Ted?"

"I'm sorry. I'm sorry for everything, for all the—for all of them. I don't know why I did it. I just—I don't want to be like that anymore, Carole. Never again, I give you my word, I swear to you—never again. I want to be a decent husband. I've been trying for years. Please forgive me, I know I don't deserve it, but please—please believe me." Daddy started crying again. "It's going to be different this time!"

"Don't," Mom whispered. "I know why, Ted. I love you and if you ask me to believe you I will. Please, don't cry."

"I'll show you, Carole. It will be different. I know this will sound stupid, that you won't believe me, but Beth and I found a church and it changed everything for me. I realized how—will you come with us? Can you keep an open mind and just listen to Loiling? For me, for us, please?"

Mom kept quiet. Beth knew she'd gone still like she did when she didn't like something. Beth was pretty sure Mom didn't want to go to Loiling's church.

But Dad made his awful sobbing sound and Mom said, "Of course, right now?"

"Right now would be perfect." Beth heard the jangle of Dad's car keys as though he'd had them in his pocket waiting. "Thank you, Carole." The door swung open, and they left. Beth stood in the hallway and hugged herself. Daddy had sounded almost happy, but they'd both forgotten her. She'd never been home alone before. For a few minutes she waited for them to remember her and come back. They didn't. Beth raced into the living room and turned on the TV. She didn't like to watch it, it was boring. She switched through the channels to the one that played music. Daddy said she wasn't allowed to listen to that kind of music. Beth liked it. She turned the TV as loud as it would go. Plopping onto the couch, she opened her Bible to read while she listened to a punk rock marathon.

CAROLE PUT BOTH hands on her knees, goose bumps prickling over every inch of her body. Ted's heart, always faint in the background, roiled with regret. Years of dishonor had infected it like an abscess, making the touch fainter and fainter. It had been a long time since she'd really wanted to touch it with hers, to claim it for her own. Lately she'd thought one day she'd come home and not be able to sense it anymore at all. This she'd never expected. As though a surgical strike had cleared away pus and dead tissue, the touch of Ted's heart had changed. Even though her father had died, Carole wondered if he'd somehow been able to talk to ilu about him. This felt real, and if it were real it would be miraculous.

Ted put the car in gear and pulled away from the curb into heavy Saturday traffic. His hand on the stick shift shook, and his breathing sounded shallow and fast. Raw regret oozed where dishonor had nested so long. Like the black dreams that sometimes plagued Carole, Ted's own sins seemed to finally claw at him. Sitting beside him she could sense agony in his battered heart. Braking, he steered the car sharply back to the curb, and sat quietly.

It was better if Beth didn't see this, Carole thought, assuming that was why he'd stopped. Ted never allowed Beth alone in Shanghai. Carole reached for the door handle, about to go back upstairs and get their daughter, when Ted spoke.

"Why did you stay? All these years, and all I've done to you, why did you stay?"

Carole put her hands back on her knees and swallowed.

"Mostly because I had no choice."

Ted shifted in his seat to look at her, and for some reason she didn't want to look back at him. It would be easier to tell him if she didn't look at him.

"But you knew, even when I tried to hide it, you knew."

"Of course I knew." She didn't say, *Your heart told me*, she didn't have to.

"You must have wanted to kill me." He spoke the last three words so low she barely caught them. She kept blind eyes on the window and considered that.

She hadn't wanted that, or maybe the truth was that she couldn't have borne it. She whispered, "I settled on watching you kill yourself." She turned her head to see his reaction.

Ted crossed his arms over his chest and leaned forward as though it could equalize the agony inside. After a few minutes of ragged breathing, he started to talk in spurts, as though pulling each word forcefully from somewhere deep and dark. "I didn't mean to—when we married—I meant to keep my vow. I thought I could. But you were so close, even that first day, I could feel you," he gasped uncomfortably. "I couldn't bear it. Like you were crawling inside me, erasing me, erasing my—first—Beth." Ted thumped a hand lightly over his heart, where beneath his shirt rested the old tattoo of his first love. He leaned forward and put his head on the steering wheel, closing his eyes. "It held you out. The other women kept you away."

Carole's heart lit with pain. She'd known this, somewhere deep inside she'd known it from the first.

"Sometimes I wanted you to leave," he admitted.

"I know," she whispered and two hot tears sprang from her eyes and slid burning down her cheeks. She turned to look out the passenger window.

"You invaded me, I couldn't bear it. How could you stay, Carole? How could you bear what I've done to you?"

A passerby peeked in the window at her, and Carole turned her head to face forward, wiping the tears away. "I love you." She wondered if it sounded stupid, desperate, and pathetic to Ted. Dropping her hands in her lap she turned to look at him as anger, packed down and kept hidden, welled to the surface.

"And love is not a transitory, changeable thing for me. I had no way to keep you out. When I gave myself to you, I gave myself to you,

Ted. What I am, that strange, weird, oddity that I am—the one you fight so hard to keep away, that woman knows how to love. Despite your rejection, I love you with all that I am. I can no more walk away from you than I can leave half my own body behind. You don't like my heart touching yours, Ted White? You don't like my strangeness or even my job? I know these things! Believe me, I wanted to leave! If it had been possible to cleave myself in half and leave you, I would have done it years ago! But I couldn't!" Carole wrapped her arms across her chest too, leaning forward, assuming the same position Ted held. It hurt. Every time she thought he couldn't possibly hurt her more, he did. Yet as sure as she knew she lived, she knew the pain of separating from Ted would be far greater. The fierce strong warrior inside her seemed to curl up in shame.

Ted grabbed her then, pulling her against his sturdy chest and wrapping husky arms around her. He held tight. It was the last straw. Torn between hope and humiliation, Carole cried. He held her there, while pedestrians looked through the window, rocking her back and forth as though she were Beth, patting her unruly hair. Carole cried until she had nothing left, until only hoarse sounds escaped. The voices kept silent, watching and waiting.

"I do know what it is like, Carole, to love someone who isn't worth it. My Beth—she never let me close. I never knew why until she died. Did you know that her death was a public scandal? My pain was fodder for the gossip mongers. Washington wallowed in my suffering. But I did the same thing to you didn't I? Shoved it in your face? I can't even honestly say I didn't want to hurt you! Half the time I think I did, as though I could retaliate through you. Oh, God, Carole, I will find a way to make it right. I will find a way to atone, I swear it to you."

Carole, feeling the distant touch of that pained heart, knew he meant every word, and she wanted to believe him, because she had no choice. The warrior inside covered her face in disgrace.

LOILING GAVE MOM her own Bible. Beth never saw her read it, but she went to church with them on Sunday morning and Mom knew all the verses. Daddy stopped crying, and Beth got grounded for watching MTV. Grounded wasn't much different from before she got grounded. The only difference was now Dad said, "Should she be doing that? She's grounded." Mom would say, "Your call, Ted." Daddy would think about it and then let her go walking with Mom, or to the library, market, the gardens, or in-line skating. After a week, Daddy stopped talking about being grounded. He put his arm around Mom a lot, and sometimes Mom smiled, not big like Daddy, just a little one that sneaked out.

They all went to the park together now, and they moved into an apartment closer to downtown. Beth started Sankle School for gifted children, and Dad drove her. He told jokes and laughed the whole way. He was the best Dad ever, and even if he really grounded her he'd still be the best Dad ever.

THE NEW APARTMENT reminded Carole of the little dump above the tattoo parlor that she'd had in San Diego, where Beth had been born. There was a guitar shop below this one which stretched halfway to the next block. They had to walk five flights of stairs up to reach the apartment, and there was no elevator. She loved it. The rent cost half of the other place, and that meant they could afford The Sankle School for Beth. Ted insisted Beth would fit right in with gifted children. Carole rubbed olive oil inside her bread pan, and dropped the bread dough inside. The telephone rang.

"Hello—Ni hao!"

"Mrs. White? This is Headmistress Ahlio. I'm afraid we need either you or your husband to come to school and pick up your daughter immediately."

"Is she all right?" Carole tried to buy time. "Did she get hurt?" Sooner or later she was going to.

"No, no, Beth is fine."

"What happened?"

"She is being dismissed from Sankle School, Mrs. White. Please pick her up or we can send her home via taxicab. Which would you prefer?"

"I'll come get her."

LEAVING BETH'S BACKPACK with her expensive new text-books on a park bench they went skating together along the wide path of the public garden. Carole waited for her daughter to speak. Beth was mad and activity calmed her.

"I didn't do anything wrong, Mom."

"Life's not fair, Beth."

"I'll say," she groused. "People steal, cheat and lie all the time! Then they lie about stealing, cheating and lying."

"Yes."

Carole slowed down so that Beth could keep pace with her. Beth glared out of the corner of her eye. "I'm not going to let them do it."

"Maybe it's not your job to stop them."

"Maybe it is."

Carole sighed. "If you really think that, you'd better be prepared to defend yourself."

Beth skidded to a stop. "They're not allowed to hit me!"

"They're going to do it anyway, Beth, if you make them mad enough. So you need to either hush, or be ready to defend yourself."

"Daddy said if someone tries to hurt me I should run away."

"That would be the same thing as hushing up and you just told me you won't do that. Do you want to learn how to fight?"

"I don't want to fight."

"Then you better learn to hush. That means that when the music teacher is kissing the principal in the art closet, you don't tell everyone about it during assembly. Do you understand?"

250

"If people didn't *lie* it wouldn't matter what I said!"

Carole pressed the back of her skate to the ground and slid to a quick stop, forcing Beth to make a clumsy stop of her own. "But they *do* lie! And it does matter! You know that! If you can't get your mouth under control you're going to have to suffer the consequences on your own. Daddy and I aren't always going to be there to defend you!"

Beth glared without quite meeting Carole's eyes. After a moment Carole moved and allowed her daughter to continue skating along the smooth path. She heard Beth whisper a defiant, "Fine!" under her breath.

Carole impatiently blew out her breath. *Guess she'll learn the hard way, just like the rest of us.*

CHAPTER
TWENTY-TWO

Republic of Indonesia —January 2002

THE BELL RANG and all the boys and girls hurried to gather their books and papers. There were only four minutes until the next class and the teachers at Public School Yong 717 were strict. Beth scooped her books into her arms and followed, smoothing the skirt of her ugly khaki uniform. They all had to wear bright red neckties too. It was a thirteen-year-old's nightmare. The only nod to individuality was their shoes; as long as they were black, they were acceptable. Most of the boys wore the coolest running shoes and the girls wore heels. Beth adored heels but she stood almost six feet tall, so she wore the lowest flats she could find. Still, she looked like a flagpole waving above the crowd of neat, petite Asians, an extra skinny flagpole from a country with a very loud flag—like Nepal or Antwerp. Beth hated her body. She walked looking at the floor and tried to blend in.

"Are you a giant? I mean is it normal to be so tall where you come from?" A perfect china doll of a girl, who managed to look adorable in her uniform, asked with a giggle. Beth cheered up. It was the first time someone had spoken to her in a week. Maybe they could be girlfriends. Dad had gotten her bunk beds just so she could have a sleepover. More than anything, Beth wanted to have a sleepover, or at least get invited to one.

"No, I'm not a giant, I'm just tall. My parents are too. My dad is six inches under seven feet tall—that is 1.9812 meters. I'm taller than my mom but not by much. I don't know if everyone in America is this tall, I haven't been there since I was a baby."

"I think I'd die if I was that tall. You look so weird."

"I am a little weird," Beth admitted and laughed. "Not a little weird, I suppose I'm a big weird—because I'm big, you know?"

"I think I get it." The perfect china doll edged away from her.

APPARENTLY HER HUSBAND wasn't trying to hide any of his secrets anymore. Fast food wrappers were tucked under the couch. Two McSatay hamburger boxes, two large fry containers, and an apple pie box. Pizza boxes littered the kitchen counter and take-out containers covered a good many surfaces. Carole had long suspected that Ted and Beth hid the evidence, but now she perused their new apartment a month earlier than expected. Passing through the house with a trash bag, she cleaned up. Inside Beth's bedroom she found empty French fry containers. It floored her. Studying the crunchy bits of fries remaining in the container, Carole decided the food wasn't dirty. It wasn't healthy, but it wasn't what the voices would call dirty either. Then she laughed out loud, relief sweeping through her. For the first time ever she knew for certain that Beth didn't hear voices.

"Oh, thank God!" she whispered like a prayer. The voices would never have allowed this. Testing her theory, Carole took a dried bit of the salty thing that had once been a potato, and popped it into her mouth. "*Degraded. Flimsy. Unnatural.*" Chuckling, she spat it into the trash.

Ted pushed the bedroom door open, his aftershave wafting over her and she fought a shiver.

"Carole! I thought I heard you laugh! Welcome home." Eyeing the trash he flushed slightly. "Er, sorry. She only eats fries fried in vegetable oil. Why is that funny?"

Shaking her head and smiling, Carole said, "I'm just surprised she can do it. She's less like me than I thought."

"Oh, she's plenty like you." Ted pulled her into a hug, his after-shave almost overpowering. "How'd you know which apartment was ours?" Then, as though realizing he didn't want to hear that answer he released her and asked quickly, "How'd you get in?"

"The door was unlocked."

"Uh-oh, Beth raced out to catch a taxi to school when I was in the shower. You know our daughter thinks everyone is as honest as she is. We overslept and I'm pretty late, but how about I make a phone call to the office and spend the day helping you pick up?"

"I don't mind getting it."

"Well, I mind. Besides, trust me, you don't want to see the bath-room." He hugged her again. "I'm glad you're home safe, and early."

DAD PICKED BETH up after school. He'd been doing it since she turned in some kids selling dope on the 94 Green Line train. "We're busted. Mom came home early."

"Uh-oh."

"She's not mad. She said she'll just never understand the whole French fry thing."

"Guess I'll be cleaning my room this weekend."

"Nope. I did it. I thought you might want to invite somebody over for a slumber party?"

Beth wailed. "I try Dad, they say no. They think I'm a tall freak."

He stepped on the brake and the car jerked to a sudden halt. The tires of the car behind them screeched as it was forced to brake suddenly. "You're a tall freak? Beth! I'm a tall freak too! We have so much in common. It's like we're related."

It made her laugh. The car behind them started to blow the horn. Dad ignored it and asked, "Do you like ice-cream?"

"Yes! Dad, you know I do."

"Oh my gosh, do you think all tall freaks like ice-cream?"

She giggled. "Mom doesn't."

More people started blowing their horns. Daddy looked in the rearview mirror at them and then back at her. "Do you think they're blowing their horns at us because we're tall freaks?"

"Maybe it's because you're stopped and they can't get out of the parking lot until you go."

"So you don't think they care if I'm a tall freak?"

"No!"

"Do you think the people walking past our car right now, and staring in the windows at me—see how they're pointing at me?" Dad waved at them. "Do you think they care if I'm a tall freak?"

"I think they think you're just a freak, Dad."

"That's another conversation, so don't try to change the topic. Today the discussion is tall freak. Do you think that that crossing guard, see him? The one who's waving his arms and getting all red in the face, do you think he cares that I'm a tall freak?"

Beth laughed. The guy was having a fit. She shook her head.

"So how many people do you think really care if I'm a tall freak?"

"I don't think anybody cares that you're a tall freak, Dad."

"Hmm, I thought they all did."

"No you didn't!" Beth accused. Not even Daddy could get away with the smallest falsehood, she heard them all.

"You're right! I know they don't care, but when I was fourteen—or almost fourteen like you—I thought they all did."

Groaning, Beth leaned back in the seat. "I get it. It will pass, I'll grow up and people won't care if I'm tall."

"It's true, Beth."

She smiled at him. Sometimes it was wonderful to hear the truth.

THE VERY NEXT day Beth found someone who didn't care if she was tall. Sitting at a table in the lunch room, eating her favorite peanut butter banana sandwich on Mom's homemade bread, she tried to avoid attention. Since there'd been no empty tables, she'd sat at a table with several other kids who also looked like they wished they were invisible. One boy had terrible acne, the other boy was enormously fat, and the other girl was having a baby and she was only fifteen years old. Everyone whispered about her. With the American giraffe in their midst it was official, this was the loser table.

Figuring if they all had to be losers, maybe they could do it together, Beth offered the pregnant girl an oatmeal cookie. "They're healthy and you probably need to eat healthy, and it's really good. My mother made it." The girl took it and smiled shyly.

"Hey, Blondie."

At first Beth assumed the boy was talking to someone else. She glanced left and then right, and finding no other blondes she looked right at him. His name was Wuan Cho and he was so beautiful. Every time he walked past her in the hall she dropped something in tribute to his handsomeness and her own awkwardness.

"Beth, right?"

"Right." She cleared her throat. It sounded froggy.

"You're American aren't you?"

She nodded mutely.

"Do you know any movie stars?"

She shook her head. Why did everyone ask that?

"You live in my building. Well, sort of. I live in the B section and I see you go into the A block. We should hang out sometime."

"Okay," she managed.

"Cool. Tomorrow? I'll meet you in the laundry room, after dinner? We can hang out, you know, do stuff."

"Cool!" she enthused. Wuan Cho was way better than a slumber party. The bell rang and she raced to science class. She forgot to slump.

THE NEXT EVENING, Beth tried on clothes for hours before she was satisfied. She settled on lots of red. It was a happy color. Her shoes were flat—of course—Wuan was at least seven inches shorter than she was, even though he was two years older. Her mini skirt was frilled and covered in red polka dots, and she wore a red top. A white with red polka dot headband pulled her long blonde hair off her face. She studied her face, and then opened her bedroom door and peeked out. Mom and Dad were in their room. She shut the door and rooted around beneath her bed and tugged a box out. Makeup.

Not very much, just some mascara and lip gloss, the strawberry kind. The finishing touch was a little silver necklace with a red gem that rested against her throat. Dad had given it to her in India. The red gem was a real ruby. Mom didn't like it, but Beth liked everything Dad gave her. Standing in the hallway she listened. It sounded like Dad was talking really low. She raced to the front door and sneaked out. Mom didn't follow.

WUAN WAS THERE waiting, sitting on a dryer and smoking a cigarette. *Ew*, thought Beth. He jumped off when he saw her, and offered it to her. She shook her head. Yes, it was gross, but he was being polite and he was still cute. Wuan had on jeans and a black tank top. He had lean muscles, and his hair was too long, his eyes a little bit slanted and very dark. He was so pretty Beth tripped in homage, and nervously smoothed her skirt. She had 100,000 rupiah in birthday money in her purse, and she was going to offer to pay for the cinema. Going to the cinema with Wuan was way cooler than a slumber party. Plus if she ever did get invited to one, they could talk about the time she went to the movies with Wuan Cho.

She swallowed and smiled, feeling extra shy. "Do you like to go to the movies?"

"I like you." He walked so gracefully. He could probably dance. She wondered if he watched MTV. She just bet he did. Maybe they

257

could go to his apartment and watch MTV. Dad would never know. *Unless he asked me.* She frowned at that thought. She'd have to tell Dad the truth if he asked her. Maybe they'd just better go to the cinema.

Wuan took her hand and tugged her towards the storage lockers. They were big and wooden and people kept sports equipment and bikes locked inside them. Dad couldn't find bikes big enough for them in Indonesia, so their locker sat empty. Wuan's fingers felt strong as he pulled her along. He was solid like Mom, like he ran all the time, and he held her hand with all his fingers interwoven through all of hers. Boyfriends held girlfriends hands like this! Dad was right, not everyone cared if she was tall. Wuan obviously didn't care.

"You have pretty hair, Beth."

"Th-thank you!" she stuttered and her heart skipped beats. "So do you." He laughed and stopped in the shadows of the big lockers. Beth tugged the string of her purse so that it fell properly and told him, "I thought maybe you'd want to go to the movies with me?"

"I want to kiss you," he whispered. Beth felt a funny twist in her belly. It wasn't a good twist.

"I don't think I'm allowed," she warned.

"Don't tell," he whispered, leaning very close.

"Oh, I don't lie—I don't think that I could even if—"

Wuan interrupted, pressing his mouth right against hers. The back of her head knocked against the door of a locker. It hurt. His mouth pressed hard and one of her teeth cut into the inside of her lip. She put her hands against his chest and pushed. Wuan grabbed her hands and slammed them against the locker really hard, holding them there. It hurt, a lot.

"Stop it!" Beth mumbled against his lips and tried to twist away. She was taller, but Wuan was really strong. He leaned against her, pressing his chest against hers, and shoving one of his legs between hers. He pushed her legs further apart and pushed his leg up against her where it shouldn't be.

Panic surged through her. Somewhere in the back of her head she thought she heard something, faint panicked voices shouting. And then Beth fought. It happened so fast, she didn't see exactly what happened. She kicked and bit. Wuan hit her back, again and again, then grabbed her shoulders and shoved her against the wooden door harder, trying to hold her in place. She screamed and shouted and he tried to cover her mouth and hold her still at the same time. She bit his hand and spit in his face, and finally managed to push him away. Beth kicked him once and ran.

━━━✦━━━

STANDING OUTSIDE HER apartment door, Beth wiped her face and cleaned off what remained of her lip gloss with the back of her hand. She fixed her clothes and hair. She could hear the TV. Daddy liked to watch shows on Saturday nights. Taking a deep breath and moving fast, she opened the door and slammed it behind her like she always did.

"Don't slam it, Bethy."

"Okay."

Beth rushed past Daddy. His eyes were mostly on the TV. Mom was doing something in the kitchen. She walked past the doorway with some boxes in her arms, but didn't look out. Beth raced for the bathroom. She locked the door and then slid down it, shaking.

Someone knocked on the door.

"Just a minute!" she said.

"Beth?" It was Mom and her voice was a whisper. "Open the door right this instant or I will break it down."

Unwilling, Beth obeyed. Mom always did what she said she would. Mom came in and shut the door behind her.

"Please," Beth started to cry, "don't tell Dad."

"I won't. I want you to tell me what happened." Mom rubbed her shoulder, just once, light and gentle. Then she went to the tub and started filling it with water.

Beth didn't want to tell. She had to if someone asked, but Mom hadn't asked outright, and never before had Beth not wanted to tell something so much. She wanted to make it not have happened. Mom didn't say anything else while the tub filled with water. Then she motioned towards it.

"I know you don't want to talk about it, but you won't start to feel better until you do."

Beth started tugging off her clothes, a hard task because she was trembling. Mom had to help her like when she was little, except only Dad used to help her then. She was glad it was Mom this time. Mom helped her into the tub and the water felt good, it was hot but it helped make the cold and shaking go away. And she talked. She told Mom everything. About freaky tall, and slumber parties, and the lunch table with the losers. She told her about Wuan Cho and the 100,000 rupiah birthday money, and that she'd lost it along with her beaded Hello Kitty bag that Dad had bought her even when Mom said not to.

It made her cry when she talked about Wuan kissing her, and she promised Mom that she didn't want him to.

"Bethy, Sweetheart." Mom never called her that. "I know you didn't want to. Please go on, if you want."

Beth did want to now. She told her everything, finishing with, "and he tore my shirt, and pinched me here and here, and it hurt but I was so scared, Mom. He tore the hem on my skirt trying to take my underpants off, and look, Mom, he gave me bruises and he pu-punched me."

"I see that," Mom said. Then she held up a fluffy towel and helped Beth dry off. She sneaked across the hall and got Beth's favorite pajamas, the ones with MTV on the front, even though she wasn't allowed to watch it. Then she tucked Beth into bed, just like she was a regular mom tucking in her little girl. It felt good. Beth lay on her side, and Mom patted her on the shoulder, leaning to kiss her cheek. "If you have bad dreams, remember to change the channel like Daddy taught you when you were little. Okay?"

"Okay, Mom. I love you."

"I love you too, Bethy. Night."

When Mom went into the living room she heard Daddy ask where Beth was.

"She went to bed early."

"Is she all right?"

"Girl stuff. She'll be fine."

"Girl stuff!" Daddy didn't like that idea. "I guess my girl is growing up."

CHAPTER
TWENTY-THREE

Republic of Indonesia—January 2002

CAROLE BRIEFLY CONSIDERED giving herself time to cool off before she paid the teenager a visit. By the time Ted's head hit his pillow and his deep breathing filled her ear, she knew that this anger wasn't the kind that would dissipate with time. Every moment that passed made it more likely that she'd annihilate the kid. The strange thing was, the voices didn't object. Even while she lay in bed planning, the voices seemed to be quietly waiting.

WUAN CHO HAD the luxury of his own bedroom, which made Carole's mission quite easy. The kid woke gasping from the weight of all 160 pounds of toned muscle strategically positioned in the middle of his chest. She flicked on his bedside lamp. His eyes lit briefly when he saw the blonde straddling him, quickly clouding with confusion when she shoved her foot against his mouth to keep him quiet. Worried recognition flickered in his eyes, and she assumed he recognized Beth's features in her face.

"Hello, Wuan," Carole whispered. "I'm Beth's mother; I see you caught the resemblance. You probably never saw me before. I'm away a lot of the time. I kill people for a living and it keeps me pretty busy!"

Wuan's pretty face twisted as he tried to get out from under her, but he could hardly move with Carole's weight on him. She used her foot to maneuver his head into the pillow. If he could barely breathe, she wouldn't have to worry he'd cry out for help. Carole used the foot for leverage, lifted herself up a bit and dropped heavily against his diaphragm, resuming her position while Wuan tried desperately to breathe. Carole reclined on his narrow body with one of her soft black shoes and one hand digging into the mattress to support her leisurely pose. The other hand took a firm grip on Wuan's man-ware, right through his briefs. She lifted her foot off his throat just enough for the kid to move his head and see her while she looked around his room. The walls were decorated with posters of popular bands, half-dressed women, and panthers.

"I like jungle cats too, they're fast," she murmured conversationally. "I never liked the way they play with their prey before they kill it though. I always thought if you're going to kill, just do it. You know what I mean, Wuan? Why make it suffer first, but that was before I met you. You've made me rethink that philosophy." She used her spare foot, hitting him in the eye with the heel, and keeping her balance by shifting her body weight onto his weakest link, still clutched firmly in her left hand. The scream low in his throat was barely audible with his neck bent near the breaking point.

"The thing I *like* about cats is that they're so sleek and beautiful. It's deceiving, you know. Like a sweet, soft little kitten you just want to pick up and put in your pocket. Not everyone feels that way though. There are some people who like to hurt things they think are help-less. There are some people who like to hurt kittens." Carole leaned heavier against his nether regions, and a whispery scream gurgled in Wuan's throat. "My favorite part about cats, though, is that looks are so deceiving. You see they're not helpless at all! Oh, maybe when they're tiny kittens, but then there's always mama cat nearby to protect them." Leaning too heavily on his boy-parts, Carole lost Wuan for a few minutes when he fainted. She revived him by shifting sides and letting him breathe a moment.

"Now where was I? Ah, yes, jungle cats—kittens—mama cat—oh, the moral of the story! That's the best part. You see, Wuan, kittens grow up. And people say that elephants never forget—and that may be true—but if they think kittens forget, they must be one of those nice people who just scratch them behind the ears and keep them safe in their pocket. You know I can't think of *anything* crueler than an angry cat, and in my line of work—I've seen plenty of cruelty."

It was possibly one of the most difficult things Carole had ever done, using restraint. She wanted to kill the kid. She settled on a beating easily recovered from, but never forgotten. The scars she left on Wuan he would carry far longer than Beth's. It was the first time she'd ever hurt someone and felt good about it, truly pleased for having inflicted pain. Slipping through the kid's bedroom window an hour later, Carole felt fairly certain he'd remain unconscious for hours.

TED HAD DEVELOPED a family routine for Sunday mornings. Breakfast out, attend church in the Indonesian Christian Church, and stroll through neighborhoods so Beth could spend hours taking notes on her favorite things. Today Carole begged off the walk and swung by a popular department store all by herself. Two hours later, back at the apartments, she rang the Cho's doorbell in the B Section. In her left hand she balanced a large platter of homemade all-American chocolate chip cookies chock full of crunchy nuts. Her right hand smoothed the hair she'd managed to wrestle into curls with Beth's hidden curling iron. Of all the disguises she'd ever worn, this one felt the strangest to Carole. A pale pink flowered dress and a very motherly white cardigan draped neatly over her trim form, and she'd even forced herself into a pair of pantyhose and pink pumps. The voices were having a fit. The door swung open and a plump, pretty Asian face appeared in the doorway. Wuan's mother had been crying. Carole didn't feel even a twinge of remorse. Drawing her brows together in concern she spoke in flawless Wu.

"Mrs. Cho? I'm Carole White, and I'm sorry to bother you today, but I heard about Wuan. He goes to school with my daughter, and I wanted to see if there is *anything* I can do, anything at all to help."

The door swung open and Mrs. Cho invited her in. Carole introduced herself again, and a third time when Mr. Cho wandered into the room. Within moments she sat on their white leather sofa and put her hands primly in her lap, listening. Mr. and Mrs. Cho informed her that Wuan had been attacked by what had surely been gang members, though they were still trying to convince him to speak to the police. Carole shook her head remorsefully and clucked her tongue, lamenting the dangers of the world, again offering any help they might need.

Mrs. Cho shook her head, "Wuan would not go hospital. We pay nurse to come wrap his ribs, stitch wounds. He not say who did this, no say where happen. Poor boy, he afraid. Wuan must be brave, learn to stay home, not go where gangs get him!"

Carole murmured words of acquiescence, sensing Wuan limping up the hallway. His father motioned him over. Clueless, the battered and bruised boy took a seat between his parents. Ignoring the plate of cookies Carole pushed towards him, he appeared to only half listen as his parents introduced her. They called her Karen and pronounced her last name as Waite, emphasizing his friendship with her daughter. Pleased with her disguise and deciding that the disgusting lipstick had been worth the extra effort, she waited patiently.

Wuan's face had turned into a mess of black and blue, and his mouth looked so swollen that chewing nutty cookies seemed highly unlikely. After listening to his parents, he nodded with feigned politeness in her direction. Mr. and Mrs. Cho began a lecture aimed at convincing their son to go to the police, during which Carole nodded emphatically in all the right places. They insisted if he stayed at home or school, and took precautions, that he would be safe from gangs. At the end of their performance, Carole rose. Crossing to Wuan's side she bent towards him, addressing him in Wu.

"Surely you realize, Wuan, that your parents are being sensible. You can't possibly be in any danger in your own home." She patted him on the shoulder, taking care to whack bruises hidden by his shirt. "You poor boy, so torn up like a wounded little kitten, I just want to pick you up and put you in my pocket." She finished in English, "Don't worry, Wuan, mama cat will take good care of you. She's always watching." Both Wuan's parents were smiling and nodding their heads. Wuan had frozen in place, not saying a word or moving. The only evidence he recognized her was the wet stain spreading over the front of his khaki pants.

"MOM," BETH WHISPERED her name.

Busy packing tomorrow's lunch Carole glanced at her daughter in the MTV pajamas. She watched Beth lean out the kitchen doorway and peek into the living room to make sure that her father still sat in front of the evening news. Beth padded to the counter on her tiptoes.

"There's a Catholic school that I could take the C bus to. It's an hour away, but I don't care."

"I do. You're going to school in the morning."

"I can't go there with him there!"

Carole studied her daughter's clear blue eyes. "You can and you will, Beth White. You go through schools fast enough without taking yourself out of them."

"But what if…what if…" Beth squeaked. Trying to come up with an argument she rested one long-fingered hand near the cutting board where Carole was chopping tomatoes. Carole lifted her razor sharp knife up, twisting it in front of Beth's pretty eyes. Beth studied it trustingly, biting her lip, obviously still working on another tactic. Carole swung the blade down, right towards Beth's hand near the cutting board. Instinct took over and Beth jerked away in time.

"Mom!"

"You must learn to fight back." Carole walked over to the kitchen door and silently shut it. She leaned across the counter and used the long knife to close the louvered shutters looking out on Ted lying on the couch. Turning, Carole leaned against the counter and met Beth's steady gaze.

"You're faster—than the average bear, Beth. I know you aren't a fighter, but if a boy tries to hurt you, you can defend yourself. I'm going to teach you how. Okay?"

"Okay." Beth's lack of enthusiasm almost made Carole laugh.

"Catch." Carole tossed the razor sharp blade into the air. Beth caught it nimbly by the handle. She looked surprised by her own prowess.

Within twenty minutes Carole decided that Beth could defend herself against Wuan, and likely a few of his friends too, if the need ever arose. Subdued, Beth scampered down the hallway without even telling her father goodnight. She definitely did not seem to enjoy a good fight like her mother did.

━━━━━━━━━

TED RECLINED ON the sofa with his evening beer. Carole stretched out beside him. He put a welcoming arm around her, pulling her against his bulk.

"What on earth were you and Beth doing tonight? I thought that the neighbors would call. Sounded like you were killing her in there."

"Girl stuff."

Ted chuckled. "Girl stuff is loud. Hey, GKI called, they're going to have a booth in the street fair next Sunday, wanted to know if you'd bake something."

Carole twisted to eye him, and Ted seemed to lose his train of thought. He ran a thumb over her cheek. "You have magnificent skin. It still looks like an eighteen-year-old's. Not a single wrinkle. The Minister thought you were Beth's big sister."

"GKI?"

Ted teased, "Church. You didn't get that?"

"I could make my bread I suppose. You like it."

"Oh, yeah, I like your bread. That's a good idea. Maybe I'll have Bethy help me bake a cake too."

"That I want to see," she teased in turn, running a hand along his neck she dipped it inside his collar, heading for his chest and the heart that beckoned.

The phone rang. Ted leaned to get it, twisting away before Carole could make contact with her goal.

"That's probably them again," he excused.

"Hello? Hello?" He waited several seconds and then hung up. It rang again, and Ted's eyes swung to Carole's. "Surely not! You just got back. It's only been a few days!"

It continued to ring, and she reached for it. Ted grabbed her arm. "Don't. Just don't answer and they'll get someone else."

"Ted, when have I ever gotten an extra month? It will probably be short."

"When have they ever been short? Carole, I hate your job."

"You did recommend me for it."

"There was little choice at the time," he growled. The phone continued to ring.

"How does it differ from what you do? The only difference between us is that you decide at a desk, or a meeting, or a party, what needs to be done, and I'm the grunt who does what needs done." Carole picked up the ringing phone. Ted disentangled himself from her, shut off the TV and went down the hall to their room, slamming the bedroom door.

KISSING YOUR DAD goodbye in front of school at nearly four-teen-years-old was the kiss of death for slumber parties. Beth knew that, but she sat in the car and kissed and hugged her Daddy. Mom had left again and he was really sad this time. The truth was she was sad too. It was hard to get out of the car and walk towards that school. Part of her wished she could go back and tell Dad what had happened. He'd let her change schools, she was certain of it. He'd also probably call the police, and go visit the boy's parents and—Beth noticed the hum of interested voices around her then. Louder than the general hum of Monday morning conversation. She straightened her uniform and peeked over the crowd of heads to see what the fuss was, almost afraid that it was just her, freaky tall, on Monday morning.

It wasn't. Wuan Cho came across the school yard. He wasn't moving with his usual cool grace. He half-limped. Both his eyes were swollen and black and blue. His long cool hair looked weird, bald in spots and sticking straight up in places. A shiver slid up Beth's spine as Wuan neared her. Some of his hair looked like it'd been pulled out. His scalp looked red and sore and torn in spots. What had happened to him? Someone else wondered that same question out loud. Wuan swore at them, and Beth thought two of his pretty front teeth were missing. She couldn't get close enough to know for sure because when she moved closer, he walked faster. It didn't seem like a coincidence.

Beth swung around, eyes searching for Daddy's departing vehicle. It was already out of sight. Had Mom told Dad? Dad worked for the marines—would marines do that? Would Dad ask them to? She didn't think marines would do that to a boy. Another thought occurred to Beth—who had taught Mom to fight? Did *Mom* ask someone to do that to Wuan Cho? A shiver rippled up Beth's long spine. When people asked, Mom said she worked at the United Nations. Beth never asked her about it because she already knew. Mom lied.

CHAPTER
TWENTY-FOUR

Mexico City—September 2005

I AM NOT going to be a freak. I am not going to be a freak. The first day of college and Beth's mind raced, repeating the words. Not being a freak seemed a simple enough mantra. She piled books in her arms, Business, Economics, Political Science, and one on Botany. Scanning the book store it was apparent she was again the tallest. *Why couldn't Daddy get transferred to some Nordic country for pity's sake?* They'd once lived briefly in South Africa, but she'd been so little it didn't count as a tall country. A nice looking, dark-skinned Mexican cut the line to stand beside her. He had heart throb good looks, and those black eyes she adored! Beth's mind raced. *Really, I could swim in them, naked preferably.* And muscles, *Oh my gosh he is ripped. I'd pay to have a look at those abs.*

He smiled with white on white teeth and said, "You're lost in thought. What are you worrying about, Economics class?" He patted that book in her arms.

Beth flushed beet red because she knew her idiot answer approached. She could feel it. And here it came, "No, I wasn't worrying, just thinking I'd pay to look at your naked abs." Stupid lived in her mouth, and it really liked to come outside and have a romp around. The kid's perfect dark brows rose, and he looked at her as though trying to place the signs of mental malfunction that he had previously missed. He waved at someone imaginary across the room and excused himself. *I am a social half-wit*, Beth thought, wishing she could die on command. *I wonder if a doctor would remove my vocal chords. I'll bet some doctor here in Mexico would do it. I read some doctor here gave a woman plastic surgery to look like a cat.*

A guy with the potential to create beautiful children cut in line, interrupting her random thoughts. He smiled and said, "What's new?"

"My books," Beth's mouth blurted because she had no control over the damn thing. The kid forced a laugh. She knew it was a tribute to the good looks she'd inherited from her mother when he stuck around long enough to try again.

"Do you like to dance?"

"Yes!" She bellowed, thrilled to be able to answer a normal question in a normal manner. "I like to dance!"

"Cool. Where do you like to go dancing?"

"In the kitchen with my father." *Kill me, Dear God, just take me now. I can hear you laughing. I know I am your plaything.* The guy darted, not even bothering with the polite wave to an imaginary friend.

Beth bit her lip. There were ways around this, and she'd been practicing them. *Run away, think before you speak—you can tell the truth without sounding like a complete head injury if you slow down!* This was her first day at college and she was nervous. Dad had home-schooled her during her last two years of high school. He said she was too smart to move at the slow pace in high school. Beth knew he was being kind. Though when he'd said it, it hadn't had that ugly sound of a lie, so he had meant it.

It was just a bit too coincidental, the timing of when her parents had decided to homeschool her. They'd been living in Columbia, and she'd alerted the hall monitors that Molito Haskell's family owned a cocaine plantation. Dad had been just trying to keep her alive. Mom loved her, she had no doubts about that, but Mom had made it abundantly clear for years that she was ready to let the real world teach her how to control her big fat mouth.

Beth only needed one semester of on-campus courses to finish. She'd managed most of her degree online while wrapping up high school. These last courses demanded attendance on campus. All she had to do was take the classes, pass, and God willing get kissed by at least one boy. Maybe there was a deaf kid on campus. She'd have to ask around.

ECONOMICS WENT WELL. The teacher seemed intelligent and very professional. He passed around the course outline, including the assignments, due dates, and how much of their grade each was worth. The course was facts. Beth loved facts. She'd failed every history class she'd ever taken because she'd found it subjective. Daddy said history was facts too, but Beth knew otherwise. History was someone's documentation, it had angles and slants and it was not absolute truth. Why couldn't other people recognize lies and disinformation like she could? At any rate, for Beth, economics rocked.

There was a list of job opportunities posted in the hall and Beth stopped to inquire about working in the library. The librarian spoke only Spanish, and after interviewing Beth briefly, promised her the job on the spot. Beth practically skipped towards her business class.

"Ssst?" The whisper came from behind. Beth glanced at the guy following her, another cutie, a bit tiny for her six-foot height, but definitely kissable. Nice arms. He held up an unlit joint. "Like to get high, Americano?"

"No. I do not." Beth stomped away. He wasn't all that cute. He followed, cajoling, offering her a free trial baggie of weed, insisting it was good, inexpensive and always available.

"Look! I don't like drugs. Take a hike!"

"Don't be hasty, you don't use means you're good for selling it. I grow it myself, good stuff, I don't use neither. You help me sell I'll give you 50% profit. No overhead, Blondie. You think on that, you look smart."

BUSINESS CLASS PROVED promising. Sitting at a table between Hunky One and Hunky Two, Beth decided she loved Mexico and height was highly overrated. None of these men seemed to mind whatsoever that she was freaky tall.

The teacher pulled her thoughts from dark, sexy eyes, as he outlined the curriculum. "The books were a waste of money—I'm sorry about that. I have to hand out something, so I just pick the cheapest one every semester. If you want to pass this class you start a business. I don't care if you're selling chocolates door to door, anything. You will give me a business plan, report costs and profits, and if you want an A—you will make a good profit."

"Does it have to be legal?" someone joked. The kid held fingers up to his lips as though smoking something furtively and most of the class laughed.

"We don't even kid about that here. So what kind of profit could be made at a school where no one does drugs?"

Beth's hand shot into the air, and unable to control it she blurted, "50%! If you don't use it, selling it is highly profitable!"

"YOU HAVE TO learn to control it." Mom's blue eyes could look right through her.

"I try! I can't." Beth leaned back in the kitchen chair.

"You like it."

Beth scowled. She didn't want to admit the truth in that, but Mom knew. Mom always knew. It was beyond annoying. Beth bit a fingernail and looked out the window. Dad had planted flowers in pots on the balcony, bright red geraniums. He always made their apartments homey.

"Why do you bite your nails?"

Beth turned her eyes to her mother and replied slowly, the words unfolding the truth that she hadn't realized until she said it. "Because it buys me time to think when I'm nervous."

"Why do you wear make-up?"

"Mom! Don't!" But Mom just waited and Beth looked over her Mom's head while she answered, the words tumbling out. "Because it makes guys really notice me."

"Why do you want guys to notice you?"

"Oh my gosh, Mom! Please?" Beth jumped up and raced down the hallway to blurt the answer loudly in the bathroom. She knew her mother was waiting at the dining room table, so she returned, embarrassed, hoping against hope that her mother hadn't heard the answer.

"No, I didn't hear it, but I can assume the gist of it, Beth. You are my daughter after all. I met your father when I was eighteen. I suppose you can do the math on how long after that before you were born."

"Kill me, Mom. Please don't tell me about your libido."

"Don't be a child. The point is I didn't actually hear you say it. Do you see? You can control it enough to keep someone from hearing what they shouldn't. I probably should have done this to you years ago."

"No." Beth put her face in her hands. "Because it's only been lately that I've been able to control it even this little bit. Mom, you can't know what it's like. I do like to do it! It feels good. I doubt drugs or even—even sex—feels as good as the rush I get when I point out the truth. At least it feels good until the consequences hit. The thing is, Mom, why do I even do it? I've read about people who blurt and I don't fit the demographics. And *how* do I always know when people are lying? I don't get it. How do I know what the truth is all the time? Why doesn't everybody know it? I don't understand!"

"We all have our cross to bear," Mom said cryptically. "You just have to learn to control it as best you can, Beth. After that you need to figure out what to do with it. It is a talent, nobody can lie to you. Now what are you going to do with a gift like that?"

CAROLE SLID ONTO clean bed sheets and curled up. There was an ache deep inside her that was sometimes hard to ignore. Lately she'd been watching Ted closely. How could it be that a man with his past could now go month after month without any physical contact? There were no outward signs that he'd been with anybody, and her heart told her he had remained faithful the past six years. She was thankful that he was no longer the toast of every town they lived in, but he hadn't let her take the place of the women he no longer went with. Not really. Once he'd hit his forties it seemed as though he'd given his affection to red meat and television.

Rolling over, Carole tugged up a sheet. As hot as Mexico City was tonight, the air-conditioning kept her fingers and toes chilled. She sensed Ted hoist himself to his feet and flick the TV off. To her surprise he headed for the bedroom. Hope kindled; it had been so long. Ted slid the door open.

"You're still up, aren't you?"

At last! She'd started to think part of him had died very young. Sitting up, she clicked on the bedside lamp. "Wide awake, I can't sleep."

"Good."

Oh, happy day. Carole sensed Beth. She sat at the desk in her bedroom studying. The faint pulse of her hideous music echoed through the wall. The coast was clear.

"Don't fall asleep," Ted warned. He went into the bathroom and Carole darted out of bed, yanking her T-shirt over her head. Digging through her dresser drawers she hunted until she found the little slip Beth had given her the Christmas they lived in Thailand. Carole had spent most of her life wearing neutral military colors, but Beth insisted her color was red. Carole stepped in front of the mirror to examine the bit of scarlet silk. It had been crumpled for years, but it was thick, good fabric and it slid over her body in a smooth waterfall without a wrinkle. She dug through a top drawer and located a lipstick Beth had given her recently, made of beeswax and olive oil and red as the slip. Carole sniffed it, it smelled nice. She leaned close to the mirror and swiped it over her lips, and discovered it felt nice too, silky as the slip. Moving back to examine her reflection, she grimaced. *Ridiculous.* Grabbing a tissue she scrubbed it off, wiping most of it away. Consoling herself, she fluffed the messy hair she still cut herself. It was her one feature that Beth approved of, at least Carole thought Beth approved. She always said, "It's you Mom. Don't change it." *Hmmm.*

Ted finished brushing his teeth and Carole darted across the tile floor and jumped into the bed, trying to arrange herself so she looked nonchalant. Not that Ted would buy that. In all their marriage she'd worn lingerie only—well, this was the first time. She was probably a pretty crummy wife. No wonder he didn't want to—the bathroom door swung open, and Ted reached for the main light switch.

"Don't shut it off," Carole pleaded. She hadn't seen Ted without his usual uniform or dress pants and shirt in ages. He stood across the room in his boxers and T-shirt, and she wanted to memorize this. It might be a long time—

"I guess I'm getting self-conscious, you're still so fit."

He had to be joking. "Ted, you're gorgeous."

"I'm almost fifty."

Ted at forty-eight stood as straight and broad shouldered as he'd been at thirty-one. Now he wore his hair in a buzz cut, in a nod to the conformity of the Marine Corp that he'd bucked for so many years. He was thicker around the middle now, even in his thighs and arms, but Carole loved every inch. She would have launched herself out of the bed and started their night on the edge of the dresser, if he would have gone for it. Ted had gotten more conservative with every passing year. His list of acceptable lovemaking had narrowed considerably.

Carole knelt on the mattress, reaching a hand out towards him. "Do fifty-year-old men have any idea how appealing they are?"

"What made you put that on?" The word *hope* flitted through Carole's mind. Ted added, "I just wanted to talk to you about the next university Beth wants to go to."

Carole dropped to sit. He wanted to talk about Beth. What would happen to them when Beth was gone and living her own life?

"Do you mean the University in Athens?"

"Yes. I've been thinking about maybe taking early retirement."

"But I thought you loved your job."

Ted leaned against the dresser and crossed his arms over his broad chest, clearly angry. "That was a long time ago, before they started transferring me around the world every six months. I'm sick of it, so I thought I could retire, maybe do some consulting work now and then."

"If that's what you want to do, I think you should do it."

"I got to thinking about the consulting work. You can choose wherever in the world you want to consult from, everyone does it. When I asked about doing it myself, they said I couldn't."

It was inevitable that he'd figure it out. Ted must have been kidding himself if he thought the transfers over the years had anything to do with his job. Then again how could he know where she'd been working? She'd been very careful those times she did manage to sneak home to catch a glimpse of them. Not even Beth ever realized how close her mother often was.

"It occurred to me that the last fifteen years hasn't been me dragging you and Beth around the planet. It's you dragging us, but I guess you knew that." Ted glared, pacing angrily back and forth in front of the bathroom door.

For years she'd dreaded when he realized it, but he seemed to be taking it rather well. Unable to confirm it, Carole simply asked, "Where do you want to be?"

"With Beth!"

She looked away. Beth would have a quite a fit. Oh, she'd smile and do her best to say something positive to Ted, but the poor young woman needed some space from her parents. As long as she stayed near cities, Carole had decided she'd be comfortable with it. Luckily Beth preferred cities. Besides, her daughter had bigger problems than the unlikely event of running into one of their kind. Until she had to suffer the consequences of her tongue without her parents to protect her, she'd never learn to control it. In the years since Carole's father had been killed in the desert, she'd traveled the globe and came to realize just how rare her kind had to be. She'd never met another, not in the jungles of a rainforest and not even in the Alps. And anyway, poor Beth needed to have a life without her parents nosing into her business anymore.

Ted said, "I'm not following her to University, Carole. I know you think I'm overprotective, but I think you're under-protective. Beth still needs us. Anyway, I've been thinking about something on the Mediterranean, a nice villa where we can enjoy life, where no one can transfer me to Bangkok two days before Christmas. Wouldn't you like that too?"

"Greece sounds nice."

"Carole, I'm not asking you if a vacation sounds nice. I'm asking you to quit and retire to Greece with me. We can spend holidays like a family, before Beth is out of school and gone."

Roaring filled Carole's ears. It wasn't the voices, they were silent. It was panic. Ted watched her, those eyes every bit as attractive as the first time she'd seen him. He wanted her to give everything up for his fantasy. Work was the only thing that had ever made her feel like she had a place in this world. What would she do with herself without work? And what of Rutak Tural's charge that she use his gift wisely? Both Rutak and her father had died so she could live. What was the point of her life if she no longer worked?

Ted stopped pacing. "I hate your job. I hate knowing what you're doing. I hate that you do it because of me. I hate the thought that you can stand in our kitchen and bake bread and then head off to God knows where and—" he mouthed the words, "kill people."

"It's not like that."

"I think I know exactly what it is like. I'm the other side of the same coin as you've often pointed out."

He waited, still and watching, while her mind raced. Would she do this for him? Could she do this for him? Ted had always hated her work. Maybe it was the reason he still kept her just outside of his heart, why he never let her closer. He just didn't know what he was asking. The choice came down to her heart or her life. The voices seemed to be listening, and even Carole didn't know her answer until she spoke.

"Okay. I'll tell them next time they call." Strangely it didn't stop her heart, and the voices approved. "*Yes, love. It is your reason for being.*" Was it? Maybe it could be. Besides, there had been questions at work. Curious comments about her ability to still keep up, not many, but it wouldn't be long before they did notice and wonder. She smiled. Yes, this felt right.

Ted's answering smile flashed. He shut out the light and shot across the room, gathering her into his arms. That night Carole felt certain she'd made the right choice.

CHAPTER
TWENTY-FIVE

Skopelos, Greece—July 2012

THE APARTMENT IN Skopelos had turquoise shutters and a wrought iron balcony with a view of the Aegean Sea. At first Beth seemed to love coming home to the white walled city for holidays. Then she stopped coming. Carole stood in the tiled entryway with Beth's monthly letter in her hands. In the past seven years Beth's life changed drastically too, and now instead of visiting she called her Dad every day, and once a month she wrote to her mother. Carole wasn't certain whose life looked better on the outside and worse at heart, hers or Beth's. Beth worked in International Banking, something to do with stocks. Carole had never really taken the time to understand it. The last two years Beth had been commuting between Amsterdam and Frankfurt by company plane, making an awful lot of money. Carole slid a finger along the flap of the envelope and tugged a folded piece of paper out. It hadn't been written on, but a photograph had been tucked inside. It showed Beth sitting inside a private plane, clad in a dark business suit, her blonde hair upswept into a professional knot. On the back of the photograph she'd written: *I found a place where people like my talent.* Carole flipped it over again and examined the photograph. Beth's eyes reminded her of her own now. She recognized pain. She dropped the picture in a drawer.

Ted sat on the balcony with the morning newspaper and his breakfast of bacon, eggs, and toast. He whistled low. "Carole, come take a look at this."

Leaning over his shoulder she looked at the latest stock market numbers. Over the past couple of years they'd made a tidy sum of money themselves. Of course they'd had a bit to begin with. She'd barely touched her income over the years, and though her salary had never been more than a Private in the Marine Corp, she'd been given bonuses that she'd never paid attention to until her retirement. Carole had been dumbfounded to find between the two of them they had over a million dollars in savings, plus Ted's comfortable pension. They'd celebrated by buying a flat of geraniums for the balcony and splurging on cinnamon ice-cream whenever they wanted. Ted seemed pleased that he could live comfortably, retired at the age of fifty-five. Every morning when he checked the stock market he announced, "This is the life." He said it this morning and stood, his chair grating noisily over the concrete flooring of the balcony. Sweeping Carole into his burly arms he danced across the tiny space into the sunny front room.

"We should go dancing every week. This is Greece, there's probably a law about it. I don't want to be thrown out over it."

Pressing her head against his shoulder, Carole felt his heart. He was happy. There *was* joy to be found in Ted's happiness. He kissed her neck, and tugged her T-shirt down, stretching the neck until it bared her shoulder and kissing it.

"You really do have beautiful skin," he whispered, marveling as he ran fingers along her face and neck. Carole tugged his shirt up and over his head. They stood in the bright light of day and Ted cradled her in his arms, his perfect lips doing things to hers that brought goose bumps shivering over her flesh. She forgot about the look in Beth's eye and her work.

"Remember the drinking fountain?" he murmured, eyeing the fountain in the corner of the large room. Water trickled from the top of the colorful mosaic fountain, dribbling down to the wide bottom. When Beth visited, she marveled over it, saying it was her favorite feature in the room. An artist had been the previous tenant and lost his security deposit for installing it.

"I remember everything about those weeks when we first met," Carole assured him. Yanking her shirt over her head and kicking her shorts off, she grabbed Ted's hand and led him to it. Sliding onto the damp edge she wrapped her arms around his torso.

"We'll probably lose our deposit if we break it," he warned.

"Let's break it," Carole pleaded, pressing her cheek against the old tattoo engraved over his heart. *Beth.* Carole kissed it, and when Ted tried to move away she held tighter, letting her heart brush over his. His heart beckoned to hers, tantalizing, always just beyond her reach. She wanted to dive into it, to know it, to claim it. Sometimes she considered claiming it against his will. Was it possible? Would it hurt him? After all this time, would he mind so much? Ted twisted, and the tattoo moved from beneath her lips. He lifted her, depositing her into an upper tier of the fountain with a splash, and began really kissing her. Distracted, Carole wrapped her arms and legs around him, pulling him closer, allowing her heart to press softly into his.

Ted shifted, adjusting her position slightly. Water spilled over the edge of the fountain in a small wave, splashing onto the tile floor. He froze. Carole glanced up at him in consternation, this was not the time to stop, and she was fairly confident the fountain could take her weight. Ted stared across the room, and she glanced over. They were reflected in a large mirror Beth had given them. It had tiled edges that matched the blue fountain. Carole reached up to touch Ted's face.

"Hey? Remember me?"

"Carole. Would you please *stop!*" Ted rarely snapped, and she stared up at him, unable to follow.

"What? What did I do? What's wrong?"

He laughed, but there was no humor in the sound. "Right now, everything. Stop with this thing." He thumped a big hand against his chest, reached to touch Carole's and seemed to think better of it, pulling his hand back. He scowled at her in the mirror.

"You never change."

Carole looked at herself in the mirror. She ran a hand over her head. The messy hair was always wild. She tried to smooth it.

Ted pulled away from her, leaving her sitting inside the fountain. "I'm not talking about your stupid hair, Carole! But since you're bringing up appearance, look at you!" He gestured towards the mirror.

"What?" She couldn't see anything to upset him.

"You still look eighteen years old."

"I do not!" she protested.

"As much as you ever did, you do. Look at me, Carole. I look like your father."

Ted grabbed his shorts and tugged them on.

"Ted! You do not look like my father! You're my husband, you're beautiful! There is absolutely nothing about you that I don't find embarrassingly delicious."

"Oh don't start. I have eyes. We look ridiculous. Look at us." He lifted her off the perch to stand, facing the mirror. Ted had gained weight over the years, he was bigger. She liked big. Running a hand over his stomach, she felt a thrill in her own. Drawn again to that heart, she leaned towards him.

"You have no idea, how—"

Ted flinched away. "Please don't, I just asked you not to do that thing. Every time I touch you, you're crawling inside me. Can we just have one normal thing in our relationship? It's not bad enough that we don't even look normal!"

"Oh come on, Ted, yes we do. You're thirteen years older than me. That's hardly abnormal."

"Just stop. Thirteen? Carole, you don't look a day older than Beth does. It makes me self-conscious."

"Why?"

"Because you're not my daughter, you're my wife."

"So what are you saying? That you don't want me anymore because I don't look old enough?" Carole said it half-joking, wishing Ted would laugh—he didn't.

Grabbing his shirt off the floor, he pulled it back on. "Of course I want you; half the guys who look at you want you."

"I don't care what other guys want! I care what you want!"

Ted picked up her clothes and tossed them at her. Crossing to the balcony, he carried his breakfast dishes into the house and put them on the tile counter while she put her clothes on. After meticulously refolding the newspaper and setting it aside, Ted finally looked at her.

"Would you be completely honest with me? Beth-like honest about something?"

"Are you sure you want me to?" *Can I be? What does he want to know?* Carole tensed, and the voices began their mantra about hiding, as if Ted didn't already know enough. She would tell him anything he wanted to know, even if she didn't want to.

"It really doesn't bother you? The difference in our ages?"

Carole opened her mouth to protest, but he held up a finger. "I know you're going to say it's only thirteen years. Please don't insult me. Does it bother you?"

Ted was right. The years between them looked more like thirty now, and she suspected in time it would only grow wider. She ignored the voices. "No, I don't care how old you get."

Candid blue eyes studied her, and it struck Carole for the very first time that Beth's gifting may have come from her father.

"Does it bother you that—apart from Beth—we have nothing in common?"

"That's not true! We have things in common!"

Ted shook his head. "No, we don't. I'm an old guy who likes to go fishing on weekends, who eats junk food and watches TV. The only thing we have in common is Beth."

"We both like cinnamon ice-cream," she said, then flushed, glancing at the floor. Ted was right. After all their years of marriage that was the only other thing she could come up with.

"I don't care," she whispered, returning his gaze. "It's not about what we have in common or looks."

Ted ran a hand over his chin, keeping his eyes on hers. "Does it bother you that more than ten years ago I made you a promise that I would find a way to make it right, to atone for the first half of our marriage, and though I've tried, the truth is there is no atonement, and what's worse is I can't ever be what you need?"

Carole leaned against the fountain, her heart sinking. She swallowed down a wave of nausea, and took a deep breath. "What do you mean?" Her voice came out a whispery quaver.

"You know what I mean, Carole. The heart thing. Does it matter that the reason I cheated, that the reason I once put so many women between us, was because it kept your heart at a safe distance?"

She crossed her arms over her chest and bent forward slightly, trying not to vomit, trying not to launch at him just to feel the satisfaction of beating him to a pulp.

"Does it matter," Ted continued, his voice low, as he took one step towards her, "That I wouldn't blame you for taking revenge even now? I had no right. I should have told you the truth long ago. Does it matter that part of me always wanted to let you in? Does it matter that it has taken me all these years to realize the truth, that I know— for a fact—that it's too late? Maybe it would have worked back in the Marshal Islands, but now it would kill me."

Sweat broke out over her forehead, and a hot flash lit from her feet and rose to prickle over her head. She glared at him. Right now she didn't care if it killed him. He'd claimed her his way long ago, what right did he have to deny her? She'd waited years!

He smiled faintly. "Does it matter that it would kill you too? To do that to me?"

"No!" she shouted, and it came out a strangled sob.

"Does it matter that that is the only reason I won't let you, Carole? Do you want to leave Beth completely alone? You're the only tether she has to—this world. Don't leave her alone like you were."

Carole stood and turned her back on Ted. Grabbing onto a top tier of the fountain, she squeezed with all her might. Bits of tile and concrete broke off in her strong hands, plunking into the pool below. She bit back a scream of fury. She sensed Ted come nearer.

"Don't touch me. I don't care about Beth right now. Don't touch me."

"So it does matter?"

"Yes," she growled.

"Does it matter that you are my heart, and I love you?"

Half the tier came down beneath Carole's hands. Chunks of concrete shattered against the tile floor, and water raced like whitewater into the lower pool, splashing over the edges and foaming over her bare feet. She spun around.

"Now you say it? After years of denying me the comfort of those words! Do you think I didn't know you loved me? I knew! You're the idiot who didn't know it! I want to hate you right now! I want you to feel my years of pain right now!"

"I've already felt it," Ted said, his blue eyes full of tears. "I shared it. I loved you from the first moment I laid eyes on you."

"Spare me!" Carole shoved past him, and ran onto the balcony. Scanning frantically, she ignored the voices and jumped. Landing easily on the street below, she ran, her bare feet skimming over rough pavement.

IN THE DISTANCE the turquoise Aegean sparkled, a brilliant backdrop to the white walls of Skopelos. At a tourist area, Carole dropped to sit at a café table. Rubbing hands over her sweaty face she rested her head in her hands, elbows digging into the scroll design of the metal table top. Her bare feet burned after running over concrete for so long, and her stomach snarled with hunger. She sensed Ted's approach, his shuffling gait as familiar to her as the continual condemnation of the voices in her head. Without a word he dropped a plate of food on the table, and slid it towards her until it rested against her elbow. Then he settled into the tiny chair beside her, holding out a fork to her. Waiting.

Dropping her hands, Carole nabbed the fork and shoveled food in, quickly chewing the mixture of beets, peppers, and rice without really tasting it. Ted watched her through sad eyes, but she refused to meet them. *Let him be sad.* Did he expect her to understand his rejection? Or to take the blame for his years of philandering? Tired as she was, ire burned in her heart again. Maybe she'd take to the water and swim. Maybe she'd get on a boat and never come back. She jabbed the fork roughly into a piece of tomato and several olives shot off her plate. So what if Ted could find her here inside the walled city? So what if his heart brushed against hers? Let him try to find her in the outside world. *Good luck with that.*

Wallowing in anger, it caught her off guard when Ted suddenly sprang to his feet, knocking the table out from under her. Instinctively Carole leapt off her chair, landing in a half crouch as a scooter shot past them, the driver's leg brushing against Ted's. One of the scooter wheels hit the table leg, flipping it over and taking out another table in the process. Several diners scattered, hurrying away from the commotion.

"Whoa!" Ted shouted after the retreating motorbike. The only response was a rude hand gesture shot in their direction. Ted reached back for her and hugged her to his side. His clean white shirt smelled like cotton and sunshine. Hot concrete burned against Carole's blistered feet, and she shifted to stand in Ted's shadow.

"General?" A man sitting at far table stood. "General White? Sir!"

Carole instantly recognized the tall black man with the fine-boned features. He wove his long body between café tables to stand by Ted.

"I'm Lincoln, Captain Robert Lincoln, do you remember?"

"Of course, Captain." There was something uncomfortable in Ted's voice, but he shook the hand offered to him.

The former leader of the Pact still looked strong, catlike and athletic, though Carole was certain the team had disbanded long ago. Lincoln wore white cotton trousers and a tunic, pegging him as a tourist.

"I recognized your polite reprimand. Only you would respond to almost being run down with 'whoa'. I'm here with my wife, a second honey—" his voice trailed off as his eyes fell on Carole, standing in Ted's shadow. "Blank?"

"White," Carole said, and hesitantly offered him her hand. "It's nice to see you, Captain." *I think*, she added mentally.

Lincoln's grin was suddenly brilliant. He didn't seem to notice her hand as his dark eyes swung back to Ted's face.

"You sly old dog you! That's why you were hunting her down! Good God, I thought you wanted—well, never mind. I sure had it wrong," he turned his eyes back to Carole. The smile stretched so widely that it was impossible for Carole not to return it. Though she had no idea what he was grinning about. He grabbed both her hands, squeezing them.

"I'm glad I didn't lie to him about where you were. Though I admit I regretted it afterwards. Spent many nights wondering why he was hunting for you." The former leader of the Pact was obviously delighted despite Ted's tight lipped frown. Then Lincoln's mouth dropped open, and he looked from one to the other, dropping Carole's hands.

"No way! That baby was yours?" He stared at Ted as though thunderstruck, then threw his head back and laughed a loud *ha*.

"Was it a boy or a girl?" Lincoln looked at Carole for that answer.

"We have a daughter. She's almost twenty-four," Ted quietly supplied.

Lincoln practically danced in the street. "I'm so glad I ran into you. I thought about you over the years, Blank. Wondered—never dreamed." Shaking his head back and forth he made a *tsk* sound while looking at Ted. "You know, General, we wondered how you managed to save her from the Judas Judge sentence. There was a wild rumor that you'd called in a favor from the President himself. Maybe it wasn't so wild?"

"Robert?" A woman's soft voice called from across the street. She stood in the doorway of a shop, in a pretty pink dress, arms loaded with packages. Lincoln looked over at her, then back at Ted and Carole.

"Well. I suppose introductions are out of the question." His eyes flitted back and forth for a moment. Then he nodded at Ted, looked at Carole and put his hand over his heart.

"All the things we could never say, huh? I'm glad you found a guy who really loves you. You deserve it." With that, Lincoln simply turned and walked away.

TED TOOK HER reluctant hand and started walking towards home. Carole ignored her burning feet and followed at his side.

"Looks like you had more than one admirer in the Pact," he murmured.

Though moments ago she'd planned never to speak to him again, she said, "I thought he hated me in the end."

With his free hand Ted scratched his nose, glancing around at the few passersby. They turned off the busyness of the main street and into the shadows of a narrow road.

"Hatred is a strange emotion. Very transitory, don't you think? Exhausting, too."

"Did you really call the President over my Judas Judge violation?"

"I told you long ago that I had to pull strings—He used to play golf with my Dad, and of course he knew who I was. Everyone in Washington did back then." Ted gave a short humorless bark. "My *mother* had an affair with my fiancé. The Washington rumor mill always got that part wrong because my dad took the rap. He was in politics. Mom drove off a bridge with my fiancée the day before my wedding. Investigators said she did it on purpose. I think the President was one of the few who truly felt for me, rather than delighted in the gossip."

"I never knew the details. Why didn't you ever tell me?"

"It wasn't something I liked to rehash. I loved Beth very much. I loved my mother too. I was thrilled they got along so well." Ted rubbed his palm roughly against his forehead. "Obviously I had no idea how well. By the time I got to a place where I could have talked about it, there didn't seem to be any point. You felt what it did to me, and you lived with my reaction." Ted avoided her eyes.

"It was a long time ago."

"You can recover from betrayal, but it does leave a mark. I imagine you know that."

Carole tried to squeeze his hand, but Ted pulled free.

"I saw your face when you looked at Lincoln. Took you back, didn't it? Your eyes never light up like that for me." Stuffing his hands into the pockets of his shorts, he glanced at her sidewise. "The world is full of men like Lincoln. Men who'd hunt with you through the jungles of Borneo if you wanted it, men who'd let you do that heart thing—"

"Why are you saying this?"

"Because I want you to be happy. I'm telling you to go find what you need. If you ever want to come back, I'll be here—alone. I'll wait for you. It seems fitting, doesn't it? After all the years I made you wait?"

Carole darted in front of Ted and stopped walking. He almost bowled her over. She put her hands on her hips, holding her ground, invading his space. "So just like that, after all this time you want me to go?"

"You were thinking it yourself a few minutes ago. What changed? Does it matter how I got the Judas Judge violation dropped? I told you long ago that I'd done it."

"You also told me you didn't know why you did it, and that you just happened to run into Lincoln who just happened to mention I was pregnant."

"I've lied to you from the first. All the more reason to leave, isn't it?"

Standing in the middle of the narrow alley, Carole crossed her arms. "What's important is why you lied. Why did you never tell me you hunted for me?"

"Because you scared the hell out of me! The truth is I tried to find you not long after I left you in The Marshall Islands. My helicopter flew over you on the way out. You were standing on the beach. I wanted to turn around, but it wasn't even an option at that point. I forced myself to wait, first a day, then a week, because I couldn't even admit to myself how I felt, or why I needed you. I was still furious with my first Beth! With my mother!"

"Do I still scare you?"

"This morning you tore apart a concrete fountain with your bare hands and then jumped out a third story window. Usually you try to hide those things from me. None of that compares to what I know,"

Ted touched his chest, "you could do here. You're completely other, of course you still scare me."

"Do you want me to go?"

"No. I—" Sorrow filled his beautiful eyes. "I love you, Carole. I always have. I can't offer you a single reason to stay, but I don't want you to go."

"Then I won't."

Ted took her hand again, threading his fingers through hers. "Thank you," he whispered, and they continued walking home.

CHAPTER
TWENTY-SIX

New Delhi, India—February 2013

THE CHAOS AND noise in the streets of New Delhi helped to revive Beth. It smelled like good spicy food, decayed flowers, and live-stock, washing the fancy luncheons, hot house flowers, and airplane air out of her lungs. On the busy streets mismatched rickety shacks leaned against each other for support. Laughter, arguing, and traffic melded into a cacophony of white noise in the hot sun. Beth felt like she'd been starving to death in posh sky-rises and board rooms as an International Stock Broker. The people she worked with loved making money, and she couldn't care less about it, but she was very good at it. At least she was very good at knowing how to make money, and who could be trusted.

Beth stopped beside a brightly painted stall selling fabric, running her fingers over turquoise silk threaded with silver. Dad and Mom paused beside her to wait. She loved the way they held hands, the way Dad tugged Mom close and whispered in her ear. Mom sipped a green smoothie from the edge of a paper cup, and tried to act casual while Dad sneaked a kiss alongside her ear. Dad draped a fold of blue mate-rial over Mom's shoulder, contemplating it. Mom offered him a sip of the sludge from her cup, and Dad backed away in mock horror. Beth laughed; she couldn't imagine Mom in a sari. She couldn't imagine

Mom in anything but her drab olive shorts and plain boring T-shirt. The entire trip Beth had been trying to get her into something with color in it.

Beth had been thrilled to shimmy into traditional Indian clothing. Rich folds of magenta fabric caressed her, though the bold colors shamed her pale hair.

"Are you happy?" Mom's voice sounded sharp and she looked right through Beth. Mom knew the answer. Instantly Beth's peace evaporated. Anger sizzled hot from the tips of her hennaed feet to the glitter she'd paid a street woman to paint into the part of her hair. Why did Mom have to do this? Of all people, she knew Beth had to answer honestly, and now Dad would be upset.

Glaring at her mother she gave her honest answer. Dad's eyes, the most gorgeous shade of blue she'd ever seen, widened in alarm. He took her arm, tugging her close. "But why aren't you happy, Bethy?" Suddenly the street noise became a headache inducing roar.

"Oh, Daddy!" The truth shot out her mouth. "I hate working with money. I don't care about money. Why would I? We never had any and I had the best childhood ever."

Dad smiled briefly. Mom pressed, "What would make you happy, Beth?"

The answer surprised Beth, though it shouldn't have. Even now she had a notebook in her hand, and she'd already jotted the locations of some of the treasures of India.

"I've always wanted to run a general store. I know that sounds dumb, but I mean a place that sells the kind of products we use, Mom. The things that nobody would be allergic to: local honey, eggs, organic foods, natural fabrics, and homeopathic supplies. You know that tea I gave you, Dad?"

He nodded. "That stuff can't be legal. I dream about that stuff."

"Where would you sell it? Online?" Mom asked.

"No!" Beth shuddered. "This is the part where it gets financially stupid. I just want one store, in a small town someplace, maybe in Scotland or someplace picturesque. I don't care about making money, just enough to survive on. I just want a quiet, boring life, and I don't want to move again—*ever.*"

Dad chuckled at that. "Good thing, I think you've run out of new places." A dog raced past so closely its toenails scratched Beth's feet. Mom jerked Dad out of the way as a blue monkey followed, racing after it. Without missing a beat, Mom continued her interrogation.

"Why don't you do it then?" Mom persisted. They were going to have words about this next time they were alone. Mom could be thoughtless about Dad's feelings and Beth was tired of it. If Mom wanted the truth, she'd give it to her, privately. In the meantime, the truthful answer to Mom's question popped out.

"Dad loves Skopelos, and what I have in mind would never work there. I don't want to be in Scotland alone. I hate being so far from *Daddy* as it is."

Always a softie, Dad's blue eyes filled with tears and he squeezed her tightly like she was still a little girl, resting his cheek on top her head.

"I could live in Scotland, Beth. Your mother is right, so stop giving her the evil eye for asking you. You two must think I'm blind! I wish I'd realized you weren't happy. Do you have any idea what that does to a father?" He lifted her hand and pressed it right against his heart. Peace slid through Beth's body, there was nothing like the reassuring touch of her father's heart.

"I say Scotland, here we come. You know what? I've never been," he said.

"ONE MORE MOVE, Carole? I hope it's my last," said Ted. The comment shot a shiver up her back. Ted tugged the scratchy blanket over her shoulder, and moved closer towards her in the hotel bed. "I only meant I'm sick of moving. I'm not that old. Sheesh. I'd just like to be settled in one place." Carole burrowed against his big chest, and not because of the cold. He smelled good.

"It's a cool night. This Indian weather is all over the map." He pressed his lips against her forehead. "Mmm," sounded deep in his throat. He smelled like some type of scented soap Beth had picked out. It was surprisingly pleasant. Carole pressed her hand against his chest, and then pulled it away when Ted's sound of pleasure abruptly faded, but he took her hand and put it back in place.

"I like it," he whispered. "I'm sorry it can't be more. If it's any consolation I'll always regret not allowing it in the early days when it was possible."

"You let Beth in," Carole whispered. It seemed safe to voice the jealous thought in the dark of the small hotel room. "That doesn't bother you."

Ted wrapped her in his big arms and pulled her tightly against him, nuzzling her hair. "Her touch bounces lightly," his voice turned husky, "Yours probes like a spear. I've both wanted and feared it from the first time it pressed against me. It would be better than sex, wouldn't it?"

"I think so."

Ted paused. "Just do it then."

Carole froze for a moment, and then sat straight up in the bed, snapping on the bedside light. It illuminated the garish striped décor.

"What? What happened to *it will kill you*? And kill me? What happened to leaving Beth alone in the world?" She glared down at him.

"I've taken so much from you. I can't deny you the only thing you've ever asked from me. Not anymore. If you want it and I want it, damn the consequences, Beth will be fine in time, she's tough."

Pulling her knees up, Carole put her face in her hands. "I'm not sure she would be. Oh, Ted, I thought this was settled."

He slid a hand up her leg. "I think sometimes you forget I'm a marine too. My heart argues with my head all the time, but I've learned to listen to my heart. You still haven't. I don't think you ever have. Don't think. For once just listen to your heart."

"Take him. Claim him for your own."

In that instant Carole understood exactly where the voices came from—her own heart, all those things she'd known instinctively, all the times her heart had argued with her mind. All her life she'd ignored her own heart. *Not any more, not with Ted.* She needed no further inducement. In one swift movement she jerked the scratchy blanket off and tossed it onto the floor, straddling Ted's torso. Digging her fingers into his hair she yanked his head up so his lips met hers, a groan of victory low in her throat. She kissed him roughly, biting his lip. Ted grabbed handfuls of her shorn hair, and wrestled her onto her back.

Carole barely noticed when they slid off the bed and onto the matted floor. It didn't matter, nothing mattered but this. Grabbing Ted's hands, she kicked against the side of the bed, sliding them across the floor and rolling Ted onto his back again. This would be done her way, and she wanted to be on top.

"You're mine!" she growled, sitting on him. "Mine." Threading her fingers through his, she lifted his hands and slammed them against the floor, hard. "You will never go with another woman again! Mine!"

"Carole! You know I won't!" Ted protested.

"I don't care! Once I claim you, you can't! You couldn't bear to!"

"I couldn't bear to anyway," he gasped and she knew he meant it.

"But you did! And you're wrong about your heart. When the women in your life betrayed you they didn't leave a mark on it. Your cheating did! It left holes! It destroyed and took what should be mine." Angrily she lifted his hands only to slam them against the floor again. "You tried to punish your betrayer by hurting me, and now I'm going to punish you for that. I will not take, I won't kill you, but I will leave a mark you can never forget." Ted fought back, not allowing her to slam his hands against the floor again. He squeezed her hands so hard it almost hurt. Carole closed her eyes and focused, shifting into position to take him. She couldn't survive killing the man she loved—the voices—*her heart* told her that, but she could claim him. She took a deep breath and concentrated. One slip would be too much and cost his life and hers.

The noise from the busy street outside faded until all she heard was Ted's heartbeat. She could feel it beating outside her own, strong but out of sync with hers, it had its own rhythm. In her mind she could see it, the heart of the man she loved. It was human and frail, ragged and wounded, but in places it was whole. It seemed as though it beat within a silver cage. Carole's heart circled his, closer and closer, searching for space. Ted moaned; she felt the vibration with her entire body. Then she found a place, and leaned forward, taking him and pressing her heart against his. She cut a shape into his heart, a shape she didn't recognize but instantly knew to be her mark. To enter his damaged heart was impossible, but this much would be hers.

Absorbed in the intimate task she shivered with intense pleasure. Years of pent up desire rippled through her. She threw her head back and felt it, the remnants of his heart. He'd wasted it whoring and running long ago, but this much she could have, and it was enough. After decades of waiting, this was enough. She finished rocking before she heard Ted's screams of pain. Carole opened her eyes, and squeezed her thighs to hold on. His back arched and his mouth stretched open wide. Fine hairs rose all over her body. Was there anything more horrible than the screams of a man in pain? In the hallway outside, she heard running. Someone banged on the door, shouting in Punjabi. Still Ted screamed, and tears ran down his face and hers. The sound went on and on, but Carole felt no regret for causing it. The simple mark would have been relatively painless once. It was Ted's fault his heart was damaged, it was his fault this hurt. Dishonor had a cost, and he was still paying it.

He shook when he finally stopped screaming, but when he opened his eyes he grabbed her around the waist and pulled her against him.

"Thank you," he groaned. "Thank you!"

BETH SLID THE salt shaker across the table towards her Dad and smirked.

"What's so funny?" he asked, applying it to his scrambled eggs. Beth went beet red, it matched her hot pink sari rather well. She looked to her mother for help. Carole bit her lip, trying to hide a smile. Beth didn't disappoint.

"Getting kicked out of a hotel because your parents are having wild sex, Dad! I don't know whether to be mortified or proud."

Ted glanced at Carole and smiled. "Be proud."

"I'm going to get more orange juice." Beth shot out of her seat and hurried across the room towards the buffet. Carole looked down at her plate of yogurt and chickpeas, her shoulders shaking with silent laughter.

Ted reached across the table and took her hand, and lifted it to his lips. "Best night of my life. But I'm going to ask you to do something more, Carole."

She stopped laughing immediately. "No! I won't, Ted. I can't. Trust me, my heart doesn't want more." He kissed her hand again.

"That's not what I meant. I want you to fix what's wrong between you and Beth. When she was younger I thought it was your fault you weren't close. You were gone so much, and you kept us both at arm's length when you weren't. I felt safer there, and I thought maybe Beth did too. Now I wonder. Did I somehow teach Beth to put distance between you? I don't like the way she treats you, and I think it's my fault. It's hard for me to know what I've cost you. Is the trouble between you and Beth because of me, or because her mother lied to her so much?" Ted whispered the last, and Carole flinched, but when she looked in his eyes there was no accusation there, and when she tried to pull her hand out of his, he held tightly.

"Don't. I've lied to Beth too, and if I'm not mistaken you used to cover for my indiscretions."

Carole stared at her plate blindly for a moment, tears swimming into her eyes. She whispered, "It's not entirely your fault."

"Isn't it?"

She looked into his sky clear eyes. He'd gotten even more beautiful overnight.

"It was partly so she couldn't feel what you were doing to me—when you went with other women." Ted made a sound like a wounded animal. Several families at neighboring tables turned to stare. Carole shook her head at him. "But it wasn't only that, Ted. Beth can't know how different I am, how different she is—it's safer this way."

"Safer! Is there something you're not telling me?"

Carole smiled at him. "Would you really want to know?"

"If it is about Beth's safety, yes!"

"What if it is safer for all of us if you don't know either?"

Ted thought about that, pushing his eggs around on his plate for a bit. Beth had apparently abandoned them. Carole could sense her on the street outside, digging through piles of spices. It was Ted who avoided Carole's eyes now. Even if she had been a normal woman, this would be hard for him. To be kept in the dark by his wife, for the safety of his family. She would tell him now, if he pressed, about her father and what she was. It didn't matter what the voices said about it. She wouldn't lie. But she hoped he wouldn't ask, because it could only put distance between them. And she would very much like to enjoy their newfound connection, at least longer than a few hours. It was all they could ever have.

"Okay, if you say so. But don't blame your secrets for the gulf between the two of you. Spend time with her. It doesn't have to involve the touch of your heart. She still needs you."

"I'm right here in India with her while she picks out silks and junk for her shop, Ted. How much more time can I spend with her?"

"Go to Scotland with her. Find her dream shop. I'll pack up the apartment in Skopelos and come when you call. But take your time, connect with her like—I don't know—I want to say like normal people do."

"Not sure I know how to do that," Carole mused.

"Learn," Ted said. "Fake it."

"I don't think Beth knows normal either."

"Learn together then." He took her hand and pressed it against his heart and smiled at her. "She's got a really terrific mother. I think she deserves to know that."

CHAPTER
TWENTY-SEVEN

Inverness, Scotland—March 2013

"HOW MANY MILES a day do you jog, Mom? I told you they stopped serving breakfast at ten." Beth stomped out the door of the Bed & Breakfast, her fashion boots clicking over paving stones. Smoothing her sweater-dress, she pretended to pick imaginary flecks off the creamy material, not quite daring to glare into her Mom's eyes. Her mother was still as toned and muscular as a seventeen-year-old jock, and her incessant running seemed borderline compulsive. Now she'd upped it to twice a day. *So much for spending time together.* Unlocking the passenger door on the rental car, Beth held it open for her.

"A shower seemed higher priority since we'll be driving all afternoon," Carole said.

Beth tried not to roll her eyes. Mom answered questions like a lawyer. Why did time alone with her mother make her feel ten again? *Sit by me Mom, talk to me.* Taking a deep breath, Beth fished in her huge leather purse. *I'm not being fair. Mom used to skate and swim with me all the time, and cook me anything I asked for, when she was home, anyway.*

Beth located what she'd been looking for. "Here, I snagged some oatcakes and fruit for you." She shoved a bag into her mother's hands. "We're going to need to find someplace with good food. The next B&B

said they won't cook special meals." She closed the door and hurried around the car, sliding into the driver's seat. Her mother sat rigid in her seat, hands clutching the paper bag, eyes straight ahead. "It's okay to relax, Mom. I'm a good driver."

"It's not you," Carole said. She reached over and tugged on Beth's belt to make sure it was secure. Beth took a deep breath. What had she been thinking to agree to this? What had Dad been thinking to suggest they scout the area alone? How could a mother and daughter have absolutely nothing in common?

At the end of the driveway her mother twisted back and forth, craning her neck to scour the empty roadway for oncoming cars. "It's safe," Carole said and jammed two oatcakes into her mouth. Beth impatiently stepped on the gas and the car lurched forward. Carole grabbed the dashboard and shot her a dirty look, chewing fast. Dad would have laughed.

"You really should learn to drive. You wouldn't be so paranoid."

"I'm surprised you actually like it," Carole said through her mouthful.

"Why?" Beth demanded. She sensed the lie coming before her mother even swallowed the food and said it.

"You just—seemed to like walking when you were little. Hikes are fun. You and I used to go on long walks all the time."

Maybe when you could carry me, she replied to the lie in her head. "It's almost two hundred kilometers to the Isle of Skye. I'm sure you could run it, but I'd prefer to drive."

"Don't sass me, Beth. Turn here." Carole pointed.

Grudgingly Beth obeyed. The rental bumped onto a rough, dirt road barely wide enough for their car. Bracken and broom brushed against the vehicle on both sides.

"This isn't the way," she complained. It looked like weeds overtook the road further ahead.

"It's a shortcut."

Beth glared at the lie and her mother actually rolled her eyes a bit.

"Technically it is longer. But it takes us away from civilization sooner, so it *feels* shorter to me. I like peace and quiet. Besides, I thought you wanted to check the nooks and crannies of Scotland."

"I do, but are you sure it's even a road? Looks like a sheep path."

"Same thing where we're headed." Carole leaned her head back and closed her eyes. Beth slowed down. For her mother to fall asleep inside a vehicle she was driving would be the ultimate compliment.

"I AM GOING to freeze to death out here," Beth fussed, half laughing as she trudged forward. "I had no idea Scotland was so bone chilling cold! Maybe I should see if I can get my job back. There's a branch in New Delhi that might not be so bad."

Carole plunged across the moor, muck sticking to her sensible hiking boots, leading the way for Beth. They were surely not too far from civilization and heat for her spoiled child. Maybe it was a good thing the car had broken down. Sometimes Beth's naivety shocked her; choosing a place to live based on a book you'd read at age twelve seemed impulsive. As much as Carole hated the voices, they'd never allowed her to be naïve. She was glad Ted hadn't come after all. While he was doing his best to be supportive of Beth's plan, he couldn't hide the fact that he preferred financial security over Beth's idea of a General Store. The last thing he needed to know was why she'd chosen Scotland. Carole stopped, turning to her daughter.

"So pick someplace different, Beth. You look happier wading through this mud than you have in the past few years. I'd say you're on the right track." And despite her daughter's whining, Beth's heart did feel happier. Carole could feel it bouncing outside her own. That was a feeling she'd learned to treasure.

Beth stopped in the middle of the road, beautiful in her sweater dress and ridiculous fashion boots. "Mother," she said, rubbing her hands up and down her arms, "I'm freezing! Where are we? We should have stayed on the main road, and we definitely should have brought a map."

"This *is* the main road, I don't need a map," said Carole.

"What do you mean you don't need a map?" said Beth.

Carole didn't answer, but she heard Beth grumble under her breath, "I thought hikes were supposed to be fun."

Carole told her, "Walking along a road is not hiking."

"Oh look! Thank goodness! Here comes a car!" Beth seemed thrilled for the interruption and jumped up and down, frantically waving her arms as though it were a matter of life and death. The driver of a little blue Mini Cooper sped up to get to her, screeching to a halt and leaning over to open the passenger door wide and welcoming. Carole had no doubt the man would be chivalrous. Beth invited chivalry, until she started speaking. Likely they wouldn't make it a mile in the car.

"Thank you so much for stopping, you're a lifesaver. Mind giving us a ride to the nearest phone?" At a soundless nod from the driver, Beth grabbed a lever and slid the passenger seat forward. She motioned for Carole to climb into the back.

"You can't be serious?"

"Come on, Mom," Beth hissed. "I'm not walking another step, there's no way I'd fit, and I'm wearing a dress!"

Carole crawled into the backseat. The seats were almost flush against the front, and she had to stretch her legs across the backseat to fit. Beth slid her long frame into the vehicle, her knees almost level with the top of the dashboard. She slammed the door shut and Carole's heart skipped a couple of beats. It looked like a clown car, but felt like a metal coffin. The murky sludge of the vehicle settled through her, making her shudder. It made her think of mud puddles with oily rainbows resting on top.

"Our car broke down miles back, and we have absolutely no idea where we are. I haven't seen a single road sign!" Beth's greeting sounded ridiculously dramatic. Carole was certain the only danger walking the moor was blisters from Beth's stupid footwear.

Carole knew there were no weapons in the car, as nothing more could possibly fit, so she tried to relax. The heavyset driver in an ill-fitting suit looked stuffed into his seat, but he didn't look dangerous. Smoothing a horrible comb-over, he put the car in gear and accelerated. Crossing her arms over her chest Carole stared out the window, trying to breathe calmly. Ninety-eight seconds. It would take over a minute to extricate both Beth and herself from this car. Unacceptable in an emergency. In the back of her mind the voices stirred, and she fought to ignore them. It was bad enough without their two cents.

Beth prattled on in the front seat. "I'm Beth White and this is my mother, Carole White. I can't tell what end is up on this moor. This is the way to Skye, right? I have reservations at a Bed and Breakfast near there, The Highlander Pottery House. My stars! I never saw anyone wear a suit coat over tartan before. Your kilt is lovely! Mother! Look at this fabric! Such beautiful wool. I've never seen the likes of it. Bet you could put that through a washing machine no worries. Goodness, I apologize for being rude. Thank you for picking us up. I'm sure glad you happened along. Where were you headed?"

From the backseat Carole got the impression that Beth was fingering the man's kilt. Did her daughter have no common sense?

"Vale. Meh naim's Doric." The man spoke in heavily accented Scots, finally managing to get a word in. The brogue so thick that his next words were muffled gibberish. Carole took an immediate dislike to him, although she was certain no man could be held responsible for his tone while Beth petted his thigh. Doric wasn't much taller than the steering wheel, and when he turned his head towards Beth his eyes were level with her breast. His head turned that way more than it looked out the windshield and the car waivered onto the bumpy shoulder of the road.

"Try not to distract Doric while he's driving, Beth." Nameless anxiety tugged in the back of her mind.

"It is possible to talk and drive, Mother," Beth sniped. "My mother thinks driving any car requires the concentration of a NASCAR race."

Again half the car slid off the road, bumping along the shoulder.

"Is something wrong with the car?" Beth asked.

"Aye, cahrk goan vale 'tis a bit jarrin'," Doric replied and he twisted the wheel, accelerating. The vehicle jerked onto the moor and Carole's head bounced against the roof violently. The car thudded up and down momentarily and then a violent whoosh slammed into it, rocking the vehicle back and forth for long seconds. Then it was over, and Doric continued coasting downhill as though nothing had happened, though his comb-over now rested upside down on the wrong side of his head.

"What on earth was that?" Beth asked, rubbing bruised knees.

Cold terror shot through Carole in waves. She already knew. *Why did I ignore the voices? My heart knew!* They'd entered a veil. Ignoring the pristine vista of Scotland sprawling green and rugged outside the windows, she turned her full attention on Doric. The man wasn't old, though he was mostly bald, and while he was very short, he wasn't fat either. The broad shoulders stretching the suit jacket were pure muscle. *Warrior.* He wagged a finger at Carole, tiny eyes staring through the rearview mirror.

"Dinna be scanning meh, Shieldmaiten. Gifs me a wicket haideck."

"Danger. He is like us, but not. He wants Beth." The voices predicted far too late what Carole could easily deduce for herself. This warrior wanted Beth—at least until he knew what her father was. How had she not noticed the vague touch of his heart? Had the touch of Beth's drowned it out? Could Beth feel it? Of course she could! No wonder she liked the creepy little man!

Beth twisted to look curiously back at her, apparently unable to completely decipher Doric's words about Shieldmaidens and headaches. Beth turned back to Doric, and matter-of-factly reached over and plopped his greasy patch of hair back into place on his even greasier head. "If this is Scottish weather, it's definitely out of the running for my shop. That was like a personal tornado! Though I'd like to buy some of that wool your kilt is made from. Is it local?"

Beth continued her one sided conversation as Carole's mind raced and she fought to reign her thundering heart in. She would have to kill Doric before he realized what they were and killed them. Had the mark she left on Ted's heart changed hers enough to let them pass safely? Did her heart feel married? Surely he would have reacted already if he'd realized she wasn't married to one of their own. Carole fought back panic. Beth couldn't know what any of this was! They had to get out of the veil before anyone else saw them, or Beth saw too much! There were only a few wooden shacks within view and no other people in sight. Carole sensed no one as far as she could scan, but the veil stretched days farther than she could ever sense. No, she had to kill this man as quickly as possible, just not in front of Beth!

A few hundred yards from the nearest shacks, the car rolled to a stop at the bottom of a slope.

"Why are you stopping?" Beth asked. Doric slid the gear into park.

"Wok," he responded. Opening the door, he began the process of disembarking.

Carole sat perfectly still, her mind racing while her daughter complained. "Was that shaking just the car then? That was weird! And now our rescue vehicle breaks down too." Beth threw her door open and climbed out. After sliding the passenger seat forward for Carole to crawl out, she straightened and stretched her lean body, griping, "Do you know what, Mom? I'm getting a cell phone. I know you don't like them, but I don't care. I don't like getting stranded." Turning towards the huts, Beth continued her oblivious monologue. "No phone lines either. Hey, Doric? Is this where you get your wool?" Suddenly she sounded excited as she pointed at the largest shack. Bolts of colorful fabric were stacked along the front porch, and a cart full of it stood to the side.

Before Carole untangled herself from the back, Beth hurried around the little car and slid an arm through Doric's. With her stiletto boots she stood well over six feet tall. Even including his flopping comb-over Doric barely made five feet. In her pale sweater dress, silky blonde hair neat as a pin, next to squat, bowlegged Doric in his kilt and a dark suit coat, they made an odd pair. Carole couldn't believe her daughter could bear to touch him. Climbing out of the vehicle, every cell of her being urged her to kill the man quickly. She wondered that he dared turn his back to her, that he didn't sense it, but both Beth and the warrior faced in the opposite direction, ignoring her.

"Oof, this place smells fantastic. Edible almost. Does it to you too, Doric?" said Beth.

"Tis clean."

"Hah, my Mom always says that, that things are clean. I know exactly what you mean though. It does smell fresh and clean. Maybe I could open my shop around here, are there any little villages nearby?"

Companionably the two of them marched towards a distant shack, Beth excitedly yammering about wool, kilts, and her shop. Carole lagged behind, her skin crawling and the voices urging escape. Outside the confines of the car it became clear that the mucky strangeness she'd attributed to the car was actually the faint polluted touch of Doric's heart. While it was recognizable as one of her kind, there was something wrong with him, something dark.

Forty-five seconds. It would take forty-five seconds to kill Doric and get out of the veil. Beth would have to take those boots off and run. How long afterwards would it take to explain why to Beth? She had no doubt her daughter would not take killing in stride, and when Ted asked Beth what was wrong—what would her daughter have to tell him? Carole's heart sank, aching. Escape could cost her both Beth and Ted, but there was no choice. The thought shot sharp pains through her heart.

Doric stopped walking and turned around. To Carole's dismay Beth jogged ahead, managing quite well in her heels, and adding precious seconds to their escape time. The wide warrior walked back to Carole.

"Dinna worrit, Shieldmaiten. Yer dah'ter not fer meh, she's fer Berwick—clan leh'er. Weh be need'n han arc. Quite ah honor fer yer dah'ter, mate 'o clan leh'er an—"

In the distance, Beth skipped up the steps of a shack and went inside. Carole moved lightning fast. If Doric saw her foot coming, he didn't respond quickly enough. With a kick to his throat, Carole interrupted Doric's speech about the honor it would be for Beth to become the mate of his clan leader. The squat warrior thudded backwards and fell. Darting forward, Carole kicked him in the head with her thick treaded boot. Kneeling, she lifted his head to break his thick neck.

Oddly the voices didn't object, but something inside her quailed. Inside her head Rutak Tural's voice whispered over the years, *droplets in the ocean*. He'd called their kind droplets in the ocean. Dropping Doric's greasy head onto the mucky ground, she stood looking down at him, wiping her hands on her pants, unable to kill him. She settled on kicking him in the side of his head, hard. Doric's head jerked roughly to the side and back, his comb-over flipped out of place again. Carole fished his car keys out of his suit jacket, ignoring the blood trickling out of his ear. The injuries probably wouldn't kill him, if warriors from his clan found him soon—and could heal like Rutak Tural had once done for her. Deep down Carole didn't really care.

CROSSING THE WOODEN floor, Beth paused and looked down. Thick plank flooring muffled her footsteps oddly. Such quality construction struck her as unusual, especially for a shack in the middle of nowhere. Her eyes slid over an ugly mannequin, then to bolts of tartan. Plaids in lovely, muted shades were stacked against all four walls, floor to low ceiling. Piles of the fabric sat on tables and long bolts leaned against shuttered windows. Grey daylight came in through the lone open window, highlighting a length of red and blue plaid partially unfurled on a table. Beth hurried over, brushing a hand over it, and groaning with pleasure. The bolt was wider than any she'd seen, the wool finer, flawless, yet she'd swear it had been hand-loomed. It took effort to upend the bolt, the weight and length making it cumbersome.

"It would need to be cut smaller to sell to the public. What a shame!" Beth unraveled a length and rubbed it against her cheek, closing her eyes. "Oh! So soft! I'd adore a bedspread made of this!"

"I'd ha'dore seeing ter tha."

Beth spun around, instinctively shoving the fabric to the floor creating a lame barrier between her and the voice, and inwardly wincing at the desecration. The ugly mannequin stepped into the light, revealing a fully kilted Scotsman. His elaborate red kilt matched the fabric barrier rolling over the tips of his boots. Grizzled ginger hair reached to his half naked shoulders, and long patches of hair dotted his jawline. Pale eyes slid admiringly over her, and Beth looked away from them. Ample sprouts of orange hair protruded from beneath the man's armpits, and she glanced at his sporran only to notice long patches of hair on his belly. Mercifully her eyes returned to his.

"I'm sorry, I didn't, er, realize you weren't a—were—real." She cleared her throat, choking back the words *creepy mannequin*. "Doric brought me. My name's Beth White and I'd be interested in purchasing quite a bit of this material." She gestured to the floor. "I'm going to be opening a shop, possibly nearby."

The man laughed, slapping meaty hands against his thighs. For the first time Beth noticed he had a sword strapped to his side. Something about it sent a shiver right up her back.

"Is there a highlander festival going on?"

The man's head tilted to the side, reminding her of a curious orangutan she'd once encountered.

"Bit o' a dialick barrier, Luv. Small mah'er, weal be speakin' har ta har soon eh'nuf."

"Pardon? You lost me after dialect barrier."

The man stepped across the fabric, his boots leaving mucky prints. Beth couldn't stop a sound of protest at the sight. He stopped a bit too close, not quite reaching her shoulders with the top of his head, and she instinctively leaned away.

"Nah worrit," he said, grabbing her forearms harshly. "Meh name be Berwick, an ah give yeh mah declah-ration."

"I don't think so!" Beth said, yanking her arms free. "I don't really care to know your name, if this is how you treat company."

"Cuhmpny?" Berwick chuckled. "Luv! I mean ter make yeh mah wife!"

Immediately Beth put her hand over her mouth, a maneuver necessary to keep *I'd rather lick your sword* from coming truthfully out of it.

Berwick smiled, gesturing towards her with an open hand. "Over-wealmed yeh, ah understand."

A giggle tried to escape her hand, and it became necessary to step on her own foot with the sharp heel of the other. *Don't laugh, don't laugh, do not laugh. You want to buy the wool don't you?*

Berwick moved forward and reached a hand up to her forearm. Gently he ran a finger down it. "Ham sorrah ta ha' bruised yeh." Turning away, he bent and easily lifted the huge bolt of fabric from the floor. Brushing muck from it, he deftly tossed it up, unfurling a large length and draping it over the table. He ran his thick square hands over the material lovingly.

Beth dropped her hands and smiled faintly. She felt the same way about that cloth. It was beautiful.

"But ah, 'spose ye'll be gettin' more'n ah few bruises t'day." Berwick patted the fabric with both hands. "Hop on up, Luv. Bes' be getting' to it."

Beth's mouth dropped open. Berwick fiddled with a clasp at his waist and his sword crashed to the floor of the cabin, echoing through the heavy wood. Tugging at his kilt, half the fabric dropped off one beefy pink shoulder.

"Are you—" Beth said a word her mother would certainly not approve of, "kidding me? Drop. Dead! You disgusting—" Turning her back on him, Beth stomped to the door, choosing from all the cuss words she'd ever heard as she moved. Without looking back at Berwick, she opened the door and slammed it with all of her might. It made a satisfying echo through the sturdy cabin. Standing on the porch for a moment, she angrily shoved several bolts of fabric off the banister—but only after glancing at the porch floor to make sure it was clean. Beth stormed down the steps and starting walking.

"Mother? Where the heck are you? I will walk all the way to the Isle of Skye, but we're getting out of here!"

STANDING OUTSIDE THE back window, Carole had heard every word. Quietly she slithered inside before Berwick could take a step after Beth. One stealthy leap and she landed on Berwick's half naked back, wrapping both strong arms around his neck, and mentally counting the seconds until he'd pass out. Ten…nine…Carole willed Beth not to turn around, but at the same time she wondered if her daughter would really mind if she saw. Beth slammed the door at the same time they hit the floor together, Berwick already unconscious. His massive weight knocked the wind out of Carole. Blinking against infringing darkness, she struggled to remain aware and sucked deep breaths. It took a full thirty seconds to maneuver out from under him. She sensed Beth's tirade on the front porch, and her daughter stomping away. Two hundred and seven seconds to get Beth and escape the veil. *Too long!*

Quickly she rolled Berwick onto his stomach and hog-tied him with his own belt, using the sword as leverage. *I should kill him! Both of them, or they'll follow,* she thought. Berwick wanted Beth. Even with the man unconscious Carole sensed it in his dim murky heart. She grabbed a handful of his hair, lifted his head and slammed it repeatedly against the floor until blood splattered. Again the memory of Rutak Tural's words made her stop prematurely. Standing she raced across the room and jumped out the window, hoping she'd never regret leaving the men alive.

BETH HAD MADE good progress. She cluelessly stalked towards the edge of the veil with long strides, nearing the dip in the earth where Doric lay tied up with strips of his own kilt. Inside the Mini Cooper, Carole pulled up alongside her daughter and shouted, "Get in!"

Beth stared through the window. "You know how to drive?" Her voice sounded muffled through the glass.

Sixty-seven seconds, if Beth stopped asking stupid questions and got in. Carole reached across and opened the door. "Now."

Beth slid in. "Mom? Are you stealing Doric's car?"

Carole hesitated briefly, the disappointment in Beth's eyes—as always—crystal clear. "Yes!" Carole huffed. "I'm stealing Doric's car. That guy is a creep, and we're getting out of here."

"Mom! Did he try something with you?"

"Let's just say he had plans I objected to."

"Oh! That's disgusting! What did he—oh, no—no, don't tell me. You're okay, right?"

Carole nodded.

"You should have seen his friend! Creepy little—did you ever see the movie Deliverance?"

Climbing uphill, the car slid a bit on the mucky ground. Carole didn't answer.

"Did Doric scare you, Mom?"

"Yes," Carole said.

"Go faster," Beth said, tugging her seatbelt across her body and securing it with a click.

They hit the edge of the invisible veil with no warning. The car jerked back and forth and Beth said a word Carole had never expected to hear come out of her mouth. At least not without that Berwick character suggesting flat-out rape.

"That's enough of that. Your father would have a fit if he heard you talking like that."

"Mother! Are you kidding? What was that, and did you smell it? Something like garbage, I noticed it when we drove in."

"It was really windy."

"I don't think so! That is not normal, turbulence doesn't happen on the ground."

"Apparently it does, Beth. Those people in Inverness warned you about the weather here."

"Yeah, they said it's cold and wet! Not—not—whatever the heck that was. There's something weird about this place! That was something—something—I don't know, but it was something."

Scanning, Carole headed across the moor, purposely plowing through brush and avoiding muddy spots. Beth twisted in her seat to look behind them.

"Do you think they'll follow us?"

Carole pushed the pedal all the way to the floor. She knew they'd follow. The little car responded with surprising speed and they trounced up and down until they hit the narrow road.

"Whoa! You're going the wrong way."

"We can't go to Skye, now. You told Doric where we were headed. I'm going back to the rental to get our stuff."

"You know we could get in a lot of trouble stealing a car."

Smiling faintly, Carole replied, "Only if we get caught."

"Go Mom!" Beth laughed, and a real smile touched her lips. "Who are you and what have you done with my real mother?"

"Just protecting my daughter."

The smile vanished and Beth went quiet.

⁓⤬⁓

IN A MATTER of minutes Carole pulled up beside the rental. Beth got out, still subdued, and walked to the sedan. Opening the door she hit a button on the dashboard and the trunk popped open. Without a word she dragged her heavy monogrammed suitcases out, pushing and shoving until each piece fit into the hatch of the Mini Cooper. Carole quickly dug through the glove box of the rental and took every bit of identifying data out. She wasn't going to make it easy to trace it back to Beth.

They returned to Inverness in time for rush hour traffic. Part of Carole wanted to ask Beth to take over, but she knew her daughter was stewing. She just hoped Beth wouldn't ask questions she couldn't answer truthfully. What if Beth asked why she could physically feel the touch of Doric and Berwick inside her own body? Surely she had been drawn to Doric on some low level. It had to have been noticeable. Beth hadn't felt the touch of one of their own since she'd been a baby. Carole wondered if it had made her daughter remember the bond they'd once shared. Every day she ached to open her heart to Beth again, but knew she never could. Beth couldn't live in that world, and it was better if she didn't know about it. Surely the touch of Doric and Berwick's hearts wouldn't tempt her to repeat the experience. Maybe it had been a blessing.

"Mom?" The sound of Beth's voice made her jump. Carole didn't look at her, and waited, trying to hide her tension.

"I'm going to ask you something, and I want you to tell me the truth. Will you?"

"If I can."

Beth made an angry sound of frustration, and rearranged her legs in the confines of the car. "Do you remember when we lived in Indonesia? I was thirteen."

That question was unexpected. "I remember Indonesia. What about it?"

"Do you remember that boy? Wuan Cho? The one who—attacked me?"

"Of course I do. Are you all right, Beth? Did those guys back there frighten you that much?"

"No," Beth replied slowly. "They made me mad. The fact that it scared you scares me."

Because if they hunt you down, they'll kill you, Carole thought. "What did you want to ask me about Wuan Cho?"

"Did you have someone hurt him?"

"Are you sure you want to know?"

"Oh, Mom! I guess I know now. I always wondered."

"You knew I never worked for the U.N."

"Well, yeah, but—wow—they really messed him up."

"He deserved it," Carole said without a drop of remorse.

To her surprise, after a moment, Beth agreed. "Yeah, he did. Does Dad know what you did?"

"About Wuan Cho? No!"

"No, Mom, I meant your work. Did Dad know about your work? Did he know you didn't work for the U.N.?"

314

"Oh, yes, he knew. Beth, I know you consider anything someone won't tell you a lie, but it's not something I can talk about."

"Were you a spy?"

"Stop it!"

"I noticed you wiped our rental car for prints. I'm not blind."

"I never saw Deliverance, but I've seen your father's cop shows." Carole would have bet anything that Doric had already located the car. She hoped he couldn't scan too well. No amount of wiping would prevent microscopic telltale evidence. "I don't want him coming after you, he's a creep."

"You should have met his friend, what a jerk. He asked me to— uh, never mind. I don't want you to go back there and Wuan Cho all over him."

That made Carole laugh.

"You're so pretty when you laugh, Mom. You don't still keep in contact with the people you used to work with do you? The kind of people who would beat up a kid?"

"I'm retired, too old."

Beth snorted. Before she could press for more information, Carole interrupted.

"So where to? For your shop? What other novels did you read?"

"Ugh, don't rub it in."

"How about the States, Beth? You've never lived in the States." They'd never lived there, not since Beth was a baby. It would be harder to trace them there.

"No place crowded. Not Dad's Washington cronies and not the west coast. I want a small town."

"There's a whole lot of country between those coasts."

"You grew up in the southwest, didn't you? What was it like there?"

"Hot," Carole replied quickly, thinking of the veil. *No place too remote.* "South Carolina is nice, lots of sunshine. You don't want to be too far from a city, do you?"

"Well, not Deliverance. I want someplace that snows, and some-place with lakes."

"New York has snow and lakes."

"Ugh, Mom. Isn't the whole place a city?"

"No, it's very picturesque. How about Michigan? It has a thousand lakes or something like that."

"Mich-ee-gen. I could go for that."

"I probably need to ditch this car. We can take a train to the airport."

"A train! Mom, I'm not riding in a train with four suitcases. People get violent about it. A taxi."

"And," Carole continued, "We'll just grab a flight to the States and have your Dad meet us there. We can all go house-hunting together."

"We're never going to get a direct flight to Nowhere, Mich-ee-gen from here."

Carole shrugged. "How about we settle for as close as we can manage? I just stole a car, remember?"

"Mom, I'm glad we came just the two of us."

Carole was glad too, and she fought the urge to touch her. Beth's heart reached towards hers, almost irresistible. She settled for shooting another smile at her daughter.

"Me too. I'm really glad. And I'm not asking you to lie, but if your father asks what we did in Scotland, I'm hoping you'll try to leave out the part about me stealing this car."

"I'll do my best to hide your crime. But mostly because you're probably the first car thief to ever take a Mini Cooper, and I'm kind of ashamed for you."

Carole's smile got wider. "Your father has wanted to buy you a car for years. If we're living in a small town in the states, I think I could comfortably agree to it—"

Beth emitted a squeal of delight worthy of a girl ten years her junior.

"On one condition," Carole continued, serious. She turned to look into her daughter's eyes. "Promise me you'll never speed."

EPILOGUE

Cleveland, Ohio—March 2013

STANDING IN THE boarding line for their flight out of the Cleveland airport, Carole felt the first stirrings of enthusiasm. The trip was almost over.

Beside her Beth hoisted two travel bags over her thin shoulder, and grinned down at her mom. "This flight will be less than an hour long!"

The gate attendant, a busty dark-skinned woman with powder blue eye shadow, issued a rote bored greeting while holding out her hand for their boarding passes.

For several moments Beth fished inside her giant silver pocketbook. "Sorry, I thought I had them right on top."

"Uh-huh," the woman replied rudely, eyeballing other first-class passengers lining up behind them.

"That's weird," Beth said, pulling her bag open wider and frowning down into it. "I don't have them."

"If you don't have your boarding passes, you're going to have to step aside." The gate attendant tried to reach her outstretched hand towards a passenger behind Carole, but Carole wouldn't move.

Beth plopped her purse onto the tall counter and insisted, "I don't have them, but we're on this flight! Can't we just get new ones?"

The woman gave an exaggerated sigh. "There's a fee to reprint. See the agent at the other end of the counter with your identification." The woman scratched her beehive hairdo with an impossibly long manicured nail.

Beth swirled one slim hand around her pocketbook again, then looked towards her mother. "The passports are gone too. Mom, I didn't give everything to you did I?"

"No, you put them in your purse at the Aberdeen airport. I saw you."

"That's what I thought!"

"Maybe they fell out during the flight," Carole said.

"Maybe," Beth replied doubtfully, chewing her lip. After a moment she shook her head, her wide eyes confused as they met Carole's. "They didn't fall out, I know they didn't."

"Ladies, you're holding up the line."

Beth stepped around the counter to a more cooperative looking attendant, and told him about her missing boarding pass and passport while one hand continued to stir determinedly in her purse.

"Your flight from Aberdeen is already airborne again, but I can have someone check for your missing passports when it reaches its destination," the male attendant offered.

"Do I have to wait here until then? I'm booked on this flight!"

"Do you have any identification at all?"

Pulling her wallet out of her purse, Beth flipped it open. Her brows tugged together and her mouth dropped open in disbelief. She displayed the open wallet to Carole. "Look at that, Mom! Everything is gone! My credit cards, even my old work badge!"

"You've been pick-pocketed."

"No, I haven't!" Beth insisted stubbornly. "I looked in my purse ten minutes ago. Everything was there!"

Carole pressed her lips together to keep from arguing. Obviously Beth had been robbed. The young man behind the counter started asking her questions, punching keys on his computer. The only evidence Beth could produce was a handful of baggage claim tickets from her pocket. She dropped them on the countertop and glanced at

Carole. "I don't know what to think, but we're going to be stuck here for a while. I can't even rent us a car without any identification."

Carole said, "Well, we could always stay here."

Beth huffed, her breath making the wisps of hair that framed her pretty face fan out. The clear blue eyes darted around until they spotted a window and she scowled. "Where are we?"

"Cleveland, Ohio."

"Mom, I wanted a small town, a *pretty* small town. Do you honestly think Dad is going to be happy giving up Greece for this?" She waved a disparaging hand towards the grey landscape outside the windows.

"The Great Lakes are beautiful. Don't judge an area based on one cloudy day."

Stubbornly Beth crossed her arms.

Carole said. "When I was pregnant with you I got stranded here in a snowstorm." She smiled at the memory. "I had the best apples here."

"But you didn't stay did you?" Beth frowned at the window. "It looks like Mexico City without the sun."

"You loved Mexico."

The young man behind the counter glanced up at them. "I can get you your suitcases."

"At least we'll have clothes," Beth said. "Maybe we can find something to eat and call Dad. He could send our birth certificates."

"Excuse me, Miss White?" The gate attendant interrupted Beth. "You need to stay with your luggage. If you'd wait right here for a few minutes until I can get it off the plane, I'd appreciate it."

"I'll find something to tide us over," Carole reassured, "at least some juice. You get the bags."

"Juice would be great." Beth leaned against the counter. "Do you have any money? Mine's gone."

Carole patted a pocket of her pants and nodded.

AT THE FAR end of the terminal Carole found a pretzel kiosk. An assortment of sugary yogurt, giant green bananas and unnaturally large oranges stood on display. Carole circled the cart, looking over the choices with mounting disappointment, spotting absolutely nothing the voices approved of.

"I have some nice apples behind the counter," the clerk offered, sliding several big green apples onto the counter. Carole grinned, fishing cash out of her pocket. *Perfect!*

"Are there a lot of apple orchards around here?" she asked, glancing down into the little woman's face. Carole froze.

It was Sister Mary Josephine. The woman's pale green eyes were fixed on the cash in Carole's hand. "I guess I'm accepting pounds sterling today." The nun spoke in a far more amiable voice than Carole had ever heard her use before. Stunned, Carole simply stared. The nun wasn't dressed in her usual habit, just an ugly green dress, and her hair—the hair always hidden by her habit—was red and twisted into a tight bun. She shoved the half dozen apples to the edge of the counter and tried to nab a bill out of Carole's fist, tugging a moment before prying it from her frozen grip.

"Sister Mary Josephine?" Carole whispered.

The woman frowned at her, jamming cat's eye glasses onto her nose. "Sister? No. My name's Abigail."

"Mom!" Beth shouted. Carole turned as her long-legged daughter raced gracefully towards her despite ridiculous heels on her boots. "Look!" Beth waved passports in one hand, and boarding passes in the other. "They were in the bottom of my bag! So was everything else!" She stopped in front of Carole, eyes wide. "I swear I looked, you saw me—but—it doesn't do us any good. It's too late. They shut the door on the aircraft, and they're not going to let us board. So we're stuck here until the next flight, which is tomorrow." She glanced over Carole's shoulder. "Oh! Those apples look great."

Carole turned. Six apples sat on the counter, but there was nobody in the kiosk. She scanned up and down the corridor, trying to locate the nun, but couldn't. *There's no way—that couldn't have been Sister*

Mary Josephine! Carole scooped the apples into her arms. "I guess we can at least get a car and a hotel for the night."

"The guy at the gate recommended a good restaurant. He said there's a bunch of nice vegan places." Beth nabbed an apple out of Carole's arms and took a bite. "Oh my word, good!" she said over a mouthful, heading towards baggage claim.

Carole looked over her shoulder, once more scanning the perimeter for Sister Mary Josephine.

"What are you looking for?" Beth asked through another mouthful of apple.

Carole shook her head, focusing her eyes forward. *That's impossible. It wasn't her.*

"You know it was," the voices whispered.

No, not the voices—my heart.

⫘

VISIT THE AUTHOR AT:

www.TheGlitterGlobe.com

www.WarrioroftheAges.com

www.facebook.com/pages/
Stephanie-Pazicni-Karfelt-Author/255103101179063

www.twitter.com/TheGlitterGlobe